The C

Previous books by Trevor Negus

The Coal Killer

The Exodus Murders

A Different Kind of Evil

Two Wrongs

The Root of All Evil

FOR RUTH

The Cause

Trevor Negus

Trevor Negus

© Trevor Negus, 2020

Published by Bathwood Manor Publishing

A CIP catalogue record for this book is available from the British Library.

ISBN 978-1-9996885-5-4

Book layout by Clare Brayshaw

Prepared and printed by:

York Publishing Services Ltd
64 Hallfield Road
Layerthorpe
York YO31 7ZQ

Tel: 01904 431213

Website: www.yps-publishing.co.uk

PROLOGUE

3.30pm 23rd July 1977
All Saints Roman Catholic School,
Londonderry

The school bell rang with a strident urgency. Its shrill tones were joined almost immediately by the sound of thirty chairs being scraped back across the wooden floor. The noise from the rumbling chairs almost drowned out the bell.

A loud voice that dwarfed both the bell and the chairs bellowed, 'Sit still! Nobody told you to move. That bell is for me, not you.'

The harsh, guttural accent of the teacher, Mr Maloney, was met with instant silence from the classroom full of ten-year-old boys.

The boys had the utmost respect for their teacher. It was a respect that was mainly born out of a deep-seated fear. Fergal Maloney was a strict disciplinarian who had joined the school from Belfast at the beginning of this term. He ruled his classes with a rod of iron.

Now that silence had once again descended in the classroom, he said solemnly, 'Right boys, listen carefully. I know you're all very excited about the summer holidays, but before you disappear for six weeks there are two things, I want you to do for me. Firstly, I want you to stay safe. Secondly, make sure you read at least one chapter of a book every day. Now be off with you!'

Instantly the boys were on the move, quickly gathering up books and pencil cases and hurling them into the bags at their feet. Grabbing blazers from the backs of chairs, they were almost running for the door. The six weeks summer holiday was a delight and for these boys it couldn't start soon enough.

Like every other boy in the classroom, Sean O'Connor was overjoyed at the prospect of not having to attend school for such a long period, but he was equally as excited at the thought of seeing his father again.

His father had been away, Sean wasn't sure where. It had been over a month since he'd last seen him and he knew he would be there to meet him at the school gates. As he made his way through the crush at the door, Sean was already thinking about the ritual visit to the local sweet shop on the short walk from the school to their tiny terraced house on the Bogside housing estate in Londonderry. Whenever his father met him at the school gates they would always call at Maisie's shop and he would be allowed to choose a bag of his favourite sweets.

Reaching the school gate, he was breathless from the sprint and disappointed that his father wasn't there, but then a broad smile crossed his face as he saw him striding towards the school.

Joe O'Connor was a huge man, standing well over six feet four inches and weighing in at close to nineteen stone. He was a big man in every sense and his long stride ate up the ground as he walked towards the gates.

With his school bag banging into the back of his legs, Sean raced towards his father. As he reached him, he was scooped up effortlessly by huge hands and then embraced in a bear like hug.

His father kissed his cheek and said, 'Hello, young fella. How's your day been?'

Sean was so pleased to see him he said nothing and just gripped his father's bull like neck, savouring the hug.

Eventually, he was lowered back to the floor and the two began walking slowly towards the Bogside.

The two of them had called in at Maisie's Sweet Shop for a quarter ounce of Sherbet Lemons and were almost home when they began to hear the sound of a disturbance emanating from the streets of the Bogside.

The noise got louder as they passed the countless white walled, terraced houses of the estate.

Sean O'Connor was starting to get nervous and began sucking furiously on the sweet in his mouth. Feeling the growing tension emanating from his son, Joe O'Connor said quietly, 'Don't worry young fella, we're nearly home. Everything's going to be fine.'

As they turned the corner into their own street, they were confronted by a wall of noise and a scene of utter devastation.

Local youths had set up a roadblock on the street, a car was on its side in the middle of the road and was now burning fiercely, acrid black smoke billowing out of the engine compartment. There were two loud bangs from inside the car and the boy flinched involuntarily.

The gathered youths numbered about fifty or so, they were throwing rocks and bottles from one side of the makeshift barricade towards the RUC policemen and soldiers from the British Army who had gathered at the other end of the street to try and restore order.

They had walked onto the end of the street where the youths had gathered and their terraced house was the other side of the burning car. Sean felt his father's huge hand grip his own a little tighter as they began to walk through the baying mob of youths. Sean lowered his gaze to the pavement and kept his head down as he walked alongside his father towards their front door.

Suddenly, the volume of noise increased. There was aggressive shouting and loud bangs all around him.

Having passed by the burning wreck Sean was now being virtually dragged towards his house by his father. The boy suddenly felt his father's tight grip on his hand lessen. He looked up and saw that his fathers' eyes were now screwed tightly shut and he watched in horror as his father started to stumble, before finally crashing to the floor, like a giant oak tree that had been felled with an axe.

As soon as his father hit the floor, he rolled over onto his back and finished up lying half on the road and half on the pavement. Sean knelt down beside him and began to hammer on his father's barrel like chest with his tiny fists, in a futile effort to rouse him.

He stared at his father's face; his eyes were still screwed shut; his mouth slightly open.

Sean began to cry and shouted above the din, 'Get up Dad! Get up!'

The bedlam continued around him as he continued to beat his father's chest.

Suddenly, he looked down at his small hands and recoiled away in horror as he saw that they were now covered in sticky red blood. It was only then that he saw the blood seeping from the huge wound in his father's chest.

Horrified, Sean leapt to his feet and ran as fast as he could to the front door of his house. He virtually ran headlong into the blue painted wooden door and started hammering on it, shouting for his mother and leaving small bloody handprints all over the door.

Instantly, the door was flung open. Standing in the doorway with horrified expressions on their faces were his mother and his two elder sisters.

His mother stepped out onto the pavement with a look on her face that was a mixture of fear, shock and a grim determination. She scooped him up in her arms and he looked back over her shoulder at his father lying still in the road. He saw his father's huge chest rise once then sink slowly back down, he could see his blue eyes were wide open now, but they were unblinking, staring lifelessly towards the sky and the pool of blood around his head and shoulders was steadily getting wider.

Suddenly, everything went black as his mother was pushed violently backwards into their home by khaki clad, British soldiers who were desperately trying to regain order and disperse the mob of stone throwing youths.

That was the last time Sean O'Connor would ever see his father take a breath.

CHAPTER I

3.30am 10th February 1989
Moorgreen, Nottinghamshire

'For God's sake JJ, will you get a fucking move on? It'll be getting light soon.'

'I'm doing my best Dec; this thing weighs a ton. How much further now?'

'Not far, just over that rise beyond the large holly bush.'

The voices belonged to Declan O'Hagan and John Joseph Hegarty.

The night was still and very cold. There was a full moon and a hard frost had formed on the ground. The exhaled breath of both men billowed out in large white clouds. Hegarty, in particular was breathing hard after the exertion of the three-hundred-yard walk into the dark woodland, carrying the black plastic dustbin.

Neither man was looking forward to digging the deep hole that would be needed to secrete the dustbin that already contained their precious but deadly contraband.

The frosted ground underfoot felt like iron.

Although a powerful man, JJ Hegarty was labouring under his heavy load. The dustbin he carried was filled with arms, ammunition and explosives. O'Hagan on the other hand, being the senior man and leader of the Active Service Unit, was only carrying two spades and a rucksack that contained small, sealed plastic bags full of various size batteries, timer units and coils of wire.

O'Hagan had previously carried out three detailed recces of this remote woodland adjacent to the Moorgreen Reservoir, near to the market town of Hucknall in rural Nottinghamshire.

It had seemed perfect for their clandestine purpose.

The woodland was dense, so wouldn't attract regular walkers. The only access to it was by Willey Lane, there was a very secluded layby set back from the lane that couldn't readily be seen.

Willey Lane was little more than a single track, so wasn't frequently used as a through route.

O'Hagan had been trained in a skill, often used by volunteers in their organisation, where natural features of the landscape were utilised to locate and identify a location. Being proficient in this skill negated the need to draw incriminating maps that might be discovered later by the security services.

It had taken him less than fifteen minutes to retrace his steps and find the location he'd previously selected to bury their arms cache.

He had used well established trees with quirky branches as the main points of reference, ending with the large, mature holly bush.

Finally, standing one yard to the left of the holly bush, he stopped.

He turned his back to the bush and faced an old, gnarled oak tree. He stepped forward five paces towards the oak tree, before driving the two spades into the hard ground.

With a smile, he turned to Hegarty and said, 'This is the place JJ, start digging.'

Hegarty carefully placed the dustbin on the ground and said breathlessly, 'That's grand Dec, but let me get my fucking breath back first, for Christ's sake.'

Reluctantly, O'Hagan agreed.

He was conscious that their Ford Sierra, rental car was parked in the layby off Willey Lane. He didn't want to leave it there unattended any longer than he had to. They needed to bury their arms and explosives and get out of there as quickly as they could.

After a couple of minutes rest, both men began to dig in earnest. This was a task they were both comfortable with. They had been employed as labourers in Derby for the last six months, working on the renovation of sections of the old Derby Royal Infirmary and preparing groundworks for the new hospital buildings that were planned for the city.

Although used to handling a spade, it still came as a relief to both men when they realised that once they had broken through the hard, top layer of frost, the ground underneath was still quite soft and easy to dig.

It had been Declan O'Hagan who first travelled over to England.

He had quickly acquired rented accommodation in the Peartree district of Derby, before gaining employment as a labourer at the hospital building site where he soon established himself as a foreman. He'd then been joined in Derby by John Joseph Hegarty and later by the twin brothers Liam and Gerry Quinn.

As foreman, O'Hagan had managed to secure employment for all three men on the same site.

The four Irishmen had quickly assimilated themselves into the community and very much kept themselves to themselves. The impression they gave was that of four hard-working men, who rarely went to pubs and never drew attention to themselves.

The reality was very different.

The four men were an Active Service Unit from the Derry Brigade of the Provisional Irish Republican Army. They had all been carefully selected for their ability to integrate themselves into society on the mainland. They were a sleeper cell that had one specific purpose. Sometime in the near future they would become active and wage a terror campaign against the British on the mainland.

After six months of patiently waiting, O'Hagan had finally been given orders that the time for the terror campaign was fast approaching.

The first part of their forthcoming campaign was supply.

Over the past six weeks, O'Hagan and Hegarty had on three occasions, driven north to a remote area of Western Scotland. At the pre-arranged meeting place, they had taken delivery of guns, ammunition and explosives from a shadowy individual whose identity was unknown to them and who was only ever referred to as, The Quartermaster.

The weapons included several handguns, a sawn-off shotgun and ammunition for both types of weapons. There had also been several blocks of the new Semtex explosive along with detonators and timer units.

The wiring and batteries that would be required to formulate the improvised explosive devices they would be making, could be purchased perfectly innocently at any hardware shop in Derby.

It was risky for the weapons and explosives to be stored at their rented accommodation in Derby and O'Hagan had been keen to find a suitable location where he could cache all their equipment. It needed to be far enough away so that it could never be traced back to them, but close enough to enable ready access.

The order to commence the bombing campaign had not yet been given, but they had received orders to try and identify readily accessible targets that were not too close to their base of operations. The targets selected were to be chosen on the basis of where their secreted bombs could cause maximum outrage and carnage.

As he dug deeper into the cold earth, Declan O'Hagan recalled how he had come to be a volunteer in the Provisional IRA.

As he matured from adolescence into adulthood, O'Hagan had never considered himself to be in any way political. Like most people in Londonderry, he had always harboured a deep-seated resentment at the presence of British Army soldiers on the streets of his home town, but had never thought about taking that resentment any further.

At thirty-three years of age he had come to the nationalist cause late.

It had been one specific, tragic incident that had pulled him into the conflict and the armed struggle. One of his younger brothers, Padraig, had been driving home after carrying out a split shift at the paint factory where he worked.

At close to one o'clock in the morning, Padraig had approached a British Army checkpoint that had been set up about half a mile from his home.

It had never been established exactly what had happened that fateful night, but for some inexplicable reason his brother had decided to drive straight through the checkpoint.

The young soldiers manning the barrier, believing they were under attack, had opened fire causing the car to swerve off the road. The small, MG sports car had hit a tree and burst into flames. Padraig O'Hagan, who was just nineteen years of age, was killed instantly.

When the post mortem revealed that his young brother had died as a result of the crash and not as a result of gunshots, Declan had been convinced of a cover up.

When no reasons, explanations or even an apology were received from the British Army or the authorities, Declan O'Hagan, a normally rational and caring man, changed overnight into being a very embittered, hateful one. He suddenly became driven by a new purpose; he wanted to avenge the death of his brother and saw volunteering to join the IRA as the perfect way to achieve this.

On the other hand, John Joseph Hegarty, JJ to all his friends and family, was a simple man who had no such moral grounds for becoming a volunteer. He only volunteered to join the Provisional IRA because all his friends had.

He was built like a body builder, short, squat and enormously strong. Although only five feet six inches tall, he was very broad shouldered and an accomplished amateur boxer. These attributes were quickly noticed by those in command of the Derry Brigade and JJ Hegarty quickly became established as the preferred option when it came to administering a punishment beating.

Hegarty had a propensity for violence; it was work he readily lapped up. As a result of his effectiveness in administering violent retribution, he was groomed from the outset by the leadership and soon made his way up the pecking order until he was selected to become a member of an Active Service Unit.

Lacking the natural intelligence and cunning of O'Hagan, Hegarty was quite happy to play the role of second in command.

The last two members of the ASU, the twin brothers Liam and Gerry Quinn, were from a family that had a long tradition of involvement in the republican cause. It had been a natural progression for both of them to follow the family tradition and become involved in the armed struggle. Both men had volunteered at an early age and had been groomed from the outset to become part of an ASU.

Their history was steeped in the cause. They had both been indoctrinated from a very early age to strive for a united Ireland. The brothers were skilled in the handling of explosives and the manufacture of improvised explosive devices. They were the designated bomb makers within the ASU.

Both O'Hagan and Hegarty were breathing hard after twenty minutes of steady digging. The hole was finally deep enough to accommodate the black plastic dustbin.

O'Hagan removed the lid of the dustbin and placed the rucksack that contained the sealed plastic bags, full of various size batteries, timer units and coils of wire inside.

The two men made one final check that all the items inside were thoroughly protected against the damp and wet before finally sealing the dustbin with black waterproof tape.

The dustbin was then placed carefully into the hole and buried until just the handle on the lid of the bin was exposed above the surface. O'Hagan placed a fallen branch over the handle so it couldn't be seen, before both men hurled handfuls of rotten, decaying leaves over the area they had been digging to hide their tracks.

O'Hagan made one last careful check of the area to ensure they had left nothing behind.

Finally, the two men set off back through the dark woodland, leaving their deadly explosives and weapons behind them.

From the edge of the woodland, they watched their hire car in the layby for ten minutes. As soon as they were satisfied that the vehicle wasn't being observed by anyone else, they approached it.

Once inside the car, Hegarty started the engine and drove slowly out of the layby. He didn't speed off, but instead kept well within the speed limit. The last thing they needed was to get stopped by a local Police patrol.

O'Hagan reached over and turned up the heater in the car, he said, 'Thank Christ that's done. All we can do now is wait.'

Hegarty replied coldly, 'We've waited this long, a few more weeks or months won't matter. The time will come soon enough for us to act, then we'll all be heroes.'

The rest of their journey back to Peartree in Derby, was quiet and uneventful.

Back in the woods next to Moorgreen Reservoir, the frost had already started to reform over the recently disturbed earth. After just a matter of hours, it was already impossible to tell that the means of so much death and destruction had been secreted in that beautiful, deserted area of quintessentially English woodland.

CHAPTER 2

10.15pm 18th June 1989
Downtown Docks, Chicago, Illinois, USA

The last of the large wooden packing crates had been lowered down into the hold of the cargo vessel, Svenska IV.

Each one of the forty crates already loaded into the vast hold, contained five of the new Barrett M82 .50 calibre sniper rifles. There were five smaller crates that carried boxes of the huge bullets fired by the specialist sniper rifle.

The consignment of arms had been purchased by the Swedish government and were on route from the Barrett Firearms Manufacturing factory in Christiana, Tennessee to the port of Gothenburg, where the Swedish army would take delivery.

The two stevedores working in the hold of the ship looked around furtively, they both knew it was now or never.

Tony 'Mac' McKenzie reached down, removed the screwdriver from his work belt and quickly got to work removing the screws from the packing crate. It took him less than two minutes to remove the lid.

His partner in crime, Stevie Costello, then carefully removed two of the green metallic cases that formed a hard-protective shell around each individual rifle. He lifted out the third of the cases and opened the lid. Inside, wrapped in a protective oily cloth was the huge sniper rifle.

Working smoothly, Costello removed an old scaffold pole from the long holdall at his feet. He quickly exchanged the rifle for the scaffold pole before placing the rifle inside the holdall.

Costello tested the weight of the green metal case with the scaffold pole inside against a case containing a rifle; they felt identical.

Both men knew that the cases wouldn't be opened again until they reached the army base in Sweden. There would be no way of knowing exactly whereabouts on the long journey the theft had occurred.

Apart from the floodlights illuminating the dock and the ship they were loading; it was pitch dark outside. There was a half-light that filtered down into the hold from the floodlights on the dockside and Costello looked on as Mac McKenzie replaced the lid of the crate and screwed it down tight.

There wasn't a trace that it had been tampered with in any way.

McKenzie then turned his attention to the crates containing the .50 calibre ammunition.

Once again, he got to work with the large screwdriver and in a matter of minutes he had removed two boxes, each box contained one hundred of the giant bullets. Two sand bags were placed into the crate to supplement the weight before the lid was replaced and screwed down tight.

The boxes of rounds were placed into the same giant holdall as the weapon.

Both men grinned at each other, all they had to do now was smuggle the long holdall containing the rifle and ammunition from the hold of the cargo ship and onto the dockside.

The two men made their way to the ladder that led from the hold to the deck. Mac McKenzie quickly scaled the ladder and looked out across the deserted deck. The crew were on shore leave, the officers of the ship were on the bridge and couldn't see the exit of the hold. The only person they had to worry about was their own dockyard supervisor, Alfie Redmayne.

Alfie was in his last few months before retirement and his eye was well and truly off the ball. He was already dreaming of moving to the sunshine of Florida where he could spend his days fishing for bluegills from the shore. All he cared about right now, was loading the ships on time and getting them out of the harbour. The security of any cargo was way down his list of priorities.

Mac could see Redmayne standing on the deck, with his back to the hold hatch, leaning on the rail looking out over the harbour.

Stealthily, Mac climbed out of the hold and walked across the deck. He stopped next to his supervisor, placed a hand on Redmayne's shoulder and said, 'Isn't that a beautiful view Alfie? What with the city lights reflecting on the harbour an' all?'

'It surely is, Mac. I'm gonna miss it when I'm gone.'

As Mac reached into his jacket pocket for his cigarettes, Costello was sneaking out of the hold behind him, carrying the large holdall.

Mac offered his open pack of Marlboro's to Redmayne and said, 'Smoke, Alfie?'

Alfie grinned, took a cigarette and said, 'Why not? Thanks Mac.'

As Costello slipped down the gangplank with the holdall, Alfie took a long drag on the cigarette before saying, 'Are you two guys almost finished stacking the load down there?'

'Yeah, we've finished, everything's squared away and distributed evenly across the hold. If it's okay with you Alfie, I'll finish this smoke and leave you to notify the crew.'

'No problem Mac, you and Stevie get yourself to the bar for a well-earned beer. I can finish up here.'

Mac took a last drag on his cigarette and flicked the butt into the ocean, 'Thanks Alfie. Do you want a cold Bud lining up?'

'Nah, I promised my old lady I'd be home on time tonight, thanks for the offer though.'

'Right, I'm out of here, see ya around Alfie.'

Mac walked purposefully down the gang plank, walked along the dock alongside the huge cargo ship, before walking away from the ship towards a small dark van that was barely visible in the black shadows on the quayside.

Stevie was already standing at the side of the van with the holdall between his feet. He was in animated conversation with a guy Mac had never seen before.

Hearing the tension in the voices, Mac quickened his stride and approached the van. Seeing him arrive, Stevie said, 'Mac, this is the guy I told you about, the one who wants to buy our merchandise. He's offered me five hundred dollars for the lot, what do you think?'

Mac turned towards the stranger, puffed out his huge barrel chest and growled menacingly, 'You'd better start getting serious here mister, you can double that and add some. Don't take too long to think about it either, the water in the harbour's very cold this time of year.'

In a strong, Boston Irish accent, the stranger said quickly, 'Okay, okay. I'll give you a grand for the rifle and all the ammunition.'

'Fifteen hundred', countered Mac

'Twelve hundred's my last offer, now let me see it.'

'Show me the cash first', said Mac.

The man from Boston held out a small brown holdall to Stevie.

Stevie opened the bag and let out a low whistle. It was full of used twenty-dollar bills.

'There's twelve hundred in there, count it if you like. Now show me the merchandise.'

Mac undid the zip on the large black holdall and opened it so the man could see the rifle and the two boxes of rounds.'

'How many rounds?'

'Two hundred.'

The man from Boston asked, 'Do we have a deal for twelve hundred?'

Stevie and Mac exchanged a quick glance, before Mac picked up the bag of cash and said, 'Yeah, we've got a deal mister.'

The man from Boston opened the rear doors of the van and asked, 'Would you gentlemen mind loading the merchandise in the back of the van?'

In one fluid movement, Stevie lifted the holdall and placed it carefully into the back of the van.

The man closed the doors, got in the van and drove away from the docks.

As the small van disappeared from the stevedore's view, Mac let out a whoop and said, 'I reckon it's time for a beer or two Stevie C!'

'Yes sir, it surely is. Being a wealthy man has given me a real thirst buddy boy, let's go!'

CHAPTER 3

11.30am 4th August 1989
West Bridgford, Nottinghamshire

Tom Naylor had been sitting on the wooden bench overlooking the small park for about ten minutes. The park formed one side of the market square in the centre of West Bridgford. The square itself was pedestrianised and was surrounded by small shops, various banks and building societies. The far end of the square afforded the only vehicular access.

Today was market day and the road into the square was already lined with goods vans of different shapes and sizes.

Tom was holding that morning's edition of the Daily Mirror, idly flicking through the sports pages at the rear of the newspaper.

To the casual observer, he hoped to appear as someone just killing a little time as he decided what to do on such a beautiful, sunny day.

Tom was dressed for the weather, wearing a loose fitting, black polo shirt, stonewashed blue denim jeans and Reebok trainers.

It was rapidly approaching midday and the sun was already high in the sky, it was going to be another very hot day.

Glancing left and right, Tom took a drink from the bottle of water he had purchased at the same time as the paper, before looking back down to finish reading the report on the Spurs v Man Utd match the night before.

Tom was looking at nothing, but seeing everything.

Although he appeared relaxed, he was feeling tense.

He was experiencing the usual pre-operation nerves. He'd been a member of the Nottinghamshire Police, Special Operations Unit for just over two years now. It was just this feeling of nervous anticipation that he had hoped for when he had applied to join the Unit.

Tom looked across at the Bradford and Bingley Building Society and saw that the woman who had entered five minutes earlier was now on her way back out of the door. She was muttering to herself as she stuffed the crisp new banknotes into her purse. She hurried away, no doubt already thinking about the next hot outfit she was going to buy.

The reason Tom was sitting on the bench, observing his surroundings so closely, was so he could carry out one final check of the plot, as the area of the planned operation was known. He wanted to be happy in his own mind, that everything about the busy shopping area was as it should be.

He and the rest of C Section had been fully briefed the night before, when the information had first come in. They had also received a further updated briefing earlier this morning, before setting out from Police Headquarters.

From his position on the bench, Tom looked towards the vehicular access into the market square. He could see the grey, Bedford van parked about thirty yards beyond the building society. It was the first vehicle in the row of vans being used by the market traders.

The Bedford van had been there since first light. It had been parked in position early, so it would be able to maintain a clear line of sight towards the front doors of the building society. It was one of the observations vans used regularly by the Special Operations Unit.

Tom knew that the two men hidden away in the back of the nondescript grey van, would be starting to curse the heat and wondering how long they would have to remain in there before the operation either went down or was aborted.

The two unlucky men inside the van for today's operation were both veterans of the Unit. Eddie Keane had been a member for three years and Wayne Hope, three and a half years. It was just bad luck for them that it was such a hot day when it was their turn inside The Box, the term used by C Section for their covert observations van.

Tom folded the newspaper, stood up, stretched and took one last look around the market square before making his way back towards the flower shop, two doors down from the building society.

There was nothing else he or the rest of the team could do now, except wait patiently.

As he walked casually back to the florists, he reflected on the information prompting this morning's operation. It had come into the West Bridgford CID office late yesterday afternoon and was from an extremely reliable source. However reliable the source, the information was lacking in some very important detail.

The general information was that an armed robbery was going to take place at the West Bridgford branch of the Bradford and Bingley Building Society shortly after midday, today. The informant had stressed that it was definitely going to be an armed robbery, but he hadn't been able to discover with any certainty, details of what weapons the lone offender would be carrying.

He could be in possession of a sawn-off shotgun, a handgun or knives.

Tom and the rest of C Section wouldn't know what weapons were involved until the offender came on the plot and the robbery started.

This had caused the Assistant Chief Constable (Ops) a major headache. He was always very reticent to send a fully armed section of the Special Operations Unit into a very busy shopping area, unless there was specific intelligence that there was an armed threat to the public.

This information fell way short of what was needed for him to sanction an armed operation.

As usual, this left the ACC with only two ways to respond.

The first option would be to park a highly visible Traffic Patrol vehicle directly outside the building society, in order to deter the would-be robber. A fine idea, but one that ran the risk of the criminal returning another day when there was no information warning of the impending offence. This could lead to a real risk of injury or worst-case scenario, a loss of life for an unsuspecting member of staff at the attacked premises or a member of the public.

The second option would be for a highly trained, team of unarmed officers to commence observations on the target premises and take the appropriate action should the offender turn up to carry out the robbery.

That appropriate action would be to identify the suspect as he approached the building society early enough for officers to intercept and arrest him. Hopefully, this could be achieved before he had the chance to enter the target premises, or use whatever weapons he may be carrying.

As usual, the ACC had decided on the second option.

Subsequently, the information had been passed on to the Special Operations Unit, for them to organise the observations and plan the arrest of the offender.

Tom walked past the outdoor market, that had already been set up on the pedestrian area, listening to the cries of the market traders advertising their various wares for sale.

Finally, before entering the flower shop, he made one last check on the team's communications.

All the team's signals were clear as a bell, so Tom entered the florists and made his way through the shop and into the store room at the back. There was no need for him to maintain a view of the building society, that job was the responsibility of the two men, sweating inside The Box.

It would be down to Tom and Matt Jarvis to respond to the signal from the observations van as soon as any suspect or suspects came into view. They would then have the perilous task of making their way along the street and intercepting the suspect, before he could get inside the Bradford and Bingley Building Society. The rest of C Section were standing by in unmarked vehicles a couple of streets away, ready to come to their assistance after they had taken down the suspect.

The only other police officers in the area, were two Traffic Officers who formed an armed response team. They were parked a few streets further out, in a marked police vehicle. The Traffic Officers had the role that Tom and Matt desperately hoped wouldn't be required.

They were there in case the suspect started shooting before he could be restrained by them. If that happened, it would be down to the armed Traffic Officers to try and contain the situation.

As well as the Traffic Officers there was also an ambulance crew on standby waiting nearby in case of casualties, together they were referred to as the disaster contingency.

As they waited patiently in the storeroom at the florists, neither Tom or Matt spent any time dwelling on that scenario.

Prior to the commencement of the operation, Chief Inspector Jim Chambers, the Special Operations Unit commander, had contacted the Chief Inspector responsible for policing the West Bridgford area and informed him that the Special Operations Unit would be carrying out an operation, targeting car thieves in the area of the market square all day and to ensure that his uniform patrols avoided the area.

Tom had used the same car thieves cover story, when he had introduced himself and Matt, to the owner of the florists that morning.

When he walked into the store room, he saw that Matt was sipping a hot coffee. Matt immediately gestured that there was a mug of coffee for him on one of the pallets containing racks of cut flowers. The hot drinks had been kindly provided by Mrs Meads, the owner of the florists.

Although it was shaping up to be a red-hot day outside, it was decidedly cool in the store room where the flowers were kept, so the coffee was very welcome indeed.

Tom nodded his appreciation for the hot drink towards the owner of the small shop, Mrs Meads. She smiled and responded by saying, 'It's a pleasure love. Let's hope you can catch some of these no-good layabouts who are breaking into people's cars.'

She grabbed two bunches of white, stem roses and made her way back into the front of the shop.

Tom glanced across the store room at his partner Matt, who was his usual calm self. Nothing ever seemed to faze him.

Matt wasn't a big man, at five feet ten inches he was probably four inches shorter than Tom, but he was a lot stockier and very strong. He virtually lived at the gym, constantly lifting weights.

He'd been a member of C Section six months less than Tom, but they had worked together on many occasions. Tom totally trusted him, knowing that if things didn't go to plan, he would have his back covered.

Both men sipped their coffees and nonchalantly checked that their radios, Plasticuffs and Asp batons were all tucked away out of view, beneath their baggy shirts.

Plasticuffs were ideal for this type of operation as they were easier to conceal. They were also very effective. Once one or two sets had been applied tightly on a suspect's wrists, there was no way they could get out of them.

The Asp baton was a spring-loaded metal cosh that was very lightweight and only six inches long. Once again, making concealment much easier than a regulation truncheon.

Suddenly, static filled Tom's left ear and the covert ear piece he was wearing crackled into life.

It was Eddie Keane, one of the men sweating inside The Box.

In a very calm voice Keane said, 'Possible suspect coming onto the plot now. He's gone by our position and is walking slowly towards the target premises. Suspect's wearing a black Benny hat, dark blue combat trousers and a zipped up black fleece. There are no weapons in view. Suspect's hands are tucked in the pockets of the fleece. He's walking very slowly and is definitely clocking points. One last thing boys, he's a proper big bastard.'

Tom knew instantly that this was their man.

The description, his furtive behaviour, wearing a zipped-up fleece and a Benny hat, it was almost thirty degrees out there already.

Tom and Matt were already moving out of the front door of the florists and began walking towards the building society. In the distance Tom could see the suspect approaching the building society from the opposite direction. He was still moving slowly and was constantly looking around him.

He was alone.

The two SOU men walked briskly past the market stalls and the glass fronted building society.

As they walked by, Tom caught sight of the building society staff inside.

A fleeting thought rushed into his head, as he wondered how the staff inside would react to the drama that was about to unfold directly outside their building.

Tom glanced forward and saw that the suspect was now less than ten yards away. He subconsciously noted that there were no other members of the public nearby.

Eddie Keane inside The Box had not exaggerated.

The suspect was indeed a very big bastard.

He was broad, looked very powerful and stood at least six feet four.

He wouldn't have looked out of place playing second row for the All Blacks, thought Tom.

Tom whispered to Matt under his breath, 'We've got to hit this fucker hard and fast. Once he's down, we don't want him getting back up, right?'

'My thoughts exactly mate.'

As they closed in on the suspect, Tom suddenly turned into a candidate for an award at next year's Oscar's ceremony.

He looked at Matt and said loudly, 'You've got to be joking mate. United are going to win fuck all this year.'

Matt responded with a jovial, 'Yeah right mate. Trust me no one's going to get near us.'

All the time they were talking, the two SOU men never stopped calculating exactly how far away the suspect was. Even though they never looked directly at him, they knew to the millimetre his exact position in relation to themselves.

When the time came, they would know exactly where to strike the suspect to cause maximum impact and pain. They wanted to stop him in his tracks.

This was not regulation police work; they knew they had to stop this man, who was armed with God knows what, before he could get into the building society and cause havoc.

Tom and Matt both knew the dangers, but it was exactly what they had signed up for when they joined the Unit.

The hammy acting hadn't been in vain.

As they drew level with the suspect, he hardly even acknowledged their presence. His eyes were fixed and staring. He was totally fixated on what he was about to do inside the building society.

This close, Tom could clearly see the two bulges beneath the fleece. This was confirmation of what he already suspected. This was definitely their man.

Matt drifted to the suspects right and Tom to the left. Forcing the suspect to walk between them. As he drew level with the SOU men, they both punched the suspect to the side of his head as hard as they could.

There was a sickening crack as their knuckles connected hard against each side of the suspect's head. This loud crack was followed by a barely audible grunt as the giant toppled to the floor. He went down like a felled tree and hit the ground hard.

Instantly, Tom and Matt were all over him, desperate to get him fully under control while they still had the element of surprise. They knew they had to restrain him before he could recover enough to use whatever it was, he was carrying beneath the zipped-up fleece.

Through his radio earpiece, Tom could hear Eddie Keane's message to the rest of the team, informing them that the suspect was down and to move in immediately to back up the arrest team.

Tom could feel the strength of the suspect as he grappled with him, he knew that if he did recover fully, he was going to be a nightmare to try and control.

Although he'd been floored by the double punch to his head, the suspect was still only dazed and was now recovering quickly. Tom could see by the wild look on his face, that he wanted to seriously damage his two assailants.

Matt managed to get one set of Plasticuffs onto the suspects wrists, but his hands were to the front and not behind his back. It was something but it wasn't ideal.

Tom moved quickly to try and get a second set on, that would ensure the suspect was fully restrained. He looped them around the suspects wrists and was just about to yank them tight, when he felt a searing pain on the top of his head.

Suddenly, he felt an unseen force pulling him backwards off the suspect. It felt like his hair was being pulled out of his head. He felt more hands join the first and felt hard punches begin to rain down on the back of his head and shoulders.

He heard a gruff voice shout, 'Come here, you horrible bastard! The cops are on their way.'

Tom desperately tried to break the grip of the men holding him. He could see now that it was the market traders who had intervened. They obviously thought they were stopping what looked to them like a mugging.

As he struggled against the market traders, Tom could see that Matt was still gamely wrestling with the suspect, trying to tighten the second set of Plasticuffs.

Tom could hear the panicked voice of Eddie Keane in his ear piece, as he shouted for immediate back up.

Tom shouted, an element of panic in his voice, 'We are the Police you dozy bastards! He's the bad fucker not us. Get the fuck off me!'

Tom managed to break free from the market traders for a second and leapt straight back onto the suspect who had just head-butted Matt full in the face.

Finally, Tom managed to tighten the second set of Plasticuffs and immediately looped another set on and tightened those too. Even though he was now effectively restrained, the suspect continued to thrash around like a man possessed.

Suddenly, there was a loud metallic clatter as two very large Rambo style knives dropped to the pavement from beneath the suspect's fleece.

It was only when they saw the two vicious looking knives, that the penny finally dropped for the public-spirited market traders. They instantly turned their attention to the suspect and began raining hard punches down on to his head and body.

Better on him than me, thought Tom.

Tom waited a few seconds, then shouted, 'Alright, alright! That's enough. Fuck off back to your stalls, we'll sort it from here.'

All the commotion in the busy square had attracted a crowd, but the onlookers kept their distance as Tom and Matt continued to restrain the snarling spitting suspect.

In the distance, Tom could hear sirens approaching.

His head felt bruised and was starting to ache. His left hand was throbbing from the punch he had landed on the side of the suspects hard head.

Tom looked at Matt as they both straddled the suspect; he could see that his partner's nose was bloodied and probably broken from the vicious head butt that had found its mark.

Matt grinned at Tom through blood stained teeth and said, 'Fucking hell mate, you look like Mr Majeeka! That tosser from the market has nearly scalped you.'

Tom grinned back and said, 'Yeah mate and you look like Rocky Balboa after the fight with Apollo Creed!'

They were both relieved to see the rest of C Section sprinting down the street towards them.

Sgt Turner quickly got things organised. The area was secured, the two knives were recovered and the suspect was transported to West Bridgford Police Station for questioning by the CID.

Local uniform police began to arrive at the scene and at the direction of Sgt Turner, they began to obtain eye witness accounts from people in the area that could be passed onto the CID.

This included the three market traders who were now looking across the square towards Tom and Matt with sheepish expressions on their faces.

As Tom rubbed the top of his head, feeling the soreness and the bruising, he was approached by the local uniformed Inspector who looked at him and Matt with an air of disdain.

The Inspector tutted and said pompously, 'Just look at the state of you two. Bloody Special Ops! It's all very well you coming down here without breathing a word about what you're doing, then turning my Main Street into the Wild West. Who do you think you are?'

Without waiting for an answer, he continued, 'I want you to get over there and apologise to those men for the inappropriate language you used towards them. They only did what any right-minded individual would do, if they saw a couple of thugs attacking somebody in the street. They don't need you swearing at them for doing the right thing. You're supposed to be Police Officers not bloody football hooligans.'

Tom couldn't quite believe what he was hearing. He looked squarely at the Inspector and growled quietly, 'I do hope you're joking.'

The Inspector glared back, 'Can you hear me laughing, Constable?'

With his head starting to throb even more, Tom tried desperately to keep his temper in check.

Through gritted teeth he said to the Inspector, 'Sir. You do realise that the upstanding citizen those men were trying to protect was just about to rob this building society right here on your Main Street! Those knives he had under his fleece weren't just for fucking show!'

The Inspector went red in the face and growled under his breath, 'Officer, you're skating on very thin ice. Now go and apologise, before I write you up for insubordination!'

Tom looked at Matt incredulously.

Matt just shrugged his shoulders, 'Come on mate, best do what he says. You're not going to win this one.'

Both men trudged slowly over to the market traders who were now chatting animatedly amongst themselves.

Tom held his hands up and in his best apologetic voice said, 'I'm really sorry for swearing at you blokes, but hopefully you understand what we were doing now.'

The guy who had attempted to scalp him grinned and said, 'What? Don't be daft mate. That's the most excitement we've all had in years. We were just wondering if you could come back next week and do it all again.'

Tom and Matt turned and trudged slowly back to the Special Ops van with the laughter of the market traders ringing in their ears, the blood congealing on Matt's busted nose, lumps visibly forming on top of Tom's head and the look of disgust from the local Inspector boring into their backs.

As he got into the Transit van, Tom turned to Sgt Turner and said, 'Any chance of a brew somewhere Sarge? I'm parched.'

CHAPTER 4

5.30am 30th August 1989
North West coast of Eire

The man shivered and pulled the thick fleece jacket he was wearing, tighter around his shoulders. It was scant protection against the chill of the dawn. The cold was something he was going to have to get used to again.

The mist that shrouded the glassy ocean was starting to clear, as a weak, watery sun slowly began to impart some much-needed warmth and dispel the damp night air.

He watched, almost trance like, as the bow wave washed relentlessly along the side of the scruffy tramp steamer. Even though there was only a slight swell he still swayed with the barely noticeable motion of the ship.

It had been two years since he had last seen Ireland and now as he got his first glimpse of the rugged coastline with its grey granite cliffs topped by beautiful lush greenery, he suddenly felt an unexpected rush of emotion course through his lean muscular body.

He stood just over six feet tall, deeply sun tanned with close cropped black hair. His eyes had a fierce intensity, they were bright blue in colour and hardly ever blinked.

The tramp steamer he'd boarded at the busy, bustling Lebanese port of Selaata had made good progress on its voyage. The journey through the Mediterranean, past Gibraltar and along the French coast, crossing the rough seas of the Bay of Biscay had seemed much quicker and far less arduous than when he had first left these shores and travelled across the ocean to the Middle East in order to further his education.

That schooling in the desert had been harsh and very thorough. Now, on his return to Ireland aged twenty, he was fully trained in every aspect of guerrilla warfare.

As the sun crept ever higher into the sky, it finally started to have some real impact and the mist began to clear rapidly from the calm, slate grey sea. As he looked towards the coastline of County Donegal, less than half a mile away, his keen eye spotted the tiny figure of a farmer emerging from his isolated, white walled cottage that was perched precariously on the cliff tops. He continued to observe the farmer and watched as the old man stretched and looked out towards the horizon at the beautiful dawn light.

Tearing his unblinking gaze away from the tiny figure on the cliff top, the man leaned against the salt encrusted, metal railing on the deck of the steamer. He stared down at the sea racing by below him and allowed his mind to drift off to thoughts of home and the painful memories of his father.

His mind took him back to the time when he was a young boy.

He was standing alone in the living room of his parent's small house in Londonderry. He was staring at his father's body lying in an open casket. His face looked waxy and a strange colour, his eyes were closed and his arms crossed over his chest, hiding the gunshot wound the boy knew was lurking malevolently beneath the charcoal grey suit.

Standing quietly in the living room, he could hear his mother's voice from the kitchen. He could tell by the tone of her voice that she was upset and was arguing with the two strangers who had come to visit. The two men had spent time with his father paying their respects, before asking to speak to his mother. The boy had been ushered out of the kitchen by his mother.

The two men had obviously been friends of his father, so he couldn't understand why they were now arguing with his mother. The boy moved closer to the living room door so he could clearly hear what was being said.

He heard a man's voice, raised and angry saying, 'Joe was one of our own Mrs O'Connor, and he's going to get the full military honours paid in respect to his sacrifice. He fought hard in the struggle to unite this country and it's only right and proper that his efforts are recognised by those who continue the fight.'

Now the boy could hear his anguished mother pleading, 'Listen Mr Macready, it was because he was in the bloody IRA that this has happened. I don't want any guns or black balaclavas at my Joe's funeral. What will the boy make of all that? He worshipped his father.'

The man's angry voice again, 'Listen to me woman, you've absolutely no say in what's going to happen tomorrow. Do I make myself bloody clear on that? It's important that people see we care about our own. We will do what we have to do tomorrow and there's nothing more to be said.'

The conversation was over and the small, angry man left the house with his companion. The boy could now hear his mother crying again. It seemed to him that she had cried constantly, ever since the day his father died.

The man was snapped out of his melancholy reverie by one of the ships crewmen.

The ebony skinned African nervously handed him a small cup of strong, sweet coffee and said quietly, 'Not long now, mister.'

The African crew of the steamer were all, in varying degrees, afraid of the deeply sun-tanned white man. They were fully aware that he was a killer in their midst, who they didn't want to cross.

The man took the coffee and without making eye contact with the crewman said, 'Thanks.'

He drank the hot, black, saccharine sweet coffee in one gulp, before making a final check of the bags and equipment that were stacked on the ships deck next to him. As he checked the weapons and explosives for the last time, he removed a small, black automatic handgun from the waxed paper it was wrapped in. He pulled back the slide and checked the action. From his fleece pocket he removed half a dozen nine-millimetre rounds and swiftly loaded the handgun.

The action of checking and loading the weapon triggered another stark memory.

His thoughts drifted back to his childhood once more. This time he was standing beside a deep, open grave next to his mother and his sisters. He was dressed awkwardly in an ill-fitting black suit, white shirt and black tie. It was a freezing cold morning; it was raining hard and the boy could feel the wetness on his face. He was glad the rain had soaked his face because he didn't want the crowd of strangers gathered there to see that he was crying and that amongst the rain, pain filled tears were also streaming down his face.

The boy looked across the wide maw of the grave and standing on the other side were six men. They stood in a straight line and were all dressed the same, wearing olive green combat jackets and black woollen ski masks that covered their faces, leaving just their eyes and mouths exposed.

The men scared the boy; they scared him even more when they all produced small, black handguns from their jacket pockets.

From behind him, there was a barked command that the boy didn't understand and suddenly all the men raised the handguns above their heads towards the grey sky. There was another shouted order and the men simultaneously fired a single shot.

The noise was deafening, the boy physically jumped and was left trembling. He could feel his mother's hand gripping his shoulder tightly and could hear her gentle sobbing.

The boy had no idea who the men were. He couldn't understand why they had guns.

The last memory, before it once again faded, was the bright colours of the green, white and orange flag of Ireland that was draped over his father's coffin.

As the memory of that flag and that dreadful day drifted away, the man carefully placed the now fully loaded handgun into the pocket of his fleece.

He made one last check of the bundles of explosives; he had previously packed into the largest of the kit bags.

Semtex explosive was the lifeblood of the Republican cause. This batch had been donated by the anti-western regime of Colonel Gaddafi's, Libya. Semtex was light, very powerful and most importantly, reasonably safe to transport and handle.

As he checked each of the plastic wrapped bundles of explosive, the man began to think about how he was going to exact a deadly revenge for the death of his father.

His father had been a prominent member of the Derry Brigade of the Provisional IRA.

As he had grown from a boy to a teenager, it had been drummed into him on numerous occasions how the British Army had taken the opportunity to shoot and kill his father when they had seen him on the streets of The Bogside during a small riot.

As a result of this indoctrination, it had not taken much to persuade him to become a volunteer himself in order to exact a revenge for what he perceived as the murder of his father. In spite of the protestations of his mother, he had willingly joined the cause.

As he'd grown from teenager to adult, he graduated from stealing cars for the older men in the organisation to burn or blow up, to being part of a gang that would administer punishment beatings at the behest of their commanders.

On the day of his eighteenth birthday, the commander of the Derry Brigade had handed him an old .38 Smith and Wesson revolver and ordered him to carry out the execution of an off-duty RUC officer.

He had readily accepted the task and had shot the policeman in the face at close range. After ambushing the policeman on the doorstep of his own home he'd calmly walked away, leaving the constable to die in the arms of his wife.

He'd been driven away from the area by other volunteers and had spent the rest of the evening in one of the pubs on the Bogside, celebrating his eighteenth birthday, with his family and friends.

It had been his coming of age in every way.

That small, frightened, weeping boy at the graveside had become a cold, stone hearted, dispassionate killer.

As he drank his first pint of Guinness in that Derry pub, he realised that he'd actually enjoyed the moment when he pulled the trigger. He liked the feeling that coursed through his body as he watched his helpless victim slump down, dying on his own doorstep.

As he had shot the man and watched him die, the only thought in his mind was the death of his own father. He no longer registered the dying policeman; all he could see was the image of his own father lying in the street, his lifeless eyes looking to the sky.

He had relished that feeling of power and couldn't wait to kill again.

As it turned out, that wait was destined to be a long one.

The commander of the Derry Brigade had recognised the killing potential of the young man and had ordered him to be sent to the Middle East, to the Lebanon, to be trained by hard-core Palestinian Militia, who were themselves taking refuge in terrorist training camps in that war-torn country.

In the heat and dust of the Bekaa Valley, he was schooled in every aspect of guerrilla warfare. He had learned hand to hand fighting techniques, field craft, bomb making skills and sniper training with the latest weaponry.

Now, with his training completed, he eagerly anticipated making the final leg of his long journey home. The Derry Brigade commander had achieved his objective, Sean O'Connor was returning to Northern Ireland as the cold and calculating killing machine the commander had hoped for.

Suddenly, the steady throb of the diesel engines ceased and the tramp steamer now lay silent and motionless in the water. The only noise that could be heard was the gentle slap of small waves hitting the side of the ship.

O'Connor watched intently as the crew readied the small launch that would carry him the last few hundred yards into shore.

The captain of the steamer, a very muscular, powerfully built Nigerian with shiny, black skin the colour of the darkest molasses and tribal initiation scars carved into his weather-beaten face was barking out orders to the crew in some native tongue that O'Connor didn't recognise.

What he could recognise was the authority in the captain's voice and he respected the man for the fear he instilled in his crew.

Finally, the small boat was ready and was now lying in the sea alongside the larger vessel.

O'Connor approached the captain and handed over a brown package, 'It's all there, Captain. Five hundred US dollars as agreed. You can count it if you want, but be quick about it, I haven't got all day.'

At first the captain scowled at the obvious disrespect in the white man's voice, but slowly the scowl turned into a broad grin, showing the five yellow gold teeth that made up the top row of his front teeth. Unlike his crew, the captain wasn't in the least bit intimidated by the skinny, blue eyed, white man. He treated him as an inconvenience, that he would rather not have aboard his ship.

Waving the brown envelope, he grinned and said, 'Mister, if you say it's all there, I believe you. Now take care getting into the launch, I would hate to see you fall into the sea now that you've paid me.'

Now it was the turn of O'Connor to glare back, as both men made absolutely clear to the other, non-verbally, how they both felt. It was a mutual dislike bordering on hatred.

Finally, O'Connor broke off the staring match and carefully placed the two kit bags into the smaller boat, before nimbly jumping in himself to join the two African crew members.

O'Connor stared at the crew member with his hand on the outboard motor and shouted, 'Come on man, move it! Get me into shore!'

The African jumped as though he'd been electrocuted and gunned the engine. The small boat responded instantly and skimmed across the calm sea, moving quickly away from the larger vessel.

O'Connor looked up and saw the face of the captain who was smiling down from the deck. For a fleeting moment he thought how good it would feel to smash a bullet through those dirty gold teeth.

As the small boat turned away from the tramp steamer, the thought disappeared as quickly as it had arrived.

O'Connor was now fully concentrating on the headland looming ahead of them, the large cliffs towering upwards almost vertically from the ocean. He knew that around that rocky headland was a small secluded cove with a tiny strip of gritty, grey sand.

It was there where he would finally step ashore.

As they rounded the headland, he glanced up at the cliffs on the far side of the cove. His keen eye had already spotted the outline of the dark coloured Land Rover on the cliff top. He could see there was one person sitting inside the vehicle, he felt his hand tighten on the grip of the handgun in his fleece pocket. He hoped it was the welcoming party he was expecting, but if it wasn't, then he would be ready for that as well.

Suddenly, the launch turned sharply and accelerated towards the shore. He could now see two figures standing on the thin grey beach.

One of the men was standing directly behind the other.

As the small boat got closer to shore, O'Connor could see that the man standing at the rear was a powerfully built man who stood easily six feet five inches tall. He had long dark hair and was wearing a Parka style coat. His hands were thrust deep into the pockets of the Parka.

O'Connor desperately wanted to see the man's hands and once again he felt comfort from the grip of his loaded pistol.

The man standing in front of this giant was a lot older and looked to be in his fifties. He had short hair the same grey colour as the granite cliffs. Even at this distance, O'Conner knew that this was indeed his welcoming party.

He instantly recognised that the older man was Eddie Macready, the commander of the Derry Brigade.

O'Conner felt a sudden surge of pride course through him as he realised that the main man himself had come to meet him off the ship.

As the launch slowed and inched towards the shore, O'Connor at last relaxed and felt his mind drift.

His thoughts briefly turned to a time not long ago, when he was enduring the sweltering heat of the Bekaa Valley in Lebanon training alongside fighters from Palestine and the Yemen. They were people who knew everything there was to know about conducting an armed struggle against an oppressive state.

From the outset, O'Connor had excelled at long range shooting. He had quickly realised that he had a God given talent, that he could use to drive the oppressive British

Army out of Ireland for good. He was now an extremely accomplished exponent of the sniper's art and his mind was suddenly filled with thoughts of taking the fight directly to the enemy.

He was brought sharply back to the present, as the shouts of the two African crewmen indicated that they had got as close as they could to the shore.

Without hesitation, O'Connor hoisted the two heavy kit bags above his head and stepped from the launch and into the knee deep, icy cold water.

He waded to the shore and heard the outboard engine of the launch roar into life behind him, the small craft was quickly turned around and began to skim across the sea back to the tramp steamer waiting offshore.

O'Connor walked up onto the gritty beach and placed the two kit bags on the ground each side of him. He then walked the last two paces towards Eddie Macready.

Macready stepped forward, embraced O'Connor and said, 'Welcome home Sean, it's good to see you lad.'

O'Connor broke away from the embrace and said, 'It's good to be back. How's my Ma?'

'It's bad news I've got lad. Your Ma passed away three months ago. We tried everything we could to get word to you, but it was impossible. I'm so sorry, I know you thought the world of her.'

O'Connor's eyes focussed on the grey sand at his feet. Without looking up he said quietly, 'How did she die, Mr Macready?'

'It was the cancer, so it was. They told your Ma in the March and by the beginning of May, she'd gone. There was nothing anyone could do. There would have been nothing you could do Sean.'

'What about the funeral? All the arrangements like?'

'I took care of everything personally. Your Ma had a wonderful funeral, we buried her next to your father. They are lying together now Sean.'

O'Connor stood quietly for at least three minutes, not saying a word. He was slowly digesting the enormity of what he'd just been told.

The old man placed a comforting hand on O'Connor's shoulder and stood quietly. Respecting the silence, he never uttered a word.

From behind him, came a grunt, 'For fucks sake Eddie, are we getting out of here or what? It's fucking freezing, come on let's go.'

O'Connor slowly raised his head and looked past the old man, his cold blue eyes focussing on the large man in the Parka coat standing behind the commander.

Macready whispered, 'Kelly doesn't mean anything by it Sean, he's an idiot.'

O'Connor said in a quiet, flat voice, devoid of all emotion, 'He's an idiot that needs a lesson in manners and respect.'

With real menace in his voice, O'Connor said loudly, 'Hey idiot, what did you say?'

A clearly disgruntled Kelly replied impatiently, 'I just said, can we get the fuck out of here? I'm freezing my arse off here.'

Eddie Macready slowly shook his head as O'Connor stepped past him and walked directly over to Kelly, who still had both hands thrust deep into the pockets of his Parka coat.

Without saying another word, O'Connor whipped the pistol from his fleece pocket and smashed the metal barrel hard into Kelly's mouth. He grinned as he felt the barrel smash through the big man's front teeth. Kelly sank to his knees on the gritty sand howling in pain and fear.

O'Connor instantly grabbed a handful of long, lank hair and yanked Kelly's head back, turning his face upwards. Once again, he smashed the barrel of the pistol into the man's already bloody mouth. This time though, he held the barrel in place. Kelly could taste blood and gun oil and was spluttering the word "sorry", only it was an incoherent mumble by the time it came out of his badly damaged mouth.

O'Connor shouted above the breaking surf, 'What did you say big man? I can't fucking hear you.'

He then dragged the now struggling Kelly back into the surf, before forcing the big man's head under the icy water. He held his head under the water in a vice like grip, his face just beneath the foaming salt water. He could feel Kelly struggling for life itself. Although he was much smaller than Kelly, two years of hard physical training had honed O'Connor's muscles into steel like whip chord. He easily held the bigger man's head beneath the water.

Finally, he eased the pressure and allowed Kelly's head to rise above the surface of the water. Kelly immediately stood up in the surf and began spluttering and coughing, gasping for air.

O'Connor gripped the front of the man's coat before contemptuously pushing him backwards into the surf and wading back to shore.

Behind him the big man got to his feet again and shouted, 'Bastard!', through his smashed teeth.

Without blinking, O'Connor turned and pointed the pistol directly at Kelly. He fired a single shot, the loud crack disturbing the still of dawn.

The round struck Kelly on his forehead, just above his left eye and a trickle of blood emanated from the small bullet hole. The tiny wound was in sharp contrast to the devastating damage that had been caused to the man's brain within his skull.

Kelly died instantly; very slowly and very deliberately he fell backwards into the sea. His body rolled over until he was face down in the surf.

The tide was on the turn and very slowly his body began to drift out to sea.

Macready spoke quietly, 'You shouldn't have done that Sean.'

O'Connor shot him a withering, dangerous look.

Macready grinned and said, 'Because, now you're going to have to carry your own bags up to the Land Rover. Welcome home Sean lad. I'm sorry for that ignorant prick Kelly. I shouldn't have brought him; he always was an idiot.'

O'Connor hoisted the two kit bags onto his broad shoulders and said quietly, 'Not any more, he isn't.'

Macready said, 'Come on Sean, let's get those bags stowed somewhere safe and I'll take you for the biggest Irish breakfast you've ever had. Well, the biggest you've had in the last couple of years anyway.'

Both men walked across the beach towards the small path that led up to the top of the headland, where the Land Rover was parked. When they arrived at the vehicle, O'Connor shook hands warmly with Macready's driver.

All three men looked down at the ocean and could just make out Kelly's lifeless body as it rolled in the surf, steadily drifting further out to sea. None of the men gave the body a second glance. All the talk was of the cause and the great work to be done, now that O'Connor had returned.

Macready took O'Connor to the back of the Land Rover and said, 'Sean, before we get your bags in the back, there's something I want to show you.'

Macready's driver opened the back door and removed a pile of hessian sacking. Beneath the hessian, resting on a bipod was the biggest sniper rifle O'Connor had ever seen.

He let out a low whistle and said, 'What the fuck is that?'

Macready said, 'It's called a Barrett M82. It's fresh from the USA and should be on its way to the Swedish Army. Our NORAID friends in Boston have excelled themselves. One of them managed to acquire the rifle and two hundred rounds of ammunition from the docks at Chicago. This beast fires .50 calibre bullets and with the right man using it, it's accurate up to a mile from the target. I've been hearing great things about your particular skill set, Sean. The rifle is yours. We have two hundred rounds and I want two hundred dead Brit soldiers.'

O'Connor said nothing, his blue eyes stared unblinking at the huge rifle.

Suddenly, all the hardship and deprivation of the last two years seemed worthwhile. In an instant, he'd forgotten about the death of his mother and the insult from that prick Kelly.

All he could think about was getting started on the mission to avenge his murdered father.

CHAPTER 5

11.30am 29th March 1990
Letterkenny, County Donegal, Eire

A low-lying mist still shrouded the deserted farmhouse as the non-descript, green Land Rover was driven slowly down the rutted dirt track.

A disgruntled moan came from the passenger sitting in the back of the vehicle, as yet again the Land Rover lurched violently, the front wheels sinking into another deep pot hole.

'Jesus Christ Almighty! Couldn't they arrange a better location than this for the meeting?'

The voice belonged to Francis Holmes, otherwise known as Frankie H.

He was the Provisional IRA's Chief of Staff and was a man with a reputation for a love of physical violence, which was exacerbated by his notoriously short temper.

The driver slowed the Land Rover almost to a crawl to try and lessen the impact of the next length of rutted track.

The man sitting in the front passenger seat of the vehicle looked over his shoulder and said, 'Another minute and we'll be there Frankie. I know it's not ideal but this place is very remote and very secure. There are no army patrols or SAS men that would dare come down this far.'

Ever since Holmes had become Chief of Staff, Ben Christie had been his personal bodyguard.

Holmes trusted Christie explicitly and always listened to his counsel, on this occasion he acknowledged his comment with a grunt and once again settled back into his seat.

Finally, the Land Rover came to a stop alongside several other 4 x 4 type vehicles in the courtyard of the crumbling farmhouse.

Standing in various recesses around the courtyard were a number of men armed with Armalite rifles and shotguns.

As the vehicle came to a stop Christie leapt out and approached the nearest armed man and said, 'I'm Christie, where's your boss?'

The man was about to reply when the door to the farmhouse opened and Eddie Macready walked out.

He held out his arms and said, 'Good morning Ben, what kept you? We were starting to get concerned.'

'There was an army patrol near the border, so we had to make a detour to get down here. Is everyone else here?'

Macready said, 'Everyone's here, you can get your man out now.'

Christie was a big man, but he moved like an athlete. He walked back to the Land Rover constantly scanning his surroundings for any possible threat. His right hand nestled around the grip of his drawn semi-automatic pistol. With his left hand he opened the rear door and said, 'It's okay Frankie, everyone's here already. Follow me.'

Holmes got out of the vehicle and walked alongside the towering figure of Christie over to Macready.

The two men shook hands and quickly exchanged greetings, before Christie ushered them both inside the dilapidated farmhouse.

The door opened directly into what many years before would have been the kitchen. It was cold and damp in the expansive room and the large open hearth of the fireplace remained dark and unlit.

In the centre of the room, set back from two small windows was a large wooden table. Sitting around that table were the men responsible for making every important decision about future operations involving the IRA.

The security implications for such meetings were obvious so the gatherings were rare events.

Francis Holmes took his seat at one end of the table.

At the far end sat Jimmy Patterson, the head of The Belfast Brigade and the man responsible for the three battalions that covered the East, West and North of that vast city.

Patterson was a brutish looking man with a badly broken nose and heavy scarring above both eyebrows. The old injuries were legacies from an unsuccessful amateur boxing career in his youth. Now well into his forties, although still physically very powerful, the inevitable middle-aged spread was starting to catch up with him. Patterson had never married, believing that he was far too occupied with the armed struggle to ever contemplate taking a wife. Although only five feet seven inches tall, he was very broad shouldered and still possessed fast hands which he was never slow in using to put his point of view across.

Sitting to Patterson's immediate right was a tall, thin man, known simply as McGuire.

Nobody knew this mysterious character's first name.

He was only ever referred to as McGuire. He was the infamous enforcer and protector of Jimmy Patterson.

Leaning against the side of his wooden chair was the black Armalite rifle that was never more than a yard from his grasp.

McGuire only ever dressed in black and this had earned him the nickname of "The Undertaker". For obvious reasons this nickname was never uttered in his presence.

Nobody knew how many murders and punishment beatings this mysterious man had been responsible for, but the usual estimate was in three figures. He very seldom spoke, but when he did it was in a very soft, lilting voice that men had to strain to hear. However quietly he spoke, nobody ever said the word 'what?' to McGuire, to do so would inevitably result in a ferocious beating at the very least.

Sitting opposite McGuire was the representative from Sinn Fein.

Eoin McAteer was an academic. An educated man who believed in the liberation of Ireland by political means. He also believed in the armed struggle and it was his role to put the political perspective on any matters raised during the meeting.

The last person to take his seat was Eddie Macready, leader of the Derry Brigade. He was responsible for the city of Londonderry, County Londonderry and County Donegal.

He was the man who had requested this meeting of the Provisional Army Council and the armed men outside were his volunteers. He was responsible for security at the meeting and the deserted farmhouse had been his choice of venue. A decision he had made in conjunction with Ben Christie.

Once Macready had taken his seat, Holmes gestured for Christie to step back and take up station immediately behind him so he could watch everyone at the table.

Macready spoke first, 'Good morning gentleman, first and foremost I want to thank you all for taking the trouble to attend today's meeting. I know it hasn't been easy to get here. There's only one item for discussion today and that is the Derry Brigade's Active Service Unit currently awaiting our orders on the mainland.'

Patterson interrupted, 'The last I heard, they hadn't even been supplied yet.'

Patiently, but with a pronounced note of irritation in his voice Macready said, 'Jimmy, if you'd let me finish my sentence, I was about to say that they are now fully supplied and are awaiting our orders to start a campaign against the British in their own backyard.'

There was a general murmur of appreciation at the last comment.

Francis Holmes raised a hand for quiet and then said, 'That's very good news Eddie. What are your thoughts on a time scale to let your men become operational? Are they ready?'

'The men have been on the mainland a long time now; they're fully integrated into the community they live. They've now been fully equipped by the Quartermaster and in my opinion they're ready to become active at any time.'

Holmes said nothing but looked down the table at Eoin McAteer.

McAteer stroked his chin thoughtfully, turned to Macready and said, 'What are your thoughts on targets for your ASU?'

Macready had been expecting this question and said confidently, 'I think that although they're equipped and ready now, I think our cause would be best served if they became fully operational later in the year, at the build up to Christmas. My proposal for the Council is this; I want to task them with attacking all the major shopping centres around the country. This tactic will not only cause mass devastation and heavy loss of life, but it will also impact massively on the British economy and furthermore will…..'

Once again, and much to the annoyance of Macready, Patterson interrupted him in mid-sentence.

In a loud aggressive voice, the Belfast commander declared, 'That's a load of old shite Eddie! If they're ready now, let them start now. Why wait until December for Christ sake?'

Macready pushed his chair back, stood up and turned on Patterson, 'You never give your brain a chance to catch up with your gob, do you Jimmy!'

Holmes knew there was no love lost between his two commanders, but he needed to nip this animosity in the bud.

He shouted, 'That's enough, both of you!'

He waited for quiet before continuing, 'Jimmy, for fucks sake stop interrupting will ya, you'll get your chance to speak. Eddie, you keep a civil tongue in your head, do ya hear!'

Macready picked up his chair and sat back down.

The two men continued to scowl across the table at each other.

Holmes once again turned towards McAteer, 'What do you think Eoin?'

A thoughtful McAteer said, 'There's merit in both arguments. Jimmy's right in as much as, we're long overdue in taking the fight to the enemy, but I think we'd gain the maximum publicity and make a far greater impact commencing a campaign on the lead up to Christmas. What you've also got to take into account, are other news worthy events happening this year. This summer will be dominated by the football World Cup. England have qualified and if they do as well as they're expected to, the news channels will give maximum coverage to that. We need to strike at our enemies when the bombing campaign won't be diluted and we get the maximum media coverage. On this occasion I tend to concur with Eddie, I think the organisation we will be best served starting the campaign later in the year. Politically, it will help to ramp the pressure onto the British government, which can only ever help our cause.'

Holmes nodded and said, 'Thank you Eoin. Jimmy, what's your considered view?'

'As Eoin has just said, taking the fight to the enemy is long overdue. I just don't think we should wait any longer. If the bombs are set in the right places and the devastation is massive the British public will soon forget about the fucking World Cup! I say start immediately, let's give them arsehole politicians in Westminster some Semtex reminders that we're still here!'

'Thank you, Jimmy. Okay, before I make a judgement on the Active Service Unit is there any other business?'

The room remained silent.

Holmes turned to Macready and said, 'Eddie, you will give the order for the Derry ASU to become operational at the beginning of April. There will be a stipulation that they're to plan their attacks to coincide with the retail frenzy that occurs during the build up to the Christmas holidays. I want your volunteers to use this time wisely and to be meticulous in their planning. I want their bombing campaign to be remembered as being a long and bloody one. You must ensure that the ASU issue a warning prior to any explosion, otherwise the press will concentrate on the fact that we didn't give one and that will deflect from what we're trying to achieve. Having said that I want maximum casualties, maximum destruction of property and maximum disruption to the economy, so any warnings given will only be made fifteen minutes before detonation. If the authorities can't evacuate their shopping centres within that time, that will become an issue for them and not us. Well, if there's nothing else gentlemen, I wish you all a safe journey.'

As soon as he'd finished speaking, Holmes immediately stood, turned to Christie and said quietly, 'Okay Ben, let's go.'

As Holmes and Christie left the farmhouse quickly followed by Eoin McAteer, it left Eddie Macready alone in the deserted kitchen with Jimmy Patterson and his henchman McGuire.

Macready couldn't resist having a sly dig at Patterson, 'Well I think that went really well Jimmy, don't you?'

Patterson stood and walked past Macready, bumping into him with his shoulder as he left the room. As the two men collided, Patterson growled under his breath, 'Fuck you, Eddie!'

Macready grinned and then allowed that grin to broaden into a wide smile at McGuire as he followed Patterson out of the farmhouse.

Macready sat back down in his chair and listened to the car engines starting in the courtyard. It felt so good to get one over that arrogant, mouthy prick Patterson, he was going to sit quietly and savour the moment.

CHAPTER 6

6.30pm 3rd April 1990
Peartree District, Derby City, Derbyshire

The message he had taken on the telephone at the rented house had been short and to the point, "Telephone your Uncle Fergus in Cork as soon as possible. Your Aunt Dolores is very ill and not expected to last the night".

As soon as Declan O'Hagan heard the coded message, he had felt a tingle of anticipation run down his spine. Had the day finally arrived to start their long-awaited campaign of terror?

The message was a pre-arranged code. It meant O'Hagan needed to contact Eddie Macready in Londonderry as soon as possible. What they needed to discuss could not be spoken about on the telephone at the rented house they were currently living in. The ASU knew all about the government eavesdroppers based at the GCHQ building in Cheltenham.

This was a call that needed to be made from a telephone kiosk.

The light was starting to fade as O'Hagan made his way through the busy streets of Peartree. There was a battered old telephone kiosk that was very rarely used, next to the small park on Corden Street. He knew it would be quieter there and it was only a short walk from his accommodation on Middleton Street.

He felt like he needed the walk anyway, to try and clear his head.

A million thoughts were racing through his mind, as well as a mixture of emotions. He was excited and apprehensive in equal measure. He had waited so long for this moment to arrive, but now it was finally here, niggling doubts were beginning to surface.

As he walked, he envisaged the carnage and loss of life he was about to unleash.

He stopped and waited for the traffic to clear before he crossed the road. As he waited, he began to chastise himself. Why was he even having these thoughts? There hadn't even been a green light as yet. He told himself to calm down, he needed to wait and see what news the telephone call brought.

He had made no mention of the coded message to the other members of the ASU. They would all find out soon enough.

He could now see the telephone kiosk; it was empty and there was nobody on the street nearby. He glanced in every direction to make sure he wasn't being observed then walked over to the kiosk and stepped inside.

From his trouser pocket he removed a handful of coins and quickly dialled the number he had memorised.

The telephone was answered on the third ring, he pushed in several coins then heard a woman's voice, 'Hello, O'Doyle's Bar, Katherine speaking.'

After taking one quick glance along the street outside O'Hagan said, 'This is Declan, I need to speak to Mr Macready.'

She replied, 'Okay, one second.'

There was a pause and then he heard Eddie Macready's familiar voice, 'Are you at a phone box?'

'Yes, of course.'

'Give me the codeword?'

'How's Dolores?'

'Dolores is fine.'

Trying to mask the growing excitement in his voice O'Hagan said, 'Do you have a message for me?'

'Yes, I have. Declan, the time's come for you and your fellow volunteers to become active. The campaign's been sanctioned and you're to start by seeking suitable locations with a view to commencing attacks during the build up to the Christmas holidays.'

'Do we have to wait that long?'

'Yes, you do. Use this time wisely. I want this to be a long campaign and the more preparation you do, the longer you will remain undetected. Do I make myself clear? There are to be no attacks until the week before Christmas.'

'Okay, is there anything else?'

'That's it. Strike deadly and strike hard.'

The line went dead and O'Hagan stepped out of the kiosk.

A grin appeared on his features and he began to stride out for home. All the doubts that had surfaced were now gone. He couldn't wait to tell his comrades the news. All he could hear were Eddie Macready's words, "Strike deadly and strike hard".

CHAPTER 7

5.30am 6th May 1990
Irish Border, Clady near Londonderry

Daylight had already been fading fast when Sean O'Connor had made his way stealthily through the tall brambles and gorse thickets that punctuated the rolling hills that overlooked the small village of Clady.

Eventually, he had found the ideal position beneath one of the gorse bushes and had remained there, lying motionless throughout the night. Only once had he turned slowly on to his side in order to urinate into the large plastic bottle that he had brought with him for that purpose. The bottle, along with everything else he used, would be removed and taken away with him once his mission had been completed. The only sign he had ever been there at all, would be a very slight indentation in the soft earth below the flattened grass.

It had been a cool, clear night and the landscape that stretched out below him had been bathed in the eerie white light of a full moon.

O'Connor had reflected how different this lush, verdant landscape was to the harsh barren lines of the Bekaa Valley in Lebanon where he had honed his deadly skills.

Now, as the first light of dawn approached, he could feel the usual drop in temperature. This sudden period of cold always surprised him, it was as if the earth seemed to resent the first rays of sunlight breaking through and wanted to keep the countryside gripped in the frigid, darkness of night.

As that initial weak sunlight crept over the horizon, the appearance of the landscape quickly altered. The surrounding hills and woodland began to take on various coloured hues and shadows began to fall.

O'Connor began to focus on one particular piece of that ever-changing landscape. Just under one mile away from where he lay hidden totally by the gorse, way off in the distance across the small valley, he could see a small gap in a copse of trees. In reality this gap in the trees was almost twenty yards wide. The way the woodland had been planted in years gone by, had formed a natural opening that had created a pathway.

It was a pathway that he knew a British Army patrol would be making their way along in roughly an hour's time.

O'Connor had previously observed Army patrols pass through this natural opening on no fewer than four occasions. Although the distance from his position was almost one mile, he knew that he could make the shot that would ensure no British Army patrols ever passed this way again.

He glanced down at his matt black wristwatch and saw that it was now less than an hour before the arrival of the ill-fated patrol.

Very deliberately, he gently pulled the large camouflaged bag forward until it was alongside him. Painstakingly slowly, he unzipped the bag until he could reach inside easily. He reached in and gripped the Barratt sniper rifle. He manoeuvred the rifle out of the bag and into position. The huge gun was now resting on bipod legs mounted below the stock and the butt nestled firmly against his shoulder.

Reaching forward with his left hand, he removed the two protective caps from the powerful scope that sat on top of the weapon. The front lens of the scope was covered in a gossamer thin muslin material to protect against any reflected glare from the polished glass.

Moving in fractions, O'Connor inched sideways until his face was resting alongside the butt of the rifle. As soon as he felt comfortable, he peered through the scope.

The gap in the trees now appeared to be as wide as a football pitch. With the weapon resting securely on its attached bipod legs, there was no shake or distortion of the highly magnified image.

Through the powerful scope he could see the detail of individual leaves on the trees that formed the backdrop curtain to the stage he had selected.

This wasn't theatre though; it was to be the stage for a violent death.

Satisfied that the weapon was set up in the right position, O'Connor reached into the breast pocket of his camouflage jacket and removed a single .50 calibre cartridge. As his cold, blue eyes looked at the huge bullet, a grim smile played across his thin lips as he anticipated the death and destruction that single round was about to cause.

Very deliberately he placed the bullet into the open breach of the rifle before slowly easing the bolt forward and down until the rifle was fully loaded, cocked and ready to fire.

Gently, he allowed the rifle butt to move from his shoulder and rest on the ground beneath him. He then raised the pair of olive-green binoculars that hung around his neck, up to his face. The lenses of the binoculars were also covered in an identical thin muslin material, to prevent any reflected glare.

Although nowhere near as powerful as the scope, the binoculars still gave him a clear view of the selected killing ground and were much more comfortable to look through and hold for long periods of time.

As he waited patiently for the army patrol to arrive, O'Connor remained perfectly still. He was like a statue frozen in time, not a single muscle twitched. His breathing was shallow and controlled so he didn't disturb the vegetation that surrounded him. He knew that his quarry would be desperately searching for any such tell-tale signs.

He was far too experienced and highly skilled to allow any such basic failings to occur.

Suddenly, there was movement in his field of vision. It had been hardly noticeable at first, as though a gust of wind had moved through the bushes causing them to shiver slightly.

He knew instinctively that the movement he'd noticed hadn't been caused by the breeze.

Slowly, O'Connor allowed the binoculars to be lowered to the ground in front of him and he moved the inch or so to his right and took up the weight of the rifle until the butt was once again nestled firmly into his shoulder.

The slow, fluid movement took less than a minute.

His actions had the same deadly grace and stealth as that of a Praying Mantis moving slowly into position before grasping its prey with lightning speed.

Once the rifle was set in his shoulder, O'Connor looked through the scope allowing thirty seconds for his eye to adjust to the increased magnification.

Less than a minute passed by before he saw the first soldier.

He could see the camouflaged lance corporal moving stealthily in a crouched position across the clearing in the copse. The soldier was carrying his SA80 rifle in the ready position. Beneath the brown and green streaks of camouflage cream on his face, the young soldier looked to be eighteen or nineteen years of age.

Through the powerful lens of the scope, O'Connor could see the trails of sweat running down the soldier's face. He could also see the fear and nervousness behind his eyes.

O'Connor knew the patrol would be led by a sergeant, he was determined that it would be the leader of the patrol who paid the ultimate price for what he saw as the unlawful and unwanted invasion and occupation of his homeland.

He allowed two other soldiers to pass through the opening before his chosen quarry finally came into view.

O'Connor made one final check of the wind; it was nil. He already knew the distance of the shot having previously made a full recce. The scope on the Barratt rifle was already set for the correct wind and distance so the deadly sniper began his routine to the shot.

He became as one with the lethal weapon, until the rifle felt like an extension of his being. His breathing was controlled and minimal. Looking through the scope he could see the cross hairs falling just short of the sergeant's right ear. Slowly, the wary soldier turned his head until he was looking directly in the direction where O'Connor lay.

Now the cross hairs of the scope fell directly on the bridge of the sergeant's nose.

O'Connor slowly exhaled and as the breath left his body, almost imperceptibly he increased the pressure on the trigger until the huge rifle barked into life and he felt the recoil drive into his shoulder.

He continued to stare through the scope of the rifle and that same grim smile played across his mouth as he saw the sergeant lifted high off the floor and thrown like a rag doll backwards. The huge round had smashed through his skull killing him instantly.

O'Connor knew the soldier wouldn't have heard the sound of the shot that had killed him so brutally and so efficiently. The high velocity round would have arrived at its target way before the sound waves generated from the shot.

Allowing the rifle to ease away from him, O'Connor picked up the binoculars and surveyed the scene of mayhem away in the distance. The young troops on the ground had no idea where the shot had been fired from and he could clearly see the look of fear and panic on their young faces as they scrambled for cover.

Very methodically, O'Connor began the task of clearing away any sign of his presence. After two minutes he began to slowly inch his way backwards out of the gorse bush. He knew the army patrol would have quickly recovered from the initial shock of their deadly contact and would now be radioing details of the attack on the patrol back to their base.

He knew that Westland Lynx helicopters would be being scrambled from the British Army base in Londonderry in an effort to locate him.

O'Connor also knew that he would have spirited himself out of the area long before the choppers arrived.

Just ten minutes after the fatal shot had been fired, O'Connor was slipping, ghost like, back across the border into the Republic. He was aware that once the British Army knew the calibre of the bullet that had been used to kill the sergeant, they would immediately attribute his death to the deadly assassin they had labelled, 'The Death Adder'.

When he had first heard the name, the British soldiers had given him, O'Connor had gloried in the infamy. He knew that every soldier he killed with the deadly Barratt rifle would make the next patrol even more reticent about leaving their large fortified bases. Those ugly cancers that the British Army had established in his beloved Ireland.

O'Connor would not rest until every British soldier in every one of those fortified bases had packed up their kit and left Ireland.

That morning, the young sergeant had become the sixteenth soldier to die at the hands of The Death Adder and his deadly Barratt rifle.

Sean O'Connor would ensure that he wouldn't be the last.

CHAPTER 8

1.00am 19ᵗʰ October 1990
Mansfield, North Nottinghamshire

Tom Naylor glanced down at his wristwatch and physically cringed when he saw that it was still only one o'clock in the morning.

The frigid night air was still, there wasn't a breath of wind and it was very, very cold. From where he lay, he could see a hard, white frost starting to form, glistening on the tarmac roads. The frosted, grey slate roofs of nearby houses reflected the ethereal white light being cast by the bright full moon.

This was the third night in a row he and his colleagues from C Section of the Special Operations Unit had spent maintaining observations in the affluent suburb of High Oakham on the outskirts of the large mining town of Mansfield.

The observations formed part of a major police operation codenamed, Operation Jackdaw. It was the brainchild of the Detective Inspector in charge of the Mansfield CID.

Following a series of high value burglaries in the area, where entry had been gained by a very accomplished and skilled climbing burglar who targeted only the highest value properties on the outskirts of the town, pressure had been building on the police to act. Several of the wealthy residents in the area had written strongly worded letters directly to the Chief Constable, demanding that their property be protected.

The Chief Constable had subsequently transferred this mounting pressure to the head of the CID who in turn had passed it on to the local CID and in particular to Detective Inspector Terry Carmichael.

In effect Carmichael, had been tasked by the Chief Constable to apprehend the burglar thereby allaying the fears of the local residents.

Detective Inspector Carmichael had galvanised his team of detectives and after a lot of painstaking work gathering good intelligence, they had finally received a breakthrough from a local informant. This career criminal had informed the CID that the series of burglaries were not down to any local villains, but was the work of a skilled burglar travelling into the area from Manchester.

The identity of this climbing burglar was unknown as was the exact time of his next planned visit to Mansfield. It had been over a week since the last offence had occurred and the frequency of offending appeared to follow a fortnightly pattern.

A decision had been taken by Detective Inspector Carmichael to formulate Operation Jackdaw. His plan would necessitate the Special Operations Unit maintaining observations on all the entrances into the High Oakham area. They would also be deployed to maintain covert observations at strategic points throughout the large suburb in the hope of observing the offender and subsequently making an arrest.

It was a good idea and a simple plan, the only factor that hadn't been accounted for at the planning stage was the fact that the weather forecast for the next fortnight was for either freezing fog or sub-zero temperatures on the clear nights.

Now on the third consecutive night of those icy temperatures, Tom inwardly steeled himself with the thought that nobody had ever said being on the Special Operations Unit would be easy.

He had been given a position monitoring the junction of King Edward Avenue and Alexandra Avenue. This was one of the burglar's preferred areas within the High Oakham suburb. There had been seven offences within this small area and vast amounts of priceless jewellery had been stolen.

Tom had taken up a position lying beneath a privet hedge on Alexandra Avenue and had a slightly elevated view of the junction.

He'd been in position since seven thirty that evening, having gone in after the main traffic and any pedestrian movement had petered out. The area itself was a quiet one and it had been relatively simple for him and the rest of the Section to take up their positions without detection.

Although dressed for the freezing, Baltic conditions, Tom was just beginning to feel the cold seeping into his bones. He could feel his core temperature dropping as he lay motionless on the icy ground. The thought of a scalding hot drink seemed a long way off. To try and take his mind off the cold, he concentrated hard on not allowing his warm exhaled breath to form a cloud that would betray his presence beneath the hedgerow.

He was grateful there was no wind. Had you added a wind chill factor to the already sub-zero temperatures, there would have been a real danger of hypothermia setting in.

The High Oakham area of the town was beautiful, with large trees lining quiet roads and very desirable, large, detached dwellings set back in vast grounds. The houses all had large driveways winding their way towards them. Some of those driveways were gated with impressive, decorative wrought iron gates.

As he lay beneath the hedgerow, Tom wondered how many years of saving it would take him to afford a house anything like some of these dwellings. He grinned to himself at his idiotic musings, the short answer was he could never afford anything like this.

Suddenly, his reverie was halted as he saw a slight movement in the shadows along Alexandra Avenue. Concentrating hard, he strained to get another glimpse of what it was that had caught his eye. After five minutes of staring into the darkness, Tom finally saw the tell-tale eye shine of a cat staring back towards him. The black cat was curled up at the base of a very large oak tree, almost completely hidden by the deep shadow.

What an idiot! Tom silently scolded himself as he realised, he'd just spent five minutes staring at a cat and not a cat burglar!

As he settled back into the rhythm of scanning his entire arc of vision, he heard an owl hooting from the same large oak tree. At least somebody thinks you're funny, Tom thought to himself.

An hour had passed since he had seen the cat and the freezing temperatures meant that Tom was starting to struggle to maintain concentration.

It was the sound of footsteps approaching that brought him back to a fully alert state. There was something about the pattern of the footfall that was wrong. This was not a person striding out for home, the steps were too small and slow. This was someone trying very hard to walk silently, and failing.

The noise of the footsteps had come from his immediate left, Tom knew that the person approaching would be passing directly in front of his position and would be no more than four feet away from him.

Tom held his breath and waited for the cause of the footsteps to come into view.

After what seemed an age, he finally saw the small figure making slow and very careful progress along the quiet tree lined road. To his relief, Tom could see that the person had crossed over the road before passing his location.

From his hidden position beneath the hedgerow, Tom had a clear view of a man dressed entirely in black from head to foot. He looked to be an average height and very slim. He moved with poise and grace, like an athlete or a dancer. His clothing didn't match the wintry conditions, he was wearing black jeans and a matt black, bomber style jacket and a black woollen ski mask that was currently rolled up exposing his features, but was ready to be pulled down over his face. On his back he carried a small, black, nylon rucksack, the type used by climbers.

The man continued to walk slowly along Alexandra Avenue, moving further away from Tom's position.

Tom waited until the man was on the very edge of his field of vision before depressing the button of his radio.

He barely breathed the message on the radio, knowing that his sensitive throat mike would pick up his whispered message, 'Stand by, stand by. Suspect now on plot at Position Delta. Repeat Position Delta. Over.'

The rest of the team were now aware exactly where the suspect was. Maintaining his view on the suspect, Tom then breathed a whispered description of the offender and his general direction of travel over the radio.

Tom knew that colleagues furthest away from his position would now be slowly converging on Position Delta, effectively closing the net.

Suddenly, just as Tom finished transmitting, the man stopped and froze like a statue. He then moved briefly, before disappearing effortlessly into the same shadow that the cat had previously occupied at the base of the oak tree. Tom strained his eyes and could just about make out the presence of the man who remained standing stock still in the shadows.

Once again, Tom concentrated hard on regulating his breathing and not making any noise that would instantly betray his presence.

After an agonising ten-minute wait, the suspect was obviously satisfied that he was alone on the street. Tom continued to observe and watched as the man made his way over to a high set of ornamental gates that formed the entrance to a large detached house set back from the road.

On one of the stone pillars that supported the gates was a grey, slate nameplate that read 'Oak Hill Towers'.

In one fluid movement, the man scaled the high gates like a human spider and was already making his way down the other side.

Tom was impressed. Scaling those gates so effortlessly was no mean feat and he realised that whoever this man was, he was an accomplished climber.

Tom immediately pushed that admiration to one side and very quickly whispered into his throat mike, 'All units. Suspect has climbed the gates into Oak Hill Towers at Position Delta. Repeat Oak Hill Towers at Position Delta. Over.'

Tom could now do no more.

He was desperate to abandon his position and move in himself to make the arrest, but he knew his role was to remain in place and observe the suspect's exit, should he manage to complete the offence and be in and out of the property before the arrival of the rest of C Section.

Through his covert ear piece, Tom could hear message after message as other police officers arrived at Position Delta, ready to intercept the human fly as and when he emerged from the driveway of the impressive house.

Fifteen minutes passed slowly by before Tom saw movement on the other side of the gates to Oak Hill Towers. The man was standing on the driveway illuminated by the bright moonlight and Tom could see him adjusting a now very full rucksack. Just as he began to scale the high gates, Tom whispered into the radio, 'Stand by, stand by. Suspect now climbing gates and exiting the property.'

As soon as the burglar's feet touched the floor after climbing down the gates, Tom witnessed what he had previously assumed to be shadows coming to life all around the entrance to the large house. Tom hadn't seen his colleagues take up their positions, but now they were moving fast he marvelled at how they had managed to get in so close without him seeing them.

It was the largest of these 'shadows' that made contact with the suspect first, Tom guessed at it being Steve Grey making the arrest. Instantly the suspect was lifted off the floor before being unceremoniously dumped hard onto the frosty pavement. A very brief struggle ensued before Steve Grey was joined by three more 'shadows', who quickly engulfed and detained the suspect without any more fuss.

Tom then heard the triumphant message through his ear piece, 'All units, suspect detained. Large amount of jewellery and housebreaking tools recovered. Over.'

The stern voice of Sgt Graham Turner now came over the radio, 'All units return to original positions and wait out. Two officers to remain with the suspect until the arrival of the CID vehicle. Once the prisoner has been handed over return to original positions and await further instruction. I want strict radio procedure maintained until we can ascertain if this suspect was acting alone. Turner Out.'

Tom felt himself inwardly sag, for a brief second, he had imagined that lovely hot drink in his hands. He knew Sergeant Turner was right. C Section would remain in situ maintaining the observations until the CID were satisfied that the man they had detained had been acting alone.

Another agonizing hour passed slowly by until suddenly Tom's earpiece crackled into life again, 'Sergeant Turner to all units, return to your rendezvous points and await collection. Over.'

Tom clenched his fist and mouthed silently, 'Yes!'

Slowly, he began to move his frozen limbs, willing them back to life. He crawled backwards out from beneath the hedgerow and very slowly stood up. He made sure he wasn't being observed himself, the last thing he needed now was to have to explain to some irate householder that although he looked like The Creature from the Black Lagoon, he was in fact a police officer, there to keep them safe.

Alexandra Avenue and the other roads in the area were totally still, there wasn't a sound to be heard. Once again, Tom glanced at his watch; it was now approaching four o'clock in the morning. He made his way slowly towards the rendezvous point, he still couldn't feel his feet or his fingers.

When he arrived at the rendezvous point, he stepped back into the shadows formed by three large trees at the side of the road. A voice whispered, 'Watch where you're treading numb nuts!'

The voice belonged to Matt Jarvis, he continued in a whisper, 'It's a good job you were a bit more observant earlier mate or we'd all still be out here freezing our bollocks off. Nice work Tom.'

Tom nodded.

At that moment the low growl of a diesel engine could be heard and Tom saw an unmarked Transit van being driven slowly along the road without any headlights on. As the van finally came to a stop, once again Tom marvelled as what appeared to be dark shadows at the sides of the road suddenly came to life and moved stealthily towards the van.

Once everyone was on board, the van driver switched on the headlights of the Transit and drove at normal speed back to the police station at Mansfield. There came a lone, disgruntled voice from the back of the van, 'Come on mate, get the heater cranked up for fuck's sake!'

Back in the parade room at Mansfield Police Station the officers gathered for a debrief.

Standing at the head of the large table was a delighted Chief Inspector Jim Chambers, a beaming Detective Inspector Terry Carmichael and a very bleary-eyed Superintendent, who had obviously been recently roused from his slumbers.

Sitting around the table were the men from C Section, still desperately trying to get warm and get the blood flowing through their frozen limbs.

It was Detective Inspector Carmichael who spoke first, 'Great job lads. It's early days, but we've definitely got him for the burglary at Oak Hill Towers tonight. The jewellery we found on him has just been identified by a very grateful householder. He assures me that he will be writing a letter to his good friend, the Chief Constable, first thing this morning.'

Steve Grey muttered to nobody in particular, 'No wonder he's looking so pleased with himself.'

Carmichael continued, 'We also found a set of Saab car keys on the suspect when he was detained and a uniform patrol has just found a Saab 900 parked unattended next to the railway lines across town. The suspects keys have been tried on this motor and they fit. We think he's been using the disused railway lines to get across town to High Oakham to avoid being seen.'

The Divisional Superintendent now chipped in to say a heartfelt thank you to all the members of C Section who still looked as if they had just returned from an Arctic expedition.

Following his little speech, the Superintendent left the room, obviously eager to return to his warm bed.

Jim Chambers said, 'Well done gents. I know it's been freezing out there, but the level of professionalism you've all shown does you credit. Rest assured, I'll be making the Chief Constable very aware exactly how this man was detained and the hardship that you've all endured over the last few nights, but then again lads, when did I ever say that it would be easy?'

Chambers grinned widely as the room filled with laughter at his last comment.

Just at that moment, Detective Inspector Carmichael appeared with a tray full of mugs of hot coffee. As the Special Ops men took a mug each, the Detective poured a large measure of malt whiskey into the mugs.

Steve Grey exalted, 'Now that's more like it, gaffer!'

It was a good end to a good job, thought Tom, but now can we go home please, I'm supposed to be moving into my new flat tomorrow?

As if in answer to his silent question, Jim Chambers continued, 'Quick as you can gents, get that brew down you and get warmed up, then let's get back to Headquarters. I don't expect to see any of you on duty again for two days, but make sure your pocket note books are completed before you go off duty. I don't want any cock ups on the statements later. Got it?'

The men nodded and very soon two vans containing a tired C Section was pulling into the car park at Headquarters ready to complete their paperwork and go off duty.

Half an hour later as they walked to their own cars, Matt turned to Tom and said, 'Do you need a hand later today with the move into your flat? Obviously, I'm going to need some kip first, but I'm more than happy to come over about two in the afternoon and lend a hand.'

'No thanks mate, you enjoy your day off. I've employed a proper removal firm to get everything from the cottage to the apartment and once it's all there I reckon me and Bailey will be able to manage. Tell you what though, if you and Kate want to come over about eight o'clock tonight with a few cans and a couple of bottles of red wine you can help us warm the place up if you like?'

'That sounds spot on, see you tonight mate.'

Tom got in his car and drove out of the car park, heading for the cottage at Linby for the last time. It had not been the same living there after the death of his girlfriend Bev. He knew he had to get out of the cottage in order to move on with his life. He knew he would never forget Bev and no way did he ever want to, but he felt drained living with a ghost. He needed to be able to try and move on to find some closure to her senseless death.

Tomorrow would be the start of a new beginning, he told himself, as he gunned the engine of his Volkswagen Golf and drove quickly away from Headquarters.

CHAPTER 9

5.00pm 19th October 1990
Trent Embankment, Nottingham

Tom Naylor smiled as the two removal men placed the last two cardboard boxes down onto the wooden flooring in his new flat.

The older of the two men stretched and said, 'That's the last of it, Mr Naylor.'

Reaching into his jeans pocket, Tom removed two twenty-pound notes and handed them to the two men. He smiled and said, 'Thanks guys, you've been brilliant. Get yourselves a drink on me for all your hard work.'

The older man said, 'That's not necessary Mr Naylor, really.'

Tom held out his hand with the cash, 'Take it guys, you've earned it. I know there's a lift, but it still hasn't been easy getting everything up to the tenth floor.'

The two men took the cash and the older man said, 'Well if you're sure, it's much appreciated. Thanks.'

The younger of the two men nodded and said, 'Cheers.'

The two removals men left the flat, leaving Tom alone in the vast apartment surrounded by what seemed like a thousand unpacked cardboard boxes. He sat down on one of the boxes and took a moment to reflect on his day so far.

It had been almost five o'clock in the morning when he'd finally arrived at the cottage in Linby. It was the home he'd shared with his girlfriend Bev, before she was so tragically killed almost three years before.

By the time he arrived back at the cottage, he'd already decided not to go to bed. The men from Pickfords Removals would be arriving in just a few hours' time to start the house move.

Instead, he had taken a piping hot shower, before putting the kettle on and making himself a large mug of strong coffee. Sipping his coffee as he went, he had then made one last inspection of the cottage to make sure he wasn't leaving anything behind that he wanted. Having done that, he then sat down amongst the myriad of cardboard boxes and waited for Pickfords to arrive.

Tom had managed to sell the cottage fully furnished and had only needed to pack up all his own personal effects. The boxes were full of clothes, pictures, books and other items of a sentimental value. There were also televisions and music systems that wouldn't be left and needed to be moved. He had been amazed at just how much 'stuff' he had accumulated over the years. As soon as he saw all the boxes it had been an easy decision to employ professional removal men to make the move.

The buyers of the cottage were an elderly, retired couple who had instantly fallen in love with the secluded cottage in the picturesque village of Linby. In particular the couple, who were both keen gardeners, loved the natural cottage garden which had looked amazing on their first viewing back in September. The buyers had recently downsized and all their furniture had been sold along with their house. They had been overjoyed when Tom suggested that the cottage be sold fully furnished. The furniture in the cottage really complimented the old building perfectly, but he was painfully aware that the same furniture would look totally out of place in the modern penthouse apartment he was purchasing.

When Tom had first been to view the penthouse apartment that overlooked the River Trent, he had been blown away with the views. It was a show apartment and he'd been particularly taken with the ultra-modern contemporary furniture, fixtures and fittings that the interior designers had used to dress the apartment.

Immediately, he had enquired how much the apartment would cost if he purchased it fully furnished. Pleasantly surprised at the amount quoted, after a brief haggle with the vendors he'd agreed to buy the apartment and all the furniture.

It would make the house move the complete fresh start he both wanted and needed.

Tom intended to share the apartment with his girlfriend Bailey. She had been spending more and more time at the cottage in Linby and had made a commitment to move into the apartment full time after the purchase was complete.

Bailey hadn't yet seen the property as she had been working in London for the last three months and Tom had hardly seen her. He knew better than to ask questions about her job. He'd shown her a couple of photographs of the apartment though and she had reassured him that she thought it all looked lovely.

He was still a little nervous that for whatever reason, she wouldn't like it.

He glanced at his watch and was suddenly shaken from his thoughts as he remembered that he was due to pick Bailey up from Nottingham Midland train station in less than an hour's time. Galvanised into action, he began unpacking boxes in earnest. He desperately wanted the apartment to have the wow factor when she walked in and saw it for the first time.

An hour later, Tom took a last look around the apartment before he went out the door. The main open plan living area was now free from cardboard boxes and it looked amazing, as did the bespoke kitchen at the far end of the large space. The large balcony was also free of clutter and once again he smiled as he took in the views. He knew there was still a large number of unpacked boxes in the second of the two bedrooms, but importantly the master bedroom was clean and tidy. He knew that the fitted wardrobes in there would need some serious sorting out once Bailey had moved all her clothes in as well.

The bathroom was looking superb; with its honey coloured travertine and marble tiles and large walk in shower, it was just perfect. The shower incorporated a huge walk in wet room that would easily accommodate two people. Tom found himself smiling again as he anticipated taking long, lingering showers with Bailey.

He suddenly exclaimed, 'Christ, Bailey!'

He looked at his watch, her train from London was due to arrive at six o'clock, in just five minutes time. Luckily the apartment was only a five-minute drive to the railway station. He grabbed his coat and sprinted out the door.

After parking the car, Tom had jogged over to Platform 5, where he waited for the express from St Pancras to arrive.

As he waited for the train, his thoughts drifted back to the first time he'd met Bailey. It had been at Liverpool

Lime Street train station, when Tom had been involved in an undercover operation to bring down a gang of armed robbers who were believed to have been responsible for the murder of an off-duty police officer.

At that first meeting, there was no way either of them could have anticipated the tragic chain of events that had drawn them so close together. Tom had always been a great believer in fate and the circumstances of his meeting and subsequent relationship with Bailey, just reinforced that belief.

The noise of the approaching express train pulled Tom out of his reverie.

Finally, the train came to a stop, the noise of the diesel engines diminished as doors burst open and passengers poured out across the platform. Desperately, he craned his neck trying to catch a glimpse of Bailey. It suddenly hit him exactly how much he'd been missing her and just how important she was to him now.

Through the crowds of people getting off the train, he finally got a glimpse of her. It was her striking, long auburn hair that he saw first, quickly followed by her large beaming smile as she began to trot along the platform towards him. She was dressed casually, in tight black jeans, black pixie boots and a figure-hugging cream coloured crew neck sweater. She was dragging a large overnight bag behind her

As he watched her trotting towards him, he experienced the same familiar stirrings that he always felt when he was with her.

Tom walked quickly along the platform until finally, they were in each other's arms. Bailey threw her arms around his neck and planted a long, lingering kiss on his lips that seemed to go on forever.

Finally, as their lips parted Tom held her close and said breathlessly, 'Mmmm, it's so good to see you.'

Bailey smiled up at him and asked, 'Have you missed me sweetheart?'

Tom answered the question with another long kiss.

'Get a room you two!', laughed a couple of young girls, who'd also been on the train and were now walking past them on the platform.

Tom and Bailey both laughed at the comment.

'Talking of rooms', said Tom, 'I've got something to show you. I hope you're gonna like it.'

Bailey smiled and said, 'Let's go sweetheart, I can't wait to see it. I haven't thought about anything else, the pictures you sent me were amazing.'

He grabbed her overnight bag and they walked along the platform holding hands. Excited about the apartment and the prospect of sharing a home together, Tom found himself grinning like a Cheshire cat and when he glanced at Bailey, he saw she was doing exactly the same.

After the short drive from the station, Tom parked his car in the secure, gated car parking area of the apartment block. He noticed the look of approval on Bailey's face as they walked across the impressive courtyard. He pressed in the code that allowed him access into the communal lobby area. They took the lift to the tenth floor and finally they both stood outside the front door of the apartment.

Tom suddenly felt very nervous, he was filled with anxiety, he was so desperate for her to love the apartment.

He unlocked the front door then grabbed Bailey, lifting her, sweeping her into his arms so he could carry her over the threshold.

She squealed with laughter, then said softly, 'Well, Tom Naylor, you old romantic.'

Tom kissed her then put her down. He grabbed her bag from the doorstep and closed the front door. He took a step back, allowing her to get her first look at the apartment.

Her eyes got steadily wider and she spoke only one word, 'Wow!'

She walked around the spacious apartment to the open plan kitchen nodding her head in approval.

Finally, she turned to Tom and said, 'This is absolutely beautiful sweetheart, the pictures didn't do it justice at all.'

With a theatrical flourish Tom swept open the large patio doors that led out onto the spacious balcony and Bailey stepped outside into the cool evening air. It was dark and the buildings either side of the river, already had lights on inside them.

Tom stood behind her on the balcony and said, 'Wait until you see the view in the morning sweetheart, it's amazing.'

'It's wonderful now', purred a smiling Bailey before continuing, 'But right now I would love to see the master bedroom. I've missed you so much Tom Naylor.'

She playfully pulled him towards her and kissed him passionately.

'Follow me', he said breathlessly as he guided her towards the bedroom.

After making love, they lay in silence, enjoying the darkness. Neither speaking, it was enough just to feel the other's presence after so long.

Bailey cuddled gently into Tom's side.

Finally, she spoke, 'This is so wonderful Tom.'

Suddenly, there was a loud buzzing noise that emanated from the open plan lounge.

Tom looked over towards the bedside alarm clock and exclaimed, 'Shit! It's eight o'clock, that'll be Matt and Kate. We'd better get dressed.'

Bailey said, 'You are joking, aren't you?'

'No, I'm not. I'm so sorry sweetheart. I invited Matt this morning as we left work. I told him to pop over later with Kate, so they could check out the new place. I never thought that we would be, well, you know.'

Bailey smiled and said, 'So, not such a romantic after all, Mr Naylor.'

'Sorry, I'd better go and let them in.'

'I think you'd better point me in the direction of the bathroom first sweetheart.'

Bailey scooped up her clothes from the floor of the bedroom before walking towards the bathroom.

Just before she went in, she grinned and said, 'One other thing Tom, try and relax will you. You look like a schoolboy who's just been caught reading Playboy by his Mum!'

Giggling loudly, she closed the bathroom door, while Tom went back into the bedroom to retrieve his clothes. He quickly got dressed, took a few deep breaths and pressed the intercom to allow Matt and his wife access to the apartments.

He said into the intercom, 'Hi Matt. Take the lift on your right. It's the tenth floor. The lift will open directly opposite the front door. See you in a minute.'

Less than a minute later, there was a soft knock on the front door of the apartment.

Bailey had now emerged fully clothed from the bathroom and stood next to Tom as he opened the door to welcome his visitors.

He took the two bottles of red wine from Kate and said, 'Hi guys, good to see you, come in.'

They both stepped inside and Tom immediately took Matt out onto the balcony to check out the view. Kate slipped her arm around Bailey and with a wicked grin she said knowingly, 'Please tell me that we haven't just gate-crashed a very private housewarming party.'

Bailey winked, smiled and said, 'Not at all, whatever gave you that idea?'

Both women laughed as they walked out onto the balcony to join Tom and Matt.

CHAPTER 10

3.00pm 20th October 1990
Glenveagh National Park,
County Donegal, Ireland

For Mickey Ryan and Richie Keane, it promised to be an exciting day.

The two friends had been picked up from their homes in Londonderry just after three o'clock that morning.

Nobody else in the battered, old Transit van had said a word as they got in. They were driven in silence from the city out into the countryside.

Half a mile out of the city, the van had stopped in a concealed layby. Another vehicle had pulled in behind the parked van and two masked men had got out. Both of these men carried pistols and ordered the men out of the Transit. With a real sense of trepidation, Mickey and Richie had done as they were told. One of the two masked men applied blindfolds to the two friends before guiding them back to their seats on the van with a terse order, 'Sit back down and don't say a fucking word!'

In total silence the two best friends had sat next to each other in the van, never once trying to remove the blindfold as the vehicle was driven off at speed.

Both Mickey and Richie had been low level volunteers in the Provisional IRA ever since they left school. As they grew older, they had graduated from stealing cars and rioting on the streets, to being involved in robberies and punishment beatings. The two men were both twenty-four years of age and today was going to be a huge step up for them. They both hoped it would lead to them being chosen to be members of an Active Service Unit sometime in the future.

Today was the first time they were going to receive instruction in the use of firearms at a secret location somewhere in the Republic.

For Mickey especially, it was an exciting day.

He desperately wanted to impress his beautiful young wife.

His wife was the daughter of staunch republican parents with a long history of being involved with the IRA. Mickey had married Bronagh Doran five years ago.

Bronagh was stunningly beautiful and Mickey knew full well that in reality she was way out of his league. He saw the way other men, better looking and more successful than he was, cast envious eyes at his young wife. He thought that if he became a member of an ASU it would impress her enough to never stray from his side.

Suddenly, the van they were in came to a skidding halt.

The driver said, 'Sit still and wait until we fetch you. You can remove your blindfolds now.'

Very slowly the men in the back of the van took off the blindfolds.

It was just starting to get light and the men could see they were now on a dirt track in very dense woodland.

Mickey looked to his left and saw a group of men wearing combat fatigues and black woollen ski masks standing in the trees. All the men were carrying black Armalite rifles.

He nudged Richie and whispered, 'Jesus Richie, look here.'

Seeing the group of armed men, Richie said quietly, 'Fuck me, I hope those boys are on our side or we're fucked.'

The group of armed men walked over to the Transit and one of them barked an order, 'Out of the van now!'

As instructed the volunteers all got out of the van and lined up.

There were eight volunteers in all.

The same man who had ordered them out of the vehicle now said, 'Today will be the first day of your education. You'll be split up into pairs and each pair will go with two instructors to learn how to handle the Armalite rifle and a self-loading pistol. Pay attention to what you're being shown and listen carefully to your instructors. Welcome to the armed struggle, men.'

Mickey and Richie had made sure they stayed together when the pairings were allocated. They had spent the day with their two instructors, stripping down the weapons and reassembling them. Practicing dry firing drills, until they were used to the weight and feel of the weapons in their hands.

As the afternoon wore on, they were finally taken to an area referred to by their instructors as 'The Ranges'. At long last they were allowed to load and fire the weapons. Much to Mickey's disgust, Richie had shown a natural aptitude for marksmanship and had received glowing praise from his instructors.

At the ranges there were several other men all firing weapons, honing their skills. One of these men had a huge rifle, much bigger than any of the others being used. This man stood apart from the other volunteers, remaining quiet and aloof, not speaking.

Mickey whispered, 'Richie, look at the size of that fucking rifle. Do you think you could fire that beast?'

One of their instructors overheard the comment and said, 'Forget about that boys, you'll never get anywhere near that rifle. That's only for use by the best of the best and you pair of fuckers don't come anywhere close.'

After a long, exhausting day, all the volunteers sat in the dense woodland enjoying a hot drink.

Mickey turned to Richie and said, 'I need a favour Richie. I've brought my little camera along and I need you to take a photo of me holding this fucking Armalite.'

'No fucking way Mickey. If they see us with a camera, we'll get the shit kicked out of us.'

'Not if we're careful. Come on man, I want to be able to show Bronagh what her husband's been up to all day.'

'I don't know Mickey, it's too fucking risky.'

'Come on, while I've still got the rifle with me. If we stand over there out of the way you can take a sly one before anyone sees us.'

Finally, Richie relented, 'Okay. But for fucks sake be careful.'

The two men walked a short distance away from where the other men were enjoying a hot drink.

Richie manoeuvred himself so he was standing on the far side of Mickey looking back towards the group.

Mickey slipped him the small camera, before holding a menacing pose gripping the black rifle.

Quickly, Richie took two photographs before handing back the camera.

A grinning Mickey slipped the camera back into his jacket pocket and the two men sauntered back to the group where the other volunteers were all casting admiring glances at the huge rifle being held by the quiet man, who still hadn't spoken a single word to any of them throughout the day.

Suddenly, the Chief Instructor shouted, 'Right men, quickly finish your drinks, then hand your weapons and any ammunition you've got in your pockets back to your instructors. Your transport will be arriving in ten minutes time, start making your way back down the track. One last thing, do not breathe a word of what's happened here today. You all know the consequences if you do.'

The men all grunted an acknowledgement and began handing in weapons.

A quarter of an hour later and with the blindfolds reapplied, the men were all being driven out of the Glenveagh National Park and back towards Londonderry in the North.

Mickey couldn't wait to get the film in his little camera developed so he could show Bronagh the calibre of the man she had married.

Beneath his blindfold he was smiling broadly, already anticipating the night of lovemaking that would follow, once Bronagh had seen the photograph of him gripping the large black Armalite rifle.

Today had been an excellent day.

CHAPTER 11

9.00am 20th October 1990
Trent Embankment, Nottingham

The morning sunlight streamed into the master bedroom and gradually roused Tom and Bailey from their deep sleep. The night before had been a fun filled, boozy affair spent with Matt and Kate. The wine had flowed as they had finished unpacking the last remaining boxes that had been stashed in the spare bedroom. It was getting late by the time their friends had finally left the apartment and an exhausted Tom and Bailey had collapsed into bed.

Now as he slowly woke up, Tom stretched and snuggled in behind a stirring Bailey.

He wrapped his arms around her and said softly, 'Good morning sweetheart, did you sleep well?'

'Mmmm, like a log.'

They lay together for another twenty minutes, not speaking, just revelling in that feeling of closeness and intimacy.

Relishing that wonderful feeling of skin on skin contact a husky voiced Bailey said quietly, 'I think we should go and try out that massive walk in shower Tom. What do you think?'

'I think that sounds like a wonderful idea.'

They walked into the shower and turned on the powerful jets. The feeling of the hot water increased their sense of intimacy and slowly they made love, enjoying their precious time together.

Half an hour later and feeling fully refreshed from the shower, they were sitting on the balcony enjoying the morning sun, dressed only in the soft, cream dressing gowns Tom had purchased for just such an occasion. He had made some freshly brewed coffee and buttered crumpets and they sat enjoying their breakfast looking out at the stunning views.

The weather was beautiful. It was one of those crisp, bright October mornings and although it was still quite cool, the air felt fresh and clean. The bright sunlight was sparkling on the deep blue water of the River Trent way down below them.

The vistas along the river were stunning in either direction. From the balcony of the apartment you could look down onto the famous Trent Bridge stretching across the wide river. To the left, the river made its way past Nottingham Forest football ground before meandering its way out of the city and into the countryside. To the right, the river made its way in a much straighter line drifting past the white stone, County Council building, looking resplendent with the bright sunlight reflecting off its green tiled rooftop. Here the river was flanked by a large park and the riverbank was blurred and hidden by large trees.

Directly ahead and away beyond the far bank, there was a clear view of the Trent Bridge cricket ground in the foreground and the rows of older Georgian style houses that made up the suburb of West Bridgford, stretched off into the distance. Beyond the houses, there was nothing but open fields as the city gave way to the countryside.

The view was spectacular whichever way you looked. It was simply breath-taking.

Bailey took a sip of her hot coffee and said, 'We're going to be so happy here, I can tell. It's absolutely beautiful.'

Tom looked at her and smiled.

She smiled back, but Tom noticed there was a faraway look and a half hidden troubled expression beneath her eyes.

He quickly said, 'What is it, what's wrong?'

'I'm sorry Tom, I didn't want to burst your bubble yesterday. I've got to be back in London this evening for a briefing.'

'What? You've only just got here. I thought you'd got a week off?'

'I know, I'm sorry. All leave's been cancelled. Something's bubbling Tom, but I haven't got a clue what it's all about.'

Unable to disguise his disappointment Tom huffed and said, 'You wouldn't bloody tell me if you did know!'

'Don't be like that. You know the score. Why do you want to behave like a child and spoil what little time we do have?'

Tom relented and said softly, 'I know, I'm sorry sweetheart, I'm just so disappointed. I've been looking forward to this for so long.'

Bailey stood and walked over to him, bent forward, kissed him and whispered, 'Me too darling.'

Tom kissed her back and whispered, 'What train do you have to catch?'

'I need to be on the two o'clock train to St Pancras, which gives us about three hours.'

She took Tom's hand and gently pulled him back to the master bedroom.

CHAPTER 12

4.30pm 18th December 1990
Metro Shopping Centre,
Newcastle, Tyne and Wear

Declan O'Hagan and JJ Hegarty blended in easily with the large crowds of shoppers who were all intent on grabbing that vital last-minute Christmas present. The only difference between them and the rest of the crowds was that they were intent on leaving a present of their own somewhere within the huge, bustling Metro Shopping Centre.

The present they wanted to leave was a harbinger of death and destruction and was made up of wires, batteries and Semtex high explosive.

Hegarty said under his breath, 'Would you look at this lot, you'd never guess there's still a week to go before Christmas.'

Looking around him at the busy crowds, Declan replied, 'I know what you mean, I can't believe it's so fucking busy. Let's move further down onto the main concourse where the carol singers are. There's sure to be a good spot near them.'

The two men walked casually along the busy mall looking into the windows of the large stores that were festooned with Christmas decorations. Both men were carrying several shopping bags. It was the Marks and Spencer plastic carrier bag being carried by Hegarty that contained the small plastic Tupperware box packed with about three pounds of Semtex and a timer device. The timer had been primed to allow the improvised explosive device to detonate at around midday tomorrow.

Today was Friday, the men had seen for themselves on their two previous visits to the Metro Centre that Saturday was always the busiest day.

O'Hagan had been instructed by his commanders that the first bomb of this campaign on the British mainland should be set to cause the maximum casualties and the most severe damage and destruction in order to create the biggest climate of fear possible.

Part of the IRA's overall plan was to cause economic disruption by fear. O'Hagan knew that the horror of this first bombing would make people think twice about venturing out shopping in the remaining days leading up to the Christmas holidays. He saw it as his mission to make the British public think that if a bomb of this size could be planted in one of the busiest shopping centres in the UK then nowhere was safe.

Neither O'Hagan or Hegarty had ever spoken about the carnage they knew they would be wreaking. They had never discussed the many innocent men, women and children that would undoubtedly be killed and maimed. Their only concern was for the success of their mission and the cause they were fighting for.

When the four men of the ASU had finally received the order from the Commander of the Londonderry Brigade to commence the bombing campaign they were overjoyed and had celebrated long into the night.

The choice of targets had been left entirely to Declan O'Hagan, the only stipulation from command was to ensure that the first bomb was detonated in the week before Christmas and that it must be a spectacular success that caused maximum casualties and maximum damage.

Having received the order to commence the campaign, O'Hagan and Hegarty had been back to the arms cache they had secreted in the woods at Moorgreen in Nottinghamshire. They had removed just enough Semtex to manufacture two bombs.

Both men knew that half of the six pounds of Semtex they took from the cache would be more than enough to cause total devastation and huge loss of life. They were unconcerned, both men were grimly looking forward to their task. They felt a sense of euphoria that they would finally have the opportunity to strike back and cause suffering to people they saw as oppressors.

Having retrieved the explosives from the cache, Declan had passed it over to the twin brothers Liam and Gerry Quinn. They were the skilled bomb makers in the ASU and it was their role to manufacture a viable improvised explosive device.

Using nothing more sophisticated than a medium sized Tupperware lunch box, electrical wire, a battery, a small detonator and a timer unit they had very quickly built a deadly device. The brothers had purchased a number of the timer units of the kind usually used by people to let them know when their car parking meter was running out.

It had been the responsibility of Gerry Quinn in particular to ensure that the timing of the explosion would be such that it would cause the maximum loss of life. O'Hagan had instructed him to time the explosion for as near to midday as possible. Gerry had used all his skills as a bomb maker to try and make the timer as accurate as possible. He had advised O'Hagan that it would be an approximation as the only parking meter timers they had been able to obtain were notoriously poor quality and were never entirely accurate.

Once the brothers had done their work they remained in Derby while O'Hagan and Hegarty travelled north to Newcastle to plant the device. It was Hegarty who had been given the task of actually carrying the lethal device on the final leg of its journey.

Both men were now meandering aimlessly along the main concourse of the Metro Centre, weaving in and out of the way of harassed looking shoppers dashing by.

'What time do you have now JJ?' asked O'Hagan.

'I make it nearly five o'clock. What time does this place close for the day?'

'It should be closing at six o'clock tonight. Let's have five and sit here for a while. We can take the weight off and enjoy the carol singers, they sound pretty good. I tell you what, leave all the bags here with me and go and fetch us a couple of coffees.'

'No problem. Do you want anything to eat?'

'That's a good shout, I'm bloody starving. See if they've any mince pies. All these carols are getting me in the festive spirit.'

O'Hagan's lips parted in a cruel smile. Hegarty grinned back, put the bags down at O'Hagan's feet and made his way to the nearest coffee shop.

As he sat there with all the shopping bags beneath his seat, O'Hagan began to take a serious look around the area he was now sitting in. The place was absolutely full of people that had paused from their shopping to listen to the efforts of the carol singers, just as he himself had done.

Directly in front of the small stage where the carol singers were performing was a large poster that declared in bold letters that the Newcastle and Gateshead Brass Band together with the Tyneside Carollers Society would be in concert here on Saturday 19th December from 11.30am onwards.

O'Hagan muttered under his breath, 'Tomorrow morning, that's perfect.'

He then began looking around the area of the stage in earnest, trying to locate somewhere he could secrete the deadly device. He needed to find somewhere it wouldn't be discovered before tomorrow morning.

Suddenly, he saw the perfect place.

On the wall to his right he could see a red fire extinguisher box. O'Hagan knew that the box would contain two fire extinguishers. One for general fires and one for electrical fires. He also knew there would be adequate space for the Tupperware lunchbox to fit in beside the extinguishers.

The only thing he had to work out now, was how to get the makeshift bomb into the fire extinguisher box without being seen.

As O'Hagan pondered a solution to this problem, Hegarty returned with two hot coffees and two of the biggest mince pies O'Hagan had ever seen.

O'Hagan grinned and said, 'By Christ JJ, who baked these fuckers, Desperate Dan?'

Hegarty laughed at the joke and handed O'Hagan a large polystyrene carton of coffee, then sat down next to him.

O'Hagan took a huge bite of mince pie then said, 'JJ, I think I've found the ideal place to leave the package. Do you see the red fire extinguisher box over there to the right? It would be perfect, so it would. We just have to figure out how to get it in there without being spotted.'

'It looks just right', agreed Hegarty.

'Let's sit here and have our coffees, wait for the crowds to thin out a little. As soon as it's a little less busy we can go over and stand by the box. You'll have to stand directly in front of me while I bend down and pretend to tie my shoe lace. As soon as I kneel down in front of the box, I can prime the bomb and open the door a fraction, just enough to place the lunch box inside. It will only take a matter of seconds, then we can get the fuck out of here. I've heard enough Christmas Carols for one day.'

Hegarty nodded enthusiastically and took a large gulp of coffee to wash down a massive mouthful of mince pie.

'JJ, you eat like a fucking pig, so you do!', said O'Hagan, grimacing.

Hegarty just smiled a pastry filled grin and the two men settled down to wait for the crowds to clear.

Less than half an hour later, both men made their way out of the Metro Centre. They walked calmly back to the car park, having successfully deposited their deadly package inside the fire extinguisher box.

The hastily thought out plan had been executed to perfection. O'Hagan had squatted down on his haunches as though he was tying his shoelaces while Hegarty stood directly in front of him hiding him from view. Having checked that the fire box was unlocked, in a flash O'Hagan had removed the lunch box from the carrier bag and in one movement had primed the bomb and placed it inside the box, where it nestled tightly beneath the two red extinguishers. Closing the door carefully, O'Hagan had then stood up and both men had casually walked away knowing that at around midday tomorrow the bomb would explode just as the brass band and the carollers were starting their concert.

O'Hagan and Hegarty knew full well that the majority of people watching and listening in delight to the brass band

and the carol singers would be young mothers with small, excited children eager to experience the magic of Christmas for the first time. Both men also knew that anyone standing within fifty yards of the explosion would be killed instantly.

Neither of them could give a shit.

Once in the car park, they placed their dummy shopping bags in the boot of the Ford Sierra then drove slowly out of the car park.

Hegarty was driving.

O'Hagan relaxed and leaned back in the front passenger seat.

He smiled and said, 'Good work today JJ, let's get back to Derby and see what tomorrow brings. I'm going to have a little kip now, when we get a bit closer to Derby if you see a quiet pub let's stop and have a quick pint, I'm gasping.'

An equally relaxed and happy Hegarty replied, 'Now that does sound like a great idea.'

The only reply from O'Hagan was a soft snore as he quickly fell asleep.

CHAPTER 13

7.30pm 18th December 1990
Kilmacrennan, County Donegal

The crunch of tyres on gravel and the flash of headlights through the lounge window of his secluded cottage was enough to make Sean O'Connor spring into action. He leapt across the room and quickly retrieved the loaded double-barrelled shotgun he had hidden behind a chest of drawers.

It was already dark outside and he wasn't expecting anybody.

He switched off all the lights and checked that his weapon was loaded. He always kept it loaded and ready, but he was a creature of habit and checked the weapon anyway.

The cottage was in the middle of nowhere, access was by a single dirt track through the forest. Only a handful of people knew he'd purchased the tiny cottage in the National Park and he never had visitors.

He squatted in the darkened hallway, with the shotgun resting across his legs.

He heard a car door slam, then the sound of a single set of footsteps walking slowly across the pea gravel driveway towards the front door.

Very slowly, O'Connor eased the hammers back on the double-barrelled shotgun and levelled it at the front door.

Suddenly, there was a loud knocking on the door and a voice yelled, 'Sean. Are you in there? It's me, Eddie

Macready. Come on lad, stop fucking about I'm freezing to death out here!'

Without saying a word, O'Connor silently moved out of the hallway and made his way to the back door of the cottage. He was only wearing a thin cotton T-shirt, jeans and a pair of woollen socks on his feet. Ignoring the freezing conditions, he crept outside and made his way stealthily along the concrete path to the front of the cottage. As he reached the edge of the building line he peered around the corner and could see a dark red Vauxhall Astra estate car, lit up by the bright moonlight.

He could see that the car was empty.

There was more loud banging on the front door and more shouts, 'Come on Sean. I'm freezing my fucking arse off out here!'

Levelling the shotgun at waist height, O'Connor stepped into view and said quietly, 'What do you want?'

A startled Eddie Macready spun round and faced O'Connor. His eyes widened when he saw the shotgun that was pointed directly at his midriff.

He spluttered, 'Jesus Christ Sean! You scared me to death. What the fuck's the shotgun for?'

'Did you tell me you were coming?'

'No, I fancied a drive out to have a chat with you, that's all. I wanted to discuss a few things.'

'Are you alone?'

'Yes, I'm on my own. For God's sake Sean, put the gun down, you're making me nervous.'

O'Connor eased the hammers of the shotgun slowly forward and finally lowered the weapon. He said brusquely, 'This way.'

He walked back around to the back door with Macready following.

As soon as both men were inside the cottage, O'Connor locked the door and switched the kitchen light on.

Macready grinned and said, 'That's a hell of a way to greet visitors, Sean.'

Putting the shotgun back behind the chest of drawers O'Connor said, 'Let me know you're coming over next time. I never have visitors here.'

'Okay I get it. You can't be too careful. Have you got anything to drink out here?'

'I don't drink, I can make tea if you want some?'

'It's fine, I won't bother, thanks.'

'Why are you here Mr Macready?'

Macready grinned and said, 'That's what I like about you Sean, always straight to the point, no messing about.'

O'Connor said nothing.

The awkward silence was broken by Macready, 'I just wanted to ask you how you felt things were progressing?'

'Fine. Sixteen kills so far. Why?'

'I just wondered if you felt there was anything else you could do? To further our cause, so to speak?'

'I'm doing what you asked me. Is there something else you want me to do? Is everything okay?'

'Yes, everything's fine. I wanted to let you know that your work is really starting to make a difference. Patrols around the border area are already lessening, which means it's easier for our volunteers to move back and forth across the border unhindered.'

'That's all good then.'

'It is Sean, it is. I just think that maybe in the future we could use your skills in a far more devastating way.'

'I don't understand.'

'How would you feel about really taking the fight to the enemy and working your magic on the mainland?'

O'Connor sat deep in thought for a few minutes before saying quietly, 'I don't know Mr Macready. I've already been away from home for a long time, I was just settling in again. I'm happy doing what I'm doing.'

'It was just a thought Sean, something that occurred to me the other day. Let's leave things as they are, shall we? Maybe that other notion is something we can consider in the future.'

'Whatever you think. Are you sure you don't want a hot drink?'

'No thanks, I just wanted to run that by you, to see what your thoughts on the matter were. I'll get going now. I don't want to be too late driving back into Derry. The Brit patrols will be out soon stopping everything that moves.'

Macready stood and walked through the cottage to the front door.

O'Connor unlocked the door and watched as his commander walked to his car.

Just before he got inside his car Macready turned, pointed at O'Connor and with a note of anger in his voice he said, 'By the way Sean, that's the first and last time you ever point a weapon at me son, got it! I'll let you know when I'm coming over next time.'

O'Connor said nothing and shut the door, immediately locking and bolting it. As he walked back into the living room and sat down his mind was in turmoil.

He thought he was doing a good job?

Why would Macready want to send him overseas again?

He had no answers. Instead he got up, walked through to the kitchen and put the kettle on, he tried not to think about the surreal meeting he had just had with his commander. As he sipped the hot, sweet tea, he vowed to be on his guard around Macready.

There was something about the grey-haired old man he didn't trust.

CHAPTER 14

8.10am 19th December 1990
Metro Shopping Centre,
Newcastle, Tyne and Wear

It was the last job of the day for Mavis Goodhew and Barbara Jenkins.

The two friends had been at work since six o'clock that morning, cleaning the public areas of the Metro Shopping Centre, ready for the expected crowds of Christmas shoppers. It was going to be one of the busiest shopping days of the year and the ladies had a certain pride in their work. They wanted the place to be spotless.

They had one final sweep through to do. The area around the stage where the brass band would be playing later that day, still needed to be mopped and swept.

Mavis was tutting furiously as she had already cleaned this area once.

All her hard work had been undone in an instant when members of the band had walked in, stomping all over her polished lino floor with wet boots. It was raining heavily outside and it looked as though the band members had found every muddy puddle before coming inside to leave their instruments in position on the stage ready for the days concert. As soon as they had dumped their instruments, they had immediately all headed back outside to the only coffee shop that was open.

The only member of the band who had remained was Geoff Riddings.

Geoff was very overweight. He was a large man in every sense, with a huge bushy beard. He was still puffing slightly after carrying the large brass tuba from the boot of his car into the shopping centre.

He needed a moment to catch his breath. He had unbuttoned his vivid scarlet and gold tunic and was now sitting with his feet dangling off the stage. As he took a few deep breaths to restore some oxygen to his body, he was staring blankly at the red fire extinguisher box.

That's unusual, he thought to himself, as he noticed that the door to the box was ever so slightly ajar.

His thoughts were suddenly disturbed by a now extremely irate Mavis Goodhew, who yelled at him, 'Howay man! Pick your feet up. I haven't got all day! We've already swept this place once ya nah!'

Geoff gave the cleaners his most benign smile and said quickly, 'I'm really sorry ladies, let me get out of your way.'

They would be the last words he ever spoke and the last words that Mavis and Barbara would ever hear. At that exact moment the parking timer completed the circuit and detonated the bomb, approximately three hours and thirty minutes early.

The explosion caused by just three pounds of Semtex was massive. Geoff Riddings, Mavis Goodhew and Barbara Jenkins were literally blown to pieces, all three killed instantly in a cauldron of hot twisted metal and debris.

The entire structure of the huge building shook with the force of the pressure wave caused by the blast. Along with the sound of the explosion itself, the air was filled with the sound of breaking glass as every plate glass window within the shopping centre was shattered by the shock wave from the blast. Each plate glass window shattered into thousands of lethal, dagger like, shards of razor-sharp glass.

Immediately after that crescendo of sound, there was an eerie silence for two to three seconds before countless alarm systems began to shrill out their useless, impotent warning.

Three people had died instantly in the blast. The only other person in proximity to the explosion was another cleaner.

Lily Fretwell, had been busily sweeping the polished floor of the main mall some seventy yards away from the centre of the blast.

She had been working with her back towards the area where her two friends, Mavis and Barbara, had been cleaning.

The force of the blast had lifted her off her feet and dumped her back down on the floor some twenty feet further along the mall. Her clothes were shredded with shards of glass and she had suffered multiple lacerations all over her body. She was now barefoot as the blast had lifted her clean out of her shoes.

Her left arm was badly broken and was now hanging at an unnatural angle at the side of her body. The hair on the back of her head had been singed from the heat of the blast. Lily was now totally deaf as both her eardrums had been perforated by the shock wave and she could no longer hear her own screams that now added to the crescendo of noise from the alarm systems.

Very slowly, a few brave men began to enter the shopping centre from outside. They were shocked and horrified by the sights and sounds that confronted them and quickly left the area again. Two men from the brass band, who had previously worked down the local mines, ventured into the shopping centre corridors that were now rapidly filling with smoke as small fires sprang up everywhere.

It was these two brave men who found a screaming, hysterical, badly injured Lily Fretwell. Very carefully, they tried to lift her from the wreckage and debris she had been covered in.

Wherever they tried to get hold of Lily it felt like they were pushing shards of glass deeper into her already bleeding wounds.

Eventually, they managed to lift her using her ragged clothes and get her outside into the fresh air where they were met by the arriving emergency services.

If the bomb had detonated just thirty minutes later as the shop workers and early bird shoppers began to arrive, the devastation would have been equally as catastrophic, but the loss of life would have been far greater.

As it was, three people were dead and another very seriously injured. Countless other people were in a state of severe shock and it was patently obvious that the repair bill for the extensive damage caused to the four-year-old shopping centre would run into millions of pounds.

CHAPTER 15

9.00am 19th December 1990
Peartree District, Derby

'Wake up Declan, wake up!'

'For Christs sake Gerry, what's wrong?'

'Nothing's wrong. You need to hear the news!'

'What fucking news? What the fuck are you talking about?'

'The bomb's gone off already, it's just been on the news, come and see!'

A now fully awake Declan O'Hagan jumped out of bed and raced downstairs to the living room where he found Liam and JJ staring at the breakfast news on the television.

Hegarty turned to O'Hagan and said, 'It's all over the BBC on Breakfast News, Dec.'

Declan stared at the television in the corner of the room. There was a very shocked reporter standing against a backdrop of smashed shop windows and shredded mannequins.

The strap line at the bottom of the screen read, "Explosion kills three in Newcastle's Metro Shopping Centre"

The reporter was talking directly to camera now, 'The reason for the devastating explosion isn't yet known. Early indications are that a fractured gas main may be the cause, but the police aren't ruling out terrorism.'

Suddenly, Declan O'Hagan erupted with a fury the other three members of the ASU hadn't previously seen. His fury was aimed at Gerry and Liam Quinn as he roared, 'Which one of you two fucking idiots set the timer?'

Gerry looked down at the floor and said quietly, 'It was me Declan. I did try to tell you that those fucking parking timers are shite, but you wouldn't listen.'

'Oh! I see, so now it's my fucking fault is it?' he said menacingly as he stepped towards Gerry. Without batting an eyelid, O'Hagan punched Gerry Quinn hard in the mouth. The force of the blow caused Gerry to fall backwards on to the floor.

Instantly, his twin brother Liam, leapt to his feet and got between Declan and his brother. Liam pushed O'Hagan backwards and shouted, 'It's nobody's fault! Not yours, Declan and not my brother's either, now fucking back off!'

There was a tense moment of silence as both men glared at each other. Eventually, Liam took a deep breath and said, 'Whatever happened to that fucking timer, we've still scored a massive blow. It said on the report that three people have been killed. There are fatalities, that's all that matters. Nobody really cares if it's three or three hundred dead. The message is now out there and that message is clear and unambiguous. The IRA are operational and none of you are safe anywhere. If we can explode a bomb in that busy shopping centre, we can do it anywhere. That's the important thing to remember Dec, not numbers of casualties.'

O'Hagan was breathing hard, his eyes still wild. Hegarty gripped his arm and said quietly, 'The lad's right Declan.'

Slowly, O'Hagan regained his composure and said, 'You're right.'

He walked over to Gerry, who was still sitting on the floor nursing a bloody mouth.

O'Hagan reached down to the injured man and said, 'I'm sorry Gerry, I shouldn't have reacted like that. I know you did your best and you did tell me that those fucking timers were shite. I'm sorry. No hard feelings?'

Gerry Quinn took O'Hagan's outstretched hand and stood up. He said quietly, 'None at all Declan. I'm as mad as you are that the fucking thing went off early.'

The two men embraced before O'Hagan reached for his donkey jacket, grinned and said, 'Right, I'm off to the phone box to let the press boys know that it was no fucking gas main. Score one for the boyos!'

'Amen to that!' chorused the other three men as they slapped each other triumphantly on the back.

CHAPTER 16

8.50am 19th December 1990
Trent Embankment, Nottingham

Tom Naylor stepped out onto the balcony of his apartment overlooking the River Trent, ten storeys below. He was wearing a towelling robe and he shuddered against the early morning chill. It was fast approaching nine o'clock in the morning and he had just come out of the shower. He needed to be leaving for work in half an hour.

He leaned on the railings and stared across the river to the City Ground, the home of Nottingham Forest Football Club. The thought crossed his mind how bizarre it was that he would have to drive almost twenty miles to Police Headquarters to report on duty when he knew that his duties would bring him straight back to this exact spot.

Nottingham Forest were playing host to high flying Manchester United today and as there was always the potential for football related violence with this particular fixture, two sections of the Special Operations Unit had been tasked to police the supporters that would be travelling down from Manchester.

Although a football fan himself, Tom despised having to police the mindless individuals who seemed hell bent on causing trouble at high profile matches such as these.

Hooliganism had long been known as the "English Disease" and had culminated in the terrible events that had unfolded at the Hillsborough Stadium earlier that year. Tom knew that changes to the way matches were going to be policed in the future would soon be coming in and he welcomed that change.

He was also very aware that it had only ever been a few moronic individuals that seemed determined to ruin England's national sport for what boiled down to nothing more than idiotic tribal differences.

The cold December air snapped Tom out of his thoughts, he pulled the heavy towelling robe closer around him and took a sip of the hot coffee he was holding. His thoughts turned to a weekend not so long ago when he had first moved into the apartment. He had spent an idyllic couple of days with his girlfriend Bailey.

That weekend had been cut short when she had to leave early and return to London for an emergency briefing. That brief moment in time with Bailey had been towards the end of October and Tom hadn't heard from her since.

He knew exactly what Bailey's career entailed; there was no way you could ask an MI5 operative what they were currently working on.

Over the last few days, he had found himself beginning to question how the relationship between them was ever going to work out. Tom knew he was falling head over heels in love with her, but he wasn't yet ready to accept the long periods when they were apart. He was painfully aware that her chosen career would mean separation on a quite regular basis.

On top of that separation, there was always the nagging fear that whatever she was involved in at any given time was dangerous. He felt a real anxiety that something could happen to her and he would never know.

He took another sip of coffee, quickly realising it had gone cold.

He looked out over the cityscape and quietly chastised himself for his negative, chauvinistic thoughts. He realised that part of the problem was what had happened to his previous girlfriend, Bev. He desperately wanted to protect Bailey after losing Bev at the hands of a psychotic madman who was hell bent on a revenge mission against him.

Tom still blamed himself for Bev's untimely death, even though he knew it was totally irrational to do so. He couldn't get away from the fact that she had been killed in a direct revenge attack for something he had done.

He knew if there was any chance of his relationship with Bailey succeeding, he would need to shake off this feeling of dread he felt every time they were apart.

As he walked back into the kitchen, he chided himself, muttering aloud, 'Get a grip man!'

Tom switched on the television in the kitchen and poured himself another coffee, before putting a couple of slices of bread in the toaster. He glanced at the wall clock as he buttered his toast. It was now nine o'clock and the Breakfast News on the BBC was full of images of Newcastle city centre.

The reporter on the news was looking ashen faced and appeared to be out of breath as he spoke wide eyed into the camera, 'Just over forty minutes ago, the Metro Shopping Centre here in Newcastle was rocked by a huge explosion. First reports indicate that there are fatalities and injuries. There are no details as yet about the exact number of these casualties, but I've seen for myself the devastation inside the shopping centre caused by the blast. It's a miracle that the explosion occurred when it did, at around eight fifteen this morning. At that time, the only people believed to be inside were cleaning staff. If the explosion had happened just half an hour later, when the shopping centre was fully open for business, the number of casualties would have been significantly higher.'

The reporter then glanced back over his shoulder allowing the camera to pan past him and focus on the main entrance to the Metro Centre. A dense cloud of thick black smoke still billowed out of the entrance, as firemen wearing breathing apparatus made their way inside.

Once again, the camera focussed on the reporter as he said, 'Although first reports from the police indicated that they believed the cause of the explosion was a fractured gas main, in a very telling statement made recently by Superintendent Jim Manley, the highest-ranking officer in attendance so far, he refused to rule out terrorism as the reason for this explosion.'

Tom again checked the clock; it was now just after nine o'clock and he realised that he had to get to work. He switched off the television, put his dirty cup and plate in the sink and said aloud, 'Bloody IRA!'

Ten minutes later and he was on his way to work.

As he drove through the city centre traffic, there was a nagging anxiety in his mind that the horrific events he had just witnessed on the television news report could somehow be connected to the absence of his girlfriend Bailey.

The more the thought lingered in his head the deeper the anxiety he felt.

Once again, he felt an all-consuming dread pass over him as he imagined Bailey pitting her wits against some shadowy IRA terrorist.

CHAPTER 17

10.30am 19th December 1990
Home Office, Marsham Street, London

The police in Newcastle knew full well that the explosion at the Metro Shopping Centre had nothing to do with a fractured gas main and had already contacted the Anti-Terrorist Branch at New Scotland Yard.

Specialist officers and forensic experts from that team were already making their way north to Newcastle in order to start the painstaking process of searching the scene of devastation for the clues that would, hopefully, one day lead to the conviction of the cold-blooded murderers of three innocents.

Three ordinary people who had arrived at the Metro Centre that morning expecting just to do a job of work, or to entertain the crowds of Christmas shoppers.

Within minutes of that call being received at New Scotland Yard, an equally urgent message had been sent from the Home Office instructing Sir Godfrey Winstanley, the current Director of MI5 to travel directly to Marsham Street personally, to provide an immediate update and emergency briefing to the Home Secretary.

Sir Godfrey Winstanley had secretly been aware that an IRA bombing campaign on the mainland could be imminent after snippets of telephone conversations emanating out of Londonderry had been intercepted by GCHQ.

In October after the first intelligence had come through, the Director had ordered MI5 personnel into Londonderry to begin trying to infiltrate various terrorist cells in an attempt to try and clarify exactly what was being organised by the Provisional IRA.

To date the operation by the security services in Londonderry had proved fruitless and now that the suspected bombing campaign had started in earnest it made it all the more imperative that good intelligence was forthcoming to identify both the people directing the operation in Londonderry and the bombers who were no doubt hiding in plain sight, somewhere in England.

The Director knew he would now face an hour of tough questioning by the bullish Home Secretary as to why this monstrous outrage in Newcastle hadn't been prevented. He would also be questioned at length on exactly what the security services were doing to ensure that no other similar atrocities occurred.

With that in mind the Director had immediately recalled all personnel back to MI5 headquarters at Millbank, London for an emergency briefing to try and prevent a full-scale bombing campaign on the British mainland. Only personnel currently engaged in undercover roles were excused the briefing.

Both the Home Secretary and the Director were acutely aware that they had been lucky this time. It was only by the grace of God, that the death toll on this occasion didn't number in the hundreds.

It was now the responsibility of both men to prevent further massacres of innocent civilians. Deep in their hearts they both knew this bomb would be the first of many. The anonymous telephone call received by a tabloid newspaper shortly after the explosion confirmed their worst fears that the explosion was the work of an Active Service Unit of the Provisional IRA.

Chillingly the message given to the press had claimed that this attack was to be the first of many and that similar bombings were planned for the length and breadth of the British Isles. It went on to say that they could strike again anywhere at any time and that nowhere should be considered safe.

As he walked into The Home Office building, the Director secretly prayed for a breakthrough from any one of the numerous agents currently working undercover across the Irish Sea in Londonderry.

Without such a breakthrough, or a huge slice of luck, it was going to be a long winter. The security services were literally looking for a needle in a haystack.

CHAPTER 18

5.30pm 10th January 1991
Fountain Hill, Londonderry

Bailey closed the door to her small bedsit on Fountain Hill. Having locked the door and buttoned up her thick coat, she made her way outside and began the walk into work. There had been flurries of snowfall throughout the day and there was still a dusting of snow on the pavements. The temperature hadn't crept above freezing all day.

Pulling her woollen scarf, tighter around her neck to try and keep out the cold, she walked carefully along the slippery pavements. It was normally only a fifteen-minute walk to the bar where she was working part time as a barmaid, but with today's treacherous conditions she would have to take her time. She had plenty of that though, as her shift wasn't due to start until six o'clock.

Bailey had been living in Londonderry since the end of October last year, after information had started to filter through to MI5 that a new bombing campaign could be about to start on the mainland. The scant intelligence suggested that the threat was credible and that it was in the advanced planning stage. The information, although very tenuous, was that this particular campaign was being orchestrated by the Derry Brigade of the Provisional IRA under the sponsorship of its militant, violent commander, Eddie Macready.

Using the undercover name of Samantha Burrows, Bailey had used the cover of being a mature student from Liverpool University on an exchange scheme studying Psychology at Thornhill College in the city.

As Sam Burrows, Bailey had managed to gain employment at the infamous O'Doyle's Bar on Abercorn Road near the banks of the River Foyle in the centre of Londonderry.

The bar was a dingy, scruffy place that hadn't been refurbished for many years. The walls were yellow, stained by the residue of a million smoked cigarettes. The floors were dark stained wood and felt sticky underfoot from spilled beer. There was one long bar that ran the length of the establishment. Inside the main bar area there were numerous small, private booths that would comfortably sit six people around a central table. Toilets were through an adjoining door at the end of the bar that led to a dark corridor. Both the Gents and the Ladies toilets were at the end of this corridor.

Although, it wasn't the most salubrious place to drink in Londonderry, it was certainly one of the busiest.

Posing as Sam Burrows, Bailey had been working there since the middle of November and had quickly become a popular, friendly face to the punters.

Speaking in her broad Scouse accent and with a very dry sense of humour, the locals, particularly the male drinkers, had taken to her sexy looks and her cheeky innuendos.

O'Doyle's Bar hadn't been chosen as her work venue at random.

The Special Branch detectives she was working closely with had briefed her fully about the type of clientele that frequented the bar and regularly drank there.

The bar was well known as being the regular meeting place for the top echelon of the Londonderry Brigade of the IRA and was a drinking hole for staunch republicans. Sam had played dumb about the politics of the place when she first went for the interview for the job of barmaid. Her engaging personality and pleasing, sexy looks meant she got the job. She had started work the same day as the interview and had pulled in four or five shifts a week ever since, telling anyone who would listen that she was a desperately poor student who needed the money to help fund her stay in Derry.

She maintained a strict policy of avoiding political discussion. If anyone tried to engage her in a political or religious conversation, she would very quickly change the subject.

Being able to play the sexy female card had been a major advantage when doing this. Even the staunchest political activist could be diverted from his zealot conversation when confronted with sparkling green eyes, a warm knowing smile and a generous eyeful of cleavage flashed their way.

Bailey knew how to play the game well. She quickly developed a cheeky, sexy persona as Sam Burrows, that she knew would have the men in the bar eating out of her hand. She promptly became part of the surroundings and very soon people felt at ease around her and would talk openly about "The Troubles" and about the Provisional IRA in particular.

Sam Burrows never appeared to be listening to a conversation and if anybody asked a question along the lines of, 'What do you think Sam?' she would always answer the same way, 'What do I think about what?'

Just before Christmas, Sam had noticed a new face coming into the bar on a regular basis. She quickly established that the handsome newcomer was in fact Danny Macready, the son of Brigade Commander, Eddie Macready. She also discovered that Danny had recently separated from his wife and had moved from Belfast back to Londonderry following a bitter, acrimonious divorce. Rumour had it that his ex-wife had taken almost every penny he had and that was why he was now living back with his father.

Danny had instantly taken a shine to Sam and often spent the entire evening just sitting on a barstool chatting to her across the bar.

He appeared to be a reserved, quiet individual with none of the bluster or arrogance displayed by his father. He didn't mix well with the other punters and seemed to live in the shadow of his infamous father. Sam had been drawn to his soft spoken, self-effacing manner and had found it both easy and pleasant to talk to him. Although he was a nationalist through and through it was obviously not the all-consuming passion it was for most of the drinkers in O'Doyle's Bar.

As she cultivated their blossoming friendship, Sam was hoping that Danny would eventually pluck up the courage to ask her out on a proper date away from all the prying eyes and ears of O'Doyle's Bar. That way she could get to know him better. Intimacy had no part in her plans, but flirting and even kissing would be on the agenda if it helped her to get closer to him. She would do anything, within reason, to try and get information about the Active Service Unit causing such mayhem and bloodshed on the mainland.

Her brief, back in October, had been that there was possibly a sleeper cell operating somewhere on the mainland and that they were volunteers from the Derry Brigade under the command of Eddie Macready. The explosion in

Newcastle before Christmas and the subsequent message left with the newspaper had confirmed this to be the case.

Sam felt that if she could get close enough to Danny then maybe, just maybe, she stood a chance of hearing a snippet of conversation that may prove significant and prevent further bloodshed.

As she made her way from Fountain Hill across the Craigavon Bridge towards the city centre, she glanced down at the black water of the river rushing by beneath her, the fast-flowing water sparkled with reflected light from the decorative lamps on the bridge. The fast currents made the river mesmerising to look at and her thoughts drifted away from Londonderry.

The wide river had sparked memories of the River Trent in Nottingham and her life in England, in particular it made her think of her boyfriend Tom Naylor. She wondered what he would think of where she was and what she was currently doing. It had been impossible to let him know where she was going. Once she had immersed herself in the undercover role, for her own safety she needed to eat, sleep and breathe the character of Samantha Burrows, student and barmaid.

She couldn't afford to even think as Bailey Masters, while ever she remained in the province, she would have to maintain her identity as Samantha Burrows.

She hoped that once she returned home, Tom would understand. It had to be this way, if she was going to survive and have a chance of protecting the public.

As she reached the end of the bridge and started to walk towards Abercorn Road and the waiting warmth of O'Doyle's Bar, she began to fully concentrate on getting back into the character of Sam Burrows. She told herself that tonight would be the night when she would be asked out by Danny Macready, on that elusive first date.

It was just after six o'clock when Sam walked into the bar. She smiled to herself when she saw that Danny was already sitting on one of the bar stools.

He smiled and said, 'Hi Sam, I wondered if my favourite barmaid would be working tonight.'

She smiled back as she undid her thick coat and removed her scarf. Her face felt flushed now that she had walked into the warm bar from the freezing cold air outside.

Having hung up her coat behind the bar she turned to face Danny, smiled again and said, 'I've got to pay the bills somehow Danny. The student grant doesn't go far and I've got no rich parents to pay my way. I'm just a poor hard up student living on Pot Noodles in a grotty bedsit.'

She leaned across the bar towards him and her blouse parted a little exposing just a tease of cleavage.

Conspiratorially she said in a breathy whisper, 'What I really need is a white knight to take me away from all this.'

She laughed out loud and leaned back from the bar.

It was now Danny's turn to lean forward, 'Seriously Sam, we get on okay though, don't we?'

He continued nervously, 'Why don't you let me take you out for dinner one evening, obviously to fit around your shifts and when you're not working? It would be my pleasure.'

Sam feigned a look of surprise and then smiled before saying, 'Do you know what Danny, I think that would be lovely, thank you.'

His face flushed slightly and he spluttered, 'Great. That's a date then is it? Let me know when you next have an evening off and I'll pick you up from your place or I can meet you here, whichever you want? It's up to you. That's just great Sam, so it is.'

Sam fluttered her eyelashes and made full eye contact as she said, 'Actually, I'm not working tomorrow night Danny, we can go then if you like?'

'Wow! That's great, fantastic. Where do you want to eat? What time shall we meet? What food do you like?'

Sam laughed out loud, 'Bloody hell Danny! One question at a time. Let's see, I like Italian food so if there's a nice Italian Restaurant around here that would be great. I'll meet you here at seven o'clock tomorrow night if that's okay with you?'

'That's bloody marvellous Sam, so it is.'

He stood up from the bar stool, finished his pint of Guinness then continued, 'I'll see you here tomorrow night then.'

'Are you off already? I've only just got here.'

'Sorry Sam, I've got loads to do. I've got to decide what to wear tomorrow and find a nice Italian Restaurant to make a reservation for my hot date', he laughed and winked at her before walking out.

The bar was now empty except for a couple of old codgers sitting in one of the booths slowly sipping pints of Guinness, trying to make them last as long as possible.

Inside, Sam was rejoicing.

Finally, she felt as though she was getting somewhere. She would contact her Special Branch liaison officer after her shift, so he could appraise London of the development.

Sam desperately hoped that Danny would only want to be friends.

He always appeared shy and was lacking a bit of confidence after his wife had dumped him. Sam was quietly confident that she would be able to keep the handsome Irishman at arm's length, long enough for her to obtain some valuable intelligence from him.

She knew that it was only a matter of time before the ASU in England continued their murderous campaign and detonated another device. Maybe this date with Danny Macready would prove to be the little breakthrough that was required. Maybe she would start getting some worthwhile intelligence on the bombers sooner rather than later.

CHAPTER 19

1.00pm 11th January 1991
Inniskeen, County Monaghan

With a wide smile spread across his ruddy face, the middle aged, barrel-chested farmer opened the front door of his secluded farmhouse to the last of his guests, extended his hand and said, 'Come in, come in it's a pleasure to meet you.'

Francis Holmes shook the farmers hand and nodded without speaking. The host showed Holmes into the dining room where his other guests were already seated around an expansive dining table.

Ben Christie turned and put his arm around the farmer's huge shoulders, guiding him back towards the door and said, 'That's great Pat, thanks. You'll need to give us a little privacy now.'

Not in the least bit aggrieved at the snub, the farmer nodded and said quietly, 'Of course Ben. Whatever you say. I'll be in the kitchen if you need anything.'

'Thanks Pat. I'll call you when the meeting's finished.'

With that Ben Christie closed the door.

Seated around the table for the Provisional Army Council meeting were Jimmy Patterson, Belfast Brigade Commander and his bodyguard McGuire. Eddie Macready, Derry Brigade Commander and Eoin McAteer from Sinn Fein.

As Francis Holmes sat down at the head of the table he said quickly, 'Right, let's get down to business. I don't want this to take all day. It's already been a bloody long trek to get down here. Eoin, you've called this meeting, what's the story with the farmer? Can he be trusted to keep his mouth shut?'

Eoin McAteer coughed and cleared his throat, 'He can be trusted implicitly. Patrick is a lifelong supporter of the struggle. His own grandfather and an uncle were killed inside the Post Office building on O'Connell Street during the 1916 Easter uprising. He can be trusted; you have my word.'

Holmes stared hard at McAteer and said, 'O'Connell Street you say! Well we all know how that bloody fiasco ended don't we! Anyway, let's get down to business. It's been almost three weeks since the Newcastle bomb. I've one question for you Eddie, why was there no warning given to the press prior to the explosion? I thought we'd agreed upon a fifteen-minute warning. All I've heard in the press is that the IRA murderers gave no warning. I made it crystal clear that there must be a warning given!'

Eddie Macready could feel the eyes in the room boring into him. He glanced over at Jimmy Patterson who had a smug smirk on his face. He could feel an anger building inside him. He took a deep breath to try and compose himself then said, 'We used the parking timers that had been recommended and to be perfectly honest Frankie, they're shite!'

Patterson couldn't wait, 'If you know they're shite, why did your boys use the fucking things?'

Holmes was already in a bad mood. He rounded on Patterson and said sharply, 'Jimmy, did I ask you to speak? No, I fucking didn't, so keep your gob shut will ya!'

It was now Macready's turn to look smug.

He waited a few seconds before saying, 'The bomb was set to detonate at midday. The ASU would have phoned the warning in with fifteen minutes to go as instructed only the fucking timer was faulty and the bloody thing went off early. Had it exploded when planned, it would have been truly spectacular. The shopping centre would have been packed.'

Holmes turned to McAteer and said, 'What's the political fallout been like?'

'We've had the usual condemnation from around the world, but the publicity has been everything we hoped for. It's put Northern Ireland at the top of the news again. Politicians are beginning to take us seriously again, so as far as that goes it's had the desired effect.'

'What about reaction in America?'

'I spoke to Michael Delaney, who runs our NORAID operation in Boston and he says it's been very positive. Fundraising has increased since the bomb. In a perverse way it's probably just as well the bomb didn't go off as planned. I don't think the United States would have been so enamoured with a lot of child casualties.'

Holmes now turned back to Macready, 'What else has your ASU got planned?'

'They've enough SEMTEX for one more device before they'll need to re-supply from their cache. They are just waiting on the order to continue. The next target's already been selected and reconnoitred.'

Holmes was thoughtful for a minute and then said, 'Okay Eddie, give them the green light, but tell them to make sure they don't fuck up the timer unit again. Bearing in mind what Eoin has just said about the effect in America, let's aim for more property damage than casualties this time.

The organisation is struggling financially, we can't afford to make any mistakes that will cut off funds being sent from America. Is that clear? No more fuck ups, Eddie.'

Macready could feel his cheeks flush as Holmes once again chastised him in front of Jimmy Patterson who was grinning across the table showing his tobacco stained teeth.

Macready was just about to ask him what he was grinning at when once again Holmes spoke, 'That's it then. The next time we meet, let's make it somewhere a little more civilised, I'm sick of the countryside and the smell of cow shit. Good day gentlemen.'

Chair legs scraped across the tiled floor as all the men in the room stood to leave. No words were exchanged between Macready and Patterson, just dark looks and muttered threats.

The meeting was over.

The bombing campaign would continue.

CHAPTER 20

3.00pm 12th February 1991
Meadowhall Shopping Centre,
Sheffield, South Yorkshire

Declan O'Hagan and John Joseph Hegarty were standing outside the celebration cards and gift shop on the main concourse of the shopping centre. Above them was the iconic dome that could be seen from the M1 motorway.

Meadowhall Shopping Centre had only been open five months and was still attracting enormous crowds from all over the country. When the ASU had looked for suitable targets, the new shopping centre in Sheffield was high on their list.

The two men were standing on the Upper Level of the centre, their eyes scanning for somewhere to secrete the small explosive device they had brought with them.

Everywhere had been decorated for the forthcoming Valentine's Day celebration, the centre was awash with red love hearts and roses. The card shop they were standing outside was suitably decorated to attract the thousands of punters that wished to express their undying love for another by buying a piece of card with a few flowers and syrupy words on.

Neither O'Hagan or Hegarty were the least bit interested in Valentine's Day, other than it seemed like a good idea to plant the bomb they had planned for Meadowhall when the already large crowds would be swelled even further.

O'Hagan turned to Hegarty and said quietly, 'Let's try inside this shop, there's nowhere suitable out here on the concourse.'

Hegarty nodded and the two men made their way inside the shop.

Inside the cramped shop it was even more chaotic than the concourse outside. Hard-pressed staff were busy taking money from customers that had formed a long queue towards the two tills. To O'Hagan it looked as though the two electric cash registers were on the point of meltdown.

The two Irishmen made their way to the rear of the shop where it was a little quieter. They soon found what they were looking for. Right at the back of the shop was a door marked 'PRIVATE – STAFF ONLY'

O'Hagan turned to Hegarty and hissed, 'Keep watch.'

Clutching the carrier bag that contained the small explosive device, he quickly stepped through the unlocked door.

Behind the door was a large storeroom with cardboard boxes piled everywhere. The sides of the storeroom were decked out with wooden shelving. Grabbing a box that would accommodate the size of the bomb, O'Hagan quickly tipped out the contents, before covering the spilled cards with other boxes.

He removed the device from the carrier bag, placed it inside the cardboard box and primed it to start the timer.

Having armed the bomb, he placed the cardboard box high up on the shelves near the back of the storeroom.

With the bomb successfully hidden, O'Hagan stepped out of the storeroom and back into the main shop.

The men browsed casually through the shelves of cards as they made their way separately out of the shop. They walked separately along the busy concourse finally meeting up outside the main entrance.

Walking back to their car, that had been parked in the yellow zone of the multi storey car park, both men were smiling broadly.

As they got into the car, O'Hagan said, 'It's a shame the bomb isn't a little bit bigger, but it'll do the job alright.'

Hegarty laughed and replied, 'It'll blow that fucking green dome to pieces!'

'I just hope the fucking timer works properly this time; I don't want another bollocking from Macready.'

'It'll be fine Declan. The brothers spent hours over this one getting the fucking thing right. What time is it set to go off?'

'If you're right about the dome, the fucking thing should be in pieces by four o'clock tomorrow afternoon.'

Both men laughed as Hegarty started the engine of their Ford Sierra and drove out of the car park.

CHAPTER 21

3.15pm 13th February 1991
Meadowhall Shopping Centre,
Sheffield, South Yorkshire

Dorothy Maitland was furious.

As far as she was concerned the fire alarm had activated at precisely the wrong time. The alarm bells had all started sounding just after two o'clock, when crowds of shoppers filled her cards and gifts shop on the Upper Level of the shopping centre.

She paid astronomical rents and rates for the shop that was located just below the iconic green glass dome that dominated Meadowhall. An hour's loss of trade at this incredibly busy time could be really damaging for her fledgling business, Maitland's Celebrations.

Dorothy had risked hiring extra staff to cope with the expected Valentine's Day demand, this was yet another expense that needed to be covered by sales and up until the fire alarm going off, it had been a gamble that was paying off handsomely.

Now she was rightly concerned.

The entire shopping centre had been evacuated and fire crews had checked the property thoroughly for any signs of fire before finally declaring it to be a false alarm at three o'clock.

At first, the Fire Chief would only allow staff to enter the shopping centre. It would be at least another half an hour before he allowed any members of the public back inside to recommence shopping.

Dorothy was livid and had vented her displeasure at a young fire fighter who was standing in the main entrance as she walked back inside. He had merely grinned and shrugged his shoulders which hadn't helped Dorothy's already angry mood. It was a false alarm for Christs sake, why did everything have to be delayed? Every minute not trading was costing her money. Money she could ill afford to lose.

As they walked along the main concourse back towards the shop she was chivvying on her staff. She had been the first person back in to the centre and now she almost sprinted along the concourse to get back inside her shop.

As soon as she walked into the shop, Dorothy started barking out orders to Glenys and Maisie her two full time staff, 'Glenys, check the tills are both okay, Maisie, nip into the storeroom and bring out some more stock for the 'Valentine's Day Wives' section. We'll be getting more forgetful husbands coming in soon looking for cards at the last-minute.'

She then turned to her two young temps and said, 'As soon as Maisie brings the boxes through, I want you two girls to start getting them onto the shelves as quickly as you can. You know which section to put them in, I showed you this morning. Come on girls, let's get cracking the customers will be arriving soon.'

As instructed Maisie walked to the back of the shop and went into the storeroom. Quickly she scanned the boxes on the shelves for Valentine's Day Wives cards.

She cursed as she saw the boxes on the top shelf of the racking, 'Bloody hell! What bright spark stacked them right up there?'

Maisie was very slight in stature and looked around for the steps. Having found the aluminium ladders, she leaned them against the racking and climbed up to retrieve the two boxes. She placed the first box on the floor and then grabbed the second box.

That's odd, she thought. This box seems so much lighter.

As she bent down to look inside the box, the bomb exploded.

Maisie was killed instantly as the blast smashed through the storeroom and out into the shop. The blast from the small bomb had been fairly contained in the stockroom that had concrete walls and a concrete floor and ceiling.

The only escape for the massive shockwave was through the door and the entire force of the blast now ripped through that small area and devastated Maitland's Celebrations.

The four women standing inside the shop were all killed instantly by the massive shockwave as it pulverised their inner organs, turning hearts, lungs and livers into soup within their bodies. The front of the shop was blown outwards onto the main concourse and flying glass and debris injured other shop workers as they made their way back inside the shopping centre.

A fire started in what remained of Maitland's Celebrations, but the small blaze was quickly extinguished by the fire crews that were already on site.

Once again fate had intervened to prevent massive loss of life. Had the bombers planted a larger bomb the concrete walls would have been insufficient to contain the blast. Had there been no technical fault with the fire alarm, the card shop would have been full of customers, the majority of whom would have perished in the explosion.

The bomb had gone off almost on time, just thirty-five minutes early on this occasion.

As the bomb exploded, Declan O'Hagan was just about to put on his coat to walk to the telephone box to make the warning call to a newspaper. The first news flash of the explosion was announced on the radio just as he was walking out of the door.

CHAPTER 22

6.00pm 13th February 1991
Home Office, Marsham Street, London

Sir Godfrey Winstanley stepped out of the grand entrance to the Home Office, onto the windy, rain sodden street and paused. His mind was in turmoil. He had just left yet another emergency meeting with the Home Secretary, attempting to brief him about the latest atrocity in Sheffield.

Intelligence was still scarce, but it was obviously a bomb that had exploded.

The phone call into the tabloid newspaper almost immediately after the device had detonated, quoting the correct codeword, confirmed that it was the work of the Provisional IRA.

Winstanley couldn't even bemoan the lack of a proper warning this time, as to all intents and purposes the centre had been evacuated at the time of the explosion. The five fatalities and dozens injured were all shop workers.

He inwardly shuddered as he considered what the death toll could have been had the shopping centre not had a fault with the sprinkler system, that had in turn tripped the general fire alarm.

'Thank God for small mercies', he muttered aloud as he walked towards the kerb edge having seen his driver approaching with the firm's Daimler.

He climbed into the back of the car and said, 'Back to the office, quick as you can.'

The car sped along the dark streets towards the MI5 building on Millbank, near the Palace of Westminster.

Staring out of the window at the wet and windy streets speeding by outside, he started to formulate a response in his mind. He racked his brain for actions he could take, he desperately felt the need to be doing something, anything. First and foremost, he would personally contact every Special Branch liaison officer working with his agents in and around Londonderry to try and stress the need for urgency. Information and intelligence were the lifeblood of the organisation and at the moment there was very little forthcoming.

He had always known that the Newcastle bomb was going to be the first of many, but the explosion at Sheffield had now confirmed his worst fears. Unless his department could get a lead on the bombers soon, another bomb would explode and this time his luck would run out and there would be a huge loss of life.

The Home Secretary had just spent the best part of an hour stressing to him the damage this scenario would do to himself, the Prime Minister and the government as a whole.

Winstanley was establishment through and through. He knew only too well that his tenure as Director would soon be coming to an abrupt end if his department couldn't locate and eliminate the bomb threat.

He stroked his temple as the throbbing headache started again.

Without a massive breakthrough from one of his agents or a huge slice of luck, he couldn't see any way to prevent the next atrocity.

The pressure he was under was enormous, he felt like a dead man walking.

The headache steadily got worse.

CHAPTER 23

11.00am 20th February 1991
Cork, Munster

The upstairs flat, just along the road from The English Market, had been empty for as long as anyone could remember.

It was perfect for the hastily arranged meeting of the Provisional Army Council, called following the explosion at the Meadowhall Shopping Centre in Sheffield. The meeting had been ordered by the Chief of Staff, Francis Holmes to discuss the ongoing bombing campaign that was already wreaking havoc on the British mainland.

It had been way too dangerous to have the meeting in Belfast. The security services were engaged in some sort of clampdown on all movement across the city. It would have been far too risky to gather everyone together in Belfast so Ben Christie had hastily searched for a suitable alternative venue. When he had suggested the empty flat next to The English Market in Cork, Holmes had readily agreed. He felt the location had a certain poetic symmetry, bearing in mind what was to be discussed.

Already waiting in the flat alongside Holmes, was Jimmy Patterson and his shadow McGuire. There would be no Eoin McAteer at this meeting as he was detained in Belfast with business at Stormont.

The three men were patiently awaiting the arrival of Eddie Macready.

At the foot of the stairs that led to the front door of the flat, stood the man mountain that was Ben Christie, Francis Holmes' personal bodyguard.

Christie could now see Eddie Macready approaching with another man.

As the two men neared the foot of the stairs, Christie stepped out and said, 'Good morning Mr Macready, who's this?'

'Morning Ben, this is my son Danny. Don't worry, Frankie knows he's coming today.'

'He never mentioned it to me and I've never met your son before, so wait here a second while I check.'

It was a comment that did not invite discussion. Nobody ever argued with Ben Christie. Eddie Macready and his son were no different. The two men from Londonderry waited patiently at the bottom of the stairs until Christie let out a low whistle from the top and beckoned both men to come up.

At the top of the stairs no words were exchanged, just a courteous nod from Christie towards Danny Macready.

Father and son walked into the tiny flat and joined the other three men already seated at the kitchen table.

Patterson scowled and said, 'What kept you Macready, we've been here fucking ages, you're late.'

Deliberately ignoring the Belfast commander, Eddie Macready directed his comment to Holmes, 'I apologise for being a little on the late side Frankie. We had a little car trouble this morning. As we discussed yesterday, this is my son Danny; he's joining us at Derry after moving down from Belfast.'

Patterson chuckled and said, 'Had a little woman trouble, haven't you Danny boy?'

Danny glared across the table towards Patterson and said flatly, 'Fuck off Patterson, that's none of your business.'

The grin instantly disappeared from the Belfast man's face and with a voice filled with menace he growled, 'Take care Danny boy, have some respect when you talk to me.'

Eddie Macready now shouted, 'Or what Patterson?'

Holmes interjected, 'That's enough! I'm sick of this constant bickering between you two. What the fuck's wrong with you? The enemy's out there, not inside this room!'

Macready and Patterson both mumbled an incoherent apology to their Chief of Staff.

Holmes waited a moment, allowing silence to descend over the highly charged, tense atmosphere. He then turned to Patterson and said, 'Jimmy when we last spoke, you outlined to me reservations you were having about the current bombing campaign being waged across the water by the Derry Brigade. What exactly are those issues?'

Before Patterson could speak, Eddie Macready mumbled under his breath, 'Jealousy.'

Ignoring the comment, Patterson said, 'I think the campaign's already showing too many weaknesses on our part. Neither of the bombs have detonated at the correct time. I've got serious doubts about the skills of the boys making the devices. If they can't get a timer to work correctly, how long will it be before we have a device that blows up while in possession of the ASU? How embarrassing would that be to the organisation? I think you should recall these Derry amateur's immediately.'

Holmes turned to Eddie Macready and said, 'Well Eddie?'

'That's bullshit Frankie! Patterson's just jealous that's it's our boys over the water taking the fight to the enemy.

When was the last time Belfast did anything worthwhile in the struggle?'

Holmes said quickly, 'There you go again Eddie. You're really starting to piss me off with this ridiculous rivalry between you and Belfast. We are the Irish Republican Army not the Belfast or Derry Republican Army. You two had better start working together or I might have to find new Commanders, this is getting beyond a joke.'

He turned back to Patterson and said, 'Is that the only concern you have Jimmy, the fact that the timers aren't that great?'

'In a nutshell, yeah. I don't want any embarrassment. It's the last thing we need at this time.'

'Your concerns are duly noted.'

He turned towards Eddie Macready and said quietly, 'Eddie, I want the bombing campaign to continue. I want you to tell your boys to seriously up the ante. That last bomb was way too small. The next one must be bigger, fuck what Sinn Fein say, I want no warning for the next device. The public are getting conditioned to small numbers of fatalities, let's give them something that will make everyone sit up and take note. Maximum fatalities, maximum casualties and maximum damage!'

Patterson looked crestfallen and scowled, muttering under his breath. Both the Macready's had beaming smiles and looked smugly over at Patterson and McGuire.

Holmes got up to leave and gave a silent warning to both men, 'I meant what I said. There needs to be far more co-operation between you two or you'll both be replaced. Do I make myself clear?'

A smiling Eddie Macready said, 'Of course Frankie, at the end of the day we're all striving for the same thing, aren't we?'

Feeling totally humiliated at being ignored by Holmes, Patterson just grimaced and nodded.

As soon as Holmes and Christie had left the flat, Patterson turned to Eddie Macready and said, 'Enjoy your moment Macready, I won't forget this day in a hurry. Come on McGuire let's get out of this fucking shithole.'

As the two men stomped out of the flat and down the stairs, all they could hear was the loud raucous laughter of Eddie and Danny Macready.

In spite of the warnings given to the two Brigade Commanders by the Chief of Staff, far from being healed, the bad blood between the men was getting worse.

Something would have to give.

CHAPTER 24

8.00pm 27th March 1991
Peartree District, Derby

Declan O'Hagan had been standing outside the telephone box on Corden Street for fifteen minutes. He was cold and was starting to get very wet as the sudden downpour got steadily heavier. He desperately wanted the young woman inside the booth to finish her call without him having to ask her to do so.

He glanced again at his watch; the call would need to be made in the next five minutes. The coded telephone call had been received at the house earlier in the day by Liam Quinn. O'Hagan had been told to call his Uncle Fergus in Cork at eight o'clock that night. Only he knew what the message really meant.

The woman didn't look like finishing her call any time soon, so Declan tapped lightly on the pane of glass with a coin.

The woman ignored him.

He tapped again.

She turned her back towards O'Hagan and continued talking on the phone.

Declan could feel his blood pressure rising as he fought to contain his temper.

He opened the kiosk door and said politely, 'Excuse me Miss, I need to make an urgent call.'

The woman put her hand over the receiver and snarled, 'And how the fuck is that my problem?'

O'Hagan was shocked at the venom in the young woman's voice, but remained calm and said, 'Could you finish your call please. Mine will only take a minute and then I'll be gone.'

'I'll be at least another fifteen minutes, me and Stacy have got things to organise, so you'd better just fuck off and find another phone box.'

The last comment was accompanied by a rigid middle finger salute.

It was the last straw for Declan O'Hagan, he slammed his hand down on the cradle, terminating the call and ripped the receiver from the young woman's hand.

As she shouted abuse at him, he yanked her bodily from the booth and said angrily, 'Fuck off, slag!'

The demented look on his face made the woman stop in her tracks. She was about to let fly with another torrent of abuse when she suddenly stopped, thought better of it and walked away. Only when she was twenty yards away from the phone box and O'Hagan was inside, did she turn and yell, 'Wanker!' at the top of her voice.

Ignoring the woman, O'Hagan closed the door to the phone booth and hastily dialled the number for O'Doyle's Bar. As the tone changed, he pushed coins into the slot. The connection was made instantly and a bored voice said, 'O'Doyle's Bar, can I help you?'

O'Hagan said quickly, 'I need to speak with Eddie Macready?'

The bored barmaid said, 'Just a second.'

The next voice O'Hagan heard was Eddie Macready. 'Hello?'

144

He said, 'Uncle Fergus is there any news on Aunt Dolores?'

'Declan! About bloody time! I was just about to leave.'

'Sorry, I had a problem with the phone.'

'You're in a call box?'

'Yeah of course, what's up?'

'I've got great news Declan. Time for the next event and this one has got to be big. This has come straight from the top. We need to send a message to the Brits. The next one has got to be huge. The last one was disappointingly small. The mindset has changed over here, this time there's to be no warning given. Maximum casualties, maximum damage. Is that clear?'

'As crystal. We can make a huge bomb with the Semtex we've still got, but we'll need to be re-supplied with explosive after this one.'

'Leave that to me, I'll arrange all that with the Quartermaster. You just concentrate on getting your boys to build the biggest device you can with what you have over there at the moment.'

'Do we have a time frame?'

'Aim for the Mayday bank holiday, that should give you enough time.'

'Will do. Anything else?'

'That's it Dec, good luck.'

The call was terminated.

O'Hagan replaced the receiver on the cradle, pressed the button below and retrieved the coins he hadn't used.

As he stepped outside the phone box, he instantly felt the driving rain lash into his face. He started to walk away and as he did so the smile on his face got broader and broader, he didn't care about the cold and the rain.

If this all went to plan, the four of them would become legends. He couldn't wait to get home and tell the others of the exciting developments.

CHAPTER 25

6.30am 5ᵗʰ April 1991
Moorgreen, Nottinghamshire

Neil Warner parked his Vauxhall Astra in the one layby available on this stretch of Willey Lane. It afforded access into Moorgreen Woods and was always Neil's favoured dog walking area.

He stretched as he got out of the car, before moving around to the rear to raise the hatchback and let his Springer Spaniel out. Slipping the lead onto the dog's collar, he spoke softly to his excitable dog, 'Calm down Logan. Yes, I know you can't wait to go diving around in those lovely wet woods, but you've got to wait a minute.'

In response to his master's words, the small dog started to leap up trying to lick Neil's face in its own show of affection.

Neil glanced at his watch and noticed that he still had some of the grime from the coalmine ingrained on his wrist. He chuckled and said aloud, 'Must have missed that bit.'

It was now getting on for six thirty in the morning. He'd just finished a night shift at the nearby Annesley Colliery, one of the few mines in the area still working after the strike in 1984. His first job after a night shift was always to take his little energetic dog for a walk in the woods to let off some steam. Neil knew that if he didn't take the dog first, he would get no sleep or rest as the dog would be howling all morning. Half an hour running mad in the woods and Logan would be okay for the day, or at least until two o'clock in the afternoon when the process would have to be repeated.

Neil didn't mind, he adored his four-legged companion. It was their routine now. Walk, breakfast then bed.

When he had surfaced from the mine that morning, his mate in the lamp cabin had told him about the terrific storm that had raged above ground all night.

As he looked at the woodland surrounding him now, he could see graphic evidence of that storm. Several large trees had been uprooted and blown over, and the ground beneath his feet was absolutely sodden.

Neil wasn't overly concerned; the winds had calmed down now and the sky was clear. He would just need to watch where he was putting his feet.

The sun was just creeping over the horizon, it looked like being a beautiful day.

He walked from the layby about ten yards into the damp woods before letting Logan off the lead.

Immediately, the dog took off into the woods at lightning pace, cavorting and racing around with all the extreme energy that breed is renowned for.

Neil never bothered to call the dog, because he knew for the first ten minutes it would be a waste of time as Logan raced around the woods exploring each new scent as it came to him.

Slowly, the miner walked in the general direction that his dog had taken, carefully stepping over upturned tree roots at every turn. The damage to the woodland from the overnight storm was greater than he had first thought.

The ten minutes playtime over, Neil started to call his dog, 'Logan! Where are you boy?'

He could no longer hear the dog crashing through the undergrowth ahead of him. Suddenly there was silence.

He shouted again, 'Logan! Come on boy, where are you?'

In response to his shout, he heard the high-pitched barking of his dog about thirty yards ahead of him.

Neil smiled and shouted, 'Wait there Logan! I'm coming, stay where you are boy.'

The little dog continued to bark.

This was a bark that carried some urgency in its tone. Neil recognised this and began to feel slightly concerned and uneasy as his dog was normally quiet. Very excitable and energetic, but quiet.

As he walked over a slight rise in the ground, Neil finally saw his dog.

Logan was barking and digging for all his worth at the base of a large, old oak tree that had succumbed to the gale force winds last night. The gnarled tree roots were now exposed to the elements and the soft earth around them had been disturbed as the ancient tree was finally toppled by the powerful, gusting winds overnight.

Now Neil understood why his dog was so animated. Where the ground had been disturbed at the base of the tree and the roots were exposed, he could see what appeared to be the top of a black plastic dustbin.

Moving closer he grabbed his little dog and slipped the lead back onto his collar. He tied the lead to one of the roots of the upturned oak and moved in to have a closer look at the dustbin.

The old miner could feel his heart beating a little faster as his mind speculated what might be in the dustbin. Something was causing his little dog to become very excited.

It has to be body parts, Neil thought. That's why the dog's going crazy.

Now that he was standing right next to the bin, he could see that the lid had been sealed on with black gaffer tape. It was obvious that it hadn't just been dumped there, whoever had left it there wanted it to remain watertight.

Neil could see where the dog had been chewing at the black tape around the lid of the bin, looking closer he could see there was a very slight opening.

With a real sense of trepidation, he began to ease a bit more of the sticky tape away until he could see inside.

What he saw made him gasp, before he took a deep breath and let out a low whistle.

Right at the very top of the bin he could see clear plastic bags that contained black pistols. Immediately below the weapons he could see packet after packet of what looked like blocks of plasticine.

Neil had worked in coalmines all his working life and knew only too well that the blocks he could see were explosives. He very carefully replaced the lid of the dustbin and grabbing his dog he walked briskly away. As he did so he took careful note of the route. As he walked back to the layby, he snapped twigs and branches as he went, so he would be able to lead the police back to the dustbin.

Ten minutes later and he was placing a very wet and muddy Logan back into the hatchback area of his Astra. The little dog was not impressed at having his playtime curtailed so abruptly and was now howling loudly.

Neil started the car and yelled harshly, 'Cut it out Logan! Shut it!'

To his amazement the dog whimpered once then lay down in the hatchback almost as if he'd gone into a sulk.

Neil grinned at the antics of his dog then drove at speed to the police station at nearby Hucknall.

Sergeant Tony Henstock was just taking the first sip of his morning tea when an ashen faced Neil Warner walked in.

The experienced sergeant, immediately sensing something was wrong said, 'Can I help you sir?'

Neil took a deep breath and spoke clearly, 'I hope so sergeant. I was taking my dog for a walk and I've just found a load of guns and explosives in Moorgreen Woods just off Willey Lane. They've been placed there deliberately in a black plastic dustbin. After those terrible bombs in Newcastle and Sheffield, it's been all over the news. If anyone sees anything suspicious, they should contact the police.'

'Are you sure that what you've seen in the bin were explosives?'

'Look sergeant, I've worked down the pit all my working life, I know what explosives look like. Trust me, it's explosives alright and there were five or six handguns in there as well. I reckon it's got something to do with the IRA.'

'Thanks for coming straight in and letting us know sir, but they really could belong to anyone, let's not put two and two together shall we? Can you show me exactly where this dustbin is?'

'I can. I marked the route out so I could find my way back in again. It's by an old oak tree that's been uprooted by the storm last night. As the tree's come down, the roots have turned up out of the sodden ground and forced the dustbin out as well. I reckon it was probably buried before.'

Sgt Henstock had heard enough, grabbing his coat he shouted, 'Pc Tompkins, get in here now!'

The young Pc immediately emerged from an adjacent office.

Sgt Henstock said, 'Tommo, nip upstairs to the CID office and grab the car keys. Get your radio and a civilian coat, we're going out.'

'Okay sarge', said the young constable quickly, before disappearing back through the office he had emerged from.

The sergeant turned to Neil Warner and said, 'You said you were walking your dog. Where's the dog?'

'He's outside in my car, I've left the windows down a little so he can get some air.'

'Will he be okay out there or do you want me to put him in our kennel for a while?'

'He'll be fine in the car for a little while, it's not hot outside.'

Fifteen minutes later and Neil Warner was again walking through the damp woods; this time he was accompanied by the two police officers.

They quickly reached the upturned oak, Neil pointed out the black plastic bin and said, 'It's over there sergeant.'

Sergeant Henstock said, 'Wait here sir'.

The experienced policeman walked slowly over to the bin. He took one look inside and knew that he was indeed looking at some kind of arms cache that could quite easily belong to the Provisional IRA.

He turned to the young officer with him and said, 'Tommo, I need you to wait here and make sure this dustbin isn't disturbed. Do not touch anything! For all we know it could be booby trapped. I'll be back as soon as I can. Right now, I need to get this gentleman back to Hucknall nick and I need to get us some specialist help out here. Are you going to be okay with that?'

'Of course, sarge. We had a lecture about explosives and how not to use your radio and stuff at Training School.'

'Good. I'll be straight back. Tommo, I mean it, do not touch anything! Understand?'

The young constable nodded and leaned back against another tree.

'Got it sarge. Do not touch.'

CHAPTER 26

8.30am 5th April 1991
Hucknall Police Station, Nottinghamshire

As soon as he arrived back at Hucknall Police Station, Sergeant Henstock had gone into overdrive. He had immediately dispatched another, more experienced, officer out to Moorgreen Woods to support Pc Tompkins and then sat a tired but patient Neil Warner down in the foyer with a hot brew, but only after the two men had taken Neil's small dog from his car. Logan had been towelled down, fed and watered and placed into the dog kennel in the rear yard of the police station.

The first of many telephone calls the sergeant had made was to the Duty Inspector in the Force Control Room.

Standing out of earshot of Neil Warner, Sgt Henstock said, 'Good morning sir. A man who'd been exercising his dog in Moorgreen Woods this morning, walked into Hucknall Police Station a short time ago and informed me that he'd found an arms cache. I've been over to Moorgreen with this chap and seen it for myself. It's a black plastic bin that had been buried until last night's storm. Inside the bin, I could see several weapons and what appears to be explosives. The explosive is in blocks, it's in plastic wrappers that has the word SEMTEX on them. I need you to contact Special Branch, the Special Operations Unit and the Bomb Squad. I've got two of my officers in the woods at the moment watching it, but I daren't do anything with it as I'm worried it could be booby trapped.'

'Where's the man who reported it?'

'He's still here at the station with me. The CID will be on duty shortly, the first detective that walks in will be getting a statement from him. His name's Neil Warner and his date of birth is 29th November 1941, would you carry out the relevant checks on him please sir?'

'I'll do the name check and get everybody travelling over to Hucknall, straight away.'

The Duty Inspector then started to set the wheels in motion. The first call he made was to the home of Chief Inspector Jim Chambers of the Special Operations Unit.

Having listened to what the Duty Inspector told him, Jim Chambers advised him to contact the Bomb Squad at Chilwell Army Barracks as top priority and get them travelling to Hucknall Police Station where he would liaise with them. He then instructed him to contact the Chief Constable at home and appraise him of the situation before contacting the Superintendent in charge of Special Branch.

Finally, he asked the Inspector to begin contacting the men from all four sections of the Special Operations Unit and instruct them to be at Force Headquarters for a midday briefing.

Jim Chambers intended to travel to Hucknall Police Station immediately to liaise with the Bomb Squad before he went to Force Headquarters to begin organising an operation that would hopefully result in the capture of the people responsible for leaving the arms cache in the woods.

There was another reason he needed to go to Hucknall Police Station first.

He had immediately realised that there was something of vital importance to the success of any plan he was starting to formulate in his brain. He wanted to stake out the arms cache and arrest anyone who came to gather articles from it and for any stake out plan to succeed he was going to need complete secrecy.

Jim Chambers realised that before any plan could commence, he needed to rely on absolute secrecy from the man who had initially found the cache, Neil Warner.

Having driven at high speeds from his Langley Mill home to Hucknall Police Station, it had taken just fifteen minutes before Jim Chambers was walking into the foyer of the station.

Striding to the front desk he produced his warrant card and spoke softly to the enquiry clerk who had just started her shift, 'Good morning Miss, I'm Chief Inspector Chambers, I'd like to speak with Sergeant Henstock please.'

The young girl smiled and said, 'He's upstairs in the CID office sir, I'll buzz the door for you.'

The automatic door latch was activated and Jim Chambers walked into the station. He was met by the enquiry clerk, 'Do you know your way to the CID office sir?'

Jim Chambers was already striding up the stairs as he said, 'Yes thanks.'

He walked into the CID office and saw a uniform sergeant talking to a detective who he recognised, having worked with him on previous occasions.

Both men stopped talking and turned to face the Chief Inspector.

Dc Hamilton said, 'Hello boss, no need to ask what brings you out here at this time of day.'

Chambers replied, 'No Dave, there isn't.'

He turned to the sergeant and said, 'I'm Chief Inspector Chambers from the Special Operations Unit, you must be Sgt Henstock. Is Neil Warner still here?'

'He's still here, sir. He's in an interview room having a cup of tea, I was just briefing Dave before he takes his statement.'

'Before you get his statement, I need to have a quick word with him.'

'No problem sir, he's through here.'

The sergeant walked in front of Chambers as he showed him to the interview rooms. As they walked Chambers said, 'How many people in the nick know about the arms cache?'

'Me, two constables and now Dave Hamilton. That's it.'

'Good, let's keep it that way. Stress to your constables that they do not speak to anyone, family and friends included, about what they've seen this morning. Understood?'

'Yes sir, no problem. Mr Warner's in here.'

'Thanks.'

Jim Chambers stepped inside the interview room and closed the door behind him. He sat down facing Neil Warner and was pleased to see that the man sitting opposite him was probably in his early fifties and looked like a hardworking, law abiding member of the general public.

Chambers said quietly, 'Mr Warner, my name's Chief Inspector Chambers. First and foremost, I want to thank you for your prompt action in reporting to us what you found in Moorgreen Woods this morning. It could be of vital importance to the safety of every man, woman and child in this country. What I'm about to tell you is secret. If we're to have any success, it's vitally important that it remains secret. Do we understand each other, Mr Warner?'

Neil Warner leaned forward and placed the mug of tea he was holding on the desk in front of him before saying, 'Please, call me Neil. Only my neighbours' kids ever call me Mr Warner. I think we both know who those explosives belong to Chief Inspector. I'm not some old lady who wants to stand gossiping over the garden fence about juicy titbits. If that stuff does belong to the bastards that blew up those shops in Newcastle and Sheffield, killing all those poor people, then just say the word. Whatever you want me to do, I'll do it.'

Chambers smiled and said, 'Thanks Neil. For what it's worth, I think you're dead right. I think the cache you stumbled upon this morning probably does belong to the IRA. At this moment in time we've got the element of surprise on our side and what I intend to do is to place a surveillance on that arms cache for as long as it takes those murderous bastards to come back to it. In order for me to do that and be successful, it's vitally important that your discovery remains unreported in anyway. I can ensure that there's a complete media blackout, but it's imperative that you don't tell a living soul about what you found today. Not close family, not friends, not your best mate down the pub, not work colleagues, it must remain a secret. If you can do this for me, I'm confident that my men will catch these bastards red handed.'

Warner had a grim expression on his face when he said, 'You've got my word, Chief Inspector. There's no reason for me to tell anyone about this. If in a couple of days, weeks, months however long it takes, I find out that you've arrested these cowardly shits I will be overjoyed. To hear that on the news would be marvellous. Most of my family still live in the

Newcastle area. I only came down here from my home town of Consett to get a job in the pits. What those bastards did up there at the Metro Centre, that could have been my family they murdered.'

Chambers stood up and extended his hand towards Neil Warner who also stood. The two men shook hands. Chambers could feel the hard calluses on the coal miners' hand as he shook it warmly.

He said, 'Thank you Neil. Thank you very much. As and when we catch these men, I'll ensure your part is recognised, if that's what you want. I'm going to leave you in the capable hands of Dc Hamilton now, he'll get a written statement from you, I've got a lot of planning to do.'

As Chambers walked to the door, Neil Warner said, 'Good luck Chief, make sure you catch the bastards.'

CHAPTER 27

1.30am 12th April 1991
Peartree District, Derby

'Okay JJ, have you got everything?'

Hegarty smiled and said, 'If by everything, you mean this bad boy, yeah, I've got it', he opened his jacket to reveal a sawn-off shotgun and held out his left hand that contained four cartridges. Ever since O'Hagan had told the other three members of the ASU about the message he'd received from Macready, the mood in the house had been buoyant and spirits were high.

Declan O'Hagan grinned and said, 'Come on then, it's time we were going. It'll take us an hour to get over there.'

O'Hagan grabbed the car keys and thrust a plastic carrier bag into the pocket of his Donkey jacket.

The two men were making the drive to Moorgreen in neighbouring Nottinghamshire, returning to the woodland where they had buried the explosives and other weapons.

They needed to recover all the Semtex that was left in the cache in order for Liam and Gerry Quinn to build the huge bomb that Eddie Macready had sanctioned.

Only O'Hagan knew that after the bomb had been built, they would be returning to Nottingham. The target for the next atrocity was going to be the Victoria Shopping Centre in the centre of the vibrant East Midlands city.

London would have been the ideal target, but security around the capital was way too tight. The provincial city of Nottingham was well known around the world and a huge bomb planted there would achieve the publicity they craved.

A bomb the size of the one they were planning would completely destroy the vast shopping centre as well as a large part of the city centre. The devastation caused would be massive and the loss of life huge.

None of that was of any concern to O'Hagan as he drove steadily out of Derby and headed for the A52, the road that connected Derby to its East Midlands neighbour, Nottingham.

Both men were in good spirits as they sped down the dual carriageway. Another three quarters of an hour and they would be at the cache. It would take less than ten minutes to remove the explosives, they were both hoping to be back home and in bed before four o'clock.

CHAPTER 28

2.30am 12th April 1991
Moorgreen, Nottinghamshire

The operation to mount observations on the arms cache in the middle of Moorgreen Woods had now been ongoing for one week. During that time nobody other than the observations team had set foot into the woodland. The weather had been atrocious, with constant heavy rain showers. Today had been the first completely dry day since the operation had begun.

To ensure the cache was kept under full observation throughout the entire twenty-four hours of any given day, all four Sections of the Special Operations Unit had been deployed at various times

The very existence of Operation Mantrap had been kept on a strictly need to know basis. Police personnel with knowledge of the ongoing operation was minimal and the only civilian who knew about the arms cache was Neil Warner, the miner who had initially discovered the explosives.

Mr Warner had agreed that until he was told otherwise, he would consider the police to be still active in Moorgreen Woods and would walk his dog, Logan at a different location.

It had been the turn of C Section to undertake the night shift observing the cache over the previous two days. This would also be the case for the next three nights shifts.

The plan had been fine tuned in the first few days and now the briefing was very short and concise. Everyone knew exactly what their individual roles were. The observations posts were well defined and in various tests carried out they had been proven to give an excellent view of anyone approaching the cache.

As the sniper team on C Section, it would be the responsibility of Tom Naylor and Matt Jarvis to be the closest in to the cache and to react to any person or persons that made an approach.

The exact location of the arms cache had been designated the codename, Position Alpha.

Also close in to the cache and working alongside the sniper team would be Sgt Graham Turner and Tony Garner. There would also be a support team, Colin Morgan and Eddie Keane, in close to assist the intercept team. Morgan and Keane would be in possession of two Dragon lights, the hand held powerful torches used by the Special Operations Unit.

The six of them, working together, would engage and arrest anyone who approached the cache. Every member of the team was fully armed with the Heckler and Koch Mp5 sub machine gun as well as personal sidearms. It was almost inevitable that anyone entering the woodland with an interest in the arms cache would be armed. The officers deployed all knew that terrorists would be prepared to do whatever it took to avoid arrest.

The most vital cogs in the operation were the observation posts.

The first one had been set up to maintain observations on the single layby off Willey Lane. Whenever C Section were on duty this role would be undertaken by the vastly experienced Steve Grey and Jack Rimmer.

It would be their responsibility to give an early warning of any vehicles using the layby and of the occupants of any such vehicles making their way into the woods. From their covert position they would endeavour to give an early indication of any weapons being carried as well as detailed descriptions of suspects.

As part of their role they would also log the registration numbers of all vehicles using the layby, even when none of the occupants got out. They would then ensure that the relevant checks were made with the Police National Computer for intelligence and any future enquiries.

There was a second covert observation post set deeper in the woods between the layby and the cache. This would be manned by Wayne Hope and Luke Goddard. It would be their role to ensure that any suspects approaching from the layby were observed as they made their way towards the cache. It was the responsibility of Hope and Goddard to give an early indication to the team waiting at Position Alpha when the suspect or suspects would be coming into their view.

Tonight, was the third night that C Section had covered the night shift on Operation Mantrap. They had been in position since ten o'clock. Weapons and communications had all been checked and the team settled down for another long shift.

The handover period was crucial; It had to be done in careful stages so that the observations could be maintained while not causing too much vehicular traffic at any one time that could arouse people's suspicions.

Fortunately, Willey Lane was very quiet and hardly ever used by members of the public.

Covert entry and extraction drills were of paramount importance and were observed rigidly. The entire changeover had taken over an hour to complete.

Luckily, tonight was a warm, dry night.

Tom and Matt quickly settled into their hide near Position Alpha, getting as comfortable as possible and making sure all the equipment and weapons they may need during the shift were close at hand.

The previous two nights had really dragged, both men knew that the need to stay alert was vital. They were both well drilled in the thirty minutes on and thirty minutes off routine that allowed one half of the team to rest for half an hour enabling full concentration for the next thirty minutes.

Every ten minutes, Steve Grey at the observation point watching the layby would update the team over the radio.

The message was always the same, 'No change, no change.'

Everyone on the team was then fully aware that comms were working fine and that nothing was happening.

Very slowly, the clock ticked round and once again the night shift seemed to be dragging. It was starting to look as though tonight's shift would again be uneventful.

Tom checked his wristwatch; it was now approaching two thirty. Another five minutes and it would be Matt's turn to take up the observations and he could relax.

Suddenly, static filled his covert ear piece, as Steve Grey calmly said over the radio, 'All units stand by, stand by. We have a Ford Sierra, registration YTO 148 X into the layby. Lights on the vehicle have now been switched off. Wait out.'

Nobody on the team uttered a word, the command to "Wait Out" meant just that. The team waited. Their concentration and alertness had just been cranked up and they could all feel the adrenalin starting to course through their veins.

Tom knew that Steve Grey would now be staring hard at the suspect vehicle through the night vision glasses that bathed everything in an eerie green glow. He would have waited to use the night vision glasses until after the Sierra's headlights had been switched off.

Once again Tom's covert ear piece chirped into life, 'Stand by stand by. Two occupants with the vehicle, both are males. They are now out of the vehicle and moving to the rear. The boot has been opened and objects are being extracted. One male has removed a spade and a carrier bag. Second male has removed what appears to be a sawn-off shotgun. Boot now closed. Both suspects remaining with the vehicle, they're clocking points and looking around them. Wait out.'

There was a painfully long pause that seemed to stretch into the darkness for ever.

Breaking that deathly quiet, once again Tom heard the calm voice of Steve Grey through his earpiece, 'Both suspects are now on the move and are crossing the lane towards the woods. Both are wearing Donkey jackets, jeans and heavy work boots. They're now entering the woodland, direction towards Position Alpha. Out of my view. Over.'

The second observation post set deeper in the woodland was being manned by Wayne Hope and Luke Goddard.

It was Wayne Hope's strong Glaswegian accent that the team heard next, 'We now have the eyeball. Both suspects are walking along the main track heading towards Position Alpha. I can confirm that the first male on the track is carrying a spade and a white plastic carrier bag, the male behind him is definitely armed and is carrying a sawn-off shotgun. Both men seem to know exactly where they're going. Still on course for Position Alpha. They will be out of our view in approximately thirty seconds. Over.'

Matt Jarvis now spoke over the radio, gently depressing the switch in his palm he whispered through his throat mike, 'All units. Intercept Team now has the eyeball. Both suspects are now at Position Alpha. Wait out.'

Having reaching the site of the hidden arms cache first, Declan O'Hagan stopped at the side of the fallen oak tree and stared incredulously at the exposed top of the black plastic dustbin.

He let out a low whistle and said, 'Jesus H Christ! Would you look at this fucker JJ? I wonder how long it's been like this? Hold the spade while I get what we came for. I think we're going to have bury the bastard thing again, before we leave.'

Hegarty took the spade from O'Hagan and placed it on the ground, then resumed holding the loaded sawn-off shotgun in both hands. O'Hagan unfurled the white plastic carrier bag and moved closer to the dustbin to remove blocks of Semtex.

As soon as he removed the lid and placed his hands inside the dustbin, Sgt Graham Turner shouted at the top of his voice, 'Armed Police! Stand still!'

The instant Turner had barked his command, the support team of Colin Morgan and Eddie Keane switched on two Dragon lights, the hand held powerful torches instantly turned night into day and fully illuminated Position Alpha.

Holding nothing more threatening than a plastic carrier bag, O'Hagan could do nothing and he stood stock still.

Hearing the words armed police, Hegarty was already moving. He stepped smartly away to the right, moving with the grace and poise of an accomplished boxer. As he danced to his right, he levelled the shotgun in the direction the shouted order had come from.

As soon as the weapon was levelled, Pc Tony Garner engaged the threat and fired two rounds from his Heckler and Koch Mp5.

Firing from a distance of less than ten yards, both rounds struck Hegarty in the chest causing him to fall backwards, dropping the shotgun as he fell. The two, nine-millimetre soft point rounds fired by Tony Garner had both smashed into the centre body mass of the Irishman, pulverising his heart.

John Joseph Hegarty was now on his back, dying.

Before the noise of the two shots had stopped reverberating around the silent woodland, Sgt Turner immediately barked another order at the terrorist O'Hagan, 'Let me see your hands.'

Very slowly, O'Hagan did as he was told. He allowed the carrier bag to fall slowly to the ground before raising his empty hands high above his head. His eyes never left Hegarty, who had fallen to the ground in front of him. He stared into his friends lifeless, staring eyes, willing them to blink.

Finally, O'Hagan accepted that Hegarty was dead and he turned his attention to the figures that were now approaching him from the dense woodland.

The four men that approached him were dressed entirely in black and were all wearing ski masks to prevent O'Hagan seeing their faces.

The IRA man immediately recognised the Heckler and Koch Mp5's the men in black were all pointing in his direction. This was the chosen weapon of the IRA's nemesis, the dreaded SAS.

With an air of defiance, O'Hagan said, 'I thought you boys shouted 'Armed Police'? You boys are SAS, so you are.'

Graham Turner said, 'It doesn't really matter who the fuck we are. All that matters to you at this moment, is that you do exactly what we tell you to do. Now get down on your knees and keep your arms outstretched with your palms facing up.'

O'Hagan never uttered another word and was compliant to every command he received.

Tom and Matt moved in quickly and used Plasticuffs to secure the terrorist. They applied plastic evidence bags to his hands to preserve any forensic evidence that may have been transferred onto his hands from the cache.

He was then walked out of the woods at gunpoint, back to the road. The layby on Willey Lane was now a hive of police activity.

Tom handed O'Hagan over to three-armed Traffic officers who placed the prisoner into the rear of a powerful Volvo traffic car. This vehicle was immediately driven off at speed, taking O'Hagan to the purpose-built specialist cellblock at Radford Road Police Station in Nottingham.

From there O'Hagan would be transferred to Paddington Green Police Station in London where he would be interviewed by officers from the Anti-Terrorist Unit.

No officers would interview O'Hagan until he arrived at the police station in London.

A low loader was already pulling into the layby to transport the Ford Sierra used by the terrorists back to Police

Headquarters where it would be the subject of a full forensic examination.

Major Crime Unit detectives were also now beginning to arrive on Willey Lane to commence the investigation into the fatal shooting of the terrorist by Pc Garner. Tom Naylor felt a pang of concern wash over him, as he saw his colleague being led away by the detectives to give his first account of the circumstances leading to the shooting.

It had been Tom and Matt who were the last officers to go through that trying process after the fatal shooting of Angela Hincks and her accomplices at Farnsfield.

Matt must have realised what Tom was thinking, because he put a hand on his friends' shoulder and said softly, 'Tony's going to have to go through the mill now mate. He'll be fine, he had no option, but to pull the trigger. I've got to admit Tom, I was starting to squeeze the trigger on my own weapon as I saw the shotgun being levelled.'

'Yeah, me too. You're right though, it's going to be a right pain in the arse for him, but he did the only thing he could do, that guy was about to fire. No doubt the detectives will be coming for our statements soon enough.'

A white van sporting the livery of the Bomb Disposal Unit then pulled into the layby to remove the ordnance from the dustbin. They had previously inspected the dustbin on the day of its discovery to ensure it wasn't booby trapped.

Evidentially, it had been necessary to leave the explosives in situ until someone turned up to retrieve them. Now they could remove the dustbin and the contents from the woodland.

Jim Chambers walked over to Tom and Matt and said brusquely, 'Right you two, don't stand around gawping. Get your weapons stowed away and get back to Headquarters for a debrief with the rest of your Section. Where's your sergeant?'

Tom gestured with his head and replied, 'He's over there, talking to the Bomb Disposal lads.'

'Okay, crack on you two!'

An hour later and Tom was sitting in the Briefing Room at Headquarters. There was a general hum of noise as he and the rest of C Section all discussed, in low whispers, the outcome of the operation. The only member of the Section not in the room was Tony Garner, he was still being debriefed formally by detectives.

Suddenly, the door opened and Jim Chambers walked in followed by the Superintendent from Special Branch. All the men in the room immediately stood up.

The Superintendent stood at the front of the room and said, 'Alright men, thanks. Sit down please.'

There was a pause, as chairs were dragged across the floor as the men quickly sat down.

When there was silence, the senior officer said, 'Great work tonight. You men have ensured the safety of every man, woman and child living in the UK today. There's an update that I want to share with you that's for your ears only. A cursory search of the Sierra yielded an address in the Peartree district of Derby. Your counterparts from the Derbyshire Constabulary have just carried out an armed raid at that address and arrested two men. They're twin brothers, Gerry and Liam Quinn. Both men are Irish and both are known to the security services in Northern Ireland. Initial reports suggest that inside the Peartree address, officers have found all the equipment needed to manufacture the type of improvised explosive device similar to the ones used in Newcastle and Sheffield. It would appear at this time that you men have just dismantled the biggest IRA threat to face this country in a long time. You need to be extremely proud of the work you've done tonight. I don't need to remind you that the press and the media generally are going to be all over this story like a rash. If you're approached by anyone from the media, please refer them to the Press Liaison Department. Remember we've still got to convict these bastards at court. Thanks again.'

He immediately turned and walked out of the room followed by Chambers.

Jim Chambers returned a few minutes later and said, 'Okay, let's ensure that we have all the necessary paperwork and reports up to date before we leave tonight. Sergeant Turner, Pc Naylor, Pc Jarvis, Pc Morgan and Pc Keane, you're all expected at Central Police Station at two o'clock this afternoon, to give your accounts to the enquiry team investigating the shooting. You know the drill, co-operate with the enquiry. Make sure your notebooks are completed before they talk to you. Well done all of you, great work tonight.'

Another hour had passed before an elated but exhausted Tom drove his car slowly out of the car park heading for his home in Nottingham and some much-needed sleep.

As he drove along the dark, deserted roads through the city his thoughts turned to Bailey. He couldn't help wondering if what had happened tonight would somehow speed up her return home. All he could do was hope. He didn't even know for sure if she was working on the IRA bombing campaign. He'd always had a nagging feeling that somehow, she was involved in trying to stop the bombings.

It was nearly six o'clock in the morning when Tom finally walked into his apartment. He climbed into bed, setting his alarm clock for midday, so that he could be at Central Police Station for two o'clock.

His head had barely touched the pillow before he was fast asleep.

CHAPTER 29

2.00pm 13ᵗʰ April 1991
O'Doyle's Bar, Londonderry

The bar was empty.

For once, the 'CLOSED' sign had been turned around to face any unwanted punters. The only people inside the bar were the four men huddled around one of the tables in the small intimate booths.

Eddie and Danny Macready were sitting opposite Aiden Cross and Glen Phelan. The two men were trusted confidants of Eddie Macready. Cross was all muscle and would readily undertake any order given by Macready. The other man Phelan, had the reputation of a thinker.

Barely able to contain his anger and frustration, Eddie Macready snarled, 'What have you heard Glen? What's the news?'

Taking account of the angry belligerent mood of Macready, Glen Phelan chose his words very carefully, 'None of this has been confirmed yet Eddie, but the word I'm hearing from sympathisers in Derby is that our cell has been compromised.'

Getting redder in the face by the second Macready spluttered, 'What the fuck does that mean exactly? Fucking compromised?'

'I've been told that the safe house has been raided by armed cops and that both Gerry and Liam were seen being led away in handcuffs.'

'No, that can't be right', came the anguished cry from Eddie Macready.

'The source is very reliable Eddie.'

Danny Macready said, 'What about Declan and JJ?'

'Again, this isn't confirmed anywhere yet, but the information I'm getting is that Hegarty's been shot dead and O'Hagan's been arrested.'

Regaining some composure, Eddie Macready snarled through gritted teeth, 'And our fucking ordnance?'

'Seized at the same time as Hegarty was killed. Apparently, Nottinghamshire Police were lying in wait for the two of them when they returned to the cache. JJ tried to fight back and avoid capture, but was shot dead.'

'Bastards', growled Macready.

To nobody in particular, Aiden Cross mumbled, 'How the fuck has this happened?'

Eddie Macready roared, 'I'll tell you how it's happened! We've been betrayed!'

He slammed his fist down on the table and continued, 'Belfast have always been fucking jealous of this campaign. Mark my words, Jimmy Patterson's hands are all over this fucking debacle.'

Danny tried to be the voice of reason, 'Patterson's a pain in the arse, but he's loyal to the cause, he would never betray us like that.'

Trying to regain his temper, Eddie Macready stared across the table at Glen Phelan, making the small, bespectacled man very uneasy.

Finally, he growled, 'Glen, I want you to get yourself over to Derby and make some discreet enquiries. I want to know chapter and verse what went wrong. If Patterson is behind this, so help me I'll….', his voice tailed off and he looked down at the table.

Without looking up he said, 'Be back here in two days, Phelan. I want a full report, understood?'

'I'll leave this evening. I can get the night ferry from Dublin. I'll find out what I can.'

'Finding out what you can, isn't good enough! I said, I want a full report and I want it quick. I need to know exactly what went wrong and who's responsible. Get going, I want you on that ferry to Holyhead tonight.'

Phelan nodded, stood up and left the bar.

Macready looked over at Cross, who was slowly shaking his head.

Needing to vent his anger somewhere Macready yelled, 'Why the fuck are you still here Aiden? You're no fucking good to me, sitting there looking gormless. Go on fuck off!'

Without speaking, Cross immediately left the bar, leaving just father and son sitting there.

Danny broke the silence, 'It won't be Patterson behind this.'

With real menace in his voice Eddie Macready said, 'Maybe he is and maybe he isn't, but I promise you this Danny, when I find out exactly who's responsible, I'll make them fucking pay.'

CHAPTER 30

2.00pm 13th April 1991
Central Police Station, Nottingham

Jim Chambers wasn't wrong, thought Tom as he walked towards Central Police Station in the middle of Nottingham. The main entrance of the station was surrounded by what looked like the world's media.

Keeping his head down, Tom marched straight up the steps and into the large stone building. Wearing a dark blue Adidas baseball cap, wraparound sunglasses, faded and torn denim jeans and a plain white T shirt, nobody associated with the waiting press scrum gave him a second glance.

He walked quickly up the stairs to the first floor and into the large canteen. He looked across the room and saw that Matt was already there. He was in an animated conversation with Graham Turner.

As soon as he saw Tom, Matt smiled and beckoned him over. He pushed out a chair with his foot inviting his friend to sit down.

Still grinning, Matt said, 'Christ mate, have you seen that lot camped on the steps outside?'

'You couldn't really miss them, could you? replied Tom.

Matt gushed, 'The media are loving it. The best headline I've seen so far was on the front page of The Sun. It said, "COPS 4 – IRA 0".

Tom grinned, then turned to face Graham and with a note of seriousness asked, 'Has there been any reaction from the IRA yet?'

'As far as I know, there hasn't been a word. No telephoned messages into the press. Nothing, yet.'

'Have you spoken to Tony?'

Graham shook his head, 'I've not been able to. I spoke to his wife first thing this morning, but Tony was still asleep. He'll be fine. He reacted in exactly the right manner. He followed his training to the letter.'

Both Tom and Matt nodded their heads in agreement.

An older man in a dark blue suit walked into the canteen. The three Special Ops men recognised him as one of the senior detectives who had initially investigated the Angela Hincks shooting at Farnsfield.

He walked across and said quietly, 'All right gents. We're ready to see all three of you now. Are you okay? Or do you need a couple of minutes?'

Graham Turner drained the last of the coffee from his mug, stood and said, 'We're ready, let's get cracking, shall we?'

The detective nodded and said, 'The sooner we get things sorted, the sooner the three of you can enjoy what's left of your day off. Follow me please.'

The three men followed the detective into an office just down the corridor from the canteen. Waiting inside this office, were two other detectives from the Major Crime Unit. The senior officer allocated a detective each to Tom and Matt, while he spoke with Graham Turner. Tom and Matt were taken to separate rooms where the detectives obtained written statements from them covering the events of the shooting at Moorgreen.

It was fast approaching six o'clock in the evening by the time Tom emerged from the interview room with the detective. The statement had been extremely detailed, painstaking efforts had been made by the detective to obtain every relevant fact.

As Tom walked along the corridor, he saw Matt emerge from another office alongside the detective who had taken his statement. The two Special Ops men made eye contact and Tom said, 'I'll wait for you in the canteen mate.'

'Okay, I won't be much longer. I've just got to sign everything up then I'm done', replied Matt.

Graham Turner had already completed his statement and had immediately left the police station to spend time with his young family. The three detailed statements would now be passed onto the Police Complaints Authority who would take on the task of fully investigating the fatal shooting of John Joseph Hegarty.

Eventually, Matt walked into the canteen.

'All done?' asked Tom.

Matt nodded.

Tom said, 'Do you fancy a quick pint? Or have you and Kate got plans?'

'I'm gagging for a beer. Where do you fancy?'

'The Fountain in town okay?'

'Fine by me.'

After a short walk through the bustling city centre that was full of late shoppers and commuters making their way home from work, the two men walked into The Fountain Inn on Bridlesmith Gate.

It was cool and dark inside. There were a few punters sat on bar stools at the bar but the rest of the trendy bar was empty.

Tom indicated an empty booth and said, 'Grab a seat mate, I'll get them in. What do you fancy?'

'Lager for me, Heineken if they've got it.'

Tom nodded and waked to the bar.

A couple of minutes later, Tom returned carrying a pint of Heineken and a pint of Guinness.

He placed Matt's lager down in front of him, sat down and took a long pull from the cold Guinness.

Matt took the top off his lager, then carefully replaced his glass and said, 'Cheers Tom. Now what is it you wanted to talk about?'

'Is it that obvious mate?'

'In a word, yes. Now what's up?'

Tom looked thoughtful, took another sip of Guinness and said, 'It's Bailey.'

'I thought it might be.'

'I'm worried, Matt. I haven't got a clue what she's up to. I don't know where she is or how long she's going to be away. She walked out of our apartment at the end of October to go to work and I haven't heard a word from her since. Before you say it, I know what you're thinking. I know that what she does isn't the sort of nine to five job, where she can tell me chapter and verse what's happening. I've got to be honest mate; all the uncertainty is driving me crazy.'

There was a pause as both men took another drink.

Matt said nothing, the silence inviting his friend to continue, eventually Tom continued, 'I'm struggling to get any proper sleep, I think she's in danger constantly. I honestly don't know if I can stand to be in a relationship like this. I love the bones of her and I know she feels the same way about me, but something's got to give. At the moment, I'm constantly on edge. I feel like I'm cracking up mate.'

Matt looked deep in thought for a minute, then the faintest smile crossed his lips, 'Tom, I know you can't ask Bailey directly what she's involved with or what she's doing, but have you thought about approaching Jim Chambers to see if he can find anything out from her bosses on your behalf?'

Tom looked incredulous.

Matt continued, 'Hear me out, it's not as daft an idea as you might think. I don't know for certain, but I reckon the boss must have some contacts with her people after the Mercer job in Liverpool. It's got to be worth a try surely? Anything is better than pulling your hair out with worry.'

Tom grinned and said, 'Matt, you're a genius. Why haven't I thought of that before now?'

'That's an easy question. Like you said, I'm a genius and you are', he paused for effect before continuing, 'Well, just thick as fuck really!'

Matt grinned, finished his pint and said, 'You ready for another?'

A smiling Tom said, 'Oh yeah, I can feel a bit of a session coming on.'

As he watched his best friend walk to the bar, Tom already felt brighter than he had for a long time. He would talk to Chambers. Maybe, just maybe he might be able to shed some light on where Bailey was and more importantly what she was doing.

CHAPTER 31

8.00am 18th April 1991
Keating's Farm, Sligo, County Sligo.

It had been a long drive from Londonderry to the small disused farm just outside Sligo.

Eddie Macready had called the meeting of the Provisional Army Council as a matter of urgency to discuss the reason for and the response to, the capture of the Londonderry Active Service Unit on the mainland.

The hour-long drive south with his son Danny, hadn't improved the old man's temper and as Danny drove the Land Rover Defender down the muddy, cratered dirt track that led to the old crumbling farmhouse, inside Eddie Macready was raging.

He didn't care how many times Danny told him that Jimmy Patterson wasn't responsible for the failure of the Active Service Unit, he still believed the Belfast commander was behind it in some way.

The rain was falling harder as Danny manoeuvred the Land Rover through the muddy farmyard to the rear of the building. Already parked behind the dilapidated building were two more four-wheel drive vehicles. Several men were huddled in the surrounding out buildings trying to shield themselves from the worst of the weather. These were the volunteers providing security for the meeting. Most of them were dripping wet and cold, desperately trying to prevent the weapons they were holding from getting soaked.

As Danny brought the Land Rover to a halt and turned the engine off, the back door of the farmhouse opened. A grim-faced Ben Christie stood in the doorway. As Eddie and Danny Macready got out of the vehicle, Christie said, 'Morning to you both. Get inside out of this shite weather. Frankie and Jimmy are already here. Nobody else is coming.'

Eddie Macready wasn't surprised that the weasel like, Eoin McAteer, from Sinn Fein wasn't there. It was too early and too wet for that snide shit to make an appearance.

It wasn't important, the two people he wanted to see were here. Francis Holmes, the Chief of Staff and his bitter rival, Jimmy Patterson, the commander of the Belfast Brigade.

As they walked towards Christie, Danny whispered to his father, 'Try and stay cool. Don't make yourself look like a fucking idiot in front of Frankie.'

'Fuck off!', was the growled response.

The two men walked into the kitchen of the derelict building.

A battered wooden table had been found from somewhere and camp chairs had been placed round it. Keating's Farm had been chosen for its remote location, not its splendour.

Seated at the head of the table was Francis Holmes. Ben Christie closed the door and walked round the room until he was standing directly behind him.

To the right sat Jimmy Patterson, standing behind him was McGuire. As usual, Patterson's bodyguard was dressed head to foot in black and was cradling an Armalite rifle.

Eddie Macready took a seat directly opposite Patterson and Danny remained standing behind him.

The windows were all boarded up and a single storm lamp cast an eerie yellow glow within the dark room. It cast bizarre shadows around the bare walls. The atmosphere inside the room was hostile and tense. Nobody said a word. The two men in charge of Londonderry and Belfast just glared across the table at each other.

Holmes broke the silence, 'Eddie, you called this emergency meeting. What's the update on your Active Service Unit?'

Patterson leaned back in his chair and for a fleeting second, Macready thought he saw the flicker of a smug smile. He bit down hard on his lip and resisted the temptation to fly into a rage. Instead, he said calmly, 'I've had one of my best men over on the mainland trying to establish exactly what happened. He returned yesterday and it doesn't make for pleasant hearing.'

'Go on', said Holmes.

'The Active Service Unit that had successfully carried the fight to the British in Newcastle and Sheffield has been destroyed. One brave volunteer, John Joseph Hegarty is dead. The other three, Declan O'Hagan, Gerry and Liam Quinn have all been detained and are currently being held under the bogus anti-terror laws. I'm confident that none of the captured men will breathe a word to the authorities. They're all high calibre operatives, who know how to resist interrogation. What I'm not so confident about is the way they were discovered and then captured or killed.'

Patterson interrupted, 'I've heard that your 'high calibre operatives' were careless where they left the cache containing all their explosives and equipment.'

'And how exactly have you heard that?', seethed a barely contained Macready.

'Belfast have always maintained sources within the various British police forces. One of our sources in the Derbyshire Constabulary has learned that Hegarty and O'Hagan were intercepted when they went to their cache.'

'And who knew they were going to the cache?'

Now it was Patterson's turn to become enraged, 'What exactly is it that you're insinuating here Macready?'

'I just think it's strange that the last time we had a meeting, we spoke about returning to the cache to get the remainder of the explosives to mount a major spectacular, then my men get bloody captured and killed at the fucking cache!'

As he spoke his sentence, Macready's voice grew louder, the word 'cache' was shouted in the darkened room

A now incensed Patterson raged back at the top of his voice, 'I had no fucking idea where your ASU had buried their explosives. You're being bang out of order Macready. I know we've had our disagreements in the past, but I would never endanger the life of a volunteer. Take that remark back right now or else!'

'Or else what?'

Danny placed a hand on his father's shoulder to prevent him standing up and Holmes suddenly barked, 'That's enough!'

The room was instantly quiet. The only noise to be heard was the clicking as McGuire fidgeted behind Patterson, moving the action on his Armalite, back and forth.

Holmes said quietly, 'Jimmy, tell your man to be fucking still. If he moves the action on that Armalite once more, Ben here, will ram the fucking thing up his arse.'

Patterson spluttered, 'For fuck's sake McGuire. Will ya stand still!'

McGuire instantly stopped fidgeting.

Holmes continued through gritted teeth, 'Eddie, I can see that you're upset about what's happened, but you're totally wrong to come to a meeting of the Council and start throwing wild, unfounded allegations around. Apologise to Jimmy right now!'

Eddie Macready could tell by the Chief of Staff's tone that this wasn't a choice, it was a command.

He snarled an apology, 'I apologise.'

'Accept his apology, Jimmy.'

Patterson stood and extended a hand across the table, reluctantly Macready took it and the two men shook hands.

Both men sat down again and Holmes continued, 'From what my own sources tell me it would appear that the authorities somehow got lucky and stumbled across the cache themselves. Obviously, they've then set up on it hoping to get a result. Unfortunately, it seems they were fortunate twice. That's all it is, bad luck. There's nothing we can do or say to prevent things like this happening.'

Patterson said, 'That's all very true Francis, but it leaves us with a huge amount of egg on our faces. An Active Service Unit undone by a bunch of provincial coppers. How embarrassing is that?'

Macready said, 'For once I totally agree with you, Jimmy. The question we've got to ask now, is what retribution we're going to take against the police who killed one of our own?'

Holmes was thoughtful and remained silent for a long time.

Finally, he said, 'That's a good question and one we all need to ponder on. I think there should be an appropriate response and it should be aimed at the police force responsible for the death of our volunteer. I want both of you to go away and give it some thought. We'll reconvene on the 5th of May. Michael Delaney, our NORAID fundraiser from Boston is flying in to Paris and plans to meet us all in Brest. I want to have some ideas on how we respond to this setback by then. Okay?'

Macready and Patterson both nodded, for the time being their differences forgotten as they turned their attention to gaining revenge against Nottinghamshire Police.

Holmes said, 'This meeting's over, see you all at the Café de Flore.'

CHAPTER 32

10.00pm 22nd April 1991
O'Doyle's Bar, Londonderry

Bailey had been working at O'Doyle's Bar for the best part of five months. She was now very well established as Sam Burrows, barmaid and new girlfriend of Danny Macready.

Because she existed in her own undercover bubble, she had not yet been advised of the recent developments in Nottinghamshire. She had received no contact from her Special Branch liaison for well over two weeks.

'Come on, budge up you lot, make room for a little one', Sam smiled as she squeezed onto the bench seat next to Danny Macready. Danny smiled and shuffled along into the booth to allow Sam to perch precariously on the end of the seat.

Following the first date she had with Danny, at the finest Italian restaurant in Londonderry, they had become really close, spending more and more time together.

Sam knew it would be a long, slow process to get Danny to feel comfortable enough to discuss IRA matters in her presence, but after the bombing at the Meadowhall Shopping Centre that time had to be cut drastically. Sam needed information and intelligence and she needed it quickly if she was going to prevent any further atrocities on the mainland.

It was almost closing time at O'Doyle's and Sam had finished her shift, so when she noticed Danny enjoying a pint with his father Eddie and four other men who she knew were all important members of the IRA, she had taken the opportunity to try and listen in to their conversation.

Whatever it was the men had been discussing, the conversation fell silent as soon as she sat down. Three of the men sitting opposite Sam, were staring across at the ample cleavage showing from within the silky cream blouse she was wearing with probably one button too many undone.

Sam had always used her sexuality as a weapon and tonight was no different, the sheer blouse and the tight black denim jeans were all designed to get the punters in the bar to relax around her. While ever they were concentrating on her female charms they would relax and maybe, just maybe, let something slip.

Danny Macready seemed to enjoy the fact that other men found Sam to be very attractive, but on this particular occasion one man, Aiden Cross, was pushing the leering just a little bit too far.

Danny leaned forward, scowled at Cross and with real menace in his voice whispered, 'If you ask her nicely, the lady might undo another button and get her tits right out, so you can have a proper look.'

Cross knew instantly that he had overstepped the mark and the last people you needed to upset in Londonderry were any members of the Macready clan.

Like a schoolboy who had been caught reading a copy of Playboy, he immediately averted his gaze and looked down at his feet. Without looking up he mumbled, 'I'm sorry Danny.'

Danny snarled back, 'Apologise to the lady, not me you shithead.'

Cross instantly looked over at Sam and spluttered, 'Sorry Sam, I didn't mean to stare.'

Sam totally ignored Cross and just smiled at Danny.

Eddie Macready turned to Danny and said, 'Never mind Aiden and his wandering eye, what are we going to do about this sorry state of affairs?'

Danny shrugged and Eddie continued, 'We've been made a laughing stock by a bunch of provincial coppers from Nottingham. I'm telling you; we've got to strike back and soon if that wanker Patterson is ever going to take us seriously again. You saw the fucking smug face on him, Danny.'

'I did, but I just don't know what we can do.'

One of the men at the table, Glen Phelan, leaned forward and whispered in a conspiratorial manner, 'I've been giving this a lot of thought and I've made some checks before I came here tonight. I've got an idea, but it's well risky and I don't know if we could pull it off.'

Phelan was a small, bespectacled individual with long black hair that he tied back in a ponytail. He was very well educated and was considered by many to be somewhat of an intellect. He never spoke much at meetings such as these, but when he did, people generally listened and took notice.

Eddie Macready whispered, 'Well don't keep it to yourself Phelan, let's hear your idea.'

All the men at the table leaned forward to catch the soft spoken, Phelan's next words. Sam snuggled in alongside Danny and cuddled in, placing her head on his shoulder.

In barely a whisper, Phelan made his pitch, 'As some of you around this table are aware, for some time now I've had access to the itineraries of some members of the Royal Family, should we ever need them. I was checking them before I came here tonight and it just so happens that the Prince of

Wales is due to open a brand-new police station in Newark, Nottinghamshire next month. It just got me thinking, how embarrassing would it be to the British establishment and Nottinghamshire's finest, if something were to happen to the Prince while he was under their care, so to speak?'

Aiden Cross was the first to speak up, 'You can't be serious, Phelan. A plan like that would never be sanctioned. You know what the feelings are within the organisation, especially Belfast, about taking action against any of the Royals. It's far too damaging with our Yankee friends. Belfast receive most of their money through donations from North America. It's a non-starter.'

Eddie Macready's face turned a livid scarlet colour and he rounded sharply on Cross, snarling under his breath, 'Personally, I don't give a flying fuck what Patterson or Belfast think. We need to show the Army Council that we're a serious part of this struggle. I think it's a brilliant idea, what else can you tell us about this proposed visit Glen?'

Phelan continued in his soft tones, 'I know that it's scheduled to happen on May 15th. The police station is already manned and being used, so a bomb would be out of the question. It would have to be shooter, but God only knows how anyone could get in close enough to pull it off.'

Macready smiled and said, 'Oh I don't know about that Glen, I think I may know just the man for the job.'

Now it was Phelan's turn to break into a broad grin as he whispered, 'The Death Adder?'

'Precisely.'

Suddenly, Sam Burrows realised that both Eddie Macready and Glen Phelan were staring directly at her and had fallen silent. She realised instantly that she had made a fundamental mistake and had been caught listening intently to the conversation.

Eddie Macready smiled at her and said, 'Who's your favourite Royal, sweetheart?'

Thinking quickly, Sam did her best to try and rescue the situation, 'Sorry, what did you say Eddie? I was just trying to hear the new Bee Gees song on the juke box.'

'Don't worry Sam, it's not important', said a smiling Macready as he stood up and made his way over to the bar.

Sam continued to snuggle into Danny's shoulder, but now also kept a discreet eye on Eddie Macready at the bar.

Her worst fears were confirmed when she saw him whispering something to two muscle bound thugs that were drinking at the bar. As Macready whispered to the two men, the younger of the two couldn't help but glance over and look at her.

At that precise moment, Sam knew her cover was blown and that she needed to get out of O'Doyle's Bar and fast.

She kissed Danny gently on the forehead and said quietly, 'Sorry Danny, I need the little girl's room, won't be long.'

Sam stood and walked quickly over to the corridor that led to the toilets. She knew that halfway along the corridor was a fire door that led to an alleyway at the side of the bar.

If she could only get through that fire door, she told herself, she might stand a chance.

CHAPTER 33

10.00pm 22nd April 1991
Nottinghamshire Police Headquarters

Ever since his conversation with Matt at the Fountain Inn, Tom had been biding his time. Waiting for the right moment to approach his Chief Inspector to ask him if he was able to get any news about Bailey.

It felt strange. Having to go to his boss to try and find out what his own girlfriend was doing at work was just weird.

As he and the rest of C Section had returned to Headquarters after an uneventful afternoon shift, Tom had noticed that the light was still on in Jim Chambers' office

The urge to know something, anything, far outweighed any feelings of nervousness or foolishness that Tom felt. He swallowed hard and knocked on the office door.

He heard Chambers' voice, 'Come in.'

Tom opened the door and stepped inside.

Chambers smiled and said, 'I was just leaving Tom, is this urgent?'

'Not really boss, but it won't take a minute either.'

'Okay, what can I do for you?'

'I haven't heard from my friend Bailey since October; as you know, she has a job that entails some secrecy. I was wondering if there was any way you could find out where she is?'

'And exactly how am I supposed to do that Tom?'

Tom felt his face flush as he realised how ridiculous his request sounded, but he pressed on, 'After the Mercer job up in Liverpool, I wondered if you'd made any lines of contact with her bosses, that are still open. I wouldn't ask, but I've really been worried sick about her, you know after everything that happened with Bev.'

Jim Chambers struck a more compassionate note as he said, 'I understand Tom. I can't promise anything, but I'll make a few phone calls tomorrow and see if there's anything I can find out. If I get lucky, I'll come and find you. Okay?'

'Thanks boss.'

'Tom, try not to worry. From what I remember of Bailey she can look after herself.'

Tom nodded. 'See you tomorrow boss, thanks.'

CHAPTER 34

10.15pm 22nd April 1991
O'Doyle's Bar, Londonderry

From the moment she realised that she was in mortal danger, Bailey was no longer thinking as Sam Burrows. She knew her only chance of survival was to get out of O'Doyle's Bar. Once outside the bar and on the streets of Londonderry, she knew it would still take a miracle for her to avoid capture and subsequent death at the hands of the IRA.

Just as she reached the fire door, Bailey heard the door that led back into the bar swing open. Glancing back, she saw the first of the musclemen come into the corridor.

She pushed down hard on the bar that operated the fire door and was relieved when the heavy door flew open. Kicking off her shoes, she bolted out into the cold night, sprinting fast down the alleyway that ran along the side of the bar.

As she ran, she could hear heavy footsteps behind her and heard one of her pursuers shout aloud, 'Oh no you don't, you fucking slag!'

Bailey reached the end of the dark alleyway and turned right, sprinting across the road, weaving in and out of the traffic, leaving car horns blaring in protest at her reckless manoeuvres. Fortunately, the traffic at that time of night wasn't heavy and it didn't hinder her progress.

She was in a blind panic and had no idea where she was running to, all she wanted to do was maintain the distance between herself and the two men chasing her. In her panicked state, she couldn't even remember the direction of the nearest police station.

The streets were all but deserted and even if they had been full of people, she knew that in reality nobody would dare to come to her aid. She continued to run blindly, weaving left and right, ignoring the pain in her bare feet. She only dared to glance back once and saw the two men about twenty yards behind her and gaining fast.

Suddenly, the Craigavon Bridge came into view and a glimmer of hope came crashing into her brain. She sucked in the cold air and sprinted even harder towards the bridge. Her lungs were burning and her legs beginning to tire rapidly.

As Samantha Burrows, Bailey had crossed that bridge every day on her way to work, she was well aware of its height and the speed of the water that flowed beneath it.

There had been many a desperate, lost soul who had taken their own life by leaping from this bridge into the black water below. Bailey had decided that by jumping from the bridge, she just might have a chance of saving hers. That is if the dark, fast flowing, freezing water beneath didn't claim her.

She sprinted onto the bridge, arms pumping, desperately trying to maintain some distance between herself and the two men.

As she ran, she heard the familiar sound of a gunshot from behind her as a pistol barked into life. The first bullet whistled past her head and she made her mind up, it was now or never.

Suddenly, without breaking stride she veered to her left and leapt straight over the waist high stone parapet. As she vaulted the parapet, she heard the sound of a second shot, this bullet found its mark.

Bailey felt the bullet graze across her left shoulder. It felt like somebody had placed a red-hot poker onto the top of her arm. The searing pain was so intense that she barely registered the black water of the fast-flowing river rushing up to meet her as she fell.

She hit the water hard and for a minute was totally disorientated as the wild, swirling currents dragged her down and spun her around. When she finally surfaced, spluttering and gasping for breath she was already about thirty yards downstream from the bridge.

The pain in her arm was made worse by the harsh, freezing cold water. She realised quickly that the heavy denim jeans she was wearing were conspiring to pull her back down beneath the icy water. Desperately, she struggled to free her legs from the clinging denims pulling on her legs, and once again she felt herself sliding below the surface.

Finally, after one more superhuman effort, she managed to kick off the heavy jeans.

Bobbing back to the surface, Bailey frantically sucked in air and allowed herself to be carried away downstream with the strong current. She had made a conscious decision that to try and fight the current would be suicidal. In any case, every second in the water getting swept downstream, created more distance between herself and the clutches of Macready and his murderous henchmen.

Bailey could feel the current sweeping her towards the far bank and in the distance, she could see the lights of houses on nearby streets.

She realised that the strong currents in the river had swept her around the area of Saint Columb's Park and that the small district of Gransha was now coming into view.

She was starting to shiver violently as the freezing cold water began to take its toll on her physically. She knew that she had to somehow get out of the water before the freezing temperatures turned her hypothermic.

It was a desperate struggle for survival now and Bailey had always been a fighter.

While she still had control over the muscles in her arms and legs, she began to strike out hard towards the far bank of the river and very slowly she began making some headway. As she neared the far bank, she felt the currents starting to subside and her progress towards the shore became easier and quicker.

It was with a palpable sense of relief that she finally felt her bare feet scrape on the shingle of the river bed.

Using the last reserves of her strength, she pulled herself out of the water and onto the grassy bank. For a full minute, she just lay on her back sucking in deep breaths, pulling vital oxygen into her cold, exhausted muscles.

As her breathing became more regular, she tried to stand. Her legs felt like jelly and the first time she stood, she promptly collapsed again. Fighting back tears of frustration she tried again and this time managed to remain upright. Slowly she climbed the grassy bank and was relieved to find that a road actually ran along the side of the river at this point. Knowing she was in a race against time to get warmed up before her body succumbed to hypothermia, she desperately looked around trying to get her bearings.

Finally, she understood where she had made landfall and using the last reserves of her energy and in a desperate bid to try and get warm, she began to slowly jog along the road. Every step she took was agony; ignoring the searing pain racking her entire body she pushed on, desperately looking for a particular landmark.

Five minutes of agony later and with fatigue rapidly overtaking her, Bailey saw what she'd been searching for. In the distance, some four hundred yards away and illuminated with bright white security lighting, was a large olive-green tower.

Bailey knew that this was the Sanger or lookout tower that she had seen many times in the distance from St Columb's Park. She knew only too well that such towers were used by both the Army and the RUC. It was either an Army base or a police station, she didn't care which.

As she got closer to the Sanger, she realised that it actually towered above an RUC police station.

Freezing cold and shivering violently, she began to hammer on the front door of the police station with her clenched fists. Eventually two uniformed police officers opened the door.

The two officers were startled to find an injured, semi-naked, soaking wet young woman who virtually fell through the door as it was opened.

Through chattering teeth that made her speech almost incoherent, Bailey managed to blurt out, 'Please, you've got to help me, I've been shot and fell into the river.'

One of the officers managed to grab her just as her legs were giving way beneath her. He dragged her inside the warm police station, as his colleague quickly removed his coat and wrapped it around her.

As Bailey felt the heat from the still warm coat envelop her shivering body, she spluttered through chattering teeth,

'I need to speak to Detective Sergeant Flynn from the Special Branch, urgently. Tell him you've got Sam Burrows here and that she's hurt.'

With that Bailey could take the pain coursing through her entire body no longer. As the shock of what she'd just endured registered she felt herself slipping into unconsciousness.

CHAPTER 35

9.00am 23rd April 1991
Waterside Hospital, Londonderry

When Bailey regained consciousness, she ached from head to toe, but she felt warm and the pain in her shoulder was now more of a dull ache than the searing pain she remembered.

She winced slightly as she tried to sit up. The bed she was in felt very comfortable, but she wanted to see her surroundings. She needed to know where she was and if she was now safe.

A gentle voice from across the room said, 'Whoa! Take your time Miss. Would you like me to call you a nurse?'

Bailey sat up and tried to focus on the man across the room who had spoken to her.

With a note of defiance in her voice, she asked, 'Who are you? Where am I?'

The white haired, elderly man in the dark suit reached into the inside pocket of his jacket and fished out a small black wallet, 'I'm sorry, my manners have deserted me, it's been a long night. My name's Chief Inspector Douglas Proctor of the Royal Ulster Constabulary Special Branch and this is the Waterside Hospital. I believe that you are Miss Samantha Burrows. Is that right?'

Bailey squinted as she tried to see the Warrant Card the man was showing her. In a voice devoid of emotion, she said, 'Where's DS Flynn? I'll only speak to him.'

'Detective Sergeant Flynn will be here shortly. I just happened to be at the police station you came into last night. I arranged for you to be brought here to get medical assistance. I've been sitting by your bedside ever since. Somebody obviously wanted you dead', he nodded towards her heavily bandaged shoulder before continuing, 'I thought it might be prudent for me to sit here to prevent any further unpleasantness befalling you. Personally speaking, I think being shot and going for a late-night swim in the freezing cold River Foyle is enough excitement in one night for anyone, don't you?'

The Chief Inspector smiled warmly.

Bailey smiled back and said, 'Thank you, I suppose I'm just being paranoid.'

'Not at all, it's always better to be safe than sorry. Anyway, Detective Sergeant Flynn will grace us with his presence in a few minutes time. As soon as he arrives, I'll leave you alone to speak with him. Can I organise you a hot drink, while we wait?'

She shook her head, 'No thanks. Water's fine just now.'

Just at that moment the door opened and a heavy-set man, well into his forties, wearing a crumpled grey suit and with dark hair that was greying at the temples stumbled into the room.

Proctor smiled and said, 'Ah! DS Flynn, glad you could join us, at last.'

'Sorry I'm late sir, the traffic out there at this time of the morning is diabolical, bloody rush hour.'

'Don't worry man, everything's in hand. I've organised a twenty-four-hour armed guard to be undertaken by Special Branch detectives. Only the attending doctor is aware that the young lady's here. I've also made her people in London aware of the situation and that she's in safe hands.'

He paused smiled at Bailey and said, 'Apparently, even though I've done all this for her, 'Miss Burrows' still only wants to talk to you.'

With a wink and a smile at Bailey, Chief Inspector Proctor made for the door. He paused at the door and said, 'My dear, I'll leave you in the very capable hands of the good sergeant. I'm off to get a well-earned coffee. Don't worry, you'll be safe now.'

As soon as Proctor left the room, Bailey began to brief DS Flynn about the IRA plans for Nottinghamshire. She was very sketchy on details as her memory had been affected by the trauma she'd been through. All she could remember was that those plans somehow involved the Prince of Wales and someone or something called The Death Adder.

CHAPTER 36

6.00pm 23rd April 1991
Nottinghamshire Police Headquarters

'Settle down! I know it's late and you've all had a long day, but the quicker we get started, the quicker we can all go home.'

The voice belonged to Sgt Graham Turner and he was addressing the men of C Section in the large briefing room at The Huts.

The men had all been on duty for ten hours having started their day at eight o'clock that morning.

Graham Turner continued, 'Right gents. I'll start with the bad news. If any of you have made plans or booked leave for the 15th of May, forget it. All leave for that date's been cancelled.'

There were a few moans and groans from some of the men that had obviously already made plans for that date. The disgruntled noises didn't last long, part of the role of the Special Operations Unit was being able to maintain a very fluid approach to the hours and shifts worked. The work always came first. If a job needed to be done, it got done, no arguments.

Every man on the Unit knew this was the case, so although there would always be a few moans initially at cancelled rest days and cancelled leave, the outcome was always the same, the men would be on duty and the job would be done.

After waiting a few seconds for the groans to abate, the burly sergeant continued, 'When you've all finished your whinging and groaning, the reason for the late change of duty is that a Royal visit's been planned for that date. What that also means is that we need to start the planning process immediately. I want to have a quick run through of the information I've just received from Chief Inspector Chambers, so that you're all up to speed. Myself and Steve Grey will prepare the Operational Order for the visit. Steve, I also want you to take on the role of Operation Controller on the day of the visit, okay?'

Steve Grey was sitting at the front of the briefing room and he nodded towards his sergeant, 'No problem sarge.'

Graham Turner continued, 'As usual, we'll provide close protection alongside Special Branch and the Royal Protection Team from the Met. Armed Traffic officers will also be deployed along with ourselves to provide an escort to the venue. Tom Naylor and Matt Jarvis, using your expertise I want you to risk assess the sniper threat and to prepare a report to cover that. Any questions, so far?'

Steve Grey asked what everyone in the room was thinking, 'Yeah, just a couple sarge, who's coming and where are they going?'

'The Royal visitor is the Prince of Wales; he's coming to Nottinghamshire on the 15th of May to officially open the new Newark Police Station.'

There were a few more mutterings now the identity of the visitor was known and where the visit was going to take place.

Sgt Turner said, 'The good news is this; as most of you will be aware, the new police station at Newark has been open to the public for six weeks already. This means that a full search and seal of the building will be required before the visit takes place as the public will have had some access. B Section and D Section will be deployed to carry out the search and seal of the building. Obviously, following our recent success against the IRA it's very likely that the threat level will have increased. That will be decided by Special Branch nearer the day.'

The news that two other Sections were to be deployed to do the building search was well received by the men of C Section. To complete a search and seal operation on a building the size of the new police station would be a massive undertaking.

Turner now spoke directly to Tom and Matt, 'I want you two to be back on duty tomorrow no later than seven o'clock in the morning so you can get over to Newark and make a start on your report about the sniper threat. I want the finished report on my desk within three days. Have either of you got any problem with that time scale?'

Matt replied, 'No Sarge, no problem, we'll be on it first thing in the morning.'

Turner now addressed the rest of the men, 'Okay, that's all for now, I want you all back here at eight o'clock tomorrow so we can get stuck into the planning properly. Any questions?'

Nobody said a word.

'That's it then, see you in the morning.'

Jim Chambers came into the briefing room and made his way over to Tom.

He said, 'Tom, I need a quick word in my office before you go home.'

Tom smiled and said, 'Okay boss.'

He had smiled because he thought his boss may have news on Bailey, but there was something about the expression on the Chief Inspectors face that was troubling.

Tom felt the energy drain from him as he followed Chambers into his office, a tangible feeling of dread washed over him as he realised that the last time he'd seen that look on Chambers' face was when he had arrived at his cottage and informed him that his girlfriend, Bev had been killed.

As Tom walked into the office Chambers closed the door behind him and said quietly, 'Sit down Tom. I'm not going to beat around the bush, what I've got to tell you isn't great news.'

A shell-shocked Tom sank into one of the chairs as Jim Chambers continued, 'Firstly, Bailey's alive. I've just received a telephone call from Detective Inspector Murray in Special Branch. He received a message on the secure line from MI5 this afternoon and was authorised by them to pass this information on to you. Bailey has been shot and wounded while working undercover in Northern Ireland. The gunshot wound isn't serious and is definitely not life threatening. At the moment that's all the information I've got Tom. I'm sorry. I tried to get more out of Nick Murray, but he just doesn't know anything else, the Security Service can't or more likely won't tell him anymore.'

Tom said nothing and shook his head slowly.

Chambers continued, 'I'm sorry I can't be more helpful Tom. I do understand what you're going through after everything that happened when Bev was killed. I want you to take a few days off until we've firmed up this information. I'll get one of the other lads to help Matt with the sniper threat report.'

Tom felt physically sick, he could feel his head spinning. For one second he had genuinely thought Chambers was going to tell him that Bailey had been killed.

His head was now full of unanswered questions; what was she doing in Northern Ireland? Where was she now? How had she been shot? Where was she wounded? Although not life threatening was her wound going to be life changing?

Chambers could see the torment behind Tom's blank expression, he opened his office door and shouted, 'Pc Jarvis, get in here please!'

Within a couple of seconds Matt Jarvis knocked on the door.

'Come in Matt', said Chambers.

The Chief Inspector quickly relayed to Matt the information he'd previously given Tom before saying quietly, 'Take your mate home and make sure he's okay. I want you to team up with Jack Rimmer on the sniper report. I want Tom to take some time off. Not a word about this to anyone Matt.'

'No problem boss.'

Matt then helped a stunned Tom out of the chair saying, 'Come on mate, let's get you home.'

The two men never spoke until they had nearly reached Tom's riverside apartment. As Matt drove his car into the small courtyard, Tom suddenly blurted out, 'I can't do this Matt. I can't handle this feeling of helplessness. When Bailey gets back, we will need to talk, but if she won't quit her job, I can't see us going much further.'

Matt stopped the car and said quietly, 'You're right, you will need to talk and you need to take as long as it takes. Don't decide anything in haste. You knew all about Bailey and what her job could entail before you got together. It's obvious that you love the girl and with that love there may need to be some compromise.'

Matt paused and then continued, 'I don't want you to think I'm speaking out of turn here Tom, but it could be that your problem runs deeper than what Bailey does for a living. It could be that it's got far more to do with your past than her present. Think about it. In the meantime, I'm sure she's not injured too badly or they would have said something.'

'But that's just it mate, nobody tells me a fucking thing and I'm sick of it!'

Matt could hear the emerging anger coming through in Tom's voice, now the enormity of what he'd just been told was starting to sink in. Matt thought better of telling his friend that he may benefit from some professional counselling. That could wait for a less raw moment.

He said quietly, 'Come on Tom, you're home now. Take it easy and please let me know as soon as you hear any more news. If you want to talk to someone before you see Bailey, just give me a call. Chambers has said take some days off, so just try and relax and think about what you want to say to her when she gets back. Are you going to be okay mate? Do you want me to come up and talk over a beer for a while?'

Tom shook his head, 'No thanks mate, I'm fine. I think I just need some time alone to think things through properly. Thanks for bringing me home and I'm sorry for sounding off at you. I'll call you as soon as I hear anything.'

Tom got out of the car and made his way slowly over to the lobby of his apartment block. He stepped inside and waited patiently for the lift to take him up to his apartment.

Matt watched his best friend slowly step into the lift and for a split second he almost switched off the car engine and followed him. He thought better of it, telling himself that space was what Tom needed now.

Matt knew Tom well enough to know that he would contact him if he needed to talk, so he turned his car around in the courtyard and drove off.

CHAPTER 37

6.00pm 24th April 1991
British Army Base, Londonderry

The huge Chinook helicopter slowly settled on the ground inside the British Army base in Londonderry. To a very nervous Bailey, it seemed as if the entire building she waited in was shaking, such was the vibration from the two Lycoming T-55L engines that powered the aircraft.

Above the din of those massive engines a woman's voice said, 'It's okay to put your blouse back on now Miss, thank you.'

The voice belonged to the British Army doctor who had been attending to Bailey's wound.

As she washed her hands in the small sink, Dr Finch said, 'You'll be pleased to know that your wound's healing perfectly. There doesn't appear to be any infection present, which is not only great news, but also quite miraculous considering the state of the filthy river water. I'm afraid you're going to have quite a vivid scar there for a number of years. The red keloid scarring is due to the fact that immediately after the wound was inflicted the area was immersed directly into freezing cold water. It should fade over time though. As there appears to be no tendon or nerve damage, you'll have full mobility within the next two weeks, although it might continue to feel stiff for some time after that.'

Dr Finch paused as she dried her hands, then said, 'I'm still a little worried about a possible underlying infection that hasn't manifested itself yet, so I want you to continue with the course of strong antibiotics I've given you. Continue taking them for the duration of the prescription until we're sure there are no complications. From my understanding, although the river looks beautiful it's quite heavily polluted, so we can't be too careful. Okay?'

Bailey nodded towards the doctor and muttered, 'Understood, thanks.'

Her mind was elsewhere as she anticipated the intense debrief that was about to happen. As the engine noise from the Chinook finally lessened and then stopped her nervousness increased. She was aware the helicopter that had just landed had only one very important passenger, the Director of MI5.

In an unprecedented move, he had flown over personally, under cover of strict secrecy, to extract from her every last detail she could remember about a possible planned assassination attempt on a member of the Royal family.

Bailey had worked for MI5 for over four years and had never met the Director. Like everyone else on the grid, she knew of his fearsome reputation. Her mind was racing as she got dressed in the medical room trying to recall every detail of the night she'd been shot. Desperately searching her mind for details of the conversation she'd overheard in O'Doyle's Bar.

Everything about that night was still vague. Memories would come to her like exploding flash bulbs. They brought with them vivid patches of detail, but they were in no order and made no sense. The harder she tried to remember, the more scrambled the memories became. She felt almost tearful with the frustration.

Dr Finch, the Army doctor who had treated her physical wounds, had tried to explain to her that eventually her memory would settle down and the reason it was so jumbled now was as a direct result of the post-traumatic stress she was suffering. It was a combination of that stress and the fact she had been unconscious for quite a long time.

The problem for Bailey was that she knew there was no time for her memory to recover naturally, in a gradual way. Time was of the essence, she needed to recall everything right now or it would mean there was no way of preventing the cold-blooded murder of the Prince of Wales. That much of the conversation she could recall. It was the important detail of the whispered plot she lacked.

Bailey had just finished buttoning up her blouse when the door to the medical room flew open. A small, diminutive man with slicked back, greying hair, wearing a smart, charcoal grey pinstripe suit, white shirt and a claret coloured polka dot tie marched brusquely into the room.

He said in a booming voice that belied his stature, 'Doctor. Thank you, but we are going to need some privacy immediately.'

The doctor quickly gathered her things and left the room, the authority in the man's voice evident.

He turned to Bailey and said, 'Please sit down, Miss Masters.' Now they were alone in the room, the man's voice had softened slightly.

Bailey did as she was asked and sat down, the man pulled over a chair and sat down directly opposite her. There was no desk or table to act as a barrier and the man sat only two feet from her.

For the first time, she noticed the cold intensity in the man's blue, unblinking eyes.

Intertwining his fingers, he said, 'Miss Masters, I know we've never met, so allow me to introduce myself. My name's Sir Godfrey Winstanley, I'm the Director. Our friends in the Special Branch here have advised me of your unfortunate experiences, so firstly I need to ask if you feel strong enough to answer my questions?'

Bailey took a deep breath, 'Sir, we haven't met but I do know who you are. Thank you for asking if I'm okay. I feel fine physically, but my memories of that night are still very confused. Dr Finch has explained to me that this is natural and that it will settle down eventually. I can tell you everything I remember now and as and when the other detail comes back; I'll ensure you know everything straight away. I fully understand how vital this is.'

Having said her piece, Bailey sighed and leaned back in the chair. She had been rehearsing her little speech over and over again inside her head, ever since DS Flynn had told her who was coming over to debrief her as he drove her from Waterside Hospital to the Army Base.

Sir Godfrey also sat back in his chair and thoughtfully stroked his chin. His eyes never strayed from Bailey's. Two minutes passed by without him saying a word, the silence was oppressive and Bailey could feel her nervousness rising by the second.

Suddenly, he sat bolt upright and leaning forward he said, 'Miss Masters, are all your belongings here? Are you ready to go?'

Recovering from the fright he had given her, Bailey replied, 'Yes Sir. What I have is in that bag over there', she indicated a small leather grip bag in the corner of the room.

Sir Godfrey was now on his feet, 'Good, good. Do you feel well enough to fly back to London with me right now?'

'Yes Sir.'

'Right, come on then let's go, there's no time to waste. Let's get you back to London and in some nice hotel where you can recover. That way you'll be able to recall your thoughts much quicker and with a great deal more clarity than you would do stuck here in this God forsaken hole.'

Bailey sat there somewhat taken aback.

Where was the fearsome debrief that she had been dreading so much? What had happened to the fearsome reputation of the Director? Why was he being so kind and considerate?

Sir Godfrey was already marching towards the door, looking over his shoulder he said, 'Come along Miss Masters, grab your bag. There's one other thing you should know. I've told Special Branch here to leak a story to the press stating that a young woman was found dead in the River Foyle and that she's been identified as Samantha Burrows. The press release will state that the RUC are treating her death as a tragic suicide and aren't looking for any other persons in connection with her death.'

He paused and then said, 'So, as of this moment, Samantha Burrows is officially dead. Another good reason, I think, to get you back to London.'

Bailey picked up the small grip bag and followed the Director out of the room, she could already hear him barking instructions to the flight crew of the Chinook helicopter.

It took a few minutes for the crew to strap Bailey into one of the seats inside the huge Chinook. Seconds later the noise of the engines rose to a crescendo and the aircraft rose steadily from the ground, before suddenly veering off to the left and rapidly gaining height.

Five minutes into the flight and Sir Godfrey tapped Bailey on the arm and shouted, 'The flight shouldn't take long Miss Masters. I've got the crew to radio ahead, there will be a car waiting to take you from RAF Northolt to the Hilton Hotel in Mayfair. A suite of rooms has been booked in advance for you. In the room next door to yours will be a specialist team on hand to debrief everything you can remember as soon as that information comes back to you. I'm aware that putting undue pressure on you could set your memory recall processes further back and be counterproductive. I'm hoping that by making you feel relaxed in safe, comfortable surroundings your memory will start to function correctly much quicker. Having said that, I don't need to tell you the urgency of the situation we're facing.'

Bailey shouted above the din inside the helicopter, 'I know, Sir. The whole thing is still a blur, like shapes disappearing in and out of a thick fog, but certain things do keep coming back. Like I told DS Flynn the only real memory I have is of someone or something called 'The Death Adder'.'

As once again her memory failed her, Bailey shook her head and tears, borne out of anger and frustration slowly rolled down her cheeks.

The Director took a starched white handkerchief from his pocket and handed it to Bailey, 'Hush now Miss Masters, it will all come back to you. Just be patient, it will come.'

Bailey wiped her eyes and settled back into the leather chair.

She stared out of the small window as the night sky began to draw in and the lights of London started to become visible way below.

CHAPTER 38

10.00am 25th April 1991
Savoy Hotel, Nottingham

Detective Inspector Nick Murray took another sip of his filter coffee and flicked to the next page of the Financial Times. The Special Branch man had been waiting patiently in the foyer of The Savoy Hotel for fifteen minutes now.

The call on the Brent emergency communication phone from MI5 last night had been quite specific. The MI5 Regional Officer, Brenda Starkey would be at The Savoy Hotel at ten o'clock sharp.

He glanced at his watch; it was now almost five minutes past ten.

The revolving door of the hotel started to move and Brenda Starkey stepped into the lobby.

Nick Murray had met with her on two previous occasions. He instantly recognised the tall, thin woman with the spartan short, grey hair, carrying a black briefcase.

He folded his newspaper and waited for her to sit down.

'Good morning Brenda, can I get you a coffee or tea?

'Tea, would be good. Earl Grey, no sugar. Thanks.'

Nick walked over to the main desk and ordered the tea and another coffee for himself. To anyone watching it looked like just another business meeting, one of hundreds that occur in hotel foyers all over the country, every day.

After the receptionist had brought the hot beverages over and they were alone they got straight down to business.

Brenda said, 'Thanks for coming Nick, this couldn't be said over the phone.'

'No problem, what's going on?'

'One of your officers is currently dating one of our operatives and we have need of him in London as a matter of urgency.'

'Okay, now I'm confused.'

'As you were informed recently, our operative was working undercover in Londonderry when she overheard a conversation where a plot to assassinate a member of the Royal Family was being discussed. Unfortunately, the poor girl was rumbled and shot.'

'Is she recovering okay?'

'She's recovering well and is now safe in London, thank God. The problem for us is that she can't remember any of the details of the conversation she overheard. My boss seems to think that getting your officer, her boyfriend, down to London as a matter of urgency, could well help speed up that process, so to speak.'

'I see. Who's the officer?'

'Pc Tom Naylor. Apparently, they met whilst working on a job together in Liverpool last year. Anyway, all that's irrelevant. You just need to ensure that Tom Naylor's in London by tonight. His girlfriend's staying at The Hilton Hotel in Mayfair. He'll be expected to arrive no later than six o'clock this evening. Can you sort all that out?'

'It shouldn't be a problem. I think I remember that job up in Liverpool. Tom Naylor's part of the Special Operations Unit. I'll talk to his boss Jim Chambers and get Naylor down to London tonight.'

'That's great Nick, thanks.'

'Any idea how long he'll need to be down there?'

'How long's a piece of string?'

'Okay, I'll get it sorted. Enjoy your tea Brenda.'

CHAPTER 39

11.00am 25th April 1991
Nottinghamshire Police Headquarters

The telephone conversation had been short and to the point.

Now, as he walked across the courtyard at Police Headquarters, Jim Chambers wondered what could be so urgent that warranted him being summoned to a meeting at the Special Branch offices.

He went into the main building, walked up the stairs to the Special Branch offices and knocked on the Detective Inspector's door.

'Come in.'

Jim Chambers walked in and Nick Murray stood and walked round his desk to meet him, 'Thanks for coming over so promptly Jim.'

Chambers was straight to the point, 'No problem Nick, but what's so urgent and delicate that it couldn't be dealt with on the phone?'

Nick Murray quickly outlined the information he'd been given earlier and said, 'So as you can see, we need to get Pc Naylor down to London today. Is he on duty?'

'No, he isn't. After that little bombshell you asked me to deliver to him the other day, I told him to take some time off, he needed it. I'll drive over to his apartment right now and make sure he gets down to London. I'm sure it won't be a problem; he'll no doubt be delighted to spend some time with Bailey. He's been worried sick about her.'

'He needs to be down there by six o'clock tonight, Jim.'

'I'll sort it Nick, leave it with me.'

'Can you let me know when he's on his way please?'

'Will do.'

CHAPTER 40

12.30pm 25th April 1991
Trent Embankment, Nottingham

Tom was waiting anxiously inside his apartment. The call from Jim Chambers had seemed extremely vague. Tom paced up and down, waves of nausea washing over him, he was literally worried sick.

The strident tone of the intercom made him jump.

He dashed across the room, pressed the intercom and said, 'Hello, who is it?'

'It's me Tom, Jim Chambers.'

'Come up boss, top floor.'

A minute passed before Tom heard a soft tapping on the front door.

He opened the door and said, 'Come in boss. What's going on?'

A beaming Jim Chambers said, 'I've got some great news for you Tom. Bailey's in London at the Hilton Hotel in Mayfair. Her people have been in touch and they want you to travel down to London so you can spend some time with her, they think you being there will help her recovery.'

'That's great news boss. Why would her bosses do that? Is she okay?

'She's fine Tom, recovering well by all accounts. I thought you'd be over the moon about seeing her.'

'I am, it's just a little unexpected. When can I go and see her?'

'Today, get packed, get yourself a train ticket organised and I'll give you a lift to the station.'

The next fifteen minutes were a blur, Tom raced round his apartment packing a small overnight bag.

At the train station he purchased a ticket for the three thirty train, travelling from Nottingham to St Pancras in London.

Having got his ticket, Tom shook hands with Jim Chambers and said, 'Thanks boss, I don't know what strings you pulled to sort this out, but I owe you, big style.'

'No problem, enjoy yourself. I'll expect you back at work in a few days' time. By the way you're now on Annual Leave, we're not a charity.'

Both men laughed and Tom raced down onto the platform to wait for his train.

He couldn't quite believe this was happening. He felt excited at the prospect of seeing Bailey again, but something was also making him feel uneasy about the whole situation.

It just didn't feel right.

CHAPTER 41

6.00pm 25th April 1991
Hilton Hotel, Mayfair, London

Bailey had been safely ensconced in the Hilton Hotel for a full day now.

She had been amazed at just how quickly, almost every detail of the nightmare that had befallen her had come crashing into her memory. The jigsaw of memories had slotted into place, as very patiently the debrief team had extracted information from her.

She had even been able to recall the conversation at O'Doyle's Bar between Eddie Macready and his henchmen. The way they had talked about the arrests that had been made in Nottingham and how the Active Service Unit had been dismantled. She recalled the anger shown by the men about the way the dismantling of the ASU had made them look amateurish. She also remembered the overwhelming need the men in O'Doyle's Bar felt to strike back quickly and in an appropriate manner.

The memory of the discussion about the Royal Family being a possible target came back sharper and she was able to tell the debrief team there had been a huge row before the decision had finally been taken to sanction killing the Prince of Wales as he opened a police station in Nottinghamshire. She was able to recall that a bomb was thought to be out of the question for the assassination and that they had decided to use The Death Adder. Try as she might she couldn't remember anything about who or what The Death Adder was or how the threat to the Prince would materialise.

At the conclusion of that days debrief, Sir Godfrey Winstanley had come to the Hilton personally. He thanked her for her efforts and told her to try and relax that evening as the debrief team would begin again in the morning.

Bailey thanked him, telling him she'd been amazed at how quickly her memories had returned once she'd arrived at the hotel and for the first time in months, felt totally secure and safe from harm.

Winstanley had just smiled as he bid her good evening.

She had come to the conclusion that as well as being fearsome and intense, the Director was a very wily old fox.

Bailey, at long last, felt completely relaxed knowing that her debrief was almost over. The only piece missing from her recollections of that night was how she had actually escaped.

She knew she had been in the river, but could not remember the events between overhearing the conversation in the bar and being in the river. She had no idea how she had got out of O'Doyle's Bar or of the events leading up to being shot and being in the river. All that part of the nightmare was still just a blur.

She lay back on the huge, soft bed and loosened the robe she had slipped on after her hot, scented bath. She let the robe slip to her sides, exposing her naked body. She closed her eyes and allowed her body to cool slowly.

A sharp, urgent rapping on the hotel door made her sit bolt upright. Very quickly, she drew in the robe tightening it around her body, before getting off the bed and walking to the door.

As she approached the door, the urgent knocking started again.

Instinctively she glanced at the clock on the wall, it was almost six o'clock at night. Who was banging on the door? All her relaxed feelings were swept away on a rushing tide of trepidation.

Nervously, she stood at the side of the door and said timidly, 'Who's there? I haven't ordered anything.'

'Bailey. It's me, Tom. Open the door.'

'Tom, is that you?'

'Yes, it's me. Come on open the door.'

Bailey immediately yanked open the heavy door. She was confronted by the sight of Tom, standing behind the biggest bunch of flowers she'd ever seen.

Tom stepped inside the room, threw the flowers onto the bed, swept Bailey up in his arms and kissed her hard on the mouth.

Finally, the kiss stopped and Bailey said breathlessly, 'Oh my God Tom, this is fantastic, what are you doing here?'

Smiling broadly, he replied, 'It's a long story sweetheart, but basically your boss phoned my boss and ordered him to order me to get my sorry arse down to London, so I could give you some much needed tender, loving care. So here I am. Orders are orders.'

She laughed and said, 'Oh my God Tom, I can't believe you're here.'

He kissed her again and said, 'Believe it, I'm here alright. God I've missed you so much, come here.'

Instantly they both fell onto the bed, crushing the flowers beneath them as they locked in a passionate embrace.

Bailey pulled away and said, 'Just a minute mister, you'd better get them roses off the bed, I don't fancy rose thorns in my backside to go along with the rest of my injuries.'

As they both laughed, Tom grabbed the flowers off the bed and threw them on the floor, before tumbling back onto the bed with Bailey.

After making love, they lay in each other's arms for a long time, not speaking. Slowly caressing each other, revelling in the special intimacy they had both been craving for so long.

It was Tom who finally broke that wonderful silence, 'How's your shoulder? Is the wound still sore? How deep is it?'

'My shoulder's fine Tom. It's really not very sore at all, just a little stiff. It's nothing more than a scratch, I was very lucky. It still baffles me; I can't remember how it happened. I've tried over and over again to remember, but I can't. It's so bloody frustrating.'

'I was so scared Bailey. I thought I'd lost you as well. When Chambers told me you'd been shot, I thought you were dead. I couldn't bear to lose you as well; it would break me in two. I know you probably don't want to hear this, but I've got to say it. I don't want you to go back to work, it's too dangerous.'

Bailey held him tight and said, 'This isn't the time or the place for this discussion. You knew what I did before we got together, I can't just turn it on and off to suit you Tom. It's what I do, it's part of me. Do you think I don't worry about you? Of course, I do, but I would never dream of asking you to stop doing your job. I completely understand why you feel the way you do; I really do.'

He slowly shook his head and said softly, 'I don't think you understand at all. It's not what you do. It's the fact that I never know what you're doing. It's that feeling of not knowing, that I don't think I can cope with. At least with me, you know where I am and to a great extent exactly what I'm doing. With you, I know jack shit, until I get a message from my boss telling me you've been shot. Months of nothing and then bang, you've been shot. I don't think I can deal with that again.'

Bailey pulled him in closer and could feel him physically shaking with emotion. She kissed the back of his neck and said, 'Not now Tom, eh? Let's just enjoy being together right now. We can talk all of this shit through later, when it's not so raw for both of us. Please, just hold me. I want to feel your strong arms around me so I know I'm safe. I'm totally in love with you Tom Naylor. We can sort this out, I promise.'

Slowly, Tom turned to face her and she could see the tears on his cheeks, gently she wiped them away and began to slowly kiss where the tears had been. The kisses moved slowly to his lips and became more and more intense.

Bailey whispered softly, 'I need you in my life Tom, make love to me sweetheart.'

CHAPTER 42

3.30am 26ᵗʰ April 1991
Hilton Hotel, Mayfair, London

The shrill scream pierced the darkness.

Instantly, Tom was wide awake, he sat bolt upright in bed and reached for the switch to turn on the bedside lamp.

The screaming had now stopped, but he could see Bailey thrashing around under the bed covers, fighting off some imaginary attacker as she lay fast asleep.

Reaching over, Tom gently shook her. Eventually, her eyes opened wide and she gasped for breath, sucking in air.

Tom stroked her sweat drenched hair and said, 'It's okay sweetheart, you were having some sort of nightmare. You were screaming out loud. Don't worry now, I've got you, I'm here with you.'

Bailey slowly sat up and reached for the glass of water on the bedside cabinet.

She drank the water thirstily, then said, 'Oh my God! It's all coming back to me, Tom. Everything. I saw it all as clear as day. I was sitting in the bar listening to them talking about the assassination. I suddenly realised that they were all staring at me and had noticed I was listening intently to them as they spoke about their plans.'

Bailey was physically shaking as she continued to recount the vivid memory, 'I watched the old man walk to the bar and have a conversation with two meatheads. I knew I was properly in the shit when the younger one looked over at me. I had to get out of there.'

She began to sob, in between sobs she continued, 'I kissed Danny on the forehead and made an excuse about needing the toilet. I made it into the corridor, but was followed by those two thugs. I managed to get through the fire door and ran for my life.'

Bailey was breathing hard and blurting it all out. Tom stared at her wide eyed and remained silent as she poured her heart out. He wondered who the fuck Danny was, but said nothing. He didn't want to do anything that would halt her recollections.

Taking a deep breath, she continued, 'I remember looking back, I could see their faces as they chased me through the streets, I will never forget those two faces. I remember my feet hurting, I was running barefoot. I could hear the two thugs gaining on me as I ran towards the Craigavon Bridge. I heard the first gunshot and knew I had no choice but to jump into the river.'

Tom tightened his arm around her heaving shoulders and cuddled her tightly. Still she blurted stuff out, 'As I jumped, I felt the bullet hit me as it grazed my shoulder. I hit the water hard and went straight under. The water was freezing and the current was swirling me upside down. I thought I was going to die, Tom.'

Finally, she was crying. The tears flooded out. Tom cuddled her close and whispered, 'That's enough now, let it go.'

He could feel her entire body trembling and heard her forcibly trying to stifle her crying until the noise was nothing more than a muffled sobbing.

Suddenly, she stiffened and the sobbing stopped, she pulled away from Tom's arms and pushed him away, 'No Tom, I've got to get it out while I can.'

Tom said softly, 'Okay. I'm here sweetheart. I'm not going anywhere.'

Bailey continued with much more steel in her voice now, 'I remember finally breaking the surface and managing to get a couple of breaths before the current sucked me under the water again. I was fighting to claw my way to the surface and managed to kick my jeans off. Suddenly, I bobbed to the surface again. I was sucking in the freezing cold air and I could feel myself slowly seizing up with the cold. I just kept fighting for my life until I reached the bank. I didn't want to die in that river, Tom.'

Tom put both his arms around her again and said, 'That's it sweetheart, it's all out now. You don't need to say another word, just hold me. I'm here now, I'll never let you face that danger again.'

CHAPTER 43

6.00am 26th April 1991
Hilton Hotel, Mayfair, London

'And you're sure that you would definitely recognise the two men who chased you and shot you before you jumped into the River Foyle?'

The man asking the question was Richard Stretton, the head of the debrief unit that had been living in the next suite of rooms along the corridor. Once Bailey had calmed down and composed herself, she had asked Tom to go and bring the debrief team to her room.

The team, and Stretton in particular, had listened patiently as Bailey recounted the final pieces in the jigsaw of what had happened to her that night. He was beaming when she mentioned that she would remember the faces of the thugs and now he wanted to clarify that was definitely the case.

Bailey looked Stretton in the eye and said, 'One hundred per cent. I'd definitely recognise them both again.'

Stretton beamed, 'That's great. If you can identify them, we can get them detained and interrogated. We might just find out who or what The Death Adder is. Excuse me, I need to let the Director know this news immediately.'

Stretton left the room.

Tom was beginning to feel increasingly uneasy.

He had a strong idea what was going to happen next. If he was right, there was no way he was going to allow it. He moved across the room and sat beside Bailey on the sofa, placing a protective arm around her shoulders. Other members of the debrief team continued to ask her questions about her ordeal in the river, trying to obtain details about what had happened once she had managed to get out.

It was the comments made by Stretton before he had left the room that worried Tom, he recognised the direction the debrief was taking and the importance he had placed on Bailey's confirmed identification of the thugs that had tried to kill her.

An hour later and there was a loud knock on Bailey's hotel room door. Tom pulled Bailey in closer to him as Stretton answered the door.

Sir Godfrey Winstanley strutted into the room, walked across to Bailey and said matter of factly, 'Congratulations Miss Masters, Stretton's told me that you've now managed to recall the entire catalogue of events in Londonderry. I've given your situation a lot of thought and I've made a decision as to how we proceed from here.'

Here it comes, thought Tom. He stiffened and stared hard at the Director.

Winstanley made unblinking eye contact with Tom and said, 'Mr Naylor I presume? I'm going to have to ask you to leave the room at this time.'

Tom looked incredulously at the diminutive man in front of him and said quietly, 'That's not going to happen, I'm staying right here.'

Without raising his voice, the Director said, 'That wasn't a request Mr Naylor, you need to leave right now. We cannot discuss what we need to talk about in front of you, your security clearance simply isn't high enough.'

Tom started to rise as he felt an anger beginning to surge through him. Bailey gripped his forearm and said, 'It's okay Tom, just leave. This won't take long I promise.'

Tom looked at her and slowly shook his head, 'Bailey, you're not going back over there.'

'It's okay, just leave. Everything will be fine, I promise.'

Tom stood up and walked slowly over to the door staring hard at Winstanley as he did so. He reached the door and looked back at Bailey who mouthed silently, "just go".

Tom stepped outside the room into the corridor.

Waiting directly outside the hotel room door were two very large, burly men in ill-fitting dark suits. They stood either side of him and one said abruptly, 'We'll direct you to the exit Mr Naylor.'

Tom tensed and said, 'That's not necessary, really.'

'We insist', came the reply.

Tom shrugged his shoulders and walked off along the corridor followed closely by the two men.

Back in the hotel room the Director looked at Bailey and said, 'Your Mr Naylor is a somewhat spirited individual, isn't he?'

Bailey replied, 'He has my best interests at heart.'

'As we all do, Miss Masters, as we all do. Anyway, I've made my decision. You will indeed be going back to Londonderry. I need you to identify the two men who attacked you. They will then be detained and interrogated by Special Branch and ourselves. Do you have any questions?'

'No sir. I've no questions, but can you make sure that Tom gets back to Nottingham safely? Will it be possible for someone to explain to him why this is necessary?'

'Naylor will be escorted back to Nottingham today. I'm not prepared to enlighten him about our future plans, Miss Masters. His security clearance isn't high enough. You're fully aware that this is the case, you shouldn't even consider breaking that protocol, let alone asking me to do it. I really don't see any future for you and Naylor. When this is over, you'll have some serious decisions to make about your career in the service.'

Bailey nodded, 'I know that Sir. When do I leave for Londonderry?'

'Immediately. Stretton's going to drive you to RAF Northolt, there's a Chinook waiting to fly you back to Northern Ireland this afternoon.'

Bailey stood and followed Stretton out of the hotel room.

The Director took out his phone and dialled a number, 'Ah, Brenda, it's the Director here. I need you to make contact with Special Branch in Nottinghamshire again, I think we may have a slight problem with Mr Naylor that will need nipping in the bud. Call me on the secure line in an hour when I get back to the office and I'll explain. I think a simple phone call over the Brent system to the Special Branch Inspector should suffice. Talk to you in an hour.'

CHAPTER 44

4.00pm 26th April 1991
Nottinghamshire Police Headquarters

Detective Inspector Nick Murray was just thinking about switching his computer off and leaving for home when the Brent telephone in the corner of his office began to ring.

He picked the phone up and waited for the person on the other end of the line to speak first.

After a few seconds a woman's voice said, 'Hello.'

Nick replied, 'DI Murray here.'

'Ah Nick! I'm glad it's you. Brenda Starkey here. I need to talk to you about Pc Naylor, it seems like we may have a problem.'

'A problem? How?'

'It would appear that he isn't over enamoured about his girlfriend's recent orders. Apparently, he caused a bit of a ruckus in London and had to be escorted from the hotel. I don't have all the details Nick, but Pc Naylor needs to be advised by his senior officer that there's nothing he can do to change anything and that his inappropriate behaviour needs to cease forthwith. I don't suppose for one minute he would, but if he did anything that jeopardised our operations so to speak, he would find himself in big trouble. You understand where I'm coming from Nick, do you think you can sort this out?'

'I'm sure I can Brenda. Naylor's gaffer is very much 'old school', he'll rein him in. I did think this was always a possibility when you asked him to go down there. I'm sure after his boss has spoken to him, he'll do as he's told, don't worry.'

'I hope so Nick, after all we don't want any unpleasantness.'

'Leave it with me Brenda, I'll sort it.'

The line went dead.

Nick reached for his landline and dialled a number.

He said, 'Chief Inspector Chambers, it's Nick Murray at Special Branch, we need to have a conversation about Pc Naylor as soon as you're available.'

The reply was equally short and to the point, 'I'm in my office now if you want to come over.'

'On my way.'

CHAPTER 45

8.30pm 27th April 1991
West Coast of Scotland

Once again Sean O'Connor found himself leaning on the rail of a ship, looking out as a rugged landscape came into view.

Instead of an African tramp steamer, this time he was aboard a small, fishing boat that had made the short trip across the Irish Sea from Larne on the northern coast of Ireland to the remote fishing village of Barcaldine on the near deserted west coast of Scotland.

The light was gradually changing from daylight to dusk and the orange hues from the setting sun made the cliffs surrounding the small harbour glow as if they were on fire. It had been a flat calm crossing and a very warm day for early Spring.

O'Connor was growing impatient to be ashore now; he was desperate to get started on his mission.

Ever since Eddie Macready had briefed him with his outrageous plan for revenge, he had felt a burning urgency to get underway. O'Connor couldn't think of a better, more spectacular way to strike back at the British, than to attack the symbolic head of the nation, the Royal Family.

He'd been relieved when Macready informed him that the girl who had been caught eavesdropping on the plan when it was first discussed in O'Doyle's Bar, had been found dead in the river.

Macready's son Danny, had been beside himself. He had taken the girl out on a couple of occasions and had insisted that the barmaid had nothing to do with the authorities and had only run from the bar because she was terrified of the two thugs his father had sent after her.

O'Connor knew that was all bullshit.

From what Eddie Macready had told him, it was obvious that the bitch from Liverpool was a Brit spy. As far as he was concerned, the best place for her was six feet under the ground in a cold grave.

O'Connor had been relieved at news of her death for two reasons. Firstly, because it now meant he was free to continue on the mission and more importantly because it meant that the British still had no idea of the outrageous assassination plot.

As the small boat got ever closer to the harbour, the fishing village of Barcaldine looked idyllic in the rapidly fading light. It was a picture postcard image of white walled cottages with blue grey slate roofs and brightly coloured doors and window frames.

Nobody in the village would give the small fishing boat entering the harbour a second glance. Every single day of the year boats such as this would enter the harbour in the evening to land their catches of cod and herring. The crews of the boats would then enjoy the hospitality of the two pubs in the village, before sleeping on their vessels for the night. The same boats would then set off out to sea again in the morning to fish on their return journey to Ireland.

Fishing like this had been happening since days of old.

The IRA had been quick to seize on this relaxed avenue into mainland Britain. All the sleeper active service units on the mainland were re-supplied via this route. The republicans knew only too well that there was just a lone police officer to watch the miles of desolate coastline around Barcaldine and other similar fishing villages along the coast.

As the fishing boat drew alongside the quay, Sean O'Connor, always the consummate professional, took the precaution of slipping into the small cabin away from any prying eyes on the dockside.

He sat down in the cabin, his legs resting on his Bergen kit bag and the long, black carry bag that contained the lethal Barratt sniper rifle.

His mind was fully concentrated on the forthcoming mission.

He knew there was a contact waiting to meet him off the boat. He'd no idea who that contact was, he only knew it was a woman who lived in Barcaldine. He would have to rely on the pre-arranged signals and passwords to identify her.

The woman waiting to meet O'Connor was Caitlin Stuart. She was born and bred in Barcaldine, the only child of Morag and Donal Stuart. When her father had died, Morag had moved in with another fisherman who lived in Oban. As soon as she was old enough, Caitlin had left to go to University. When she later dropped out of further education, she moved back to Barcaldine to live on her own.

She despised the English and was a devout Catholic, as well as a militant member of the Scottish Nationalist Party. She felt a strong kinship towards her Irish neighbours and what they were being forced to endure as they struggled to rid their country of the English invaders.

She was still young, only twenty-two years old, but she'd already served a twelve month prison sentence for arson after being convicted of burning two holiday cottages owned by English families to the ground.

Caitlin had been out of prison for over two years now and had deliberately avoided all contact with the law since her release. She'd behaved impeccably and hadn't featured on the local police officer's watch list for well over a year.

From the outside, it appeared to everyone in the close-knit community that Caitlin had been very immature and had made a stupid mistake as a youngster. They considered the arson offence was just a foolish episode of a young girl's life who at the time was both very young and very impressionable.

Following her release from prison, she'd obtained work in a local guest house through a prison release scheme. The job came with a small flat that was just two streets back from the harbour. She had worked hard and been pleasant to everyone in her community.

In reality, she was still a troubled young woman who was waiting patiently, biding her time, for the next opportunity to strike out at the establishment.

Daylight had now disappeared completely, the quayside was lit by two lamps that both emitted a feeble, white light that reflected back off the grey cobbles.

Caitlin waited in the shadows that had been formed by those two dull, white lights. From those dark shadows, adjacent to the ice houses she stood motionless, watching as the fishing boat drew alongside the quay. She knew that this particular boat, sailing out of Larne had no fish to land this evening. Instead it was carrying a very important passenger.

As she had been instructed, Caitlin was wearing a dark green, woollen hat that would identify her to the man she was to meet off the boat. She'd been told nothing of this stranger, she only knew that he was coming into the country without the knowledge of the authorities. She had no idea of the reason for his visit to the mainland and she didn't want to know.

It had been explained to her, that her role was to assist this man in any way she could. She was to offer him transport, food and lodgings. Basically, she was to provide anything and everything he wanted.

The old man who had approached her with the task was a regular visitor to the guest house where Caitlin worked. She had often spoken to him in the past about politics and life in general. She had quickly realised that the old man was a supporter of Irish nationalism and their conversations often turned towards the Troubles. The old man revelled in the talks, pleased to find someone who felt the same way as he did.

Ever since she had been tasked by the old man, she'd felt a growing tension rising within her. It was a mixture of apprehension, fear and excitement.

It was the moment Caitlin Stuart had been waiting for.

It made her feel alive again.

From a young age, she had always been fascinated by the armed struggle of small groups of individuals against mighty nations. She had spent her brief spell at St Andrews University studying the written works of various terrorist leaders.

Like everyone else on the campus she had read various articles on subversive activity, but unlike the other students Caitlin had also studied how to make rudimentary explosive devices and weapon handling.

Caitlin wasn't a confused, immature young woman, she knew exactly what she wanted to achieve in her life. Notoriety was her single goal; she longed to be remembered as someone who had taken the armed struggle forward and had made a difference by positive action.

Now, as she waited in the shadows by the side of the ice house, she could see that the fishing boat she had been watching had finally been moored. The two-man crew had made the vessel secure by tying two large ropes to the quayside and had then jumped ashore.

She watched as both fishermen walked off along the quay laughing and joking, already anticipating their first pint and a good, hearty meal at one of the two pubs.

Caitlin remained in the shadows until she was sure nobody else was loitering in the area. Once satisfied that she was alone, she stepped forward and stood below one of the two white lamps for a few seconds, before quickly stepping back into the shadows.

O'Connor had been peering from the small cabin on the boat waiting for just this action. As soon as he saw the woman step back into the shadows, he moved stealthily off the boat carrying the two large bags with him.

He moved directly into the same black shadow he had seen the woman step into.

Caitlin spoke up softly but confidently, 'Liam is that you? Liam from Donegal?'

O'Connor knew the pre-arranged passwords and responded immediately, 'Yes. Is that Katie from Inverness?'

Caitlin now stepped forward to properly greet the stranger.

As they both stepped out of the shadows and into the soft white light, for the first time she got a good look at the tall, handsome, dark skinned, muscular stranger.

Instantly, she experienced what felt like a mild electric shock, as a tingling sensation surged through her body.

Slightly breathless, she said quietly, 'Welcome to Scotland Liam. Let's get off the quayside and away to my flat in the village.'

O'Connor never said a word, he just hoisted the Bergen onto his broad shoulders and picked up the rifle carry case.

As he followed Caitlin through the dark, cobbled alleyways he spoke for the first time. In his soft Irish brogue, he commented, 'Nice hat, by the way.'

Caitlin immediately whipped off the old woollen hat, exposing her long auburn hair, shaking it free with a flourish. She smiled at the softly spoken Irishman and could feel her face blushing when he smiled back.

After a brisk two-minute walk they arrived at the door to her flat. It was on the first floor, above a derelict chandler's shop. The paint was peeling from the old sign hanging loosely above the large bay window on the ground floor.

O'Connor quickly glanced around; it was perfect. Very secluded, a quiet corner of a quiet village.

They went inside and climbed the narrow flight of stairs to the first floor. O'Connor placed his bags on the floor and looked out of the bay window that mirrored the one on the ground floor. From the elevated position he could see across the rooftops of the single storey ice houses to the harbour less than fifty yards away. The inky black sea, now illuminated by a bright full moon.

Caitlin switched on the light and pulled the heavy drapes in the bay window.

'Can I get you something to eat?' she asked.

'That would be great, I'm famished.'

Looking around her tiny flat she said, 'I'm sorry it's only a small flat, but it comes with my job at the guest house and the rent's very low. You can have the bedroom; I'll sleep on the sofa in here.'

'That's very sweet of you Katie, but I'm used to sleeping on much worse than that sofa. That will do me fine until we're ready to move down south.'

O'Connor saw the girl's eyes widen and he realised that she had absolutely no idea what his mission entailed.

'Listen Katie, I don't want to insult you, but it's obvious to me that you've no idea why I'm here. What have you been told?'

'Nothing at all, and I don't want to know either. All you need to know is that I'm willing to help you in any way I can, Liam.'

He could now see the burning passion in her eyes and for the first time he noticed how stunningly beautiful she was, with her long, ruby red hair and green eyes sparkling with a ferocity he hadn't encountered for quite a while.

He laughed and said, 'I just know that you and me are going to get on famously, darling.'

She smiled, 'Will egg and chips be okay for tonight?'

'That would be perfect with a nice hot cup of sweet tea. Now is there anywhere safe I can leave that bag over there?', he nodded towards his rifle case.

'If you mean the long bag? That should fit easily under my bed, if that's okay?'

'Just promise me one thing Katie, don't ever touch that case and never look inside. Do you understand?'

For the first time Caitlin caught a glimpse of the coldness behind those sparkling blue eyes and she noticed how quickly the smiling demeanour of the stranger had changed to a deadly seriousness.

'Okay, I promise.'

She walked into the kitchen to prepare his meal and as she began peeling the potatoes, a smile played across her lips as she anticipated just what might happen between her and the handsome, enigmatic stranger who had just come into her life.

CHAPTER 46

6.00am 28th April 1991
Nottinghamshire Police Headquarters

The telephone call the night before had been short and to the point. When Tom had answered the call at nine o'clock, he'd half expected it to be the Duty Inspector with a call-out for a job. Instead, he had been shocked to hear the voice of his boss, Jim Chambers.

He had been even more surprised to hear the edgy tone in the man's voice.

The instruction had been terse and delivered in a very clipped fashion, 'Be at The Huts at six o'clock tomorrow morning. We need to talk', Chambers had told him coldly.

Now, as he drove his car into the deserted car park at headquarters, he could see that The Huts were in total darkness, except for a solitary light burning behind the opaque glass. Tom knew that light was shining from Jim Chambers' office.

His boss was already here and waiting. Tom wasn't too surprised; he'd often thought Chambers lived at The Huts and was married to the job.

As he locked his car, Tom's mind was racing. Why had he been summoned so brusquely for what was obviously going to be a private meeting? What was going on?

Tom opened the door to The Huts and walked along the main corridor towards Chambers office. Before he got to the office door, Chambers voice boomed out from inside, 'Get yourself a brew if you want one Naylor, then get in here. We need to talk.'

Once again Tom's mind was in a turmoil. Why was the comment so abrupt, bordering on aggressive? He was puzzled, he had never heard Chambers like this. It was almost as if his boss had been rattled by something.

Tom didn't want a coffee so he carried on walking and knocked on the office door, before walking in.

Without looking up from the papers spread all over his desk Chambers said, 'Sit down. We need to get a few things sorted out.'

As he sat down, Tom looked closely at his boss. It looked like he'd been at his desk all night. His eyes were bloodshot red, there was tell-tale stubble on his face. The shirt he was wearing was unbuttoned at the neck and looked grimy. There were also the remains of four half-drunk cups of black coffee on the desk.

Tom sat down and said, 'What's this all about boss?'

'You may well ask, Naylor. I've been asking myself that same question ever since Special Branch took a telephone call from London a couple of days ago. As you're fully aware Naylor, shit always rolls downhill and it's ended up here on my fucking desk. What the fuck happened between you and Winstanley?'

'Nothing happened. I just told that old spook exactly what I thought of him and his fucked-up plan to send Bailey back over to Northern Ireland. The man's a sanctimonious, self-serving prick who's using her for his own ends. Before our conversation got too heated, I was asked to leave anyway, so what's the problem?'

'And did you leave?'

'I didn't have a lot of choice, I was physically ushered out of the hotel and taken to the train station by two of Winstanley's muscle bound goons. It's disgusting boss, they're just using Bailey and she can't see it.'

Chambers sat back in his chair and let out an exasperated sigh, before placing his face in his hands and slowly shaking his head from side to side. After a few seconds he looked up with a worried expression on his face.

Using a softer tone, he said, 'Tom. Take it from me, you've no idea what you're dealing with here. These aren't your normal, average people. That whole institution is staffed by people with only one thing on their minds, the safety and wellbeing of a nation. That "old spook" as you referred to him, is himself driven by those very ideals. He wouldn't hesitate for a single heartbeat to put any of his staff in harm's way, if he felt it was for the greater good. More importantly, what you need to understand is the fact that he will not hesitate to remove any obstacle to achieve that aim. Can you grasp what I'm telling you?'

'You're telling me that I'm in danger of becoming just such an obstacle.'

It was a statement not a question.

Chambers sighed again, 'Look, I know how much you care about Bailey and how much she means to you. I'm also fully aware of your history, I understand why you're so protective towards her after what happened to Bev, but you've got to back off and let Bailey do her job. If you don't, you will be perceived as interference and you'll be removed from the equation.'

With a look of incredulity on his face Tom asked, 'Am I being threatened here?'

Chambers responded angrily, 'Don't be so fucking melodramatic man! Understand this Naylor, from this moment on, you're to have no further contact with Bailey Masters, until she contacts you. Is that clear enough for you?'

His own voice filled with anger, Tom replied vehemently, 'Until you call me into this office and inform me, ever so apologetically, that she's been injured or killed in the line of duty. Is that how it goes?'

The anger had risen within Tom as he realised the futility of his situation. Deep down he knew he was powerless to change anything.

Jim Chambers adopted a more conciliatory approach, 'Tom, I've worked with you for a number of years now and I respect you both as a man and as a police officer. So, on this one occasion, I'll allow you that show of ill manners and disrespect. I'm truly sorry about the situation and if I'd known it would end like this, I would never have agreed to their request for you to go down to London to spend time with Bailey. I'm sure this situation will work itself out and that she'll be in touch with you very soon. I think you both need to then take some time to consider your futures.'

Tom slowly shook his head, stared directly at Chambers and said quietly, 'With respect, sir, you're no better than Winstanley. I thought you'd arranged for me to visit Bailey because you cared how I felt after I found out she'd been wounded. It turns out you were just dancing to Winstanley's tune all along. You've used me to help them get the information they needed, which has led directly to the person I love being placed in harm's way, again. How do you sleep at night? You're right about one thing though, we'll both have some serious decisions to make once this is all done.'

'I'm sorry you feel like that. Just for once, try and see the bigger picture here. If that bomb in Newcastle had exploded just thirty minutes later, hundreds of innocent people would have been killed or injured. It would have been carnage. You and Bailey both know the cruel, indiscriminate way these terrorists operate, she understands the threat they present to the public and that's why she's ready and willing to place herself in danger to stop them. Nobody's forcing her to do anything against her will. If you want my honest opinion and seeing as how we're speaking man to man, I think this has nothing to do with Bailey. This is all about you, it's baggage from your history and the circumstances that surrounded Bev's murder. You can't change the past Tom. It's already happened. You either put it to one side or allow it to cloud every decision you make for the rest of your life.'

Tom could feel himself shaking as a volcanic rage built inside him. He'd never been spoken to like this. He would never have allowed anybody else to talk to him so bluntly, so coldly.

Chambers was in full flow now, 'I'm not being cruel for the sake of it. Contrary to what you may believe at this moment, I do care deeply about you and Bailey, but I have to weigh that care and compassion against the responsibilities I have to the safety of the general public. I know that deep down, you understand what I'm saying Tom.'

Slowly, Tom could feel the anger within him subsiding as he realised that every word Chambers had said made perfect sense. He realised that his over protective attitude towards

Bailey was irrational and had more to do with the fate that had befallen Bev.

Seeing that Tom was calming down Chambers pressed on, 'Do you honestly think Bailey welcomes your interference in her career? I'm sure she would prefer you just to be proud of her efforts.'

Rubbing his eyes to try and alleviate the stinging sensation he was experiencing, Tom spoke quietly, 'Of course I'm proud of her, she knows that. I know that my protective feelings are irrational and I know where they come from. I'm trying my best to deal with that. I also know that whatever happens next is Bailey's choice and that she's deeply committed to the fight. I'll take on board what you've said this morning. I'll just keep my head down, get on with doing my job and let Bailey get on with doing hers. Tell Winstanley and his cronies that I won't be a problem they need to worry about.'

'Thanks Tom.'

'Just promise me one thing, please keep me fully posted if you hear anything from either Winstanley or her immediate bosses. You know anything you tell me will go no further. I give you my word that I won't try to contact Bailey in any way.'

Chambers stood up and offered his hand which Tom readily took and the two men shook hands.

'Thanks boss.'

'I knew you'd get the bigger picture Tom. You need to get home; I believe you're on an afternoon shift later today. I don't want you to be late.'

'Don't worry boss, I'll be here.'

CHAPTER 47

10.00am 5th May 1991
Cosquer, Brest, France

The small room above the dingy Café de Flore on the Rue de Pont-a-Louet was heavy with thick blue smoke from the countless cigarettes that had already been smoked that morning. The walls of the small windowless room had a permanent yellow staining, residue from the countless cigarettes smoked during the many meetings held there.

The café situated in a province just outside Brest had, for the past ten years, been used regularly by the Provisional IRA to hold clandestine meetings away from the prying eyes and ears of the Security Services.

It was impossible to imagine how many bombings and shootings had been sanctioned from this very room and how many innocent lives had been lost as a result of those decisions.

At the head of the table, as usual, sat Francis Holmes, the Chief of Staff flanked by his bodyguard Ben Christie. Holmes had the final say on all matters of policy and strategy. Without his approval and sanction, nothing could happen.

To his right sat Eoin McAteer, the Sinn Fein representative who never missed one of these meetings in Northern France.

Sitting on the left of Holmes was Michael Delaney.

Delaney was the man responsible for raising funds across the USA. He had been instrumental in the acquisition of the

Barratt rifle that had been used with such deadly effectiveness in the border counties.

He now lived permanently in the States and had flown into Charles de Gaulle Airport, from Boston two days ago, specifically to attend this meeting. He would milk the expenses from the organisation and spend another couple of days in Paris after the meeting. He was in no rush to get back to Boston.

Delaney was a very polished individual who took care over his appearance, he always wore a smart, tailored suit, shirt and tie. He was very dapper and considered himself to be a lady's man. He was now forty-six and still single, due mainly to his philandering ways.

As a result of the good life he enjoyed in America, where he was feted as a minor celebrity around the Irish Bars that were so popular in Boston and New York, he had recently started to pile on the pounds.

This was due to an idle, indolent lifestyle, far too many large meals and copious amounts of alcohol. The powder blue, Armani suit he was wearing for the meeting was now very tight fitting around his corpulent waist and the rolls of fat on his neck were starting to spill over his shirt collar.

The man from Boston detested smoking and being in the small room filled with secondary smoke was aggravating him and making his eyes water. He'd never been comfortable in these surroundings and longed for the meeting to be over so he could drive his hired Citroen back to the swanky Hotel de Crillon in the centre of Paris.

He found the petty arguments between men he considered to be no better than criminals and gangsters to be tedious and very boring.

Delaney was also switched on enough to know that he had to play the game. If it was ever perceived that his usefulness had come to an end, he knew that would mean only one thing. An anonymous shadowy figure stepping out of some dark alley in Boston one night firing a bullet through the back of his head.

Across the table from Delaney, sat Eddie Macready and Glen Phelan from Londonderry. Both men fidgeted, obviously uncomfortable in this company.

Phelan was simply scared shitless and nervously kept stealing a glance across the room at McGuire who simply stared back never uttering a word.

Macready, on the other hand, was just totally pissed off. Once again, he felt as though he'd been forced to attend this meeting, just so he could be told what he could and couldn't do, like some errant schoolboy.

The Londonderry man had been summoned to this so-called strategy meeting after word had somehow got back to Francis Holmes about the planned assassination attempt on a member of the Royal Family.

Macready was convinced that the plan had been leaked to Holmes by Aiden Cross and he made a mental note to deal with Cross on his return. Macready considered Cross to be a weasel of a man who could no longer be trusted and that meant only one thing. In the very near future Aiden Cross would be disposed of. Any man who could not be trusted implicitly was a liability and there was only one way to deal with a problem of that kind. Cross would be taken from his home one night in the very near future and executed. It was as harsh and as simple as that.

After Macready had been told by Holmes to provide the meeting with detailed plans of the targeted assassination, his proposal had already been the subject of discussion for thirty minutes.

Patterson lit yet another cigarette, took a deep pull from it and spoke as he exhaled the blue smoke, 'Look Eddie, it's simply out of the question. You know where we all stand on the Royals. We rely heavily on the money from NORAID to arm ourselves and continue the struggle. Without that funding from our American supporters we'll be left with nothing more than rocks and bottles to throw at the Brits.'

Macready looked scornfully at Patterson, 'I know that's the position in Belfast Jimmy, but over in Derry we have our own ways of funding the struggle.'

'By robbing a few banks, you mean. How long's that going to last?'

'We need to make a statement that strikes at the very head of the establishment after our recent bad luck. We had stockpiled a lot of explosives and arms, all gone. We have lost four good men, one dead and three captured. All this achieved by a few local cops in a sleepy backwater like Nottingham. Just the newspaper headlines alone were a huge embarrassment. We need this strike to regain some credibility.'

Delaney now spoke with an air of disdain in his voice that carried more than a hint of a Boston accent, 'Eddie, do you honestly think that by killing a member of the Royal Family you're going to gain credibility? Have you any idea how well respected the Royals are in America? You'll set our cause back twenty years with this crazy idea. We'll no longer be welcomed anywhere; we'll be unable to raise funds and any political goodwill we currently enjoy in the States would be wiped out as fast as the bullet used to kill the Prince. It's a ridiculous idea that shouldn't be sanctioned.'

Macready could barely disguise his loathing of the fat pompous man from Boston. Glaring across the table he said, 'You sit there and speak of our cause as if you know something about it. What exactly do you know about our struggle? When was the last time any of your family were interned without trial? When was the last time your home was invaded at three o'clock in the morning by British soldiers with guns, scaring your woman and kids shitless? You know nothing my fancy friend, so sit there and keep your fucking gob shut while me, Frankie and Jimmy sort this fucker out. Okay?'

As Macready's voice rose to a crescendo, McGuire leaned forward on his chair. Patterson shot him a glance and the giant settled back on his chair again.

It was Holmes who spoke next, 'Eddie, there might be a grain of truth in what you just said to our friend Delaney. Maybe he's a little out of touch with the everyday suffering of our people at the hands of the RUC and British soldiers, but he's the only man in this room who can speak about the political will and cash flow from America that we as a movement rely upon. He's had a long, arduous journey to be here, to offer his considered advice, so when you talk to him, do so with a little more respect.'

Macready fixed Holmes with a cold stare, then shot the same look towards Patterson before saying quietly, 'Don't lecture me about who I should or shouldn't respect. I couldn't give a shit how far he's travelled. The man is nothing more than a pompous prick who's sponged off this organisation for far too long. I'll not listen to any of his so called considered advice. As far as I'm concerned, he's got nothing to add to this conversation.'

Delaney leapt to his feet, 'Pompous prick, am I? You seem to have forgotten that it was me that supplied you with the sniper rifle that you intend to kill the Prince of Wales with. Fuck you, Macready.'

As the arguments got heated and voices were raised, once again McGuire became agitated.

Macready said menacingly, 'Jimmy, you'd better tell your man to stop eyeballing me or this meeting is going to end very badly.'

Delaney sat back down and Patterson said, 'Eddie, calm down for fucks sake! We're all on the same side here. Let's try and deal with this rationally. We've all listened to your plan and although I haven't witnessed his skills first hand, I've heard great things about your man, Sean O'Connor. Personally speaking, I'm sure your plan would work and that O'Connor would be successful. I couldn't give a shit if the entire Royal Family were all killed tomorrow, but this is not about us personally. This is simply about what's best for our struggle in the long term. It's never been about some quick fix to repair damaged reputations. Our struggle has been ongoing for a hundred years, we're playing the long game, we always have. We don't deal in hastily hatched revenge missions. This isn't personal Eddie, but I'm totally against this mission.'

Macready sat back and grunted.

Holmes said, 'Eoin, what's the view of Sinn Fein?'

McAteer said quietly, 'We're totally against pursuing this course of action, we feel it would do irreparable damage politically. It shouldn't be sanctioned.'

Holmes leaned forward and said, 'I've listened to everyone. I think it's a good plan that would have every chance of a successful outcome, however at this time I feel that it's not in the best interest of our organisation and I cannot sanction this operation. Eddie, you must contact O'Connor immediately and tell him not to travel to the mainland. His mission is aborted, at this moment in time any attempt on the lives of the Royal Family is forbidden. I'm sorry.'

Macready stood up and walked towards the door, quickly followed by Phelan, who couldn't wait to get out of there. As he reached the door, Macready turned to face Holmes, he grinned before snarling, 'I'll do my best to call O'Connor off, but he's already over the water. If I can't get in touch with him there'll be no stopping him. As you're all aware, the man's a killing machine.'

Holmes had heard enough, he stood and shouted, 'Listen to me Macready, this is no longer up for fucking debate. I've made my decision. You get this half-arsed revenge mission stopped and you do it today, or the consequences for you personally and for the Derry Brigade will be dire. I'm not fucking about; this mission does not happen. Do I make myself clear?'

Macready chuckled and said mockingly, 'Yes Francis. Anything you say. I'll call him off today.'

Macready left the room closely followed by Phelan. Quickly, they made their way down the narrow flight of stairs and out of the café. They stepped out into bright sunshine that made both men squint as they walked back to their hire car. A twenty-minute drive would take them back to the harbour in Brest, where a fishing boat was waiting to ferry them back to Cork.

Phelan gunned the engine of the Peugeot and drove out of Cosquer. As he drove, he said, 'Jesus, Eddie. I thought for one minute you were going to refuse to call it off. How soon do you want me to contact O'Connor?'

'Are you fucking mad? I'm not calling anything off. I've taken orders from Holmes and that fat prick Patterson for the last time. We've got our own fundraisers; we don't need pathetic handouts from that sly piece of shit, Delaney. We do alright from our own people in Boston and New York, we don't need his money. Sean O'Connor will continue his mission. I just wish I could be there to see the look on that arrogant shit, Patterson's face when he reads the paper the morning after the Prince of Wales has become the latest victim of The Death Adder.'

Macready chuckled to himself at the thought of that image. Phelan, ever the thinker, sat quietly with a worried expression on his face as he drove the car towards Brest.

Back in the upstairs room at the Café de Flore, Delaney said, 'Do you believe him Francis? Do you think he'll call off O'Connor?'

A very concerned looking Holmes said, 'Not a prayer, he's a total loose cannon these days. He gets angrier and more belligerent every year that passes. He's rapidly losing focus on what we're trying to achieve. The movement just can't afford to allow this killing to proceed. If Macready isn't going to stop O'Connor, then I must. I've got to act for the good of the cause or I'd be failing in my responsibilities.'

Eoin McAteer nodded in silent approval.

Delaney said, 'I don't understand, how are you going to stop him?'

Holmes replied, 'Michael, you've got a long journey back to Paris. Why don't you let me worry about the details? Keep up the good work over there, we're all relying on you.'

The two men shook hands and hugged each other before Delaney left the room, quickly followed by McAteer.

Holmes waited a few minutes and then addressed the three men left in the room, Patterson, McGuire and Christie, 'Does anyone know Sean O'Connor?'

In his soft lilting voice McGuire said, 'I knew his father, he was a good man. I've only met Sean on one occasion and I found him to be a very capable man and an accomplished sniper. Without doubt, he's one of the best I've ever seen. I wouldn't like to think I was ever in his cross hairs.'

Francis Holmes knew that coming from a man as formidable as McGuire, that was high praise indeed.

Holmes said, 'Anyone else got anything to add?'

The room remained silent.

Holmes was deep in thought, slowly digesting what McGuire had said. Eventually, the Chief of Staff looked directly at McGuire and said, 'Right McGuire, this is my thinking. I'll do everything in my power to lean on Eddie Macready to get O'Connor back from the mainland and the mission aborted. Thanks to Aiden Cross, we know where they intend to carry out the hit. If we can't get O'Connor back, I want you to be in position to take him out. It's a bad situation, but at this moment in time we just can't afford for anything to happen to the Royal Family. It will set our movement back massively. Why couldn't that idiot Macready target a politician, nobody gives a fuck about any of them lying arseholes!'

McGuire's expression didn't change, 'I'll leave this evening and be in England by tomorrow night', he said softly.

Patterson said, 'Go to our sleeper cell in Hammersmith, everything you'll need to stop O'Connor will be waiting for you there. I know this will be difficult, but it's vital O'Connor is stopped. Do you understand?'

The big man nodded, picked up the Armalite rifle, slipped it under his long black coat and left the room.

Patterson lit another cigarette as he followed McGuire down the stairs. His thoughts turned to Eddie Macready. It was time the Chief of Staff addressed the problem and did something about the permanent friction between Derry and Belfast caused by Macready and his old-fashioned ideas.

Patterson decided there and then that if the Chief of Staff wasn't prepared to deal with it, he would. No matter how this debacle with O'Connor ended, Macready would be removed, sooner rather than later and in one way or another.

CHAPTER 48

1.00pm 7th May 1991
Newark, Nottinghamshire

It had been ten days since Sean O'Connor had arrived in Scotland. After two days of lying low, cooped up in Caitlin Stuart's two roomed flat in the small fishing village of Barcaldine, he'd travelled south with Caitlin to the historic, tourist city of York in North Yorkshire.

The plan was for them to travel together posing as newlyweds who were spending their honeymoon in the picturesque city. The reality was far different, it was to be the forward reconnaissance base for their planned atrocity in Newark, Nottinghamshire.

The first leg of the journey had been made in Caitlin's battered, old Vauxhall Viva. They had driven down as far south as Newcastle. Once there they had left the Vauxhall Viva parked in the free long stay car park of the railway station. They had then walked a short distance to a back street car hire firm where they hired a metallic blue Rover SD1 saloon to complete their journey south to York.

As soon as they arrived in the medieval city, they found a small bed and breakfast in Heworth, not far from the city centre. From the leaded light windows of their bedroom they could see the impressive York Minster towering above the walled city.

For the first couple of days they had acted out the role of loved up tourists, visiting all the sights the city had to offer, strolling around the tops of the fortified walls and enjoying quiet evenings in small, romantic restaurants and quaint, quirky pubs with low ceilings and roaring open fires.

Caitlin could never have imagined just how quickly her life was going to change when she had agreed to meet the mysterious Irishman off the boat in Barcaldine.

She had realised very early on that she was falling in love with the tall, handsome stranger with the piercing blue eyes and soft Irish accent.

The two days spent with him after they arrived in York had been the happiest of her short life. What had at first been a pretence, acting as a romantic couple had quickly become reality.

The first night spent in the cosy bedroom of the bed and breakfast had seen Caitlin take the initiative. Very tentatively she had kissed the man she knew only as Liam softly on the lips.

He had responded fully and the kisses had gradually become more and more passionate, until eventually they were caught up in the moment and were desperately pulling at each other's clothes, falling on to the soft bed where they made love throughout the night.

Love was an alien concept to O'Connor, but he enjoyed the physical process of sex and Caitlin was a beautiful woman with a stunning body. It had been a long time since he'd experienced sex as good as it was that first night with the gorgeous red head from Barcaldine.

O'Connor was fully aware that the young woman was falling deeply for him and although he hadn't set out to deliberately hurt her, he knew that when the time came to leave her behind, he would do it without a second thought.

After spending two idyllic days in York, O'Connor decided it was time to move the mission on and to start planning their attack in earnest.

Early on the morning of their third day in York, the two of them had taken the A1 road to Newark. Caitlin had driven while Sean did his best to navigate. The journey had been filled with laughter and it was only as they approached Newark that their mood turned serious. O'Connor in particular suddenly became sullen and fixated on why they were there.

After parking the metallic blue Rover in the car park next to the ruined castle, they had spent the day wandering around the ancient market town, holding hands, window shopping, looking every inch like a young couple lost in love.

They had quickly located the brand-new police station and saw a quaint coffee shop directly across the road from the main entrance. They spent an hour sipping hot cappuccino coffees as they watched the comings and goings of police officers and members of the public.

It was an extremely busy police station; the planners had been right to instantly reject a bomb as the method of assassination. There would be no chance of getting any sort of device anywhere near the building without being detected. A device could be left further away, but the odds of success would be very long indeed.

Quickly making up his mind that the only feasible way to be sure of success was to utilise his considerable skills as a sniper, O'Connor immediately set about the task of looking for a suitable vantage point from which to take the shot.

As they slowly meandered around the old market square, looking for tall buildings that could afford a view of the new police station, Caitlin suddenly stopped walking, cuddled into O'Connor and said, 'Liam, can we get some lunch? I'm starving.'

He nodded and without speaking they again walked hand in hand from the market place back down to the River Trent. As they approached the river, Caitlin saw a beautiful French style bistro on the far bank.

'Can we go over there, it looks beautiful?', she asked.

'Okay, it does look nice. I'm glad it's quiet too, there are a few things I need to tell while we have lunch.'

For a fleeting second, a look of concern came over Caitlin's face, but O'Connor quickly smiled and put his arm around her shoulders to reassure her as they walked over the old bridge that spanned the river. She looked up in awe at the ruins of the enormous castle that towered above them as they made their way to the bistro.

Although still early May, it was a beautiful warm day with hardly a hint of any breeze. They chose a table outside that had a view of the tranquil, slow flowing river below them. The tablecloths were a crisp, red and white check cotton. On the tables were cut glass salt and pepper pots and a tall, glass vase containing a single white carnation. The cutlery was neatly wrapped in white cotton napkins.

The menu was written in French with an English translation below.

It was charming and more importantly virtually deserted. It was still quite early in the day and the Bistro was experiencing that quiet period between breakfast and the main lunch time rush.

A young blonde girl with a smart, black uniform approached them, 'Can I take your order?', she asked politely.

Caitlin said, 'Could you give us a couple more minutes while we look over the menu? Thanks.'

The girl nodded, smiled and said, 'Whenever you're ready to order, I'll just be inside.'

With that she hurried back inside.

Once the young waitress was out of earshot, O'Connor had a quick glance around him. As soon as he was satisfied that nobody could overhear him, he leaned forward and said softly, 'Katie, I need to tell you a few things about what I'm trying to achieve here. I've thought about this and I think that you're just as committed to my cause as I am. You're taking the same risks as me, so I think it's only fair that you know who I am and what I'm about to do.'

Caitlin was shocked and she spluttered, 'Liam, you don't have to explain anything to me. I'm happy to…....'

O'Connor cut her off in mid-sentence, 'My name's Sean, not Liam.'

'Oh!', said a surprised Caitlin.

He continued, 'Listen to me, I've been sent over here to kill somebody. Somebody very, very important. I'm telling you this because I know I can trust you and I think you may be starting to have deep feelings for me. I don't want you to get hurt and there'll come a time soon when I have to leave you behind. I wanted you to understand the reality of the situation. If after I've explained everything you want to leave and let me get on with it, I'll understand. I know I can trust you and that you wouldn't compromise my plans.'

Caitlin was more than a little shocked and sat deep in thought.

When she eventually spoke, she chose her words very carefully, 'Okay as long we're being honest with each other, my name isn't Katie, it's Caitlin. I'm pleased you've told me your real name, but as for the rest of it, I already had some idea that you were over here to be involved in something huge. I've only got one question; will killing this person make a difference to the struggle in your country? Will it really change things?'

O'Connor grinned and said, 'That's two questions Caitlin. Trust me, what I'm about to do will reverberate around the world. It will make a difference all right.'

This was music to Caitlin Stuart's ears; all she had ever wanted, was to be part of something that everyone in the world would remember.

'Sean, I want to stay with you, always. Whatever you're about to do I'm with you and whatever you want me to do I'll gladly do it.'

O'Connor smiled and beckoned over the waitress, 'We're ready to order now, thanks.'

Half an hour later and they were relaxing at the table after finishing a wonderfully light and fluffy mushroom omelette and crisp green salad.

Now slowly sipping their milky café latte's they sat quietly, taking in the lovely views of the ruined castle towering over the slow-moving, dark blue river.

O'Connor suddenly stiffened, 'Do you see what I see?'

Caitlin smiled and said, 'The sunlight sparkling on the river?'

'No, better than that. Can you see the derelict looking building on the far bank way over there? I need to get in there and have a look around. I won't be long. Order another coffee and have a piece of pie with it.'

With that, he stood up smiled and was gone. She watched him striding over the bridge, back towards town to check out the derelict buildings that backed onto the river bank.

As soon as he was out of sight, she beckoned over the waitress and ordered another coffee, feeling full from the omelette, she decided against the pie.

CHAPTER 49

2.30pm 7th May 1991
Newark, Nottinghamshire

Sean O'Connor took one more careful look around the area, as soon as he was satisfied there were no prying eyes watching him, he squeezed through the small gap in the corrugated iron fencing that had been put there to keep youngsters out of the derelict and dangerous building.

Once behind the fencing he relaxed a little and looked around. On the side of the crumbling building was a fading painted sign that read, Swainson and Blackley Mills in large letters.

O'Connor moved swiftly across the waste ground that had once been a bustling car park for the mill employees.

This side of the building was secure. All the doors and windows had metal grilles or covers to prevent people gaining access. Each metal grille had a plastic sign attached that read simply, DANGER – DO NOT ENTER.

Moving quickly, he made his way around to the far side of the deserted, building that backed onto the river. He made his way carefully along the river bank looking for a way inside the property. After a few minutes he found what he'd been searching for. Hidden behind a large growth of bulrushes and an overhanging willow tree he saw a small, wooden door that was hanging on by just one hinge.

Taking care not to slip on the muddy bank, O'Connor moved stealthily into the doorway, careful not to disturb the hanging door. He squeezed through the small gap and into the darkness of the disused building.

Once inside he stood stock still, allowing his body to become attuned to his new surroundings.

He listened intently for any other signs of life within the building. He knew that old, abandoned properties like this one, soon became magnets for rough sleepers trying to find shelter from the elements. The last thing he needed today was a confrontation with an angry, unwashed vagrant who thought someone else was trying to pinch their place to sleep for the night.

After waiting for what seemed an age, O'Connor slowly made his way through the dark building. All the windows on the first three floors of the six-storey building had been boarded up and there was an all-pervading smell of damp throughout the decrepit structure.

Finally, he found a crumbling staircase. Placing his feet carefully he began to ascend the dangerous staircase, taking care not to stumble and fall into the unguarded stairwell. Having reached the sixth floor of the building, O'Connor quickly got his bearings and began searching the skyline for the new police station.

Making sure he placed his feet on the joists so as not to fall through the rotting floorboards, he approached the far end of the building until he was at the furthest point away from the river and the hanging door where he had gained access.

Because it was so far above ground level, none of the windows on the top floor had been boarded up. Virtually every pane of glass had been smashed and there was a constant moaning noise as gusts of wind were sucked into the building.

Looking out from this far end of the building, away in the distance across the rooftops of the historical, market town he got a glimpse of the modern police station.

O'Connor was pleased to see that from this high vantage point, he had a clear unobstructed view of the main entrance to the police station. He estimated the distance to be approximately eleven hundred yards.

At that distance and across rooftops with a swirling, gusting wind it would be a tough shot for anyone. O'Connor had always been confident in his own ability and he knew it was a shot he could accomplish using the Barratt .50 Cal sniper rifle.

A cruel smile flashed across the face of the Death Adder, as he felt the thrill and anticipation of taking the shot rising within him.

'Perfect', he muttered to himself, before retracing his steps out of the building and making his way back across the river to the bistro and a smiling Caitlin.

CHAPTER 50

10.30pm 7th May 1991
Londonderry, Northern Ireland

The knock on the front door of Aiden Cross's semi-detached house on the Creggan Estate had been polite but insistent. As he walked towards the front door he shouted, 'Alright, alright I'm coming!'

He unlocked and opened the door and was a little surprised to see Glen Phelan standing on his doorstep.

'Bloody hell! It's you Glen, it's a bit late for a social call, what's up?'

'Eddie wants a word at O'Doyle's, says it's urgent. Something to do with this O'Connor business.'

'Can't it wait, I was just about to turn in?'

'You know what he's like Aiden, best not to upset the man.'

'Jesus! I'll grab my coat.'

Aiden Cross grabbed his black bomber jacket from the bannister in the hallway and shouted to his wife, 'Popping down to O'Doyle's, bit of business.'

A woman's voice shouted back, 'At this time of night? Okay, well don't be long love, I've got an early start tomorrow so I won't be waiting up!'

'Okay love, I won't be long.'

He stepped outside, closed the front door and followed Phelan down the road to where he had parked his red Ford Sierra.

Phelan took the car keys from his pocket and walked around to the driver's door while Cross waited by the passenger door.

As Cross waited patiently for Phelan to unlock the car doors, four masked figures carrying handguns, stepped out of the shadows behind him.

With the handguns pointing at Cross's back the men stealthily approached him.

At the last second, Cross sensed their presence and turned.

It was too late.

A revolver was thrust into his face and a guttural voice said, 'Don't move a muscle, you fucking tout!'

Cross froze with fear. One of the masked men stepped forward and placed a black, cloth shopping bag over his head while another secured his hands with cable ties.

Finally, finding his voice he yelled at Phelan, 'What the fuck's all this about Phelan? I'm no fucking tout!'

His voice was muffled by the bag and Phelan either didn't hear him or couldn't be arsed to respond. Cross could now feel rough hands grabbing him and dragging him across the road. He heard the sliding door of a van open just before he was lifted and thrown inside. His head struck the metal floor of the van hard and he felt dazed and disorientated. He could sense other bodies getting into the back of the van with him.

He was panicking now and cried out, 'This is bullshit! I haven't done anything.'

The same man who had spoken before said menacingly, 'Shut it, tout!'

'I'm no fucking tout!'

In response to his angry outburst, Cross received a hard punch to the back of his head. He felt dazed and sick to his stomach. Questions flooded his brain, what was going on? Why was he being treated like this?

He heard the diesel engine of the van start up and felt the vehicle lurch as it was driven from his street.

The same man who had spoken before said, 'Where are your Belfast friends now?'

Cross was now terrified; he knew exactly what this was about and he inwardly cursed making the telephone call to Patterson. There was nothing he could do now; he would wait until they got to O'Doyle's Bar. He had always been able to talk to Eddie. That's what he would do. He would beg his Commander's forgiveness at the Bar.

Hopefully, Eddie would let this one mistake pass and let him go home to his wife and kids.

Thirty minutes passed before the van finally stopped.

He heard the sliding door open and felt hands grabbing him. He was pulled from the van and made to kneel. He could feel the damp from the soil he was kneeling on seeping through his jeans and he knew instantly that this wasn't O'Doyle's Bar.

The black bag was yanked from his head.

He was kneeling in woodland, directly in front of him was a shallow grave.

Standing to the right of the grave were Eddie and Danny Macready.

To the left of the grave were three men still wearing balaclava masks. He could sense there was a fourth man standing directly behind him. He daren't turn his head to look behind him.

If he had, he would have seen the masked figure of Mickey Ryan standing behind him holding an old, Webley revolver in his right hand.

Ryan was breathing hard; he was desperately hoping that this was all being done to terrify Cross. When Eddie Macready had called him, and three others into O'Doyle's Bar earlier that evening, he'd been shocked at what Macready had asked him to do. To be handed the revolver and ordered to kill the tout would mean a definite promotion up the hierarchy of the organisation. He knew his wife Bronagh would be impressed at his promotion so at the time he'd been glad to have been given the responsibility of offing the treacherous grass.

Now that Aiden Cross was actually kneeling in front of him and he was holding a loaded gun to the back of his head, doubts about what he was about to do were flooding through his brain. He was sweating profusely under his mask and was desperately hoping that Macready wouldn't give him the order to shoot.

Eddie Macready said menacingly, 'Do you know why you're here Aiden?'

Cross nodded and said, 'I didn't mean any harm Eddie, I just felt the organisation should know about your plan. I didn't think it would be a problem. It's not like I touted the information to the Brits. I'm not a fucking grass. I just did what I thought was best for the organisation. I'm sorry.'

In a mocking tone Macready said, 'When did you ever think Aiden? It seems to me that you've no loyalty towards Londonderry or me. You say you're not a grass? What do you call a person who goes behind another's back and tells tales?'

Cross was pleading now, 'It wasn't like that. I did what I thought was best for our cause. I've learned my lesson Eddie, just let me go home, please. I've got three kids still at school. I'm sorry.'

Macready snarled, 'It's too late for sorry. You've caused a fucking shitstorm and made me look like a fucking idiot. You're going to pay tonight. Do it Mickey!'

Ryan sucked in a quick breath, then squeezed the trigger of the Webley.

The bullet smashed into the head of Cross, pulverising his brain and killing him instantly. The force of the shot caused him to topple forward into the grave.

One of the other masked men stepped forward and took the revolver from Ryan, slapped him on the back and said, 'Well done Mickey, good lad.'

Danny Macready looked down into the shallow grave and said, 'Get that tout covered up before you drive back to Derry.'

Two of the men grabbed spades from the rear of the van and began to throw damp soil over the body of Aiden Cross.

CHAPTER 51

10.30pm 7th May 1991
Heworth, York, North Yorkshire

McGuire sat in his van on the dark side street in the middle of York and smiled. He was pleased with his days' work.

Having obtained everything, he needed for the operation from the safe house in Hammersmith, he had immediately driven north to Newark in the battered Ford Escort van.

As soon as he arrived in the Nottinghamshire market town, he made his way to the new police station, where he waited patiently for his quarry to arrive. He had counted on O'Connor visiting the police station first. It was after all the ground zero for his assassination attempt.

He hadn't been disappointed.

He watched with interest as O'Connor had arrived at the coffee shop with the red-haired woman on his arm. He had observed them drinking coffee as they checked out the comings and goings at the police station. He had then followed them through the quaint streets as they walked hand in hand in front of him.

The young couple had been oblivious to his presence and he had found it all too easy to avoid the pathetic attempts at anti-surveillance techniques employed by O'Connor. He'd expected a far higher standard from Derry's finest. It quickly become obvious to McGuire, that O'Connor believed none of the law enforcement agencies were aware of his activities and that he wasn't being as cautious as he should be.

The man in black had chuckled to himself as he watched the couple holding hands and stealing the odd kiss. O'Connor was being distracted from his field craft by the beautiful redhead. McGuire considered all women to be a distraction, they had never been high on his list of priorities.

Patiently, he had observed them as they ate their romantic meal at the side of the slow flowing river. He had then followed O'Connor, at a discreet distance, as he checked out the deserted mill. He had already identified the tall derelict building himself as being one of only three possible venues where O'Connor could take the shot.

McGuire had watched through a small set of binoculars, as O'Connor peered out from the sixth floor of the building.

He had then looked around and made a mental note of other buildings that overlooked the side of the mill building O'Connor had looked out of. He already knew this was the side of the building that offered the only view of the new police station.

He had then followed O'Connor back to the Bistro where the woman had sat waiting for him. Judging by their reactions, it was obvious that O'Connor had made his decision. The assassination attempt would be undertaken from the top floor of the derelict mill.

McGuire had retrieved his own vehicle and then followed the young couple as they walked slowly back to the car park next to the castle. He watched them get into the blue Rover. It had then been an easy task to follow them, at a discreet distance, as they drove north along the A1 road, back to York.

He had followed them into York and watched as they parked up outside the bed and breakfast in Heworth. He waited for fifteen minutes after O'Connor and the redhead had gone inside, before he was satisfied that they were not coming out again and that this was indeed the place they were staying.

McGuire knew that all he had to do now, was watch them carefully and prepare his own killing ground should it become necessary.

One of the buildings he'd seen that faced the mill building in Newark was a multi storey car park across the other side of town. It was well away from any view of the police station and because of this he knew there would be very little security covering that location on the day of the Royal visit as there was no threat from that direction.

McGuire still hoped that Holmes and Patterson would be able to persuade Eddie Macready to call O'Connor back and abort the mission. The last thing he wanted to do was shoot and kill a committed republican.

He may not have wanted to do it, but McGuire knew if Patterson ordered him to take O'Connor down, then he wouldn't hesitate to do it.

CHAPTER 52

5.30am 10th May 1991
North Yorkshire Moors

Ever since that first trip south with Caitlin, O'Connor had been making the same journey from York down to Newark on a daily basis, albeit at various times of the day and night.

He had taken Caitlin for company on some of the trips and he'd been amazed at just how passionate and enthusiastic she had been during the planning process.

Indeed, it had been Caitlin who suggested the answer to the last part of the planning puzzle. He had struggled to think of a way to get in to Newark, successfully bypassing what would be stringent security, on the day of the Royal visit. Even more important was the question of how to get out after the assassination, when every road in the county would have a police roadblock.

The answer to both questions had come to her one evening in Newark as they were strolling over the bridge to their favourite bistro.

Suddenly, she stopped and looked over the bridge down at the gentle flowing river below, 'That's it Sean!' she exclaimed before continuing, 'Every time we've been here, we've literally been staring at the answer.'

He had replied tersely, 'What's the answer? What have we been staring at? What are you going on about?'

'The river, we can use the river. I'm not sure how yet, but that's got to be the answer.'

He had looked at her thoughtfully before smiling and saying, 'Caitlin, you're a genius. Have I ever mentioned to you that I'm a dead keen angler and that there's nothing I'd like better than a little trip along the River Trent fishing from a small boat?'

Money had never been a problem on this mission and O'Connor had quickly purchased a small wooden boat along with oars and a trailer from a boatyard further down the river at Fiskerton. It had been a simple enough task to find a back-street garage in York that could weld a suitable tow bar on to the Rover. With the tow bar fitted the trailer could easily be towed behind the hire car.

O'Connor had stored both the boat and the trailer in the unused garage at the bed and breakfast in Heworth. He had spoken to the landlady after breakfast one morning and asked if it was possible as they had bought the small boat intending to move on to the Lake District after they had finished sampling the delights of York. The landlady was more than happy to allow him to use the empty garage. She had confided in Caitlin afterwards, that it hadn't been used since her husband died as she didn't drive and had never owned a car.

Time was pressing now; the day of the Royal visit was fast approaching and O'Connor had one more vital task to complete before that day arrived.

The Barratt rifle needed to be checked to ensure its accuracy had not been compromised during the journey across the Irish Sea. It had been a relatively calm crossing, but O'Connor was never one to leave anything to chance.

The shot he was about to attempt in Newark was incredibly difficult so he desperately needed to fire a couple of test rounds to zero the weapon.

Having checked a map of the area around York, he had decided that the best place to do this would be somewhere in the vast area of deserted moorland that lay to the north of the city.

At five o'clock that morning he had set off from the bed and breakfast leaving Caitlin fast asleep. He had furtively left through the back door of the premises and quickly placed the black, carry case for the huge rifle in the boot of the Rover.

He stopped on the outskirts of the city at an all-night petrol station where he purchased a four-litre plastic container of screen wash. The contents were irrelevant, he had only bought it because he needed a target and the container was bright yellow in colour.

After a half hour drive, O'Connor found himself in the middle of bleak moorland. He stopped the Rover in a small layby, got out and took in his surroundings. There wasn't a building to be seen in any direction. Whichever direction he looked, all he could see was an endless expanse of undulating terrain covered in gorse and heather. It was totally deserted, the perfect location for his purpose.

He got the yellow container from the back seat of the car and set off across the moorland. He carefully paced out a distance of eleven hundred and fifty yards. This in itself was no easy task over the rough, boggy terrain, but it was something he was familiar with and skilled in. He had regularly paced out distances, when preparing sniper attacks on British troops back in Ireland.

Having placed the yellow container on an exposed piece of limestone, he then retraced his steps back to his vehicle, once again carefully counting the eleven hundred and fifty paces as he went.

As soon as he was back at the Rover, he took the time to look around him. He checked fully three hundred and sixty degrees and only when he was completely satisfied that there wasn't another living soul to be seen, did he open the boot of the vehicle.

From inside the boot, O'Connor took the Barratt rifle out of the carry case and picked up the two rounds of ammunition he had brought with him for testing.

It was beginning to get light now as the sun slowly began to edge over the horizon. The night sky was changing from pitch black, through different purple coloured hues until finally becoming a soft orange colour directly above where the sun would eventually emerge over the moor.

O'Connor walked fifty yards away from the vehicle, before settling down onto the damp, peaty earth. He positioned himself facing west so that the sun would rise directly behind him. He had chosen this direction so that the first rays of the morning sun would pick out the bright yellow container eleven hundred yards away across the bleak moor.

As he waited for the sun to rise, he set the Barratt down onto its bipod and made the weapon ready to fire. He wanted to get this task done as quickly as possible, he knew that every second he was exposed on the moorland in possession of the huge rifle was a grave risk.

As the first rays from the sun finally broke over the horizon, O'Connor got down in the prone position and took the rifle into his shoulder. He looked through the powerful scope just as the yellow container became illuminated by the sun.

He reached into his breast pocket and retrieved the first of the rounds he had brought with him. Placing the huge .50 calibre bullet into the breach of the rifle he made ready to fire and began his pre shot routine.

This routine never changed. It was always exactly the same, whether he was making a killing shot or as today just zeroing the weapon. Everything stayed the same, even down to the amount of breaths he took before he squeezed the trigger.

Peering through the scope, O'Connor placed the cross hairs directly on the centre of the distant yellow container. He then controlled his breathing before gently exhaling and exerting a gradual pressure on the trigger until the rifle roared into life and he felt the massive recoil drive into his shoulder.

Remaining perfectly still as the round was fired, he continued to look down the scope. He saw the tell-tale splash of earth, a yard to the left of the container as the huge bullet slammed into the soft peaty soil missing the limestone outcrop.

Quickly adjusting the scope by two clicks, he re-centred the cross hairs, reloaded and followed the same routine to shot.

Once again, the huge rifle roared its presence across the still moorland. Again, he felt the satisfying thud of the weapon driving into his shoulder. This time as he looked through the scope, he saw the plastic container disintegrate as the huge round smashed into it.

That's better, he thought and with a grim smile of satisfaction, he quickly stood up and picked up the rifle.

'That's some rifle you've got there, son.'

The voice had come out of nowhere and O'Connor cursed himself for being so careless. He knew he'd made a bad mistake by not checking his surroundings more often and now he'd been seriously compromised.

O'Connor was shocked to see the man standing only twenty yards to his right. He was obviously either a gamekeeper or a poacher. He was wearing a weather-beaten camouflage jacket and dark corduroy trousers. More concerning was the fact that cradled over his right arm was a double barrelled, twelve bore shotgun. The weapon had been broken open in the safety position.

Quickly regaining his composure, O'Connor replied, 'Yes, it is. I use it for competition shooting. I've an international competition in Manchester tomorrow and I needed to zero the telescopic sight. As I've been staying with friends in York, I thought this would be the safest place. There aren't many ranges that can accommodate this beast. Do you want a closer look? You look like you're a gun enthusiast', O'Connor smiled and nodded towards the man's shotgun.

The man approached O'Connor.

As he got closer, O'Connor quickly assessed the man and what level of threat he posed. He could now see that the stranger was in his early fifties and quite portly with a ruddy complexion that spoke volumes about the amount of time he spent outdoors, exposed to the elements. His greying hair was just showing at his temples beneath the olive-green Benny hat he was wearing.

As he approached, the stranger stared in awe at the huge rifle being carried by O'Connor.

He grinned at O'Connor and said in a broad Yorkshire accent, 'Bloody hell kid, it's massive! Where did you say your competition was? I don't think I've ever seen a rifle that big. It sounded like a cannon when you fired it. I don't mind telling you I nearly shit myself when you fired that first round.'

O'Connor laughed and said, 'You can have a go if you like? I've got a couple of spare rounds.'

'Are you sure? That would be great. Are you over from Ireland for the contest then? That's quite a strong accent you've got.'

'Yeah. I came over on the ferry from Dublin two days ago, that's why I needed to zero the rifle, because of the motion of the boat. It was quite a rough crossing.'

O'Connor placed the Barratt on the floor, resting the weapon on its bipod. He gestured for the man to take up a firing position. As the man carefully placed his double-barrelled shotgun on the heather, O'Connor noticed the brass ends of the two cartridges that were still in the barrels of the broken weapon. The weapon was still loaded and O'Connor smiled to himself, knowing everything was now going to be okay.

He turned to the stranger and said, 'Get yourself comfortable and I'll pass you a round, it's a simple bolt action to load it.'

The man got down on his knees and then lay in the prone position at the side of the rifle, but before he could touch the weapon, O'Connor stepped forward and kicked the man hard in the head, his heavy boot striking the man on his temple. The force of the vicious kick knocked the man away from the rifle.

The rifle didn't move, remaining steady on the bipod.

O'Connor swiftly stepped forward and followed the first kick with a second. This time the boot landed flush in the man's face and knocked him over onto his back where he remained perfectly still, having been knocked unconscious.

Picking up the man's shotgun, O'Connor quickly closed the weapon making it ready to fire.

By the time he'd taken the three paces back to where the man lay, he'd started to regain consciousness and was beginning to groan loudly.

As the fog cleared from his vision, the man looked up and saw that the tall Irish stranger was now standing over him holding his shotgun. To his horror he saw that he was now looking directly up into the twin black holes of the barrels.

The terrified man blustered, 'There's no need for that son. I won't tell a soul what I saw. You can trust me son, just let me go. Please.'

Disregarding the man's pitiful pleas, O'Connor squeezed one of the triggers on the shotgun, blasting the man full in the face from point blank range. The effect was devastating and virtually decapitated the man. O'Connor instantly pulled the second trigger and again a myriad of lead shot smashed into what was left of the man's head.

He looked down at the dead man and could see that his arms and legs continued to twitch even after the second cartridge had been fired.

Using the butt of the shotgun, he scraped a shallow indentation into the soft, peaty ground. When the hole was deep enough, he rolled the man's body into it and began to pile the black soil over the body until it was covered. He then hurled the shotgun away onto the deserted moorland, where it would lie undiscovered and slowly rusting.

O'Connor swiftly picked up his Barratt rifle and marched silently back to the Rover. He lifted the boot of the car and placed the now zeroed weapon back into the carry case.

As he drove from the moors back towards York, he wondered how soon the dead man would be missed. He wasn't unduly worried; the day of the Royal visit was fast approaching; he and Caitlin would be leaving York within the next couple of days.

CHAPTER 53

8.00am 13th May 1991
Heworth, York, North Yorkshire

O'Connor had regularly checked both television and radio news bulletins to see if there were any reports about the man he'd killed on the moors, three days before.

There had been nothing, no mention of any missing person.

Only two days now remained before the planned royal visit to Newark. O'Connor was making the final checks of his detailed plan to assassinate the Prince of Wales.

He had risen early and eaten breakfast alone, leaving Caitlin to sleep. Once breakfast was over, he'd left the bed and breakfast and was now striding out towards the telephone box, two streets away in the centre of Heworth. He had previously arranged with Londonderry to be at that particular telephone box at eight o'clock this morning to get any last-minute updates.

One of the first things he had done when he arrived in York, was to pass the number of this telephone box back to Glen Phelan, his contact in Londonderry. The public telephone box was secure from government listening posts and was always the chosen method of communication.

He was now walking quickly, almost breaking into a jog. He had to ensure that he was there waiting when the incoming call came in. It would be a disaster if the call was picked up by some random passing stranger.

O'Connor reached the telephone box in good time, with ten minutes to spare. He was getting anxious, he glanced at his watch. It was now five minutes past eight and still no call.

Suddenly, the telephone rang loudly. He snatched the receiver from the cradle on the second ring and said, 'Liam from Donegal.'

To O'Connor's surprise, the voice that answered wasn't Phelan's, it was Eddie Macready who had made the call.

Macready said, 'Good morning Sean. How's it all going? Is your plan coming together?'

'No problems this end. I'm good to go.'

'That's good to hear son. Unfortunately, we do have a problem over here. Frankie Holmes and Jimmy Patterson aren't too happy about our plan. I've told them to go fuck themselves, but I think enough of you lad to tell you that there could be a shit storm of trouble waiting for you back here if you decide to carry on with your mission. You'll always have my full backing, but under the circumstance it's got to be your choice Sean.'

There was a long silence, before Macready spoke again, 'Obviously I'd be delighted if you carried on. I genuinely believe that once you've been successful, and those two see the positive reaction in the media, I think they'll come on board too. Like I said son, the choice has got to be yours now you know the situation.'

This was a calculated gamble by Macready. He believed that O'Connor would desperately want to complete the mission and take all the plaudits that would follow. He had deliberately withheld the strength of the Army Council's feelings.

He was using O'Connor, playing him.

O'Connor was silent and deep in thought. This was indeed very worrying news. Questions flooded through his brain; What was the reason for the Army Council's reticence? Would they come on board after he'd killed the Prince? Could he trust Macready? Did he want to continue?

After a full five minutes weighing everything up, O'Connor growled, 'Fuck them two, it's still on Mr Macready.'

'Good luck, son', said a smiling Macready before he hung up the telephone.

O'Connor was deep in thought as he walked slowly back through the deserted streets.

His thoughts were of Caitlin, he didn't want her involved in any messy fall out after the mission.

By the time he reached the bed and breakfast his mind was made up; she would have to leave for Scotland today.

When he got back to the room, Caitlin was making a cup of coffee. She looked stunning, wearing one of his t shirts and a smile.

She turned and said, 'Would you like a coffee?'

He fixed her a steely glare and said, 'Leave that Caitlin, get dressed and get your gear packed. I want you on the next train back to Newcastle, I won't need your help to finish what we've started. It's going to get more and more dangerous from here on in and I don't want you involved any more than you already are.'

There was a look of shock and disappointment on Caitlin's face and she said angrily, 'You'd better tell me what's going on Sean, or I'm going nowhere.'

There was an awkward silence for a few minutes as O'Connor wrestled with whether or not to explain everything to Caitlin, or to just fuck her off.

Finally, he decided to tell her about the telephone call. He explained to her the problem about the Army Council not being happy with the proposed assassination. He also told her what he knew about the long-standing dispute between Macready and Patterson.

Tears of anger and frustration welled up in her eyes and she said angrily, 'Can't you see how Eddie Macready's using you? He knows that if you go through with this without the sanction of the Army Council, you're effectively signing your own death warrant!'

'It won't come to that. Once the Prince of Wales is dead and they see what a massive reaction there is, everything will be okay.'

'For Christ's sake Sean, don't be so naïve. You know what I'm saying's right. If it's not sanctioned and you disobey them, they'll kill you.'

O'Connor was angry and frustrated over his decision to tell her. It had been the wrong thing to do.

He shouted, 'That's it, pack all your stuff. We're going to the railway station right now and you're on the next bloody train to Newcastle.'

Caitlin could see that she'd pushed him as far as she dared, so she said softly, 'Okay Sean. I'll do what you say, I'll pack my stuff and catch the train to Newcastle. Once I'm there I'll do what you want me to do. I'll get my car and drive back to Scotland to wait for you, but if anything happens to you, Macready and Patterson will pay. They're both bitter, sad, old men who are playing you. I don't want you to do this, can't you see I love you?'

She started to sob and blurted out, 'There's no need for you to do this, you can strike back another way, don't let the petty squabbling of these two bastards cost you your life sweetheart.'

O'Connor was tight lipped as he threw her bags onto the bed and said quietly, 'Get your gear packed, now.'

In his heart he knew that she was right.

CHAPTER 54

10.00am 13th May 1991
York Railway Station, York, North Yorkshire

The silence was heavy as O'Connor waited with Caitlin on the platform at York Railway Station. Neither seemed willing to break that silence as they waited for the express train that would take her back to Newcastle.

Suddenly, the platform was filled with noise as the train thundered alongside the platform, before coming to a stop amidst a crescendo of screeching brakes and hissing.

It was as if the sudden noise of the express had galvanised Caitlin into action, she flung her arms around O'Connor's neck, kissing him hard on the mouth.

She broke away from the kiss and said breathlessly, 'Please don't throw away what we have Sean. Before we met, all I'd ever been bothered about was making a statement that the world would remember Caitlin Stuart by. I realise now that was pointless, all I really want is to be with you for the rest of our lives.'

Tears were streaming down her face now, but tears were wasted on Sean O'Connor.

He pushed her away and said sharply, 'Get on the train Caitlin. When you get back to your flat in Barcaldine, pack all your belongings and get a fishing boat over to Donegal. Go to my cottage near Kilmacrennan in the Glenveagh National Park, the one we spoke about. The key will be where I told you I always leave it. Wait for me there and as soon as I've finished what we've started, I'll join you there. Look in the bag I left at your place. It's under your bed, use whatever you like from inside. Don't worry about me Caitlin, I'll be in touch before you know it.'

Reluctantly, Caitlin wiped her face and stepped on the train.

As the Newcastle express train pulled away from the platform she looked out of the window, smiled at O'Connor and mouthed, 'Take care sweetheart. I love you.'

O'Connor waved and half smiled back at her.

There was a feeling of dread in the pit of her stomach and she felt as though this would be the last time, she ever saw him.

As the train pulled away and she watched him getting smaller and smaller in the distance, she vowed there and then that if anything happened to her love, the people responsible would pay a heavy price.

CHAPTER 55

10.30am 14th May 1991
Abercorn Road, Londonderry

Bailey shuddered, feeling a shiver pass through her body. She wondered if it had been caused by the cold, damp weather outside the van she was in, or the fact that she was back outside O'Doyle's Bar in Londonderry.

The place where she had come so close to being killed, just three weeks ago.

She took slight comfort in the knowledge that she was very well hidden from sight, sitting in the back of a van that had been cleverly disguised to look like a vehicle used by one of the local telephone repair companies.

Immediately behind the van was a red and white striped tent that had been erected above an open telephone switch box. Inside the tent were two Special Branch detectives, pretending to be busily repairing some non-existent problem with the exposed telephone wires.

The van had been in position on Abercorn Road since eight o'clock that morning. It was a typically drab Londonderry morning. The weather was foul with a cold wind and heavy drizzle falling steadily. It felt more like a winter's day than late spring.

It was now almost ten thirty in the morning and Bailey knew that O'Doyle's Bar would be opening soon. She began to concentrate even harder, looking through the one-way glass of the van at every person who approached the door to the bar. Most of the people walking by had their heads bowed into the strong wind, trying the best they could to shelter from the incessant drizzle. They all appeared to be concentrating on getting to where ever their busy lives were taking them.

For the observations team the inclement weather was a Godsend, people were much less inclined to question why the repair tent had been there for so long.

The only down side was because of the fine drizzle it often became difficult to get a clear view of the entrance to the target premises. The small darkened window in the van's side panel that Bailey was looking through, constantly became covered in a fine film of moisture.

In less than thirty minutes time, the doors to O'Doyle's Bar would open for business.

It was the bar where Bailey had worked as a barmaid, whilst undercover as Samantha Burrows. As soon as the doors were opened, she knew the usual clientele would immediately start drifting in. It was as much a meeting place as it was somewhere to get a beer.

Bailey had been flown back to Londonderry to try and identify the two men who had chased her from the bar three weeks ago. The men had tried to kill her, twice firing handguns at her as she fled barefoot through the streets from O'Doyle's.

It had only been the desperate act of leaping from the Craigavon Bridge into the fast-flowing River Foyle that had saved her life that night.

As the observations van had been driven into position that morning, they had travelled across the same bridge.

As she looked down into the swirling, muddy brown water rushing beneath the bridge, Bailey wondered just how she had managed to survive.

She knew that the two men ordered by Eddie Macready to kill her were only small fry within the organisation, but the director of MI5, Sir Godfrey Winstanley was very keen to have them identified, detained and subsequently interrogated.

He was hopeful that either one or both of the men may unwittingly provide some nugget of information or intelligence that would help them to identify the person who had been tasked by the IRA to assassinate the Prince of Wales.

Everyone in the security service knew it was a long shot, but it was one they all felt was the worth the effort. After all, at the moment they knew nothing whatsoever about the mystery assassin.

Sitting alongside Bailey in the observations van, was Detective Sergeant Niall Flynn of the RUC Special Branch. If she was successful and was able to identify the men it would be his task to coordinate the surveillance teams who would follow the men away from O'Doyle's to their homes. He would also supervise the detention of the two suspects and the subsequent thorough searches of their home addresses.

Bailey was hoping either one or both of the men would show up sooner rather than later. As far as she was concerned, the less time she spent in Northern Ireland and Londonderry in particular, the better.

She didn't know if it was because she felt nervous about being back on Abercorn Road, but she felt distinctly nauseous this morning and had already been sick once, prior to setting off in the back of the observations van.

As the drizzle steadily turned into heavy rain, the noise of the raindrops pounding on the metal roof of the van was making the headache she already had more and more painful.

Half an hour slowly ticked by and finally the rain began to ease.

A heavily built woman with greasy, long black hair tied back in a tight pony tail, suddenly appeared at the door to O'Doyle's. Bailey recognised her instantly, she turned to Niall Flynn and said, 'That's Tracy Donoghue, she's the bar manager.'

Flynn nodded.

Bailey continued to watch Donoghue as she bent over and placed a wooden wedge under the front door, ready to welcome the first customers of the day.

One of the first people to turn up at the bar was Danny Macready. His head was down, bowed against the wind and the rapidly easing rain. Without pausing he strode purposefully inside.

Bailey visualised Danny sitting down on the same bar stool and ordering his usual pint of Guinness. His head had been bowed because of the inclement weather, but she could see that he looked totally miserable and dejected. She wondered if his black mood had anything to do with the reported demise of Samantha Burrows.

She muttered to Niall Flynn, 'That was Danny Macready.'

He nodded and said, 'Good, looks like some of the players are starting to arrive at last.'

Flynn was relishing the responsibility of running today's operation. He dearly wanted to nail the two bastards who had come so close to murdering Bailey.

Flynn had been Bailey's Special Branch liaison officer during her time spent undercover as Samantha Burrows in O'Doyle's Bar. During their brief time working together, he had really come to like the bubbly girl from Liverpool and her infectious humour. He was eager to make amends for what he perceived to be a failing on his part, when she'd been almost killed by the very people she was trying to infiltrate.

Bailey had gone to great lengths to explain to Flynn, that it was nothing to do with anything he had or hadn't done during the undercover operation. The reason she'd been compromised was solely down to her. She had broken one of her own cardinal rules and had been spotted paying far too much attention to one particular conversation.

Even with all her reassurances, Flynn still felt the need to exact a revenge, especially against the two thugs who had almost killed her.

As two more customers walked into O'Doyle's, Flynn growled in his guttural Belfast accent, 'What about these two shitheads?'

Bailey said nothing and just shook her head dismissively.

Finally, the rain stopped completely and it became easier to look through the one-way glass. After a further twenty minutes, a man came into view carrying a dark brown leather holdall. He looked to be in his early twenties and had long dark hair, cut in a mullet style. He was very muscular and was dressed for the gym, wearing a white Adidas training top, navy blue Adidas bottoms and black training shoes.

With no trace of emotion in her voice, Bailey said quietly. 'Niall, he's one of them.'

Flynn immediately began speaking urgently into his radio, informing the rest of the surveillance team that one of the suspects was now inside O'Doyle's Bar. He began by providing the team with a very detailed description of the suspect.

Less than ten minutes later, Bailey saw a second man approaching the front door of O'Doyle's. This man was slightly older, had short brown hair and a goatee beard. He was also very muscular and looked like a body builder. Quite a bit shorter than the first man she had identified; this man was wearing a black Cargo coat and blue jeans.

Having got a good view of his face as he turned and looked at the van, Bailey said, 'That's the other one.'

Once again Flynn began passing a detailed description of the man over the radio, followed by a series of instructions to both the surveillance team and the waiting arrest teams.

As soon as he'd finished organising everything he turned to Bailey and said, 'Right, I think your work here's done. Let's get you back to base. We can take it from here and I'm sure you'll be quite relieved to get out of here. Am I right?'

'As always, you're spot on Niall. The sooner I'm out of here the better.'

Almost immediately, the two detectives outside who had been pretending to work on the non-existent problem with the phone lines replaced the cover of the signals box and began to pack up the red and white tent.

Within fifteen minutes the observations van's engine rumbled into life and it was slowly driven along Abercorn Road away from O'Doyle's Bar.

Bailey looked at Niall Flynn and said quietly, 'I've got to tell you Niall. I don't care if I never see that bloody place again.'

'Can't say I blame you', said Flynn as he listened intently to the radio pressed tightly to his ear.

A different vehicle, disguised as a delivery van, had now replaced the local telephone repair van. A detective waited patiently inside ready to give the surveillance team confirmation that their targets were leaving O'Doyle's Bar.

For the rest of the journey back to the police station in the observations van Bailey and Niall Flynn sat in silence, exchanging the occasional smile.

Flynn listened intently to the radio traffic as the surveillance teams began to get ready to detain the two men identified by Bailey.

Both men had now been seen to leave O'Doyle's and had gone their separate ways.

A broad smile played across Flynn's face as he imagined the arrest teams smashing their way into the suspect's houses in a little while from now.

He thought to himself, they wouldn't be so cocky then, would they? They wouldn't be dealing with a frightened young woman then, would they? We'll see just how big and brave you really are then, won't we?

'What are you smiling at Niall?' asked a bemused Bailey.

'Oh, nothing in particular. I was just thinking that sometimes I really do love my job.'

CHAPTER 56

10.30am 14th May 1991
Londonderry

Richie Keane hated this weather.

As soon as he stepped outside O'Doyle's the rain had begun falling hard again. He pulled the hood of his white Adidas training top tight around his face, gripped his leather holdall a little tighter and waked briskly through the near deserted streets, heading for his small terraced house.

As he strode out purposefully, he thought to himself, what was the point of working your bollocks off in the gym to build muscle, if it was constantly hidden beneath your training top.

After his gym session that morning he'd popped in to O'Doyle's Bar for a swift half of Guinness. It had been deserted in the bar, so he hadn't stopped long. He was walking out the door just as his best mate Mickey Ryan came in. He had a quick ten minute conversation with Mickey and then left the bar. He was starving and needed food. He always felt ravenous after a good workout at the gym.

He kept his head down and walked as fast as he could, thinking about what he was going to have to eat when he got home. He was completely unaware that he was being followed and that his every move was being closely monitored.

He was totally oblivious to the fact that a British Army patrol in an armoured Land Rover was shadowing him. Driving parallel to him, but a couple of streets away.

As he reached his house, he got the Yale key out of his tracksuit bottoms pocket and opened the front door. He walked in, slammed the door behind him and dropped his gym bag on the floor in the hallway. He pushed the hood back off his head and made his way into the kitchen.

He switched the radio on and began to sing along loudly to a classic song from The Undertones.

He opened a tin of baked beans, dropped the contents into a saucepan and placed a couple of slices of bread in the toaster. He began to stir the beans and was belting out the lyrics of 'Jimmy Jimmy' along with Feargal Sharkey.

Suddenly, there was tremendous crash as the front door to his terraced house was smashed completely off its hinges.

Within seconds, three British soldiers armed with rifles had stormed their way into his tiny kitchen. The first soldier through the door grabbed him and threw him bodily onto the floor, the second soldier drove the butt of his rifle straight into Keane's mouth, smashing his teeth and knocking him senseless.

By the time he came around, he could smell burned toast and was flat out on the floor, his wrists tightly bound with Plasticuffs.

The soldier who had smashed the rifle butt into Keane's face snarled, 'Right Paddy, you're nicked.'

'Fuck you', was all that Keane could manage to say through his badly damaged mouth. He could hear his house was being ripped apart upstairs as the Army patrol systematically ransacked the place, upending his possessions as they did so.

Suddenly, Keane became aware of a man in the kitchen dressed in a sharp navy-blue pin stripe suit.

Keane shouted at the man, 'Who the fuck are you? Fucking Special Branch?'

The reply was clipped, 'Never you mind who I am sonny. Get on your fucking feet. We need a chat.'

'I've got fuck all to say to you, you treacherous bastard.'

'We'll see about that, shithead.'

The Special Branch detective nodded towards the soldiers who immediately dragged Keane out of the house and bundled him unceremoniously, into the back of their armoured Land Rover. As soon as the back door slammed shut, punches and boots began pummelling into Keane. After a couple of minutes, he lay bruised and battered on the floor, the sound of soft moaning escaping from his bloodied mouth.

CHAPTER 57

11.00am 14th May 1991
Londonderry

Ten minutes after Richie Keane had left O'Doyle's Bar, Mickey Ryan finished his Guinness and decided to go home to his beautiful wife Bronagh. He'd been married for five years and there wasn't a day went by when he didn't thank his lucky stars for meeting her. She was absolutely stunning and Mickey knew other men cast envious eyes in her direction when they were out together.

Basically, he worshipped the ground Bronagh walked on.

Having left O'Doyle's, he nipped into the betting shop on the way home, mainly to dodge the worst of the rain, but also to place a couple of bets on that afternoon's horse racing at Linfield.

Just like Richie Keane before him, Mickey Ryan had been totally unaware that his every move was being monitored and that he was being followed by a full surveillance team.

When he arrived home at the terraced house he shared with his wife, he made himself a mug of tea and settled down on the settee in the living room to watch the horse racing on the television.

Suddenly, he heard the rumble of diesel engines being driven at speed towards his house. He heard the squeal of brakes as the armoured Land Rovers screeched to a halt directly outside his front door.

Instantly, Ryan knew it could only mean one thing.

Ever since the night he had shot Aiden Cross, he'd been worried that somehow the police would find out who had pulled the trigger. He was surprised it was this quick though, he didn't think the touts body had even been found yet.

He shouted, 'Bollocks!', and leapt off the settee, his mug of hot tea spilling all over the carpet.

He had reacted quickly, but he was still too slow.

The front door of his house came crashing inwards as it was smashed off its hinges. He caught a glimpse of khaki clad soldiers bursting through the splintered wood of the smashed door.

Desperately, Ryan tried to run from the lounge through into the kitchen, where Bronagh was busy doing the family laundry.

Just as he grabbed the handle of the door into the kitchen, he felt the full weight of a rifle butt strike him between his shoulder blades.

The force of the blow, knocked all the wind from his body and sent him hurtling through the kitchen door. He collided heavily with his wife and both of them ended up in a heap on the kitchen floor.

The same soldier who had struck Ryan with the rifle butt stepped into the kitchen and aimed a kick at the prostrate Ryan. The heavy boot landed just behind Ryan's ear and knocked him senseless.

Bronagh was now on her feet and screaming at the soldiers in her kitchen, 'Leave him alone you Brit bastards!'

A detective wearing jeans and a leather jacket walked into the kitchen. He immediately handcuffed Ryan, then turned to Bronagh, put his face directly against hers and shouted, 'Sit down and shut the fuck up! You're giving me a headache.'

Ryan's pretty wife slumped to the floor next to her husband and began to cry hysterically as he groggily tried to console her.

The detective turned to one of the soldiers and said, 'Get that Fenian piece of shit out of here, the rest of you turn this place upside down. You know what you're looking for. Look lively before the natives start getting restless.'

Mickey Ryan was dragged out of the house and thrown into the back of one of the three Land Rovers parked on the narrow street. The vehicle was quickly driven off leaving the two remaining vehicles parked directly outside the house. More soldiers had already deployed from the vehicles, as crowds of disgruntled youths began to gather at both ends of the terraced street.

Inside the house, the remaining soldiers, under the guidance of the detective, were systematically searching the house, ripping up floorboards and tipping out the contents of drawers and cupboards as they did so.

Already the sound of the first half house brick clanging off the side of one of the armoured vehicles outside was a warning that the crowd had now become overtly hostile to the presence of the Army.

The search of the house was quickly concluded and the soldiers left the house. The detective carried out evidence bags containing items that had been seized. As they left the house they were met with shouts of abuse and a hail storm of rocks and bottles. A couple of the youths jeering and throwing rocks managed to get themselves too close to the departing soldiers. They were instantly grabbed and clubbed to the floor. The rifle butts leaving them bloodied and writhing in pain on the pavement.

In less than a minute, the troops and the detective were back inside the two remaining armoured vehicles. They were immediately driven off down the street, the drivers steering the heavy vehicles directly at the baying crowds that quickly scattered in front of them.

As soon as the two armoured vehicles disappeared off the narrow street, the gangs of youths that had gathered began to disperse. This was an everyday occurrence in this part of Londonderry. None of the youths taking part in the stone throwing knew what Mickey Ryan had done and none of them really cared. They were all aware that he had connections with the IRA and that was enough.

They knew they would either see him tomorrow with a few cuts and bruises after a night at the police station, or he would be interned and they wouldn't see him for a while.

Only Bronagh, his pretty wife really cared. She'd been left sobbing on the floor of her kitchen. She couldn't even contemplate getting up to look at the wreckage of her once beautiful home.

To everyone else, it was just the way things were.

CHAPTER 58

1.00pm 14th May 1991
Londonderry Police Station

Chief Inspector Proctor of the RUC Special Branch stood next to Sir Godfrey Winstanley, the Director of MI5. Both men were observing, through one-way glass, the interviews of Richie Keane and Mickey Ryan, the two men detained earlier in the day.

They were at the Specialist Interview Unit at the main Londonderry Police Station. So far, the interviews were going nowhere, both men had adopted the usual protocol of IRA personnel and were refusing to speak, just blankly staring at the wall.

'Not going too well, is it Douglas?', said Winstanley

'It's very early days yet, we haven't really started working on them yet.'

There was a pause and then Proctor said, 'I want to show you something we retrieved from the search of Ryan's house. It was hidden under the floorboards in one of the spare bedrooms. I think you'll find it very interesting.'

The detective handed over a very battered looking photo album.

Winstanley quickly flicked the pages, scanning photographs of Ryan dressed in various Paramilitary uniform and showing off various weapons for the camera.

As he turned the pages, Winstanley said, 'It's a tad unusual for one of your 'boyos' to keep souvenirs isn't it, Chief Inspector?'

'Very unusual, but I guess Ryan has quite an ego.'

Winstanley continued to scan the photographs, turning the pages quickly.

Suddenly, he stopped and his eyes widened as he looked at the detail on one particular photograph.

The photograph had been taken in a woodland setting, it showed Ryan in the foreground holding aloft an Armalite rifle in triumphant pose.

It was the image in the background of the photograph that had made Winstanley stop dead in his tracks. Standing immediately behind Ryan and half turned away from the camera was a tall, sun-tanned man holding an enormous rifle. It was obvious that this particular individual had been unaware the photograph was being taken.

Winstanley said matter of factly, 'Unless I'm mistaken that weapon is the American made, Barratt sniper rifle.'

'You're not mistaken, Sir. It most definitely is the .50 calibre Barratt rifle. I believe that's the weapon that has been used to such devastating effect on the border by an individual trained as a skilled sniper. We've only found out this morning that British troops patrolling the border area have nicknamed this shooter, "The Death Adder". We believe that weapon, used by this individual, has been responsible for countless murders of soldiers over the last couple of years.'

Barely able to contain his excitement, Winstanley whispered, 'Who's the man holding the rifle? Do you know him? Can you get him identified?'

'Right at this moment, we don't know who he is, but I think that's about to change. Follow me, I'm going to show you a proper interrogation. I know Mickey Ryan's Achilles heel and If I'm not very much mistaken, he'll be telling us exactly who this sniper is shortly.'

'I don't care what it takes, Chief Inspector. We need to identify this man.'

Ryan had already been questioned by Special Branch detectives and MI5 operatives for well over two hours. His face was a livid purple colour that evidenced the countless punches and slaps he had endured during that time. The rules governing such interrogations were regularly flouted and the sound of another slap punctuated the silence when Ryan refused to answer another question.

He hadn't spoken a single word throughout the entire time he'd been detained. As questions were asked and the physical assaults started, Ryan continued to stare, unblinking, at the wall.

Leaving Winstanley in the corridor to watch through the one-way glass, Proctor entered the interrogation room and gestured for the two Special Branch detectives to step away from Ryan.

The two burly detectives stepped back and stood at the side of the room.

Proctor leaned forward and with his soft, gentle voice, he whispered in Ryan's ear, 'Mickey, Mickey. I admire what you're doing, so I do. Just let me spell one thing out to you, so you understand exactly where we're both at. Okay?'

There was a pause before Proctor continued in the same soft-spoken voice, 'If you continue with this macho bullshit, you're never going to see that beautiful wife of yours again. Do you understand me?'

Again, he paused for effect, then said, 'Unless you give me the name of the man holding the rifle in this photograph, I'll arrange for your wife, the beautiful Bronagh, to be snatched off the street tomorrow and disposed of. Trust me Mickey, I'm not fucking bluffing.'

For the first time since his detention Ryan made eye contact with the person questioning him.

Proctor held out the photograph showing the man with the Barratt rifle and said softly, 'I know you couldn't care less if we batter you all day and all-night, but how will you feel if you know you could have saved Bronagh and you didn't. Could you live with that Mickey?'

Ryan glared at Proctor his face full of naked hatred, 'Leave Bronagh out of this, you treacherous shit. If you touch a single hair on her head, I'll fucking kill you!'

Douglas Proctor let out a chuckle, then turned to Ryan and with real menace in his voice said, 'Ah! Mickey. So, all of a sudden, you've found your voice. Do you think your threats mean jack shit to me, boy? I've had harder, bigger men than you threatening to kill me, you Fenian scum. Give me the name boy, or believe me I'll give the order for Bronagh to disappear tonight!'

Tears borne out of a mixture of hatred and frustration formed in Ryan's eyes and rolled down his bruised and battered face.

He spat out the words, 'You really are the devil, old man, one day soon your time's going to come.'

Proctor leaned forward and with his mouth less than two inches away from Ryan's ear, he bellowed, 'When it comes, it comes! Rest assured it won't be before I've made your wife disappear. This is war, you maggot! Don't you understand I'll do whatever it takes? Give me the name boy. Now!'

Flinching away from the deafening shouts in his ear, Ryan said, 'Alright, you bastard, I'll tell you. Promise me that Bronagh will be safe and you won't go near her.'

Knowing that he had now broken Ryan, Proctor turned towards the one-way glass and smiled at Winstanley.

He said softly to Ryan, 'Give me the name and your wife will not be touched. I give you my word.'

Ryan mumbled through sore, swollen lips, 'His name's O'Connor. Sean O'Connor.'

Proctor nodded at the two detectives standing by the wall and immediately left the interrogation room and joined Winstanley in the corridor.

The Director who had witnessed the entire interrogation smiled and said, 'Chief Inspector, that was a masterful demonstration of the interrogator's art, it was a delight to witness your skills at close quarters. I've heard great things about your powers of persuasion and I'm pleased to see I haven't been misinformed. I appreciate the service you continue to give towards the security of our great nation. Ryan and this other man Keane, need to be detained indefinitely until we can locate Sean O'Connor.'

'Ryan and Keane are going nowhere. I'll put my best detectives on researching O'Connor. I can guarantee in two hours' time, I'll know everything there is to know about Sean O'Connor.'

Winstanley stared at the grainy photograph of the tall, sun tanned man holding the huge sniper rifle and said, 'I hope we've still got time to find him and stop him.'

'I hope so too. The enquiries I made earlier with the Army suggest that this man's skills are second to none. That "Death Adder" nickname they gave him, wasn't given lightly.'

'We're going to need every scrap of information and intelligence you can find on him, Chief Inspector.'

'I need two hours, Sir.'

'I'll be waiting, detective.'

CHAPTER 59

1.00pm 14th May 1991
Barcaldine, West coast of Scotland

It had been less than a day since Caitlin Stuart had said her emotional farewell to Sean O'Connor at York Railway Station, as she boarded the express train to Newcastle.

After the long drive from Newcastle back to Scotland she was exhausted. Since walking into her small flat in the fishing village of Barcaldine, she had hardly moved, she felt totally bereft. All she could think about was how cruel a mistress fate was. When she had first agreed to meet the man off the boat from Ireland, she had no idea how quickly and how deeply she would fall in love with him.

Caitlin stood and walked slowly across to the bay window that looked out over the harbour. Wiping the condensation from one of the small panes of glass she looked out at the activity down on the dock. Fishermen were busily landing their mornings catch. The boats had been out since before first light and although it was now only approaching one o'clock in the afternoon, they had already landed enough fish to be back in the harbour and looking for a buyer for the trays full of fresh herring and cod.

One boat in particular caught her eye. She recognised the tiny fishing trawler from Ireland that had first brought Sean O'Connor into her life. As she thought about Sean, she felt an overwhelming sense of dread and despair at what his fate would be.

Those feelings of dread quickly turned to anger as her thoughts turned to the two old men, Eddie Macready and Jimmy Patterson, the puppet masters pulling all the strings. Two powerful men whose petty feuding could mean that the only man she had ever loved would be cruelly snatched away.

She walked through to the bedroom and sat down heavily on the one battered, old armchair in the room. She sat with her head in her hands feeling helpless, not knowing what she should do.

She glanced across at the bed, and was instantly transformed back to the quaint bedroom in the bed and breakfast in York where she had first experienced every pleasure a woman could know with the handsome stranger from Ireland.

She tried to banish those thoughts from her mind and her eyes strayed from the top of the crumpled, unmade bed wandering down to the large black grip bag that was sticking out from underneath the bed.

Suddenly, galvanised into action she was on her feet and pulling at the heavy leather holdall.

She could hear Sean's voice in her head saying, "Look in the bag I left at your place. It's under your bed, use whatever you need from inside". It was the same bag he'd forbidden her to touch or look inside when he had first arrived.

Caitlin knew that the large rifle previously kept in the bag had been removed along with the carrying case and was now with Sean in York. Even without the rifle, the bag was still heavy and Caitlin struggled to lift it onto the top of the bed.

Finally, she managed to get the bag up onto the bed. Stepping back, she sat back down in the armchair and just stared at it, wondering what was still inside.

After a full ten minutes, spent gazing at the Pandora's Box on her bed. Caitlin suddenly jumped up and pulled the two large zips that fastened the bag until they were fully open.

With a growing sense of trepidation, she looked inside.

As she inspected the contents her jaw dropped and her eyes widened. Inside the large bag were a number of small, black handguns and boxes of ammunition. There was also a plastic bag full of batteries, wires, timer devices and detonators. At one end of the bag were four large blocks of a yellow plasticine like substance. These blocks were individually wrapped in plastic and were labelled:

EXPLOSIVE PLASTIC
SEMTEX-H

Caitlin didn't recognise the material, but she did recognise the name on the clear wrapping. In bold letters on every block was the word SEMTEX. She had read enough books during her short spell at University to know that she was looking at everything she would need to build a crude improvised explosive device that would cause an enormous explosion with devastating effects.

Finally, at the very bottom of the holdall in two clear plastic bags was a huge wad of banknotes. Carefully, she opened the bags and counted the money. In total there was just under twenty thousand pounds, the majority of which was in used twenty-pound notes.

Quietly, Caitlin zipped up the large bag and replaced it below the bed before sitting back down in the armchair.

An hour passed and Caitlin hadn't moved, her mind was spinning out of control. She felt sure that this was a sign given to her from Sean. She now knew her destiny.

If any harm came to Sean as a result of him being manipulated by men too old and too scared to take any risks themselves, then she would avenge the death of her lover and soul mate.

Caitlin walked over to her wardrobe and took out a cardboard box containing keepsakes from her University days. At the bottom of the box was a battered book. She began to read avidly, quickly flicking through the well-thumbed pages.

She soon realised that she could remember most of the contents of the book, but it felt good to revise the main problems encountered when constructing an improvised explosive device.

As soon as she had finished reading the book, Caitlin started to pack her belongings. There was no time to waste, she needed to go down to the quayside to arrange passage on one of the small fishing boats across the Irish Sea to Donegal.

She had made the decision to do exactly what Sean had asked her to do. She would travel across to Ireland and wait for him to come home to his cottage near Kilmacrennan, she would take the black holdall and all its deadly contents with her.

CHAPTER 60

2.30pm 14th May 1991
Newark, Nottinghamshire

McGuire stepped into the telephone box and dialled the number he had committed to memory. There was a delay before he heard the tones indicating the need for him to pay for the call. He quickly placed coins into the payphone and the call was connected.

A gruff voice said, 'Patterson.'

McGuire said, 'It's me, what's the update?'

'Do you still have O'Connor in sight?'

'I'm in Newark now, watching him have his lunch. Is he going to be called back?'

'It's bad news. Francis hasn't been able to talk any sense into old man Macready and we're rapidly running out of time; the visit's scheduled for tomorrow. You're going to have to do whatever it takes to stop O'Connor. Understood?'

'Understood.'

'Do you have everything you'll need?'

'Yes.'

'McGuire, listen to me, I want you to leave it to the very last minute, but make sure you stop this happening or we'll all be in the shit. I'm relying on you.'

'No problem.'

McGuire replaced the telephone, stepped out of the phone box and got back into his Ford Escort van. He peeled a banana and began eating as he continued to watch O'Connor at the bistro in Newark.

CHAPTER 61

6.30pm 14th May 1991
Farndon, Nottinghamshire

Sean O'Connor lifted the small trailer carrying the wooden rowing boat away from the tow bar on the Rover car. Effortlessly, he wheeled the trailer down the boat ramp towards the river. He had selected the secluded boat ramp and jetty at Farndon very carefully.

He had spent two days observing the ramp and noted that although it was always busy during the daytime, as dusk drew closer it was never used.

It was perfect.

He slipped the small boat from the trailer into the water, secured it to the wooden jetty at the side of the ramp, then returned the trailer to the car. He locked the trailer in position on the tow bar. From the boot of the car he removed several items, carrying them down the ramp to the boat.

It was a fine, windless evening. The sun was low in the sky, but was still giving off some warmth. The last rays of the rapidly setting sun were glinting on the surface of the slow flowing water of the river, as it meandered its way from Farndon towards the impressive ruins of Newark Castle in the distance.

He had made his final journey down from York earlier that day and enjoyed a hearty lunch at the bistro where he'd spent so many wonderful hours with Caitlin.

The thought of Caitlin snapped him out of his reverie and he scolded himself. He had neither the time nor the inclination to appreciate the beauty or tranquillity of his surroundings. He busily returned to the task of placing the items he had taken from the car boot into the well of the boat.

At the very bottom, he placed the long, black carry case that contained the Barratt sniper rifle and ammunition. Immediately on top of the carry case, he placed a thick sleeping bag. The last items to go in were a couple of fishing rods already made up with reels attached, ready to fish. A wicker basket containing items of fishing tackle and a thick, warm coat.

O'Connor had no intention of doing any fishing.

The fishing tackle was just a precaution in case he encountered any security and was challenged as he made his way downstream towards the old mill. He was hoping that by coming down the river the evening before the day of the Royal visit he would avoid any security that may be about.

In the pocket of his navy-blue fleece jacket he carried a Glock 9mm self-loading pistol with a full magazine, as his final insurance.

The last item he stowed onto the boat was a leather grip bag containing two bottles of fresh water, a couple of ham and cheese bread rolls purchased from the bistro earlier. Two bars of plain chocolate, a set of binoculars, a Mini Maglite torch and a large hunting knife in a leather scabbard.

He knew the visit was scheduled for eleven o'clock tomorrow morning, so he would need food and water to sustain him overnight, while he waited patiently for the Prince of Wales to arrive and meet his destiny.

Having stowed all the equipment, O'Connor untied the boat and stepped carefully on board. He sat down and using the oars he pushed the boat away from the jetty and out into the gentle current.

Only using the oars to steer the boat, he made slow progress down the river. He placed one of the fishing rods against the side of the boat so it would appear to the casual observer that he was fishing as he drifted slowly downstream.

As the boat meandered its way along the tranquil river, O'Connor thought of Caitlin Stuart. He'd been disturbed by what she said to him at York Railway Station as they parted company. He couldn't get out of his mind what she'd said about Macready and Patterson, about them using him for their own personal gains and not for the advancement of the cause. What if she was right? What if he was embarking on this massive undertaking for nothing?

Ever since Caitlin left, he'd been weighing up his options. He desperately wanted to strike at the very heart of the British establishment and the killing of a prominent member of the Royal Family would definitely do that. What he didn't want to do was carry out a mission that in the long term would jeopardise everything they were fighting for. What if Caitlin had been right all along? What was Macready's agenda? Could he trust him?

The time for such ponderings was rapidly drawing to a close as the time of the visit drew closer.

Suddenly, O'Connor came to a decision.

Fuck Eddie Macready and fuck Jimmy Patterson!

He wasn't going to take the risk of being hung out to dry by the Army Council. He'd thought about his choices long and hard, he knew that every time a prominent member of the Royal Family visited anywhere, they were always accompanied by the Lord Lieutenant of the County and the Chief Constable of that particular county's police force.

O'Connor knew that he was more than capable of firing two accurate shots in rapid succession. He was confident that he would be able to despatch both the Lord Lieutenant and the Chief Constable in a matter of seconds. This attack would still strike a huge blow against both the establishment and the Nottinghamshire Police Force in particular.

The outrage and embarrassment to the security services would be enormous, but without all the political fallout that would have followed the assassination of a prominent member of the Royal Family.

Having made his decision, O'Connor felt as though a massive weight had been lifted from his shoulders.

A grim smile played across his lips as he began to formulate the strategy needed to kill both of his selected targets. The Chief Constable would be the first to be taken down, then the Lord Lieutenant. O'Connor knew that after the first shot there would be pandemonium. He knew the Lord Lieutenant was, generally speaking, always an elderly man who would be very slow to react to the threat and someone who would make an easy, static second target.

After the first shot, the focus of all the security teams would be the protection of the Prince of Wales, nobody would really give a fuck about the Lord Lieutenant.

O'Connor wished he'd still got time to contact Caitlin and let her know his plan. He knew how pleased she would be. For the first time in a couple of days, O'Connor allowed himself to think of a life with Caitlin after the shooting.

In the distance he could see the stone bridge that crossed the river just beyond the ruined castle and he knew he was closing in on his destination. As he slowly approached the bridge in the fading twilight, he saw a bright orange inflatable dinghy tied up immediately below the bridge. There were two men sitting in the dinghy.

Instantly, he recognised the small dinghy.

It was being used by police divers.

They were obviously checking under the bridge for improvised explosive devices.

Steering his boat to the far side of the river away from the police divers, O'Connor grabbed the fishing rod in one hand and played out some line over the side. Allowing the boat to drift with the current under the bridge.

One of the divers in the boat saw the small boat containing the lone fisherman and raised a hand in acknowledgement. He'd obviously just surfaced from below the cold water and was more interested in the hot cup of tea in his hands than any possible threat posed by the angler.

O'Connor waved back and slowly passed under the bridge out of the diver's view. Only when he was completely out of sight of the police officers did he relax his grip on the Glock pistol in his fleece pocket.

He threw the fishing rod back into the bottom of the boat and hastily grabbed the oars to prevent the boat from colliding with the bank.

After drifting for another couple of minutes, he finally saw what he'd been looking for. In the distance, about fifty yards ahead he saw the hulking shape of the disused mill building appearing out of the gloom.

The twilight was now being complimented by the orange glow of street lights coming on in the distance and wisps of mist were starting to rise from the cold waters of the river as night began to fall.

He carefully steered the boat towards the overhanging willow tree that he knew hid the partially open door that afforded the only access into the mill.

O'Conner jumped from the boat on to the bank and cursed under his breath as he slipped on the damp, muddy surface. Regaining his balance, he quickly secured the boat, tying it to an overhanging branch of the willow tree. This part of the river wasn't overlooked and the boat was well hidden from view.

Without wasting a moment of the twilight, he removed the grip bag and the carry case containing the rifle. Everything else was left in the bottom of the boat. If everything went according to plan, he would need it all again tomorrow as he rowed back upstream to the boat ramp at Farndon, after the two fatal shootings.

CHAPTER 62

6.30pm 14th May 1991
Nottinghamshire Police Headquarters

'Good evening gents, let's get cracking, shall we? We've all got an early start in the morning.'

The voice belonged to Jim Chambers, he was meeting with Detective Inspector Nick Murray from the Special Branch and Superintendent Tremaine Wilks, the Close Protection Officer for the Prince of Wales.

'Okay Nick, what's the latest threat level update?'

'It's not good. I've just had a conversation with my Regional Officer from the Security Service and she's informed me that there's a real and credible threat to the principal's life, at this time.'

Chambers said, 'Can she be any more specific? Do we know how that threat is likely to manifest itself? Are we talking about a bomb? A shooting? What, for Christ's sake?'

'All she could say was that they were still working hard to pinpoint the threat, that's it.'

Chambers looked worried, 'Well, that's it, we need to cancel the opening ceremony.'

Tremaine Wilks now spoke up, 'That's totally out of the question, I'm afraid.'

At the best of times the royal protection officer's plummy tones always aggravated Chambers, this was the worst of times and his patience was wearing thin.

He turned to the Metropolitan Police Superintendent and said, 'What do you mean, out of the question?'

'Exactly what I said Chief Inspector. The Prince of Wales will not be seen to bend to these threats. Rumours such as these are constantly coming to our notice, in one form or another. Quite rightly, the Prince refuses to let them change his schedule.'

Murray said, 'With respect sir. This is a lot more substantial than a rumour. This is one step down from a dead certainty. Someone's going to try and kill your principal tomorrow, surely it's down to us to take the appropriate steps to prevent that happening?'

Looking down his nose at the Detective Inspector, Wilks said, 'It's not up for discussion. I've already received this particular threat report from our liaison at MI5. I've relayed it to the Prince and he's chosen to disregard it. The visit will continue and he will open Newark Police Station tomorrow. I suggest we're all on our toes a little bit more than usual. Now if there's nothing else as regards timetables and the like I'll get back to the Prince? He's a dinner engagement this evening at Chatsworth House with the Duke and Duchess of Devonshire and I need to get back to the hotel and sort my tux out.'

An exasperated Jim Chambers shook his head, 'Everything's in hand.'

Tremaine Wilks stood, brushed down his very expensive Savile Row suit and said, 'In that case gentlemen, I'll see you tomorrow morning.'

As soon as Wilks had left the room Chambers said under his breath, 'Arrogant tosser! Nick, I need you to keep chasing your Regional Officer. I want to know what this threat is before tomorrow morning. Can you do that?'

'No problem boss, I'm on it.'

Nick Murray got up and left the office, leaving a very worried Jim Chambers to sit and wonder what tomorrow would bring.

CHAPTER 63

8.30pm 14th May 1991
Newark, Nottinghamshire

As soon as he was inside the building, O'Connor made sure all his equipment was safe and well above the water level before taking time out to attune to his surroundings. He squatted down on his haunches and remained stock still, allowing his senses to take in the noises and smells of the old, dilapidated building.

He remained motionless in the darkness for twenty minutes.

It was time well spent.

He soon realised that he wasn't alone. From above, he could hear noises and a shuffling that betrayed the presence of somebody else inside the mill.

Taking the Glock 9mm handgun from his fleece pocket he checked the action and ensured the weapon was loaded and ready to engage any threat that lay above.

Before setting off to investigate the noises, O'Connor reached inside the grip bag he had brought in with him and retrieved the large hunting knife with the serrated edge. He put the leather sheath for the knife onto his belt then slipped the wicked looking blade inside the sheath. He checked that the knife was secure, before slowly ascending the crumbling staircase.

Every few steps, he would stop and listen intently for the tell-tale noises, locating the source was a priority.

He reached the third floor of the mill and stopped again. He quickly realised that the other occupant or occupants of the derelict building were on this floor.

Very carefully, O'Connor opened what was left of the heavy fire door gaining access to the third floor. He stepped inside the large open plan room and squatted down at the side of the fire door, allowing his eyes to adjust to the even darker confines of the large deserted room.

At the very far end of what had once been a busy and thriving mill room employing countless men and women in the hosiery trade, he could see what looked like a small office attached to the room. At one time it would have been the domain of the supervisors running this area of the factory.

Now that his eyes had become adjusted to the low levels of natural light, he could just about make out the flickering orange glow of a small fire from within the tiny office.

As he moved closer, he could hear the shuffling noises far clearer now.

O'Connor grinned; this is what he had hoped he would find. It looked as though a tramp had come in during the day looking for a place to shelter from yet another cold night.

Steadily and methodically, he approached the room taking great care where he placed his feet so that he wouldn't be heard by the vagrant. After what seemed like an age he stood outside the open door to the office.

Peering quickly around the door frame, he could see a man sitting on a wooden box. The man had his back facing the door, he sat in front of a small fire he had made from pieces of wood that had once been an office chair. The fire was burning slowly and the orange glow from the flames silhouetted the man.

O'Connor could now see that the other occupant of the disused mill was an elderly man with a bushy, unkempt grey beard. He was dressed in the dirty, ragged layers of the homeless and had straggly matted hair protruding from the dark, stained woollen hat he was wearing. There was an overpowering stench of stale urine and sweat emanating from the man.

Gripping the handle of the hunting knife on his belt, O'Connor slowly pulled the weapon from its sheath. He held the knife out in front of him and the orange glow from the fire glinted on the honed edge of the razor-sharp blade.

Silently, he moved into the room until he was standing directly behind the tramp. The rancid smell coming from his ragged clothes was now almost overpowering. Without a moment's hesitation, O'Connor slammed the large blade of the hunting knife deep between the shoulder blades of the tramp.

He felt the strong blade punch through the multiple layers of rags and eventually through bone and cartilage. The old man gasped and sat bolt upright. O'Connor gave the blade a sharp twist and felt the steel grind against the man's ribs.

The tramp fell forward and O'Connor once again gave the knife another sharp twist back the other way, before pulling hard at the weapon to retrieve it from the body.

As he withdrew the weapon, O'Connor could feel the warm blood start to ooze from the catastrophic wound as the old man's life ebbed quickly away.

Stepping away from the body, he stamped on the small fire to extinguish the flames before making his way back down the stone steps to the entrance of the mill. As he descended the stairs, he thought how nobody was ever going to miss the old tramp.

Back down on the ground floor, he stepped outside the mill into the cold night air. There was a clear sky and a bright moon cast an ethereal light over the black water of the river. Bending down, he washed the tramp's blood off the blade of the knife in the cold river water. He then dried the blade on the sleeve of his fleece before slipping the knife back into the sheath, its deadly work done.

Satisfied that he was now alone in the mill, he carried the Barratt rifle and the rest of his equipment up the crumbling stone steps to the sixth floor. He set up the rifle looking out from the point he had previously recced several days ago. He rolled out the thick sleeping bag and retrieved his binoculars. Sitting cross legged on the sleeping bag, he peered through the binoculars looking across the rooftops of the medieval market town at the brightly illuminated police station away in the distance. He glanced at his wristwatch; it was now almost ten o'clock. There was still time for something to eat and drink before he slept.

He had perfected the art of being able to sleep for set periods of time. It was a skill he'd mastered during those far off days in Lebanon. His thoughts drifted to those hot days and freezing cold nights spent in the desert.

Right now, he looked up at the clear, star filled, night sky and waited patiently for tomorrow to arrive.

His day of destiny was fast approaching.

CHAPTER 64

5.00am 15th May 1991
Newark, Nottinghamshire

It was fast approaching five o'clock in the morning as the eight, plain white, Ford Transit vans of the Special Operations Unit roared into the car park at Newark Police Station. It was still dark outside so the bright white lights that illuminated the secure car park strained the eyes of the armed officers inside the vehicles.

Preparations for the visit of the Prince of Wales had been in the planning stages for weeks and now the day had finally arrived for him to ceremonially open Newark Police Station.

Members of the Special Operations Unit had been on duty since four o'clock that morning, drawing weapons from the armoury and preparing all the kit they would require to ensure the visit passed by without incident.

The Prince of Wales and his entourage were due to arrive at the police station at eleven o'clock that morning, there were still the last-minute final searches and security procedures to be completed prior to them arriving.

The Close Protection Officer for the Prince, Superintendent Tremaine Wilks had been working closely alongside Chief Inspector Jim Chambers and Detective Inspector Nick Murray of Special Branch, during the planning of the visit to ensure the complete safety of the Royal visitor.

As soon as the eight vans came to a stop in the secure yard, officers got out and started to make their way inside the new police station carrying all the equipment they would need.

Inside the building, the large Parade Room had been set aside and would be utilised as the control room for the operation. It would be from this room that individual officers were deployed to carry out their various tasks.

All the weapons being used by the officers of the Special Operations Unit were now being carried overtly at all times and as they made their way through the corridors towards the Parade Room, they received some wary looks from the police officers who worked at the station on a daily basis.

Tom Naylor and Matt Jarvis were the last two men to alight from the second of the C Section vans as they had the most equipment to carry. Both men carried the large bag that contained the M77 Remington sniper rifle. They also carried a Heckler and Koch Mp5 sub machine gun as well as all their sundry kit, body armour, binoculars and night vision equipment.

Matt Jarvis had been the officer responsible for carrying out the detailed recce of the town in relation to any possible sniper threat. He had painstakingly highlighted every building within a five-hundred-yard radius that had a clear and unobstructed view of the main entrance to the police station and therefore had the potential of being used by a sniper.

His recce had highlighted only three buildings that had the necessary clear line of sight to the target area. Each of these buildings had been sealed off overnight to prevent anybody gaining access.

One of the three buildings highlighted was the tower immediately below the spire of the impressive Church of St Mary Magdalene. The granite and stone church first used in the year 1180 had already been used by worshippers for hundreds of years before Oliver Cromwell's New Model Army laid siege to the city during the English Civil War. Cromwell had issued a personal order not to destroy the beautiful church during the siege.

It was a beautiful building, but both Matt and Tom were only interested in it as a potential firing point for a would-be assassin. They both spared a thought for the four officers who had spent the previous ten hours on the top of the tower, exposed to the elements throughout a bitterly cold night.

As soon as the final briefing had been delivered in the Parade Room, officers began leaving to carry out their designated tasks. Tom and Matt together with a two-man sniper team from A Section would relieve the officers on the church tower and maintain a covert observation post that covered the entrance to the police station. The ancient church tower offered a three-hundred-and-sixty-degree panoramic view across the rooftops of the historic market town.

The only other two buildings that offered any kind of shot opportunity were the roof of a local night club and a newly built office block. There were no windows at all on the night club building so the only opportunity would be the roof. The office block was actually just over the brief that had been given to Matt. At six hundred metres it was still an option for a skilled sniper so he had included it in his report.

Both buildings had been secured the day before and would remain secured until after the Royal visit. Officers had been deployed at both locations to ensure their security.

The final briefing had taken just over fifteen minutes to deliver. It had been given by Jim Chambers and Nick Murray and was both detailed and precise. At the end of the briefing there had been a brief input from Tremaine Wilks. The duties for individual officers ranged from searches of surrounding properties to the close protection of other dignitaries in the Royal party such as the Chief Constable and the Lord Lieutenant.

A number of contingency plans were also delivered in the event of any hostile act taking place and this included the allocation of a designated safe room and exit strategy for the Prince of Wales.

Tom and Matt, along with the A Section sniper team of Johnny Watson and Tim Piper, carried their equipment to the transport waiting to take them to St Mary Magdalene Church. The A Section team were very capable snipers and made a good team, there had always been a healthy rivalry between the four men as to who were the best marksmen on the Special Operations Unit. That rivalry was always put to one side when they were tasked to work as a cohesive single unit.

It was almost six thirty by the time both rifle teams had set up their equipment on the tower immediately below the majestic spire and began their counter sniper observations.

As the sun's rays started to push back the dismal, grey light of early dawn, it soon became obvious that it was going to be a glorious day. There wasn't a cloud in the clear blue sky and not a breath of wind.

Four hundred metres away from the church tower, the front of the new police station was already a hive of activity as crash barriers began to be erected by council employees.

They would help control the large crowds that were expected to welcome the Prince of Wales to the historic market town.

Tom and Matt had been tasked to watch the side of town that included the entrance to the police station, Johnny and Tim the other side. Both pairs of riflemen employed the same observation techniques.

Using high resolution binoculars one officer would do a slow sweep left to right, painstakingly scanning every detail of the buildings spread out before them. The other officer would then repeat the process but sweeping from right to left. This method ensured that the two officers were never concentrating on the same area at the same time. Their brief was to look for anything unusual, activity on a rooftop, a window that suddenly opened a fraction, anything that just didn't appear right.

All four rifles being used by the two teams were loaded and ready to engage any threat seen from their vantage point. They had been strategically placed on their bipod legs within an arm's length of each sniper.

Three unremarkable hours had passed when suddenly a breathless Jim Chambers spoke quickly over the secure covert radio to the C Section sniper team, 'Chief Inspector Chambers to Charlie sniper team, leave your position at the church tower and return to the Control Room immediately. Over.'

Both men acknowledged receipt of the message, quickly packed their kit and made their way down the internal spiral staircase before stepping out of the side door of the ancient church. Immediately outside the door, parked on the road with the engine revving loudly was a powerful Traffic Patrol car.

The young, white capped, traffic officer jumped out and said, 'Get in gents, you're needed back at the Control Room sharpish.'

The snipers carefully placed their rifles in the boot of the car before getting in the rear of the car, their Heckler and Koch sub machine guns slung across their chests. No sooner had they fastened the seat belts than the car lurched away, speeding through the narrow lanes on the short journey back to the police station.

The Volvo screeched to a halt at the front door of the station.

As the two men undid their seat belts the traffic officer looked at Tom through the rear-view mirror and said, 'Leave the rifles in the boot and get straight inside. Your gaffer told me urgent meant urgent.'

Tom was about to protest, but something about the look in the eye of the traffic man told him to just get inside and find out what was happening.

As they ran through the corridors back to the Parade Room, Matt said, 'Christ Tom, what the fuck's going on? I've never been pulled out of an observations post like that before.'

'Me neither, but it doesn't sound good. Something's happening.'

Both men burst into the Parade Room and saw an ashen faced Jim Chambers clutching a fax message. Chambers walked towards them, thrust the fax message towards Matt and said, 'Matt, I know you did the anti-sniper reconnaissance for this operation and we've just received some hot intel from the RUC Special Branch that I want you to see. I think it may alter your opinion as to whether we've done enough.'

Grabbing the fax message from Chambers, both men started to quickly read the contents:

URGENT FAX MESSAGE — 0930 — 15.05.91

There is now confirmed intelligence supporting the threat of an attempt to assassinate HRH Prince of Wales.

The assassin is believed to be a specialist sniper, responsible for the deaths of sixteen British servicemen over a period of eighteen months. Ballistic tests have confirmed that all sixteen deaths could be attributed to the same weapon. An American made Barratt .50cal sniper rifle.

Troops based in the border area refer to this sniper as 'The Death Adder'

This man has now been positively identified. He is Sean O'Connor (see photograph)

Ten of the sixteen deaths occurred from shots fired from a distance of over 1300 yards

END OF MESSAGE

At the foot of the fax message was a grainy photograph of a tall dark individual looking away from the camera, holding the unmistakeable Barratt rifle.

'Well Matt, has our planning been thorough enough?' asked a very worried Jim Chambers.

Still staring at the photograph of the Barratt rifle, Matt answered quickly, 'Nowhere near enough. Sir, you need to get this visit stopped immediately. My reconnaissance brief was to a distance of five hundred yards. If you extend that distance to thirteen hundred yards, there are any number of tall buildings out there that would offer a sniper of this class the opportunity to get a shot into the front of the police station.'

Matt paused for that information to be taken on board before continuing, 'To consistently make successful shots like that over a distance of thirteen hundred yards? Jesus, that's some awesome shooting. No wonder the squaddies have nicknamed him Death Adder!'

'I'm afraid that calling off the visit is not an option.' The plummy tones of the voice made it instantly recognisable.

Superintendent Tremaine Wilks continued, 'The Prince of Wales will not bow down to terrorists. The visit will go ahead and it will be down to all of us to do whatever it takes to keep him safe.'

'And if we fail?', asked Chambers.

'Don't fail, Chief Inspector. I'm just leaving for the Newark Showground so I can meet the Prince of Wales when he arrives in the Queen's Flight helicopter. The visit will be going ahead. Like I said, don't fail, Chief Inspector', said Wilks as he walked briskly out of the Parade Room.

Chambers shook his head, then turned to Tom and Matt, 'I want you two back out there immediately. I want you to make a note of every building that overlooks this place for as far as the eye can see. You're going to need more staff to get all those buildings checked, I know that. I'll be getting that manpower organised while you're doing a quick recce. I need that list of likely buildings as fast as you can get it. Now move it, get out there on the front steps of this nick and start scanning with your binoculars. I want that list of buildings!'

Without a word Tom and Matt sprinted for the door and raced through the corridors back to the front of the building. Once outside the main doors they stood side by side, using their high-resolution binoculars to scan the panorama of buildings spread out in front of them. As each high building was identified on the map, Matt quickly wrote the name and the location of the building down.

It took fifteen minutes, but by the end of the process they had identified a total of nine buildings that all had a view of the front of the police station and that were all well outside the five-hundred-yard perimeter.

Tom immediately got on the radio and informed Chambers that they had a total of nine buildings to clear. He gave details of all the buildings and their locations then said, 'Me and Matt will take Pc Jenkins, the Traffic cop who picked us up and check out the three buildings on the list that are the furthest away. Using the Traffic Patrol car will be the quickest way to get around them all. We'll check the roof of the Municipal Baths on King Street first, then the roof of the Black Prince pub on Fletcher Gate and lastly the derelict building that used to be Swainson and Blackley Mills. The old mill is right on the limit at approximately eleven hundred yards, but it will still need checking. Over.'

Chambers replied, 'Thanks Tom. I'm organising three other search teams to clear the other buildings. Keep me informed as and when you've cleared your three. Over.'

Tom turned to Matt and Pc Jenkins, 'Let's go. We'll start with the nearest and work our way out. The first one is the Baths on King Street. How much time do we have?'

Matt looked at his watch and said grimly, 'Not enough.'

Pc Jenkins gunned the engine of the Volvo and drove at a maniacal speed through the narrow lanes to King Street.

As the buildings flashed by outside the car, Tom wondered if they had any realistic chance of checking all nine buildings before the Prince of Wales arrived? Other questions raced through his mind; If the Death Adder was out there, would he have noticed all the extra police activity? If he had, what would he do about it?

CHAPTER 65

10.00am 15th May 1991
Newark, Nottinghamshire

From his lofty perch on the sixth floor of the derelict building, that was once the bustling, thriving business of Swainson and Blackley Hosiery Mills, O'Connor had been observing the increased police activity since just before first light.

His powers of concentration were enormous, he hadn't moved a muscle since the eight white vans thundered into the secure car park of the new police station.

He had watched the armed officers unload all their equipment from the vans and make their way inside.

As the poor light of early dawn had slowly turned into full daylight, he had watched the four-man sniper team deploy on to the tower at the base of the high steeple of the ancient church. He had considered this as a possible option to take his own shot, but had quickly discounted it. It was not suitable for his purpose in any way, it was way too close to target and was far too obvious. He thought it would be the first place the police would check on the day of the visit. He had been proved right.

Once again, his well-honed skills had stood him in good stead. He had also made a mental note of the weapons the sniper teams were carrying. He recognised the Remington M77 sniper rifle. It was a solid, reliable weapon but at only .243 calibre it was restricted on distance. Although lethal at a greater distance, it could only ever be relied upon to be accurate up to a distance of five hundred yards.

He had taken comfort from the fact that even if the sniper teams on the church tower did by some fluke see him, they wouldn't be able to effectively engage the threat he posed. He would have ample time to either neutralise them or make good his escape.

What had been of concern to him was the unusual behaviour of two members of that four-man sniper team. Without any obvious reason they had suddenly packed up all their equipment and left the tower. O'Connor knew this was definitely against usual practice. Protocol dictated that a three sixty observation post such as the church tower, would generally be manned by four people.

Looking though his binoculars, he'd watched as the two snipers were met by a fast patrol car and taken back to the police station. Both men had then sprinted from the car into the station, minus their rifles. He continued to observe the front door of the police station and ten minutes later he saw the same two snipers emerge and start scanning the skyline in front of them using their own binoculars, making notes as they did so. They were definitely searching for something in particular.

As he watched them, O'Connor whispered to himself, 'These boys are on to something.'

He wondered exactly what had changed. He checked his watch and saw that it was now almost ten o'clock.

One more hour to wait before the Prince of Wales arrived.

Sixty minutes, before he made the shots that would cause chaos down below him. Only then could he finally start the long journey home back to Derry, where he would be greeted as a hero.

CHAPTER 66

10.35am 15ᵗʰ May 1991
Newark, Nottinghamshire

The Traffic Patrol car screeched to a halt at the side of the corrugated iron fencing that surrounded the disused mill building that was located adjacent to the banks of the river.

As the two Special Ops men jumped out of the car and raced across to the fence, Tom said, 'We've checked the Municipal Baths and the Black Prince pub; Do you really think this building is even an option? It must be closer to twelve hundred than eleven hundred yards, this place really is on the limit mate.'

Matt answered, 'You read the fax message, this guy is lethal at thirteen hundred yards. It's our only option. The other search teams have cleared all the other possible locations that a sniper could use. How much time do we have left?'

Tom glanced at his watch as he began to climb the fence, 'It's twenty-five to eleven already, we've got twenty-five minutes.'

Pc Jenkins, helped the two snipers over the corrugated iron fencing before passing their weapons over to them.

As soon as he landed on the other side next to Tom, Matt turned and shouted to Pc Jenkins, 'Let the Control Room know where we are and that this is the last possible building where the suspect could be. If there's nobody in here then unless we've missed something glaringly obvious then this hit man isn't in Newark. If, on the other hand, the shit hits the fan inside the building and you hear gun shots, do not come into the building. Just call it in and get back up here immediately. Do you understand me?'

The young Traffic officer nodded and ran back to his car to update the status of the two Special Ops men.

Both men checked the actions of their Heckler and Koch Mp5's, made sure they were loaded and that the safety was off. With the weapons check complete they made their way across the waste ground towards the derelict mill. Their approach was identical to the route taken by Sean O'Connor when he had first recced the building. The men made their way to the rear of the building and began to skirt along the side of the river bank looking for somewhere to gain access.

On the top floor of the building, O'Connor was busy carrying out his own weapon check. Checking the action of the Barratt rifle and peering down the scope to check the sight picture. There were two huge bullets at the side of the rifle ready to use. O'Connor was superstitious and only ever liked to have the correct amount of ammunition to hand that would be used to kill his targets. On this occasion it would be two rounds.

If he needed a weapon for any other contingency, he had his Glock to hand and that had a full magazine.

He began preparing mentally for the double shot he was about to take. The first bullet was destined to kill the Chief Constable, then in the ensuing chaos the second would end the life of the Lord Lieutenant of Nottinghamshire.

Out of his view and unbeknown to O'Connor, down on the ground floor the two Special Ops snipers continued to scout the perimeter of the building.

Tom and Matt were very carefully negotiating the slippery bank of the river. As they approached an overhanging willow tree, Tom suddenly saw the half open door, hanging from its hinges.

He squatted down and raised his right-hand signalling for Matt to stop.

Tom turned and whispered to Matt, 'Just ahead, there's a door half hanging off. It looks like it could be a way inside.'

He continued to make his way forward, as he pushed through some tall reeds and bulrushes, he was suddenly confronted by the small wooden boat containing the fishing tackle that had been tied to an overhanging branch of the willow.

Looking down, Tom could see fresh footprints in the black mud of the river bank.

He turned to Matt and said, 'Call it in Matt. I reckon O'Connor's inside.'

Matt grabbed his hand-held radio and said quietly, 'Pc Jarvis to control. We have reason to believe that the subject, Sean O'Connor, is inside the derelict Swainson and Blackley Mills off Fraser Road. Repeat the Swainson and Blackley Mills off Fraser Road.'

All that came back was a hiss of static.

Instantly, Tom grabbed his own radio and transmitted an identical message. This too was answered by the white noise of static interference.

'Shit, we're in a bloody radio black spot', said Tom as he looked quickly at his watch. He could see there was now only fifteen minutes to go before the Prince of Wales would be getting out of his car outside the police station.

There was no time to get back to Pc Jenkins and the Traffic car radio to summon assistance. If Sean O'Connor was inside, they had no other option but to locate him and engage the threat of the Death Adder by themselves.

Tom gave Matt a steely look and said, 'You ready mate? We're going to have to do this ourselves. There's no time left.'

'Ready as I'll ever be', said Matt as once again he quickly checked the magazine and safety catch of his weapon.

Stealthily, they entered the building. They had no time to attune their senses to the surroundings. They gave themselves just one minute for their eyes to adjust to the gloom, they could just make out the crumbling stone staircase they were at the foot of.

Matt whispered, 'What do you think. Straight to the top floor, shit or bust? or do we clear each floor?

'We haven't got the time to clear each floor, we've got to gamble and go straight for the top. If I was taking a shot from this distance, I'd want as much elevation as possible.'

Tom led the way and began to stealthily climb the crumbling stairs, closely followed by Matt.

After five minutes of careful climbing they were at the bottom of the final flight of stairs that would take them to the sixth floor.

Tom began to move slowly up the concrete stairs, keeping his back in close to the wall, trying to move as silently as possible. The Heckler and Koch nestled tight into his shoulder; the end of the barrel pointing in the direction he was looking at all times.

As Tom neared the top, Matt was almost halfway up.

Matt took another step and placed his weight on to his right foot, with a sickening feeling he felt the crumbling stair lurch to one side. Suddenly, with a grinding noise the stair he was standing on, fell away.

He did his best to regain his footing but it was too late, Matt fell into the open stairwell landing heavily on the concrete steps ten feet below.

Instantly, Tom looked down into the black void where the stairs had previously been. As the dust settled, he could see Matt lying still on the rubble, his right leg twisted at an unnatural angle.

He started to make his way down the steps towards his badly injured colleague, but Matt raised a hand and said quietly through gritted teeth, 'I'm okay. There's no time left. Go on.'

Tom turned and made his way back up towards the old fire door that led into the large, open plan, top floor of the mill.

Sean O'Connor had heard the crash of falling masonry as the stairs had given way beneath Matt.

He moved like a panther away from the Barratt rifle and into the shadows at the side of the room. He crouched and waited, his right hand firmly gripping the Glock pistol.

Stairs didn't just collapse by themselves; he knew he had company. He would deal with the threat first and then make the shots, there was still time, just.

Waiting in the gloom, he watched silently as a black clad figure entered the vast room. He waited for the figure to get further in. Nobody followed him into the room. He must be working alone, thought the Death Adder. Time to deal with the problem.

Very slowly he raised the Glock and took careful aim, for the first time catching a glimpse of the intruder's face. He recognised the figure as being one of the two snipers he had observed leaving the church tower earlier.

I was right, you were onto something, he thought, before taking up first pressure on the trigger of the Glock.

As Tom entered the room, he took a few seconds for his eyes to adjust to the gloom. At the far end of the room he could see what appeared to be the outline of a man lying next to a large rifle. Feeling the Heckler and Koch secure in his shoulder he advanced a little more into the room and took aim. Just as he was about to squeeze the trigger, he realised to his horror that what he had first thought was a man, was in fact a rolled up sleeping bag.

Instinctively, Tom crouched low and moved sideways. This movement saved his life, he instantly felt red-hot pain searing through his right shoulder and at the same time heard the deafening crack of a pistol being fired.

The bullet from O'Connor's Glock, had smashed into Tom's shoulder, just to the side of his body armour. It spun him around causing his Heckler and Koch Mp5 to fly from his grasp. As he was falling, he heard the weapon clattering across the concrete floor away from him.

Tom landed in a heap and remained stock still, not moving a muscle. He could feel the burning pain in his shoulder and the warmth of the blood as it started to trickledown his sleeve beneath his Kevlar body armour.

Tom knew his only chance was to play dead and let whoever had shot him think that the first bullet had found its mark.

For the first time, Tom saw Sean O'Connor as he emerged from the shadows at the side of the room. Without even looking at Tom, O'Connor darted back to the Barratt rifle at the end of the room.

Tom looked at his watch, it was now eleven o'clock.

That was why O'Connor hadn't bothered to check to see if I was dead or not, thought Tom. He's almost out of time.

Tom now looked on helplessly as O'Connor got down on the floor next to the huge rifle. He watched as the sniper placed a huge bullet into the breach of the weapon.

Knowing that time was almost up, Tom looked around and saw his own weapon lying about ten feet away.

Painfully slowly and without ever taking his eyes from the Death Adder, Tom began to drag himself across the cold concrete floor towards his weapon.

He saw O'Connor push the action of the Barratt rifle forward. With a sickening feeling in his stomach Tom realised that time was now up; there was nothing more he could do. The Prince of Wales was about to be murdered in cold blood before his very own eyes.

Grimacing against the pain, Tom stood up, desperately lunging for the Heckler and Koch.

Suddenly, there was a loud slapping noise and Tom saw O'Connor lifted violently up and away from the Barratt rifle. He could see that the Irishman had himself been shot in the head with a high calibre round that had caused catastrophic injury to his skull.

Sean O'Connor had died instantly.

Instinctively, Tom threw himself to the floor as he had no idea where the high velocity round that had killed O'Connor had come from. Very slowly, he crawled over the concrete towards his own Heckler and Koch machine gun. Having retrieved his weapon, he stood up slowly and made his way over to where O'Connor lay. The Irishman was now on his back, the top and one half of his head had been completely blown away.

That's some Karma, thought Tom.

From outside the derelict mills, Tom could hear sirens approaching. Pc Jenkins had obviously remembered the hasty briefing given by Matt, "If the shit hits the fan inside the building and you hear gun shots, do not come into the building. Just call it in and get back up here immediately".

Leaving Sean O'Conner exactly where he was, Tom made his way back to the stair well. Looking down into the gloom he could see Matt with his Heckler and Koch still in his shoulder, manfully trying to pull himself up the crumbling staircase dragging his shattered leg behind him. He was gritting his teeth and grunting against the pain as he moved.

Tom shouted down, 'Stay where you are mate, the troops are on their way.'

'Tom it's you. Thank fuck for that. I thought you were a dead man when I heard that handgun go off.'

'So, did I mate. My shoulder's well and truly fucked though. How's the leg?'

'Busted! Where's O'Connor? Has he fucked off? Is there a different way out?

'O'Connor's dead.'

'But I only heard one shot and it was a pistol. What the fuck's happened?'

'Don't ask me. I haven't got a clue, but Sean O'Connor is still up there and he's as dead as a doornail. Another sniper has taken him out clean, with a headshot.'

'I don't understand Tom. How?'

Tom shrugged and starting to feel a little light headed, he allowed himself to slowly slide down the wall until he was sitting on the concrete steps.

As he waited for assistance to arrive a million questions were racing through his mind. Who had fired the shot? It couldn't have been a police sniper, could it? Who had the weapon or position to have made that shot?

Tom gave up surmising, at this moment in time he really didn't give a fuck how it had happened or who had fired the shot, he was just relieved they had.

CHAPTER 67

11.05am 15th May 1991
Newark, Nottinghamshire

Across town, some four hundred yards from the mill building on the fifth floor of a multi storey car park, the engine of a dirty Ford Escort van sparked into life. The vehicle had occupied the same parking spot all this morning and all of the previous night.

McGuire had followed O'Connor from the bed and breakfast in York, observing him continuously as he drove his Rover car towing the trailer and the boat to the boat ramp at Farndon.

He had looked on intently as O'Connor loaded his rifle into the small boat before rowing off downstream towards Newark, the town centre and the castle.

McGuire had known exactly where O'Connor was headed, so he abandoned his observations and drove directly to the multi storey car park. He drove to the fifth floor and stopped in front of the row of No Parking cones that had blocked three spaces.

He got out of his vehicle, retrieved the cones and threw them into the back of the van. He then reversed the vehicle into the centre one of the three spaces he'd previously selected.

As soon as the car park emptied McGuire had locked the front doors of his vehicle and climbed over the two front seats, getting into the rear of the van. He then placed a piece of hardboard behind the front seats to prevent anyone seeing inside the rear compartment of the vehicle.

He then opened the rear door slightly and using binoculars had observed O'Connor as he set up his killing position on the top floor of the now derelict, Swainson and Blackley Mills building.

Unlike O'Connor, McGuire had not slept. He had remained alert all night, both to observe O'Connor and also to ensure he wasn't compromised.

Only once during the long night had a curious car parking attendant come over and checked the parked van. McGuire had heard him approaching and quickly closed and locked the rear doors. After finding that the van was all secure and was displaying the twenty-four-hour ticket the attendant had moved away.

It was lucky for the attendant that he had decided not to investigate further, as McGuire lay in wait inside the rear of the van gripping the bone handle of his hunting knife.

As dawn broke the following day, McGuire had continued to observe O'Connor as prepared to take his shot.

From his location in the multi storey car park, McGuire had seen the Traffic Patrol car pull up outside the disused mill. He watched as the two, armed officers scaled the fencing and made their way across the waste ground towards the mill building.

A fleeting hope that he may not have to shoot O'Connor flashed through his mind.

He maintained his observations on O'Connor and had seen how quickly he had moved when something had startled him. McGuire knew it was the presence of the armed police officers. Through his binoculars McGuire had witnessed O'Connor shoot the first cop who came into the room, he watched the cop fall and remain still on the floor. There was no sign of the second cop.

O'Connor had quickly returned to his rifle and begin to make ready for the shot that would assassinate the Prince of Wales.

McGuire had his orders; he could not and would not let that happen.

He opened the rear doors of the van another inch, just wide enough for the large noise suppressor on his sniper rifle to clear the van doors.

Peering down the powerful telescopic sight, McGuire held the cross hairs steady on the forehead of O'Connor. He waited until his target actually slid the bolt of the action forward inserting a round into the breach of the Barratt rifle before exerting a gradual pressure on the trigger of his own French made, Nexter FR F2 sniper rifle.

There was hardly any noise, but the recoil into his shoulder was enormous as the suppressor did its job forcing the energy from the high velocity round back into his shoulder. The rifle bucked high in his grasp, but he maintained sight picture through the scope and saw O'Connor lifted away from the Barratt rifle as the bullet found its mark.

The round had smashed into O'Connor's forehead, McGuire knew instantly that he had killed his fellow Irishman.

There was no emotion shown by the big man.

He wasn't happy.

He wasn't sad.

He was just McGuire.

Having taken the shot, he never wanted to take, McGuire sprang into action. He placed the Nexter rifle on the floor of the van, covered the weapon with an old blanket and removed the piece of hardboard from behind the front seats. He then climbed back into the front of the van. Opening the passenger door, he climbed out and walked to the rear of the vehicle quickly looking around him for unwelcome, prying eyes. There was nobody about so he opened the rear doors of the van and retrieved the spent cartridge from the rifle.

He closed and locked the back doors, before placing the spent cartridge case that had contained the bullet that killed O'Connor carefully on the concrete floor at the rear of the van.

McGuire wanted the cartridge case to be found so the police would know where the fatal shot had been fired from.

He got in the driver's seat, removed the blue latex gloves he'd been wearing, throwing them into the rear of the van. He turned on the ignition and slowly drove the van out of the multi storey car park.

The action of killing Sean O'Connor had left a bitter taste in McGuire's mouth. All he wanted to do now was make the long drive to Stranraer, dump and torch the van and the rifle, before catching the ferry to Belfast as a foot passenger.

He wanted to be back home in Belfast, with a pint of Guinness in one hand and a Bushmills chaser in the other.

CHAPTER 68

1.00pm 15th May 1991
Newark, Nottinghamshire

Two hours had passed since Sean O'Connor had been shot dead and Tom Naylor and Matt Jarvis injured on the top floor of the derelict Swainson and Blackley building. Police officers and detectives were now all over the building trying to make sense of what had occurred and gather any evidence they could find.

As the armed back up had arrived at the mill, after being alerted by Pc Jenkins, they had painstakingly cleared every floor as they slowly advanced to the top of the building.

The armed teams had made the grisly discovery of the body of the tramp murdered by O'Connor the night before. The small office where the body lay had been cordoned off and everything left in situ to await the subsequent arrival of the CID and the Scenes of Crime department.

Finally, the armed teams reached the stairwell at the top of the building, where they discovered the two injured Special Ops men.

Tom had quickly appraised the raid team on the death of O'Connor and that there was no longer an armed threat on the top floor.

Support teams and paramedics were quickly rushed through the derelict building by the armed officers so their colleagues could receive the medical attention they both needed. Their speed was tempered by caution at the state of the crumbling structure.

Matt Jarvis had immediately been removed from the building by the first attending paramedics after discovering that he had broken both the tibia and fibula of his right leg. He was carried out of the building on a stretcher by colleagues from C Section. As he was lifted from the ground, he sucked oxygen through a mask to try and ease the pain his injuries were causing.

Although in a lot of pain, the prognosis for Matt was good.

Neither of the breaks were complicated and although it would take a long time, with countless hours of rehabilitation and physiotherapy, he was expected to make a full recovery.

The second attending team of paramedics treated the bullet wound to Tom's shoulder. Fortunately, there was no damage to the bones of his shoulder and no tendon damage. The small, nine-millimetre bullet had passed through the fleshy part of the arm around the top of his bicep. He would need to be seen at the hospital later to clean the wound thoroughly, but bleeding was minimal so he had elected to remain at the mill building to debrief Jim Chambers.

As soon as the raid teams had declared the building clear, Jim Chambers made his way up the crumbling staircase to the top floor where he found Tom Naylor standing to one side of O'Connor's body.

Chambers looked at the massive head injury sustained by O'Connor before turning his attention to the huge rifle still on the bipod legs about five metres from the bloody corpse.

Chambers turned to face Tom and said, 'Jesus Tom, that rifle's like a bloody cannon.'

'That's the infamous Barratt fifty. Made in America. I've only ever seen pictures of it before today. It's accurate at distances over a mile and the fifty calibre bullets it fires are enormous.'

He gestured to the single bullet lying next to the weapon and continued, 'If you're hit with one of them, you're a dead man, simple as that. They'd cut you in half.'

The two men walked over to the edge of the building and looked through the smashed windows out across the rooftops of the town facing in the direction of the police station.

'As a sniper yourself Tom, what would be your best guess as to where the shot that killed O'Connor came from?'

Tom looked out across the rooftops of the old market town, staring at the angular pitches of high slate roofs, standing next to modern concrete office blocks that all towered above the narrow-cobbled streets below.

'The way his body was lifted up and away from the rifle when the bullet struck his head, I reckon it has to have been from a building on a similar level, or just below this one. The only building of the right height facing this way is the multi storey car park across there.'

'Do we know who owns that car park?'

'I think it's owned by the local council; the control room will tell you for sure, boss.'

Chambers made the enquiry on the radio. It was quickly confirmed that the car park was council owned and Chambers immediately requested officers be despatched to that location to begin a search of the property. Especially the areas that overlooked the old mill.

Chambers then turned and said, 'You need to get to the hospital now Tom. Get that shoulder properly cleaned up and sorted out, you don't want to risk an infection. We can take it from here. You and Matt both did well today.'

Tom smiled to himself and said, 'Well done? I didn't do anything boss. I was a dead man. O'Connor had the drop on me completely. If he hadn't been so hellbent on getting his shot at the Prince away, I would by lying here as dead as he is now. I don't know who shot him or why they did, but I do know that if they hadn't, we wouldn't be having this conversation.'

'Well the fact is we are having this conversation and the Prince of Wales is safe and sound, so as far as I'm concerned, I don't really give a toss what happened. I'm just grateful for whatever divine intervention took place today. We all need a little luck at times, now get yourself away to the hospital. Pc Jenkins is still where you left him. He's on standby to take you to the hospital. The doctors have already been notified that you're on the way, so you'll be seen straight away when you get there.'

As Tom started to walk towards the fire door, he heard a message through his covert ear piece that was directed to Chief Inspector Chambers, but on the open channel. The message informed Chambers that a spent casing for what looked like a high calibre rifle, had been found on the fifth floor of the multi storey car park where it overlooked the mill. The strange thing was it had been left standing on its end as though the sniper had deliberately placed it there.

Tom turned to Chambers and said, 'That's bizarre boss. Why leave it there? It's almost as if whoever pulled the trigger wants us to know what they've done.'

'My thoughts exactly. It's not something for you to worry about though, now get to the hospital. Go.'

After a shaky walk down the many stairs of the mill on legs that felt increasingly like they were made of jelly, Tom finally arrived back at the corrugated iron fencing that now had a massive hole in it, opened up by the raid.

Standing next to his Volvo on the other side of the hole was Pc Jenkins.

Tom smiled and said, 'Well done for getting the back up here so promptly mate. I've been told you're taking me to the hospital?'

'That's right, how's the shoulder?

'Mate, it's hurting like a bastard, quick as you can eh?'

'Jump in', said a grinning Pc Jenkins, pleased with the praise he'd just received.

As soon as Tom was in and his seat belt was fastened the young traffic cop gunned the powerful engine and sped off with the blues and twos blaring. Within four minutes they were pulling into the ambulance bay of Newark Hospital's Accident and Emergency Department.

A porter pushing a wheeled stretcher emerged accompanied by a doctor in a white coat and a male nurse.

'On the trolley', said the doctor before continuing, 'Let's get you inside and thoroughly checked over. I don't know why you've delayed getting here, you should have come here immediately, we need to clean this wound properly. The biggest danger you face is infection and the sooner the wound is cleaned the better. Then we can properly asses for nerve damage and any other soft tissue damage internally. I'm really not happy with you officer', the doctor scolded.

Tom frowned, he hated hospitals and he hated doctors.

He grimaced as he sat down on the trolley, 'Alright Doc. Calm down, calm down. I'll live.'

CHAPTER 69

3.30am 16th May 1991
Daily Mirror Offices, London

Ever since he had scribbled down his first story as a small child, the only job Andy Minson had ever wanted was to be a reporter for a national newspaper.

He dreamed of delivering that big news story and now at the tender age of nineteen years he felt he had taken the first step onto the ladder.

Instead of going to University after school like all his friends, he had opted to take the hard route and work his way up from the bottom at the Daily Mirror newspaper. When he first left school, he had applied for and got a job at the newspaper as a junior office clerk.

The job amounted to being little more than a glorified tea boy. Throughout the day he would be sent on puerile errands and in between times he would make countless cups of tea and coffee for everyone and their dog.

Andy always maintained a boundless exuberance and soon became popular among the staff. He would never turn down any request, no matter how mundane or menial the task. Eventually his willingness and pleasant disposition started to get noticed and people started to refer to him by his first name. Some of the reporters, who Andy idolised, even started to throw him the occasional smile and a nod as they passed by.

He had been doing the same job for almost two years, then two weeks ago just as he was about to head home for the night, he was called in to the Assistant Editors office.

She offered Andy the opportunity of manning the news desk during the graveyard shift. This entailed him being alone in the news room between the hours of midnight and five o'clock in the morning, seven days a week. His duties included answering the telephones to take incoming calls of any breaking news stories. It would also be his responsibility to alert the correct people if any major stories broke overnight.

It was a thankless, soul destroying job that nobody wanted.

Nobody except Andy Minson, who jumped at the chance.

All he needed now was for something big to happen, a momentous story to break overnight. He would be the person taking the important call that would get him noticed by every reporter at the newspaper. It would be his big chance to start working alongside the journalists he so admired.

For the first two weeks the telephone hadn't rung once and Andy was starting to feel impatient for something to happen.

Glancing at the clock on the wall of the newsroom he saw that it was now three thirty in the morning. Not long to go now, he thought.

At least when the cleaning ladies started to arrive to do their daily char work he would have some company. They were always cheery and always made Andy a nice cuppa before they started cleaning.

He started to fold a sheet of paper into yet another paper aeroplane. He was absolutely bored rigid.

Suddenly, the big red telephone that was on the desk in front of him burst into life. Its shrill ring tones reverberated around the deathly quiet of the newsroom.

On the third ring Andy snatched the receiver off the hook, 'Daily Mirror Group, how can I help?'

'Don't speak or ask questions, just listen. Have you got a pen and paper to hand?'

The voice was male and carried the strongest Irish accent Andy had ever heard. It reminded him of the guttural tones of the Reverend Ian Paisley who he'd seen ranting on the news on countless occasions.

Impatiently the voice asked, 'Have you got a pen and paper yet? Are you ready?'

'I'm ready, I've got a pen and paper', said Andy confidently.

The man from Northern Ireland spoke slowly allowing Andy the time to write down word for word the contents of the message.

The voice then said, 'Right sonny, read the message back to me.'

Andy took a deep breath and said, 'Okay. This is a message from the Irish Republican Army. At eleven o'clock on the 15th May in Newark, the Provisional IRA prevented the assassination of the Prince of Wales. This action was taken because the IRA are seeking to achieve a united Ireland through political means. Although in the past we have seen the Royal Family as legitimate targets, this is no longer the case. We expect to achieve our aims by targeting either political or economic targets. A member of a splinter organisation not affiliated to the IRA was attempting the assassination to destabilise our organisation. Without our intervention the assassination attempt would have been successful.

This message is not to be made public or published in any way by the media. It has been passed to you as per agreed protocols so that you can pass it on immediately to the security services only. The agreed code word currently being used is "HAWK 77". That is the end of the message.'

The phone line went dead immediately.

Hastily, Andy read the message again.

He couldn't believe what had just happened. This was it. His big opportunity had finally arrived. He imagined himself working alongside one of the chief political correspondents as they prepared this breaking news story for print. Very soon everyone at the newspaper would know who Andy Minson was and just how erudite and efficient he was, not to mention talented.

He glanced at the clock on the wall and quickly wrote the time next to the message. According to the briefing he had received when he started this job, the first thing he needed to do following a message of this nature was to contact the Editor himself.

He selected the Editor's home phone number from the roller desk in front of him, picked up the receiver again and dialled the number on the card.

Andy had never even spoken to the Editor, Sir Christopher Walford, and now here he was calling him on his private home number at quarter to four in the morning.

After five rings the telephone was answered and a muffled voice said, 'Walford speaking.'

Andy blurted out, 'Minson here sir, from the Night Desk. I've just taken a call from the IRA.'

'Who did you say? Minson?'

'Yes sir. Andy Minson. I've been on the Night Desk for two weeks. The IRA have just called and left a message for the security services.'

'Minson.'

'Yes sir.'

'Have they given you a code word?'

'Yes sir.'

There was a long silence before the Editor exploded, 'Well? What the fuck is it?'

Andy could feel his face burning, this call wasn't going at all well, 'The code word they gave was Hawk 77, sir.'

Suddenly, Sir Christopher Walford was wide awake and paying full attention. He said brusquely, 'Was the message the warning of a bomb threat?'

'No sir, it was nothing like that.'

'Okay Minson, very slowly, read back to me exactly what the caller said, verbatim.'

Andy took his time and very slowly, he clearly read the entire message back to the Editor, exactly how it had been said to him.

'Well done Minson. This is what I want you to do now.'

'What's that sir?'

'This message will keep until I get to work at nine o'clock. Seal the message in an envelope, put my name on the envelope and place it on the desk in my office. Understood?'

'Don't you want me to start calling reporters from the Irish Desk and the Political Desk ready to start work on the story?'

With a weary note to his voice the Editor said, 'No Minson. What I want you to do is what I've just told you.'

Andy started to say, 'But......'

Once more, Sir Christopher became enraged, 'You're not fucking listening man. I want you to do fuck all, apart from put the message in an envelope on my desk. Don't you fucking understand English?'

There was a pause before he continued, 'And Minson, you do not breathe a word about this fucking message to anybody. Is that clear?

A very deflated Andy Minson said quietly, 'Yes sir.'

Andy sealed the envelope containing the message, wrote the name of Sir Christopher Walford on it and placed it on the desk in the Editors office.

As he closed the office door behind him, Andy came to a decision.

As from tomorrow, they could stick this fucking job right up their arse.

CHAPTER 70

3.30am 16th May 1991
Barcaldine, Scotland

It was three thirty in the morning, the wind driving in from the Irish Sea was bitingly cold and outside the harbour walls it was whipping the tops off the waves creating white horses.

Over towards the east, the first purple coloured hues of the dawn were starting to break over the hills that surrounded Barcaldine.

Lifting the large black holdall from the quayside onto the deck of the fishing boat, the young Irish fisherman said, 'Is that the last of your bags Miss?'

Caitlin nodded, smiled and said, 'Yes that's everything, thanks. How much do I owe you for taking me across to Donegal?'

The fisherman smiled and said, 'My Dad said it's twenty quid, is that okay? I hope you've got your sea legs; it looks like it could be a choppy crossing today. That wind's quite fresh.'

Caitlin reached into her purse and handed over the twenty-pound note. She made no comment on her prowess, or lack of it, as a sailor, she didn't want the crew of the small fishing boat to change their minds about taking her. She knew they wouldn't want to wet nurse somebody who was badly sea sick. She just hoped it wouldn't be too bad.

Pocketing the note, the fisherman said, 'Make yourself as comfortable as you can in the cabin. As soon as the tide's right, we'll be underway. Once we're clear of the harbour I'll make us all a brew.'

'Thanks', she said and made her way down the steps into the tiny glass fronted cabin where she sat on a slatted wooden bench.

Although all very irregular and unofficial, these crossings from the wilder, more remote regions of Scotland's west coast across the Irish Sea to Ireland had been happening for as long as men first had boats. It was an easy way for the fishermen to make some much-needed extra income when the fishing wasn't great and good catches were scarce.

After seeking out a suitable boat to make the crossing on the previous afternoon, Caitlin had gone home from the quayside and packed. She had managed to fit almost all of her worldly goods into three holdalls. She had left no photographs of herself in the flat and had packed her up to date passport and driving licence.

On the coffee table in the lounge of her flat she had left several travel brochures. All of which she had left open on pages covering the Almeria region of southern Spain.

Caitlin knew it was only a matter of time before she was linked by the authorities to Sean O'Connor and anything that would help throw them off the scent of where she had gone would be a good thing.

Ever since eleven o' clock yesterday morning she had listened intently to every news programme waiting for news of the assassination. When nothing had been broadcast, she realised that either Sean had aborted the attack himself or something had gone disastrously wrong. She speculated on what could have happened.

If Sean hadn't aborted the assassination himself, he must have been discovered before he could strike at the Prince of Wales. All she could think of, was that he'd been betrayed by the hierarchy of his organisation. The two old bastards who didn't give a toss about him and who would gladly betray him if it suited their own ambitions.

She recalled the conversations she had with Sean while they were still in York. How he had spoken so disdainfully about Macready and Patterson. She had found it difficult to comprehend how two men supposedly fighting for the same cause, could be so at odds with each other when they had a common enemy.

When it had been time to leave her flat, she had struggled down to the quayside with her heavy bags. It had taken her two trips to carry the three holdalls as well as the large black bag that had belonged to Sean. Even the young fisherman had struggled with the weight of that particular bag, but he didn't ask any questions about the contents.

A hard, flinty look crossed her features as her thoughts focussed on the two IRA commanders, first Eddie Macready in Derry and then Jimmy Patterson in Belfast. Both were very powerful men who had purposefully made decisions that put her one true love in harm's way.

She vowed to herself that if Sean had come to harm because of anything those two unforgiving, old men had done, she would readily avenge him.

As she sat in the darkness pondering her future, she heard the diesel engines below her suddenly throb into life. She felt the motion as the boat lurched away from the harbour wall, its moorings released.

As the fishing boat moved steadily away from the quayside, Caitlin looked out of the dirty, salt smeared cabin window at the streetlights of the small village she had called home for most of her life. She felt a tear roll down her cheek as she realised, she would never return to Scotland. Her life, her future would be spent in the small cottage near Kilmacrennan in the Republic of Ireland.

She desperately hoped that future would be spent with Sean O'Connor. Hope was still beating strongly in her heart. Until she heard officially that he'd been killed, she would continue to believe that he was still alive and would soon be returning to his cottage in Ireland.

Caitlin knew that the crossing would take around five to six hours depending on the weather. The crew had told her they were not fishing on the return journey so it would be a straight, uninterrupted crossing.

In just a few hours' time, she would be arriving in the small secluded fishing port of Rathmullan in Donegal. The sea crossing would be the first leg of her journey to a new life.

CHAPTER 71

10.30am 16th May 1991
Hyde Park, London

Sir Christopher Walford felt uneasy. He hated all this 'Boys Own', cloak and dagger stuff, why a simple telephone call wouldn't suffice was beyond him. He was a very busy man and could do without all this clandestine bullshit.

Now well into his sixties with a florid face that belied too many business lunches eating Michelin star food and a love of good malt whisky, Sir Christopher had squeezed his short, rotund frame into a Crombie style overcoat to keep out the unseasonal cold wind that was blowing across the park. With a black bowler hat perched precariously on his large, round head he looked every inch the city gent.

He had contacted the private number for the security services as soon as he walked into his office at the newspaper that morning. The upshot of that succinct conversation was the meeting he was now waiting to have with the Director of MI5. The arrangement was that he needed to be here at ten o'clock sharp and to wait on one of the park benches that overlooked the band stand.

He glanced at his Rolex watch that showed it was now ten minutes past ten o'clock.

He tutted and muttered aloud, 'Bloody poor form.'

As the Editor of the Daily Mirror, he was fully aware of his responsibilities to act promptly on such messages received from various terrorist organisations across the globe who felt the best way to communicate with the establishment was via one of the red tops.

At least it kept a vital communication channel open.

Sir Christopher hadn't really understood the message about the assassination attempt on the Prince of Wales when he had first heard it and he hoped that the clown who had been working the Night Desk had got the details right. The last thing he needed was to be made to look an idiot in front of Sir Godfrey Winstanley. The two men had known each other since they were first year students of Peterhouse College at Cambridge University.

Sir Christopher had never really liked the pompous, arrogant Winstanley during their days at Cambridge. That hadn't really changed since. Although their paths had crossed on many occasions over the intervening years and they were both now knights of the realm, Sir Christopher would never consider Godfrey Winstanley to be anything other than an acquaintance.

Looking to his right along the pathway, surrounded on both sides by rhododendron bushes in full bloom, he saw the Director approaching.

He was dressed almost identically, the only difference being that on Sir Godfrey, the Crombie overcoat and bowler hat looked impeccably smart.

Walford stood to greet his acquaintance and the two men shook hands before they both sat down on the wooden bench.

Sir Christopher said, 'Really Godders, is all this subterfuge absolutely necessary?'

Hating the use of his varsity nickname, Winstanley said abruptly, 'Yes, it is. Do you have the message?'

Somewhat taken aback by the curt reply, Walford reached inside his overcoat and retrieved the envelope containing the message Minson had taken down verbatim that morning.

He handed the envelope to Winstanley who opened it and quickly read the message.

Folding the paper containing the message and putting it in his own pocket Winstanley said, 'Who else knows about this message?'

'Just me and the Night Desk staffer who took the original message. Why, is there any truth in it?'

'That doesn't concern you.'

'Excuse me Godders, I've fulfilled my obligations by giving the message to you. Technically, what I do with the contents of the message is up to me. I could set a few reporters on researching what's happened? Establishing the Prince's movements over the last week? Noting any incidents around them? That sort of thing?'

'You could Christopher, unless I order you not to.'

'And are you?'

'On this occasion, yes I am. It's in no one's interest to pursue this story, trust me.'

'Do you have any idea how much I hate it when you say, trust me? It's like a red rag to a bull.'

Adopting a slightly more conciliatory tone Winstanley said through gritted teeth, 'Suffice to say Christopher, I would really appreciate it, if you didn't chase this story. All I will tell you is that a certain Royal had a very narrow escape. His family in particular would hate to see any of this being made public knowledge.'

'Now you've said that, I'm getting more and more interested.'

Walford knew he was in no position to investigate the story, not least because he didn't want to jeopardise any chances he might have of a peerage in the future. However, he enjoyed winding Winstanley up, making the arrogant tosser squirm a little.

He pressed on, 'I think I'll make few tentative enquiries, put my best man on it.'

Finally, Winstanley took the bait and snarled, 'You bloody well won't do any such thing Walford! I'll have your fucking job! Never forget that you fucking print what we fucking tell you, got it?'

Walford raised both hands in mock surrender and said, 'Okay Godders, whatever you say. The message from our Irish friends never existed.'

Winstanley muttered something incoherent under his breath stood up and marched away.

Sir Christopher Walford chuckled as the diminutive Winstanley stormed away. Having enjoyed his sport for the morning, Sir Christopher stood up slowly, stretched and walked away in the other direction.

As he strolled through the park, heading back to his office, he wondered just how close the close shave for the Royal had been.

CHAPTER 72

10.00am 16ᵗʰ May 1991
Irish Sea

The crossing hadn't been as bad as she'd first feared.

The howling wind made the sea a little choppy when they first left Barcaldine, but as they got further out into the Irish Sea the wind dropped and the sea became calmer.

Sitting in the small cabin on the boat, Caitlin pondered over her next move when they finally reached the small port of Rathmullan. She planned on either hiring a car or buying a cheap runner and then driving out to Sean's idyllic stone cottage outside the village of Kilmacrennan. He had named his cottage, 'Hunter's Lair'.

Caitlin felt as though she already knew what the cottage looked like after listening to Sean describe how beautiful it was, with its white washed stone walls, grey slate roof tiles and ancient dark wooden doors and window frames.

He had described the cottage to her as they lay in bed, cuddling closely during that beautiful warm glow that follows love making.

He had told her of the wonderful crisp, clean air and the spectacular views of the Glenveagh National Park that surrounded the isolated cottage.

It was the perfect secluded retreat, more importantly, only Eddie Macready was aware that Sean had purchased the cottage soon after his arrival back in the country.

She couldn't wait to spend idyllic days and nights with Sean at Hunters Lair.

Her beautiful thoughts were suddenly shattered as the sliding door of the cabin was roughly yanked open. The swollen wood of the door screeching on the salt encrusted runner. The young fisherman, who didn't look to be a day over sixteen years of age, stuck his head around the door, beamed a smile and said, 'I've brought you another brew, Miss. We shouldn't be much longer now; we'll soon be tying up in Rathmullan.'

'Thanks, a mug of tea would be great. Do you know if there's anywhere I can hire a car in Rathmullan?'

The young lad thought for a moment and then said, 'I reckon, Fat Gerry who owns the garage, may have a couple. I think he hires them out to punters that have come over for the fishing. His garage is on Miller Street not far from the harbour. I'll point you in the right direction once we've tied up.

'Thanks.'

'It's no problem. If you want to leave your bags on board until you get sorted for a car that's fine. Me and Dad will be on board sorting the gear out for at least a couple of hours when we get there.'

'That would be really helpful, thanks. Can you drive a car right down to the quayside then?'

'Yes Miss, no problem. The fish merchants drive their vans onto the quayside all the time.'

Caitlin smiled and said, 'Please, you don't have to keep calling me "Miss". My name's Caitlin, you and your Dad have both been very kind.'

The youngsters face flushed a deep crimson colour, beneath his shock of red hair. He grinned and blustered, 'That's alright Caitlin, it's been a pleasure.'

With that he screeched the sliding door closed and went back on deck, leaving Caitlin alone with her scalding hot mug of tea and thoughts of a new life in Donegal.

CHAPTER 73

10.00am 22nd May 1991
Nottinghamshire Police Headquarters

The conference room at Headquarters was already smoke filled when Jim Chambers walked in. He'd been summoned to the meeting by the Assistant Chief Constable who was overseeing enquiries into the attempt on the Prince of Wales' life.

Already present in the room to discuss progress was the Head of CID, Detective Chief Superintendent Neil Wilkinson and Detective Inspector Nick Murray from Special Branch.

The ACC, Paul Crawford, had only transferred to the Nottinghamshire force from Devon and Cornwall six months ago and he still spoke with a strong West Country accent.

A heavy smoker, he took a drag on his cigarette, gestured for Jim Chambers to sit down and said, 'Grab a seat Jim, we're just getting started.'

He waited for Jim Chambers to sit down next to Nick Murray and then said, 'First and foremost, Jim. How are your two constables?'

Jim Chambers said, 'Sir, Pc Naylor is recovering well. His wound was superficial with no underlying damage to either tendon or bone. He's at home on sick leave at the moment. Pc Jarvis is still in the City Hospital. He's undergone surgery to reset the broken tibia and fibula and he's also recovering well. Both men are expected to make full recoveries and return to full duties in the near future.'

'That's good news, both men did a cracking job. They acted in the highest traditions of the service. The Chief Constable's already informed me that he will be giving official commendations to both men.'

Crawford then turned to Nick Murray and said, 'Right Inspector, let's start with you, shall we? Have you had any updates from your Regional Officer at MI5?'

Nick Murray replied, 'I had a meeting with her two days ago. The security services are still working hard alongside the RUC, trying to establish more facts about Sean O'Connor. Very little is known about him. His father Joe O'Connor, was a leading figure in the Londonderry Brigade of the IRA. It would appear that he was shot dead during a demonstration in Londonderry when Sean was still a child. There's a record of Sean O'Connor as an adolescent, getting into scrapes at various demos, but nothing serious. He was implicated by an informant into the shooting dead of an RUC constable around his eighteenth birthday. There was no evidence and he was never arrested. After that there's nothing. No intelligence, nothing from informants. It's as though he just vanished.'

'Does he have any family?' asked Crawford.

'His mother passed away a couple of years ago and Sean never turned up at the funeral. He has two sisters. Apparently, when he didn't attend his own mother's funeral it caused a huge rift within the family and the sisters no longer want anything to do with him. There's no record of Sean O'Connor anywhere. There isn't even any intelligence on where he lives. He doesn't appear to own any property, it seems he stayed at various people's homes, constantly sofa surfing. He was very well regarded by everyone in the Londonderry Brigade, in particular by the leadership.'

He paused before continuing, 'Obviously, what's happened to O'Connor hasn't been made common knowledge in the province yet. Nothing has been released by any of the media about what he was suspected of trying to do. Information is still coming in from the RUC and MI5, but it's very sketchy. It's still early days sir.'

'Okay, thank you Inspector.'

Crawford then turned to Detective Chief Superintendent Wilkinson, 'Neil, how are you progressing with enquiries this end? First and foremost, do we think Sean O'Connor was acting alone?'

'Right sir. On the day of the shooting after the small boat was found we had search teams scouring the riverbanks, checking all jetties and boat ramps. In Farndon we found a Rover motor car with an empty boat trailer still attached. Checks on the PNC revealed that this car was in fact a hire car and had been hired from a private car hire firm in Newcastle. The name on the licence used to hire the car was Caitlin Stuart. We've carried out extensive enquiries into this woman. We located her address to a small fishing village on the west coast of Scotland. After liaising with the Scottish police, we sent an arrest team to Barcaldine to check that address. It was a very small flat and was empty. A full search of the address was made and there's evidence to suggest that she may have gone abroad to Spain. Checks have been made with manifests on both flights and ferries, since the dates of the shooting. These checks have revealed no record of Caitlin Stuart booking on board either a flight or a ferry, so either she's lying low somewhere here in the UK, or she's travelling under a different name using forged documents.'

Crawford asked, 'Does she have a UK passport and if so, have we recovered it?'

'She is on record as having a current passport but we haven't found it in her flat.'

Crawford made a quick note then nodded indicating Wilkinson should continue, 'We've also made extensive enquiries with regards to possible sightings, CCTV etc. There is one possible sighting of O'Connor with a red-haired woman walking through Newark on May 7th, about a week prior to the Royal visit. From tentative enquiries we've made in Barcaldine, it would appear that Caitlin Stuart is a red head. She hasn't been at her job, waitressing at one of the small hotels in Barcaldine, since the 27th of April.'

'Thanks Neil. Top priority, I want Caitlin Stuart traced.

'Okay sir,'

'Let's move onto the death of O'Connor. What do we now know about the shooting?'

'Following input from PC Naylor on the day, I organised a full search of the multi storey car park that overlooks the mill building where O'Connor died. As you know a single 7.62 cartridge case was found. A full forensic and ballistic examination has now been made of that cartridge case and although not definitive, the ejection port markings left on the cartridge case lead us to believe that it was fired using a French made, Nexter FR F2 sniper rifle.'

'Have we recovered the weapon used?'

'No sir.'

'Extensive enquiries were carried out with staff who work in the car park and one of the night attendants recalls seeing a small van parked on the fifth floor overnight. There was nobody with the vehicle but it was parked in the vicinity where the cartridge case was found. Checks have been made with the car park security cameras and they show a Ford Escort van arriving the evening before and exiting again five minutes after the shooting of O'Connor.'

'Can we see the driver or a registration plate?' asked Crawford.

'The quality of the camera is dreadful; images are very grainy. I've tried to get the images enhanced but the best I can tell you is that the vehicle was driven by a white male dressed in dark clothing, that's it.'

'Registration plates?'

'Both plates, front and rear were caked in mud, I'm sorry to say that none of the numbers or letters were visible. We've checked the Police National Computer and there are no reports of such a vehicle being stolen in Nottinghamshire during the week leading up to the shooting.'

Crawford was deep in thought, 'Do you think it's worth pursuing this vehicle?'

'I've thought about it sir, but it's a case of where do you stop? If we had a partial plate, that would be something we could work with, but we've got nothing. I've had detectives looking at CCTV from around the town for the week prior to the shooting. There's no sign of a similar vehicle. I think it's a dead-end sir.'

'Thanks Neil. I want you to make a check with forces where there are recognised ferry ports to both Northern Ireland and the Republic for any records of abandoned vehicles around the ports since the day of the shooting.'

'Yes sir. I've already got that enquiry in motion; I'm just waiting to get responses from the Forces involved.'

Crawford said, 'Excellent work Neil.'

He then turned to Jim Chambers, 'Is there anything you want to add Jim?'

'Only this sir, all the officers that were involved in any way on the visit have now been fully debriefed. The only thing to come from these interviews is one of the dive teams tasked with checking bridges for ordnance recalled seeing a lone fisherman travelling downstream from Farndon towards Newark town centre in a small boat that matched the description of the one recovered at the rear of the mill.'

'Thanks Jim.'

Crawford paused, then said, 'Okay. Gentlemen, I want all the stops pulling out to find this mysterious, red-haired woman. We need to speak to Caitlin Stuart as a matter of urgency. I'm of the opinion that she was involved in this heinous plot and I want her found sooner rather than later. There's a distinct possibility that while ever she remains at large, the Prince of Wales could still be in danger. Neil, let me know if there's any progress with the abandoned vehicle enquiry as soon as possible please.'

Nick Murray remained tight lipped; at their recent meeting he'd been informed by Brenda Starkey about the message from the IRA. He was well aware that the Provisional IRA had claimed responsibility for shooting O'Connor, but he'd also been informed by Starkey that the information was classified under the Official Secrets Act. He had been reminded by her that he was not at liberty to divulge that information to anybody and in particular to his senior officers.

Crawford stubbed out his cigarette and said, 'That's it for now then, gents. We'll reconvene in a week's time. If there are any significant breakthroughs prior to that, don't hesitate to contact me at any time day or night. Thanks.'

CHAPTER 74

10.00am 30th May 1991
Tyler's Farm, Drumkeen, Donegal

Francis Holmes lit another cigarette as he waited in the small room of the decaying, unused farmhouse just outside the small village of Drumkeen in rural Donegal.

Every drag of the cigarette he took, the Chief of Staff was getting steadily angrier and angrier. His thin face was now a livid red colour and his features pinched. He constantly clenched and unclenched his fists in a losing battle to try and control his rising temper.

Also sitting around the table in the dingy, cold room that had once been the kitchen of the now derelict farmhouse, were Jimmy Patterson and McGuire.

McGuire had finally arrived back in Belfast a week ago and had immediately given his report to Patterson and Holmes. Sean O'Connor had been shot and killed just as he was about pull the trigger to assassinate the Prince of Wales. His report had been delivered in an unemotional, matter of fact way. It was a statement about the taking of a life, but McGuire considered that to be a perfectly normal event.

The men waited in the gloom for the arrival of Eddie Macready and his son Danny.

Following the disastrous assassination attempt that had resulted in the death of one of the IRA's most deadly and dangerous volunteers, Francis Holmes had made a decision.

Eddie Macready would be replaced as the Derry Brigade commander. His loose cannon approach would no longer be tolerated. He would stepdown, one way or the other.

The Chief of Staff had given the problem a lot of thought and had come up with a plan that he hoped would placate the old man enough to make him step down without a fuss. Holmes' plan was for Eddie Macready's son Danny to take over as Derry Brigade commander with immediate effect.

Danny Macready had always been a major player in the Belfast Brigade, prior to his marriage ending in divorce and him moving back to Derry. Since moving back, Danny had taken a back seat. He had no involvement in the planning of the disastrous Death Adder debacle.

Holmes would only make the offer once.

If Eddie Macready agreed to stand down, so much the better as that would mean there would be a smooth transition of power and all the damaging infighting between Derry and Belfast would stop.

If Eddie Macready didn't agree to the plan, Holmes knew he would be left with only one option. That option would be left with his bodyguard and enforcer, Ben Christie, to deal with.

Eddie Macready would be removed from the farmhouse at gunpoint today; driven out to some remote woodland and given a bullet to the back of the head. There would be no second chances.

Jimmy Patterson was aware of the Chief of Staff's plan, he secretly hoped that Macready would decline the offer to go quietly. He'd made contingencies for three of his own men to be armed and waiting outside ready to assist Ben Christie to remove the problem, should it become necessary.

Suddenly, the farmhouse door opened with a bang and in strutted Eddie Macready, followed by his son Danny.

An angry Holmes snarled, 'Sit down Eddie!'

Macready growled back, 'This had better be good Frankie. I'm getting sick of you clicking your fingers and expecting me to dance to your tune.'

'Eddie, the time for all your bluster and bullshit is over. The mission you sponsored in England, against my specific orders, has been a disaster from start to finish and has resulted in the death of one of our most feared and effective volunteers.'

'The only reason Sean O'Connor's dead is because Patterson's man McGuire killed him before he could accomplish his mission.'

Holmes raged, 'No Eddie, O'Connor's dead because you ignored everything we spoke about in Brest. You ignored all the reasoned argument that was given to you at that meeting as to why we couldn't allow an attack against the Royal Family at this time. More importantly, you totally disobeyed a direct order from me.'

Macready flushed, 'And just who the fuck do you think you are, to give me orders?'

'Fuck off Eddie! You know the score and you sure as hell know how the hierarchy of our movement works. I'm the Chief of Staff, I make the final decision on all operations. If you're not happy with that situation then it's time for you to stand down.'

'What?', shouted an incredulous Macready.

Raising his voice to the same volume as Macready's, Holmes shouted back, 'You heard me Eddie. It's already been decided. As from this moment you'll stand down and your son Danny will take over command of the Derry Brigade with immediate effect. And Eddie, I do mean immediate effect. Have you got anything to say?'

Before Macready could answer, the door behind him opened and Ben Christie flanked by Patterson's men all entered the room with pistols drawn. McGuire also stood up and levelled a pistol at the chest of Eddie Macready.

Danny Macready stood up quickly with his hands raised and his arms outstretched, 'Whoa Frankie, there's no need for all this. Why don't you let me talk to my father and sort this out?'

Ignoring Danny Macready's pleading, Holmes stared hard at the old man and snarled, 'Well, what's it to be Eddie? Are you going to stand down or are you going for a short drive with my man Ben?'

Eddie Macready knew he had been backed into a corner and had only one choice to make. He suddenly felt very old and insecure. He could feel an unusual sensation rising from the pit of his stomach. As soon as he recognised that the unfamiliar feeling was fear, he made up his mind to stand down.

Ignoring the smug looks from Jimmy Patterson, Macready looked Holmes in the eye and said, 'Alright Frankie, have it your way. I'll stand down and allow my son Danny to take over as commander of the Derry Brigade with immediate effect, but I want it recording that I'm only standing down in an effort to unify our cause.'

Sitting to one side, Patterson allowed a cruel smile to play across his lips as he recognised that the old man was in fear for his life and was blustering to the end.

With a resigned air, Holmes said, 'Whatever you say Eddie.'

He then turned to Danny and said, 'Danny, as of now you're calling the shots in Derry. I'll give you my word that provided your father does what he's committed to today and no longer has any say in operational matters he'll not be harmed. I also want to place on record the thanks of the Republican movement and my own personal thanks for all the dedication and sacrifice Eddie Macready has shown for our cause previously.'

As soon as the Chief of Staff stopped speaking, the men standing behind Eddie Macready holstered their weapons, only McGuire continued to aim his pistol at the chest of the former Commander.

Danny helped his father to stand and both men left the farmhouse. Danny looked at his father, he appeared to have aged twenty years in the time the meeting had taken. He'd transformed into a shadow of his former self.

The two men walked in silence back to their car. It was only when they got inside the car and Danny started the engine that he saw the single tear running down the cheek of his father.

As Danny drove the car out of the farmyard he said, 'Don't worry, nothing's going to change. I'll still be coming to you for advice about things. Holmes doesn't need to know.'

Eddie sat in silence for a few minutes and then suddenly blurted out, 'Fuck Holmes! Fuck Patterson! and fuck the cause!'

The rest of the car journey back to Londonderry was made in stony silence.

CHAPTER 75

10.30am 31st May 1991
Hunters Lair, Kilmacrennan, Donegal

Two weeks had passed since Caitlin had first driven along the winding country lane from the pretty harbour village of Rathmullan to Kilmacrennan.

The small hamlet of Kilmacrennan in rural Donegal consisted of fourteen grey stone houses, a village shop, a bakery and a tiny pub. The place was idyllic, surrounded on all sides by green rolling hills with higher ground away to the west.

Three quarters of a mile from Kilmacrennan on the road to Glenveagh National Park, set back in the woods was Hunters Lair.

The cottage lay at the bottom of an unmarked dirt track seventy-five metres from the main road. The track stopped outside the gate to the property. Once through the gate the cottage was surrounded by gravel within low granite walls.

On the day Caitlin had first arrived at the cottage, it was afternoon and the sun was shining brilliantly on the white washed walls and the grey slate roof still glistened with the moisture from a recent shower. The cottage sat against a backdrop of beautiful rolling green hills. The contrast of the white and grey against the vivid emerald green was breath-taking.

Caitlin had stopped the hire car immediately outside the gate, got out and stared at the cottage for ten minutes, drinking in its captivating beauty. Eventually, she opened the gate and walked towards the cottage, her eyes searching for the ornamental milk churn with ivy growing around it. Sean had described to her how he kept a spare front door key hidden beneath that churn.

She found the milk churn at the side of the cottage and as she rolled the heavy object to one side, she saw the large mortice key on the floor. Quickly retrieving the key, she placed the milk churn back in position and made her way to the front of the cottage.

The bulky key slid easily into the lock of the oak door, with a heavy clunk she felt the ancient tumblers drop as the key turned in the lock and with a twist of the door handle and a strong push, the heavy door opened inwards.

Caitlin had stepped out of the bright sunlight and into the house. Although the entrance hall itself was quite dark, as she opened the interior door to her left she saw that the quaint and cosy sitting room was bathed in light from the afternoon sun that streamed through the windows.

The sitting room was sparsely furnished with one large comfortable sofa that took up all of one wall, two chairs in one corner and a pine sideboard below the window. On the far wall was a huge inglenook fireplace with a log burner set into the recess.

On the sideboard sat a silver framed photograph of a very large man standing next to a raven-haired woman both smiling at the camera. Caitlin had guessed this couple were Sean's parents.

The only object on the walls was an ancient wooden crucifix with a set of confessional rosary beads hanging from it.

It was a beautiful room and Caitlin had tried that first day to imagine what it would be like at night with the log burner going and the two lamps at either end of the big sofa switched on.

She had opened the door that led from the sitting room into the kitchen and had been pleasantly surprised at just how modern all the appliances were; the room contained everything needed to equip a modern kitchen.

The only other two rooms in the cottage were the bathroom and a single bedroom. The bathroom contained a bath, a toilet, a sink and a shower. Again, she had been surprised at how modern the room was. It had obviously been recently refurbished and was tiled entirely with black Welsh slate. It was stunning.

The last room she had ventured into was the bedroom. The room was the same size as the sitting room and was dominated by a huge double bed covered in a dark brown, fur throw. The window in the bedroom offered a panoramic view of the hills of Glenveagh National Park away in the distance. The only other furniture in the room was an antique looking chest of drawers with a matching wardrobe and a tall, grey metal cabinet standing in the corner of the room. This metal cabinet had a keyhole at the top and the bottom.

Caitlin had quickly checked the two drawers in the bedside cabinet and found two black keys. Trying the two keys in the metal cabinet, she hadn't been surprised to find that the cabinet contained a small arsenal of various weapons along with ammunition for each weapon.

She had immediately relocked the cabinet and placed the two black keys onto her key ring.

Two weeks had now passed since she had first walked around the beautiful cottage. She had experienced the cosy nights with the log burner and the lamps, but there was still no sign of Sean returning.

With each passing day, Caitlin had slowly begun to think that Sean was never going to return to Hunters Lair.

Every morning, she made the long walk from the cottage into Kilmacrennan. There she would buy fresh bread from the bakery and milk and a newspaper from the local shop. The newspaper was always the most important purchase, Caitlin was desperate for news of Sean O'Connor.

It seemed pointless to take the car each day, when she really did have all the time in the world. She enjoyed her daily walk, the countryside and the fresh air were both so beautiful, it really would have been a crime to drive.

There was still plenty of cash left over from the wads of banknotes she had found in Sean's holdall that had lay hidden under her bed in Barcaldine.

That cash was now kept in the locked gun cabinet. As the days had passed, she alleviated the boredom by trying out the various rifles and handguns that were in the cabinet. The secluded woodland was the perfect place to practice firing the various weapons.

Today had been no different, she had risen from her bed early and made the hour-long stroll into Kilmacrennan where she had purchased her usual groceries and a paper. The young girl who worked in the village shop had packed the groceries for her and had placed the newspaper at the bottom of the carrier bag.

Now back in the kitchen of the cottage she unpacked the groceries. As she placed the newspaper on to the table, it flopped open onto the front page.

Caitlin shuddered as she read the banner headline, "Royal assassination attempt foiled by UK Police"

Her heart felt as though someone had plunged an icy hand into her chest and squeezed.

She sat heavily onto one of the chairs next to the table, all feeling in her legs deserting her. Without even reading the article fully, she knew that her lover and soulmate, was dead.

Eventually, she steeled herself to read the article. It told how the reporter of a newspaper in the Republic of Ireland had been contacted by the Provisional IRA. He had been told by the IRA source that there had been a plot to kill the Prince of Wales, but that the British police had shot dead the would-be assassin before he could make an attempt on the Prince's life. The article stated that at the time of writing nothing further was known about the assassin. It went on to say that no one else was harmed during the police operation.

For a long time, Caitlin sat motionless staring at the newspaper on the table, allowing the message it carried to slowly burn its way into her brain. Thoughts were racing through her head; how had Sean been compromised by the Police? He was so professional, so careful, had he been betrayed? Who had betrayed him?

Finally, she stood up, made herself a strong coffee and sat on the sofa in the sitting room where she pondered on what Sean would have wanted her to do now.

Suddenly, she felt a warm glow that had nothing to do with the piping hot coffee she was sipping. She knew only too well what Sean would have wanted her to do; she could feel her heart rising in her chest and a smile played across her mouth.

CHAPTER 76

9.30am 14th June 1991
Londonderry

The shouts emanating from inside the smart bungalow on the leafy street were getting louder. The argument had been raging for well over half an hour. People outside walking their dogs to the nearby park, quickly crossed over the road in case the argument suddenly spilled out onto the street. Local residents knew only too well who lived in the pretty, brick-built bungalow and nobody wanted to get involved in a row with the Macready family.

Suddenly, the front door of the bungalow was hurled open by an old man with short, steel grey hair. He slammed the door shut behind him with such force that the windows shook.

The grey-haired man turned swiftly and stomped angrily down the driveway towards the Vauxhall Astra parked at the roadside.

Eddie Macready walked as if he had the weight of the world on his shoulders. His hands were thrust deep into the pockets of his brown leather jacket. He muttered under his breath as he walked.

No sooner had the door to the bungalow slammed shut than it was flung wide open again. Danny Macready emerged from inside clutching a slice of toast in one hand and his jacket in the other.

Through a mouthful of toast, Danny shouted, 'For fucks sake, wait a minute. I'll drive you into town.'

The answer he got was short and terse, 'I don't want fucking company, especially yours, you fucking idiot!'

'You've got it wrong Dad; Sam wasn't working for the Brits; she was a sweet girl who didn't have an ounce of harm in her body.'

'Son, when it comes to women, you've got shit for brains. You always have had and you always will. The bloody woman was a fucking spy and she had you hook, line and sinker, boy!'

'Go to hell! Sam was just another example of how fucking far you'd lost the plot. It's a good job you're no longer in charge or the whole thing would go to ratshit.'

'Danny Macready, the fucking big shot! You'd know all about that state of affairs wouldn't you son. Rat shit should have been your middle name. Now piss off and leave me alone!'

Danny gave up the fight, 'Tell you what Dad, drive your fucking self to town.'

With that Eddie Macready jumped into the Astra, slammed the door and immediately turned the key in the ignition.

The only sound was an ominous click.

There was a split second for Eddie Macready to start to say the word, 'shit', before the entire car exploded in a ball of flame, hurling molten metal fragments high into the air. The flash of the explosion was followed instantly by a thunderous bang. The shock wave of the blast lifted Danny Macready off his feet and sent him hurtling backwards into the wall of the bungalow.

Eddie Macready died instantly. The Vauxhall Astra car was reduced to a burning, twisted wreck.

The small, but very effective, Semtex bomb had been placed under the vehicle directly beneath the driver's seat. It had been activated on the turn of the vehicle's ignition switch. Every day for the best part of the last ten years, Eddie Macready had diligently checked beneath any vehicle he was travelling in. Today, because of the argument with his son and the deep-seated feeling of indignation he had felt ever since the meeting at Tyler's Farm in Drumkeen, he hadn't bothered to check under the vehicle. Today, that single omission had proved fatal.

Very slowly, Danny picked himself up off the floor, he could feel the warm blood trickling from his ears. He was stone deaf, the blast wave from the bomb had perforated both his ear drums. His face had been shredded with tiny fragments of glass from the exploding windows of the bungalow. His right arm hung limply by his side, he looked down and could see a sliver of metal from the Vauxhall embedded in his arm. The shrapnel from the exploding car had gone straight through his jacket and his shirt before piercing the flesh of his arm.

He turned around and surveyed the burning wreckage of the Vauxhall Astra and knew instantly that his father was dead.

Once again, Danny Macready slumped down to the floor. He was tentatively approached by a woman he recognised as one of his father's neighbours. He couldn't hear a word she was saying, but he could lip read enough to know that she was telling him an ambulance was on its way.

The last thought that flashed through his mind, before the pain of his arm overtook him and he passed out, was to kill Jimmy Patterson as soon as he could.

From the other side of the small park, a petite, red haired woman watched the unfolding drama outside the Macready's bungalow. She leaned against the driver's door of her car and gasped as the Vauxhall Astra erupted into a ball of flame. She saw the younger man thrown backwards into the bungalow walls, like a leaf in a strong gust of wind.

She smiled as the Astra turned into raging inferno. She was thinking of her lover looking down from above and she muttered to herself, 'You see Sean, I told you I'd get even, just Belfast to deal with now.'

CHAPTER 77

10.30pm 30th June 1991
The Harp Bar, Belfast

Inside the Harp Bar, the air was thick with acrid, blue cigarette smoke. The lively bar was full of the sounds of Irish music and men and women who had been drinking steadily all night. It was now almost closing time and the traditional Irish folk band were well into their final set. The rhythm of the music was pumping and it was very loud. A few of the more sober drinkers were trying to dance the quick-fire steps of the traditional dance. Others propped each other up, kissing each other with varying degrees of passion.

The Harp Bar was a long single storey building that had an entrance door at each end. Like most bars in semi-rural Ireland, the bar inside ran the entire length of the building and the stage area was on the opposite wall. There was a small dance floor in front of the stage and tables placed in the remaining space. There were private booths at each end of the room near the entrance doors

In one of these private booths sat a heavy-set, bruiser of a man with a ruddy complexion and huge shovel like hands. He was nursing his seventh pint of Guinness.

The man was Jimmy Patterson, other people in the bar knew who he was and what he stood for. The vast majority of punters in the bar feared him, he sat drinking alone and that was how he liked it. As far as he was concerned the people in the bar were all plebs who danced to his tune, not the band's.

He smiled to himself as the thought of people dancing to his tune came into his head.

As was his habit, Patterson had sat with his back to the end wall so he could see the entire room as well as who was coming in and going out of the bar. Tonight, he'd been even more cautious after what had happened to Eddie Macready over in Derry, two weeks ago. Patterson had explained at length to Danny Macready that he was not responsible for his father's death and that he was as shocked by what had happened as he was. Patterson had explained to Danny how he believed the attack on his father was the work of the SAS, under direction from British Intelligence exercising some sort of revenge attack for the attempt on the Prince of Wales life.

Patterson drained the dregs of the now warm Guinness from his glass and rose unsteadily to his feet. Grabbing his leather jacket, he made his way to the door.

The bar was located on the outskirts of Belfast and was a regular haunt for staunch republicans. Patterson wanted some fresh air before he was picked up by McGuire for the fifteen-minute drive back to Belfast city centre.

Patterson stood in the shadows outside the bar, far away from the single white light that illuminated the entrance door. He took a cigarette from the packet and lit up, drawing the smoke deep into his lungs.

From the darkness came a woman's voice, 'Excuse me darling, have you got a light?'

The voice was thick, like syrup and carried the accent of rural Donegal.

A stunning looking woman with long, ruby red hair approached him holding a cigarette to her full red lips. Patterson looked her up and down, she was wearing very tight black jeans that clung to her firm thighs and narrow waist, calf high leather boots and a black leather jacket.

Beneath the black jacket she wore a sheer blouse. The jacket was slung back on her shoulders so that her full breasts were thrust forward. Patterson could see her breasts were not restrained by a bra; he could clearly make out the erect, dark nipples as the cold night air took effect on the woman.

He spluttered, 'Yes', and quickly reached into his jacket pocket for a lighter.

Patterson had paid so much attention to the woman's beautiful, full breasts, he had failed to notice that the hand not holding the cigarette to her lips was still in her jacket pocket.

As she leaned forward to reach the flame from the gold plated lighter, Patterson used his huge hands to shield the tiny flame from the breeze. He was mesmerised as the woman leaned in closer, her perfumed fragrance rushing forward to meet him.

He was staring intently at her full lips at the base of the cigarette, her mouth was amazing. Now that her face was lit by the flame from the lighter, he got a first glimpse of her exquisite green eyes.

As their eyes locked, Patterson experienced feelings he had long forgotten, he was completely engrossed by the woman and failed to notice that she had now taken her other hand from inside her jacket pocket.

Crucially, he also failed to see the small .32 Ruger self-loading pistol she held in her tiny hand.

Patterson could feel an unfamiliar stirring in his loins, as thoughts of kissing her full lips and caressing those voluptuous breasts, flooded his alcohol befuddled brain.

By the time he felt the cold steel of the gun barrel pressed against his temple it was too late. The beautiful woman smiled as she squeezed the trigger. There was a sharp crack as theRuger.32 was fired, followed instantly by a sickening thud as the bullet slammed into Patterson's head from point blank range.

The bullet smashed its way into his skull, tearing through his brain. He collapsed to the floor, blood spouting like a fatal fountain from the neat hole in his temple. The big man was dead before he hit the floor.

Quickly, the woman stepped away from Patterson's body, putting the gun back in her jacket pocket. As she walked back to her car she looked up to the sky and said softly, 'All done now Sean, all done.'

She started her car and drove slowly out of the car park.

McGuire had driven into the car park just as the woman had raised the gun to Patterson's head. He'd been powerless to prevent her pulling the trigger and killing his Commander.

He braked hard and the car skidded to a halt. He jumped out and raced to the boot, but by the time he'd retrieved his Armalite rifle, the woman's car was disappearing down the road and drinkers were starting to emerge from The Harp Bar and gather around the body of Jimmy Patterson.

He knew it would only be a matter of time before the place was crawling with the security services.

He quickly changed his mind about firing the black rifle at the woman's car as it disappeared into the distance. Frustrated, he threw the rifle back into the boot of his car and jumped into the driver's seat. He started the engine and desperately tried to manoeuvre his car in the tight car park, trying to turn the car around. By the time he finally drove onto the main road there was no sign of the woman's vehicle.

He beat the steering wheel in frustration.

He thought about the woman, there was something about the long red hair. The recollection of where he had seen that long red hair before came to him in a flash. He pictured a recent memory of that woman walking over the stone bridge in Newark, hand in hand with Sean O'Connor.

CHAPTER 78

10.30am 7th July 1991
O'Doyle's Bar, Londonderry

Danny Macready had been shocked when McGuire had phoned and asked for a meeting two days after the shooting of Jimmy Patterson. He had been very wary; he knew just how much McGuire had worshipped Patterson and he didn't want to end up in the cross hairs of the 'coffin maker'.

Very reluctantly he agreed to that initial meeting, but he had been the one dictating the time and location where the meeting would be held. He stipulated that the meeting should be held in Derry and had put in place several safeguards. Macready had been shocked how quickly McGuire accepted all the protocols he laid down.

At that initial meeting he'd been equally as shocked by what McGuire had told him. He had sat open mouthed as McGuire recounted how he'd seen the red-haired woman gun down Jimmy Patterson outside The Harp Bar and how he'd recognised her from his time surveilling Sean O'Connor.

McGuire had gone on to say that he believed the same woman was probably responsible for the death of Danny's father, Eddie. He thought that both killings were something to do with the death of Sean O'Connor.

McGuire had seemed a little on edge at that first meeting, almost panicked.

Danny couldn't make up his mind if the man in black was rattled by what had happened to Jimmy Patterson or if he was worried that he would also be on the woman's hit list. After all, it had been McGuire that had actually pulled the trigger and killed O'Connor.

McGuire had asked Macready to try and find out if Sean O'Connor had any property in Derry, where the scheming red haired bitch could be laying low planning her next move.

Danny Macready had gone through his father's private papers and soon found the deeds to a cottage called Hunters Lair. There was also paperwork that suggested this property had been purchased on behalf of Sean O'Connor.

The cottage was located just outside the town of Kilmacrennan and within the boundaries of the secluded Glenveagh National Park.

Intrigued by this discovery of a property his father had never spoken about, Macready had driven to County Donegal and soon found the cottage called Hunters Lair. Sitting in his car he had watched the cottage for hours, undecided whether or not to go and knock on the door. He was about to approach the cottage when he had seen a small car approaching from Kilmacrennan.

He hunkered down in the driver's seat of his car and watched the vehicle turn off the small road into the driveway for Hunters Lair.

He watched in amazement as he saw a red-haired woman get out of the car and use a key to open the front door of the cottage. The mysterious red head was just as McGuire had described.

Whoever she was, she was definitely living alone in O'Connor's cottage, Hunters Lair.

After seeing the woman for himself, Danny Macready had arranged for his men to watch the cottage day and night. They had quickly reported back how every morning the woman would walk from the cottage into Kilmacrennan. She was, by all accounts, a creature of habit.

His men had kept watch on the cottage for three days now. Satisfied that she was living there alone, Macready had arranged another meeting with McGuire for this morning at O'Doyle's Bar in Derry. Once again McGuire had been happy to travel to Derry and had agreed to the same protocols as the first meeting.

Sitting in a private booth, Danny Macready glanced at his watch. It was fast approaching ten thirty. He began to feel a real sense of trepidation at the prospect of seeing McGuire again. There was no getting away from the fact that the man was a stone-cold killer, just being in his company made Danny's skin crawl.

Suddenly, the door to the empty bar opened and McGuire stepped inside. He had already been searched outside the bar as per the agreed protocols.

Seeing Danny in the booth, McGuire walked over and sat down opposite the Derry man.

In his soft, lisping voice McGuire said, 'Have you got news for me Danny boy?'

Danny bristled at being called Danny Boy, but ignored the remark. He said firmly, 'I do McGuire. I've found your mysterious red head.'

'Well don't keep me in suspense, where is the murdering bitch?'

'It seems that Sean O'Connor had a property in the Glenveagh National Park.'

'Whereabouts?'

'It's a small cottage called Hunters Lair, it's in the forest just outside the town of Kilmacrennan.'

'How can you be sure the woman's there.'

'I've seen her for myself McGuire. When I discovered the paperwork for the cottage in my father's documents, I drove over to Donegal. I saw a woman exactly as you described, use a key to get into the cottage.'

'Who else is living there?'

'Nobody. I've had my men watching the place for the last few days, she's there alone. It appears she's a creature of habit. Every morning she leaves the cottage early and walks into Kilmacrennan, then spends the rest of the day at the cottage.'

'And she's definitely there alone?'

'One hundred percent.'

'Good.'

'What are you thinking McGuire?'

'I think it's time for the bitch to pay the piper!'

CHAPTER 79

6.30pm 15th July 1991
Karikari Peninsula, North Island, New Zealand

This was the second week Tom and Bailey had spent in the beautiful, secluded White Sands Apartments next to the beautiful Rangiputa Beach on the Karikari Peninsula of the North Island.

After the stress of the last six months, they had decided to take an extended break as far away from home as they could. They both needed to recharge their batteries and make some serious decisions about their future.

The intention had been to tour the North Island of New Zealand, but after arriving at Rangiputa Beach, they realised they had found exactly what they were both looking for.

The days had been spent taking long walks along the beaches, looking out over the crystal-clear waters of Kohanga Bay. The evenings were spent eating the delicious sea food on offer at the apartments and reaffirming their love for one another.

After eating yet another delicious meal, they had decided to take an evening stroll along the beach just as the sun was setting. As they walked arm in arm, barefoot in the soft sand it was Tom who broke the silence, 'I know we've touched on this briefly a couple of times while we've been here, but I think we need to have a serious conversation about where we both see our future. I want to say that for my part, I think meeting you has been the best thing that ever happened to me and I definitely see our future together.'

Bailey squeezed her arm around his waist a little tighter, smiled and said, 'Wow Tom, that was all a bit heavy straight after dinner. How long have you been preparing that little speech?'

Tom stopped walking and faced Bailey, 'I'm serious. I know how I felt at the time you were working over in Ireland. I know it's your career and that you love it, but I don't know if I can cope with not knowing where you are and more importantly if you're safe. I'm being honest with you about how I feel. I've tried so hard to make sense of what happened to Bev and you've really helped me to come to terms with that devastating loss. I just don't think my sanity would remain intact if, God forbid, anything like that ever happened to you as well.'

Bailey could hear the emotion in Tom's voice and she said, 'Christ, you really mean this don't you?'

'Yes, I do. I don't want to lose you Bailey. I love you. I'm more than willing to give up my career with the police as long as it meant I could be with you and make sure you're safe. I'm seriously thinking about resigning.'

'It won't work Tom. Whatever you did after the police, you'd still be wondering where I was or what I was doing.'

Tom looked down at his feet and shrugged, 'I don't know what else to say.'

His voice was cracking with emotion, Bailey brushed the single tear from his cheek and said softly, 'Don't worry Tom. You're not the only one who's been thinking hard about our situation. I haven't told you this, but I still wake up some nights in a cold sweat after having the same nightmare. Each time it's exactly the same; I'm leaping from that bloody bridge and I can see the cold, black water racing up to meet me. I'm never going to put myself in that position again. My days working for the Firm are over. I could never operate under that much stress now, I'm damaged goods. I'm resigning when we get home.'

Tom was reeling, moments ago he thought their special relationship was doomed to fail.

Bailey could see his torment and she continued, 'What I want most of all is for us to be together for the rest of our lives. We've both suffered our share of tragedy and heartache, it's time we had some joy and happiness. It would be so wrong to pass on our chance of a life together.'

Tom was beaming now, 'Do you really mean it, you're quitting? Is it what you really want? You're not going to regret this decision in years to come, are you?'

'It's not a decision I've taken lightly Tom, but the time's right. I've served my country and I think it's now time for us.'

As the sun was setting over the ocean behind them Tom said, 'Marry me?'

Bailey laughed and said, 'I thought you'd never ask. Of course, I'll marry you.'

EPILOGUE

7.30am 30th July 1991
Hunters Lair, Kilmacrennan, Donegal

Caitlin Stuart had made her mind up the day before.

She had spent another lonely day in the cottage. As soon as she returned from her morning walk into Kilmacrennan, she had stepped through the front door of the cottage and could feel the melancholy gradually descending upon her.

The pain of living in Sean's beautiful cottage without him was just too much to bear. It had been almost midnight when she finally stopped crying. She had wiped the tears from her face and began packing her meagre belongings.

She accepted now that it was impossible to stay.

Caitlin knew if she remained cooped up in the cottage, she would slowly lose her mind to the all-pervading grief and deep sense of loss she constantly felt. In that instant she had made the decision to drive into Kilmacrennan the next morning and look for a fishing boat to take her back to Scotland.

She knew full well that her decision to return to Scotland carried a lot of risks. After the failed assassination attempt there was every possibility that the authorities would have identified her and be actively searching for her.

Caitlin had made up her mind. She would much rather take the chance of being captured and thrown into prison, than remain a single day longer in Sean's cottage, thinking of the happiness that had been so cruelly snatched from her.

She finished her cup of coffee, placed the keys for the cottage on the kitchen table and took one more look around each room before opening the front door and walking outside to her car.

It was a cold morning, the dark clouds above looked heavy with rain. The weather matched her dark mood.

As the first gentle rain began to fall, Caitlin unlocked the car and raised the boot, before stepping back inside the cottage for the last time. She quickly retrieved the two large grip bags from the kitchen floor and stepped outside. The cash left by Sean was in the largest of the bags. She felt confident that she would be able to evade the authorities and start a new life somewhere in the remote highlands using the money he had left her.

She placed both the bags in the boot of the car and closed it. She turned to the front door of the cottage and slowly shut it, not bothering to lock it. She could feel tears starting to sting her eyes as thoughts of the life she could have had with Sean came flooding into her mind.

Brushing the tears away with the sleeve of her coat, Caitlin stepped around to the driver's door and got in the car.

Just as she was about to put the key into the ignition, she heard what sounded like massive hail stones slamming into the car.

The glass in the driver's door window suddenly shattered and she felt an intense burning pain in her side.

The hailstones were bullets and they were smashing into the car, piercing the metal and shredding upholstery and clothing before slamming into her soft yielding flesh.

Suddenly, the noise stopped.

All she could hear now was the gentle sound of raindrops starting to fall on the roof of the car and the sound of her own ragged breathing.

Her left hand reached across to her right side and she felt warm, sticky blood oozing from the several wounds in her chest and stomach. She could barely breathe now; she was gasping for air unable to draw much needed oxygen into her destroyed lungs. Slowly she turned her head to the right and was aware of a sinister, dark apparition approaching the car.

Her vision was starting to blur now, but through hazy eyes she saw the figure was a tall, thin man with a gaunt face, dressed entirely in black. She suddenly feared she was staring directly into the eyes of the grim reaper and reached up to her neck for the rosary beads that had belonged to Sean.

She began to wheeze a last prayer, when the dark figure suddenly yanked the door open.

Caitlin hadn't realised she'd been leaning on the shattered door, but as soon as it opened, she spilled out of the car landing heavily onto the white gravel drive.

She lay on her back and stared up at the menacing figure, standing over her. For the first time she saw the black rifle he was holding. Bizarrely, she noticed the wisps of dark smoke curling from the end of the barrel.

Caitlin knew she was dying; she could feel her life quickly ebbing away. Suddenly she no longer cared about dragging in another painful breath, she shuddered once and felt a feeling of warmth envelop her entire body

She saw the smoking barrel of the gun directly in front of her face and heard a soft lisping voice say, 'Your day has come, bitch.'

With a grim smile of satisfaction on his face, McGuire fired a single round directly into the face of the mystery redhead, killing her instantly.

Shouldering the Armalite rifle, he could smell the acrid stench of cordite still escaping from the hot barrel. He raised the collar of his black Reefer coat and began walking down the driveway away from Hunters Lair.

COMING SOON:

The NEW Danny Flint thriller
BENEATH THE CITY

Nottinghamshire 1987

A fourteen-year-old girl mysteriously disappears without trace on her way home from school. Emily is the precocious daughter of Dominic and Rebecca Whitchurch, two highly successful barristers from the Mulberry Chambers in the city of Nottingham. Det Chief Insp. Danny Flint is facing an uncertain future following the death of the Chief Constable and the appointment of a new Chief and Head of CID.

Det Ch Supt. Adrian Potter is determined to see the staff from the Major Crime Investigation Unit integrated back into Divisional CID and has plans to abolish the MCIU.

Potter delegates the task of finding the missing girl to the MCIU after pressure is brought to bear on the new Chief Constable by the Head of the Mulberry Chambers.

It soon becomes apparent to Danny and his investigating teams that many people hold grudges against both the barristers but are any of those grudges enough to make someone want to abduct and harm Emily Whitchurch.

When a sinister ransom note is received, the enquiry takes on a heightened pace, but in the honeycomb of caves that lie beneath the city there are a thousand places to hide a young girl.

As the real reasons behind the abduction are finally revealed the detectives face a desperate race against time and atrocious weather to locate the girl before the dangerous subterranean recesses claim her for good.

PREVIOUS BOOKS BY THIS AUTHOR

1st TRILOGY

BOOK 1) THE COAL KILLER
BOOK 2) THE EXODUS MURDERS
BOOK 3) A DIFFERENT KIND OF EVIL

THE COAL KILLER – NOTTINGHAMSHIRE – 1984.

The county's in the grip of a bitter strike called by the National Union of Mineworkers. Jimmy Wade is a coal miner and Mick Reynolds is a sergeant in the Metropolitan Police. When Reynolds is sent to police the strike the two men are thrown together. Recognising each other's murderous natures, they embark on a brutal killing spree, using Wade's natural cunning and Reynolds knowledge of forensics and police procedures to evade detection. The killers revel in playing games, taunting the police. As the police close in, the story reaches a thrilling climax.

THE EXODUS MURDERS –
NOTTINGHAMSHIRE – 1986

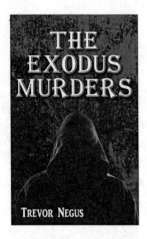

Two brutal murders are discovered on the same day at different ends of the county.

An identical series of letters and numbers has been daubed on the walls at both scenes using the victim's own blood. After discovering the meaning of the code left at the murder scenes; detectives realise they are in a race against time before the cold-blooded killer strikes again.

A DIFFERENT KIND OF EVIL – NOTTINGHAMSHIRE-1986

The body of a young boy is discovered at a secluded beauty spot. The post mortem reveals that the child had been sexually assaulted and suffocated. As the police investigation takes them into a murky world of child exploitation at Children's Homes across the county, they are also tasked with investigating the escape of psychopath Jimmy  Wade from Rampton Hospital. The two investigations set Ch Insp Danny Flint his toughest test yet. As he closes in on his quarry the story hurtles towards a thrilling and breathtaking climax.

2nd TRILOGY

BOOK 1) TWO WRONGS
BOOK 2) THE ROOT OF ALL EVIL
BOOK 3) THE CAUSE

TWO WRONGS –
NOTTINGHAMSHIRE, 1987

Barry Tate the man who had controlled the distribution of illegal drugs across the county for over a decade has finally been jailed for life. Dealers strive to fill the void and violent drug related crime soars in Nottinghamshire. Standing in their way are the Special Operations Unit, the armed response teams of Nottinghamshire Police.

This war on crime takes an unexpected and personal turn when the wife of a serving SOU officer is abducted. As the police struggle to keep up with developments a burning question is left unanswered. Can two wrongs ever make a right?

THE ROOT OF ALL EVIL –
NOTTINGHAMSHIRE 1988

Fanatical animal rights activists are planning the murder of the Company Director of UK Pharmaceutical Ltd. They have a ruthless attitude and will use firearms to achieve their aims. Standing in the way of this plot are armed officers from the Special Operations Unit and an undercover officer from the Metropolitan Police. Meanwhile, in Liverpool

a gang of armed robbers kill an off-duty officer during a raid on a security van in Liverpool. The sickening, cold blooded murder is captured on CCTV. The graphic images of the killing cause Pc Tom Naylor to confront a ghost from his past and lead him into undertaking a dangerous undercover role. As tragedy strikes, Tom is left facing unpleasant truths that make him question everything he ever believed in.

The Author – Trevor Negus

Trevor Negus is a retired Police Officer who spent 30 years working with Nottinghamshire Police. He spent six years as an authorised firearms officer and was a sniper on the Force's Special Operations Unit. The last eleven years of his Police career were spent as a detective on the CID, involved in numerous murder enquiries. He was trained as a specialist interviewer involved in the planning and interviews of murder suspects.